A KINGDOM'S HEART

CHAPTER ONE

WILLIAM

The theatre in Eldenmark always smelled of candle wax and rain.

The walls were old stone, veined with moss, and the air held the hum of a hundred voices waiting for the play to begin. I had come alone. Tomorrow I would kneel before the king and rise as a knight, but tonight I only wanted quiet. The world before duty.

The lights dimmed. The wooden stage glowed gold, the painted curtains rippled like flame. Actors moved across the boards in silks and rough linen. They prepared to speak lines from *The Song of the Willow Bride,* and my chest ached at the sound of it. My parents had read me that story long ago. I still remembered my mother's voice, soft and steady, turning sorrow into something holy.

The play began with the queen in disguise, the farmer's son by the river, and the willows trembling with their secret.

The play moved like a prayer. Each voice carried me further from the world outside. I might have forgotten the crowd entirely, until a flicker of movement caught my eye. Near the back, half hidden in the shadows, stood a girl in a dark cloak that brushed the floor. The hood couldn't hide the way light caught her hair, pale as wheat beneath the torchlight. It fell long, all the way to her waist. Her face was soft, almost unreal, with the delicate look of something carved too finely for this world, and her eyes were bright blue, like the summer sky.

She looked nothing like a villager--not with skin that untouched, nor posture so straight. Yet she wore simple cloth boots and a cloak patched at the edge. Maybe she had borrowed them. Maybe she wanted to disappear.

The crowd clapped when the farmer's son spoke of love lasting beyond exile, but I barely heard. The stage and the crown I would serve come morning vanished from my thoughts. All I saw was the girl.

Her head turned. Our eyes met.

It was no more than a breath of time, yet it felt longer. A flicker of surprise crossed her face, and she turned away at once. Her hood shifted, catching the glow of the torches, and I saw her hands tighten around the folds of her cloak.

The play carried on, though I could hardly follow it.

The farmer's son was betrayed, the queen's cries went unanswered, and the king's blade fell. The crowd gasped, then broke into applause. Tragedy always pleased them when it wasn't their own.

I stood when the clapping began to fade. The torches guttered as the applause began to fade. She was already slipping toward the exit, her steps quick and careful. For a moment I simply watched her, then found myself following, unsure why.

The corridor outside was narrow, lit by torches that hissed and guttered against the chill. The crowd spilled into the hall in bursts of laughter and talk. Boots scraped the stone. The scent of wine hung in the air, thick and sweet.

The girl moved faster now, her cloak brushing the wall as she tried to slip through the press of people. For a heartbeat, I lost sight of her in the throng. Then the way ahead opened, and two men stepped from a side door, broad and flushed with drink.

One blocked her path with a lazy grin. "Where is a pretty thing like you running off to?"

The other laughed. "Take off that hood, love. Let us see the face hiding under it."

She tried to move past them, but the first caught the edge of her cloak. His hand dragged the fabric, not hard, but enough to make her stumble. She froze.

"Let go," she said. Her voice was quiet, but the words were steady.

The man only smiled. "No need to be shy."

For a moment I stayed where I was. Training held

me still. I had been taught to weigh before I acted, to measure strength against treason. But the sound of his voice cut through all of it.

The torches hissed. The hall felt close, the air too thin to breathe.

Something inside me snapped.

I stepped forward. "That is no way to treat a lady."

Both men turned. One sneered. "And you are?"

I met his gaze but said nothing. The hall had gone quiet save for the hiss of the torches. The men smelled of ale and sweat, making me take a step back because of the stench.

The one nearest me took a half step closer. "You believe yourself a hero?" He leaned in, his breath hot and sharp with drink. "Go back to your seat, boy. This is not your concern."

He reached out, maybe to shove me, maybe to show off. That was when I moved.

I caught his wrist mid-swing, twisting until I heard him hiss. The second lunged, cursing, but I blocked his arm and drove my fist into his gut. He bent double, wheezing.

For a moment, no one moved. The fight had left the air heavy. One torch sputtered, its flame bending low in the draft. The men staggered back, muttering under their breaths.

I looked back, expecting to see the girl standing there so I could ask if she was alright.

But she wasn't.

The space where she had been was empty. The

corridor was thinning with people drifting out into the night. The archway gaped open, dark and wet with rain. I took a step toward it, half hoping to catch a glimpse of her cloak in the lamplight, but there was nothing—only the sound of water running in the gutters and the faint, steady tapping of rain against the stone.

A hollow feeling settled in my chest.

"You will pay for that," one of the men spat, clutching his stomach. The other glared, still rubbing his wrist. They stumbled away, muttering curses under their breath.

I watched them go, the sound of their boots fading against the stone. The torchlight flickered across the wet floor, turning the puddles to shifting gold. For a long moment I stood there, listening to the rain and the echo of my own heartbeat. Then I breathed out, long and slow, and turned toward the stables.

My horse waited near the post, restless but patient. He was a massive black stallion with a white streak down his nose, gifted to me by the castle as a token of the title I would recieve tomorrow. I had named him Corven.

He was one of the largest in the royal stables, bred for strength and endurance. I needed that. At six foot three and weighing around two hundred and thirty pounds of pure muscle, I wasn't easy to carry. Corven didn't seem to mind. His muscles shifted beneath his sleek coat as I approached, and his breath came out in small clouds of mist.

"Easy," I murmured, running my hand along his neck. The tension in my chest eased just a little.

I mounted and turned him toward the road. The rain had begun again, soft and steady, tapping against the saddle and my cloak.

The torches of Eldenmark dimmed behind me, fading to orange glows in the fog.

For a while I rode in silence. The rhythm of hooves and rain filled the world, and my thoughts drifted, circling the same place: the girl.

I could still see her standing in the torchlight, the edge of her cloak caught in someone's hand, her eyes bright with both fear and defiance. I had seen courage before, on the training fields and in the faces of men who meant to die, but nothing like that. Hers was quieter. Truer.

The image stayed with me, even as the road darkened and the city disappeared behind the hills.

It was a long ride to my home, but I did not care. The theatre played *The Song Of The Willow Bride* once every year, and I wouldn't miss a chance to see it.

My home stood in a secluded stretch of land, far from the city. It took time to reach, but the ride always cleared my mind. The house rested in the middle of an open plain, the grass dark with rain. My father had built it himself, plank by plank, before the plague took him and my mother eleven years ago when I was only nine.

The wood was weathered now, silver-gray under the

moonlight, but it was sturdy. He had built it to last, and it had.

I dismounted and led Corven into the small stable beside the house. The smell of wet earth filled the air. The rain whispered against the roof, steady and low.

Inside, the hearth was cold. I hung my cloak and set my sword beside the wall. Tomorrow I would kneel before the king and rise as a knight of Elarion. Yet, in the quiet, my thoughts returned only to her—the mysterious girl who vanished before I could ask her name.

CHAPTER TWO

IRIS

Father would be furious.

He always was when he found out I had slipped beyond the castle walls. His punishments were never light. Last time, I spent a week helping Raven clean the healers wing, scrubbing blood from the floors until my hands ached. Yet I did it again.

My best friend Raven had told me that the theatre in Eldenmark would be performing *The Song of the Willow Bride.* I had begged her for details until she finally sighed and told me the truth. That was all it took. I needed to see it.

It was the story I had loved most as a child, about a farmer's son named Mike who fell in love with a queen. She walked among her people in disguise, and he never knew her name. Their love was quiet, pure, but the king found out. The boy was exiled, and the queen was forced to watch him leave. I used to read it over and over, pretending I was the queen. Pretending love could be stronger than duty.

It was foolish, I suppose. But I had always found comfort in that story. It made the walls of the castle feel less like a prison.

Now the rain poured hard, soaking through my cloak and dress as I rode. My horse's hooves struck the muddy road in a steady rhythm. The torch I carried sputtered in the wind, its flame barely holding. The fields stretched endless and dark around me.

I muttered a curse under my breath when I realized I had gone the wrong way. The storm had blurred the path, and the forest looked unfamiliar. My heart quickened. The castle should have been visible by now, its towers were usually bright even through rain. But there was nothing ahead but darkness and the sound of rain striking leaves.

I pulled the reins and slowed the horse. "Wonderful," I said softly, though there was no one to hear it. The air was cold against my skin, my hair clinging to my neck. I tilted my head back, staring at the sky, and laughed once, quietly. "You have done it now, Iris."

The torch sputtered, its flame shrinking to a single glow before it vanished into smoke. Darkness swallowed everything. I cursed angrily, clutching the reins tighter.

The road ahead was invisible now. I could only hear

the rain, heavy and relentless, pounding against the trees. The storm rolled closer. Each rumble of thunder seemed to echo through my ribs.

"Please," I whispered to no one, "do not let the lightning find me."

I rode slower, guiding my horse with what little sense of direction I had left. The forest pressed close on both sides, and the night felt endless. My cloak was already drenched. My hands were numb. I had been riding far too long.

The world felt different in the dark. The silence between thunder made me uneasy, and every shadow looked like movement. I thought of the men at the theatre, their voices, their hands. I swallowed hard. The last thing I needed was to meet more like them out here.

A sudden flash tore through the sky, white and violent. The light blinded me, and before I could breathe, another followed, closer this time, splitting the dark with a deafening crack.

My horse screamed. Her muscles tensed beneath me, her head jerking hard. "Easy, girl," I called, trying to steady her. "Easy!"

She didn't listen. Panic took her. She reared once, then bolted down the path, hooves pounding against the mud. I gripped the reins with both hands, my heart racing, the world blurring past.

"Stop!" I shouted, but she wouldn't. The wind tore at my hood, rain cutting against my face. Then another flash burst above us, so close it turned the world white. The thunder came instantly after, shaking the ground.

The horse jolted sideways. My balance slipped. I was falling. The reins slid through my fingers. Then I hit the ground hard and the air was knocked from my chest.

Pain flared through my shoulder. I gasped and rolled onto my side. My horse was already running, her dark shape disappearing into the rain.

"No!" I cried, my voice breaking. "Come back! Stop!"

But she didn't. The sound of her hooves faded into the storm until I was alone, lying in the mud, the rain cold and merciless against my skin.

I scrambled to my feet, mud clinging to my dress. My shoulder throbbed with every movement, but I forced myself upright and turned in a circle, searching the darkness for any sign of shelter. The rain came in sheets now, sharp and cold, stinging my face.

"Hello?" I shouted, my voice raw. "Is anyone out there?"

Nothing. Just the wind moving through the trees.

I tried again, louder this time, but the storm swallowed my words. My heart pounded. The forest looked endless, every tree twisted and black against the flashes of lightning. I wrapped my cloak tighter, though it was soaked through. My teeth began to chatter.

Another flash tore across the sky, so bright it turned the world white again. The thunder followed again, closer and more violent. I flinched and stumbled back, a shiver running through me.

I needed to move. Standing still meant freezing. So I

walked. Step after step through the mud, as my boots sank into the earth. My hands trembled, my breath came in short, uneven bursts. I prayed under my breath that I'd find someone, anyone, before the night swallowed me whole.

The rain fell harder. The trees pressed close. Their branches were heavy with water. Each breath I took burned in my chest.

Then something changed.

A flicker through the dark, so faint I almost missed it. I stopped and blinked against the rain. There it was again, a small, steady glow between the trees.

Light.

My heart kicked against my ribs. I pushed forward, branches scraping my arms, mud pulling at my feet. The glow brightened as I neared, gathering shape and color until I could see it clearly.

A cottage. The windows shone warm against the dark, with soft gold through the rain.

Relief hit so sharply it almost hurt. I let out a broken laugh, half disbelief, half gratitude, and kept walking toward the light. Then I started running.

Branches scraped against my cloak as I hurried forward. My legs ached, but I did not care. The closer I came, the brighter the light grew. It looked lived in. Safe.

Once I reached the door, I knocked gently at first. "Hello? Is anyone there?"

No answer.

I knocked again, harder this time, my hand trembling. Still nothing. The rain beat louder against the roof, and panic rose in my chest.

"Please," I called. "Someone, please."

I hit the door again, rougher, desperate now. The latch rattled, and I tried it myself. The door was locked. I pushed once more, ready to call out again, when it swung open.

A figure filled the doorway. He was tall and broad-shouldered. The light from inside caught the edge of something in his hand.

A sword.

I froze where I stood.

He did not speak. He only watched me. Water dripped from his dark hair, tracing lines down a face I could barely see. His grip on the hilt tightened and he shifted his weight forward as if he expected an attack.

The air grew thin. My pulse thundered in my ears.

He looked ready to kill.

Before I could speak, before I could even breathe, the world seemed to hold still.

CHAPTER THREE

WILLIAM

No one ever came here. Not this late, not in weather like this. My home was far from the village, surrounded by open fields and the dark line of the forest. Even traders rarely passed by. So when someone began pounding on my door, hard and desperate, I froze.

The sound came again, sharper this time. Whoever it was wanted in.

I reached for my father's sword on the wall. The leather grip was worn smooth where his hands had held it for years. He had taught me how to use it, taught me to defend what was mine, taught me never to strike a woman no matter the cause. I remembered that as I lifted the blade and went to the door.

The rain hit the walls in sheets, the wind howling

across the open field. I pulled the latch and opened the door.

I expected a beast, or a thief, or maybe some poor soul from the village who had lost their way. But what stood there made me pause.

A small figure stood with her head lowered, hands raised slightly in front of her. The hood of her cloak dripped with rain, the fabric clinging to her frame. For a moment, she said nothing, only breathed hard, trembling from the cold.

Then I saw she was a woman.

I lowered the sword at once. "Who are you?" I asked.

Her voice came soft, shaky. "I am sorry. I did not mean to startle you. I lost my way in the storm. I saw your light and thought..." She hesitated, then swallowed. "I thought I might ask for shelter, just until the rain passes."

I studied her in the dim light. Her voice sounded young but careful, her words too smooth for a common traveler. I was about to speak when she lifted her head.

Our eyes met. Blue, clear even in the dark.

For an instant, the world narrowed to that single color. My heart skipped a beat. The memory came rushing back to the theatre, the torchlight on her straight, long, pale-blonde hair, and the way she had vanished into the rain.

It was her.

The sword slipped from my hand and struck the

floor with a dull sound. I took a step back, half in disbelief, half in relief.

"You," I breathed. Then, quickly, "Yes, of course. Come in."

She hesitated with an uncertain look. Her eyes flickered past me toward the light within. Her hand gripped the edge of her cloak as if she might turn and flee.

"It is alright," I said quietly. I made myself soften my tone. "You will catch your death if you stay out there. Please, come inside."

For a moment longer she waited, then stepped across the threshold.

I closed the door behind her. The latch clicked, and the storm fell away to a muffled roar against the roof. The air inside seemed to shift with her presence, warmer somehow. For the first time in a long while, the house felt different. Alive somehow.

I turned to face her. "You are soaked through. Sit by the fire."

She looked around the room as though uncertain whether she belonged here. Her eyes moved slowly over the shelves, the wooden table, and the sword rack on the wall. When they came back to me, pain flared behind my ribs. My heart was beating too fast, and I wasn't sure why.

I had imagined her face a hundred times on the ride home, and yet seeing her here, standing in my doorway, felt unreal. The same girl from the theatre. The same eyes that had caught mine before disappearing into the night.

I forced myself to look away. My hands moved automatically, gathering bits of kindling from beside the hearth. I knelt, struck the flint, and coaxed a flame from the dry twigs. The fire caught, spreading slow and steady until the room began to glow with a soft orange light.

"Sit," I said quietly, glancing up at her. "Warm yourself."

She hesitated for a moment, then nodded. The cloak clung to her shoulders as she crossed the floor, her steps light but uncertain. She sat near the hearth, holding her hands toward the flame. Her fingers were pale, trembling slightly as the warmth reached them.

"Thank you," she said at last, her voice barely above a whisper.

I leaned against the wall, watching her. The firelight danced across her face, turning her blonde hair to gold and casting long shadows behind her. She kept her eyes on the flames, silent, her cloak slowly drying against her shoulders.

I wondered how she had come to be here. How she had made it all the way from the village in this weather. The forest roads were rough even in daylight. At night, in a storm like this, they were dangerous.

Neither of us spoke for a while. The sound of the rain filled the space between us, unbroken but not uncomfortable.

At last I said, "Are you alright?"

She looked up at me, startled, then nodded quickly. "I am fine."

I studied her face for a moment, unsure if I believed it. "Even after the theatre today?"

Her eyes widened. For a heartbeat she looked as though she might deny it, then her shoulders dropped. "Oh," she said softly. "You recognized me."

"I did," I said.

Color rose faintly in her cheeks. "Thank you," she murmured.

"For what you did. I did not get to say it earlier."

I shook my head. "You owe me no thanks. Those men were drunk and cruel. Anyone would have stepped in."

Her gaze dropped to the fire again. The light flickered over her hands, pale against the dark cloth. "Not everyone would have," she said softly.

The words stilled me. For a heartbeat, I only watched her, uncertain how to answer. She said it like someone who had learned the truth of it too many times.

Something inside me shifted. The ease I had felt began to fade, replaced by the slow ache I could not name. I had thought of all the times I had turned away from another's pain, or stood silent when I should have spoken. Perhaps she was right. Perhaps not everyone would have, so I was glad I did.

When she looked up again, our eyes met. There was something steady in her gaze, something that made it hard to look away. She looked serious.

"Where did you learn to fight like that?" she asked.

"My father taught me first," I said. "Then others,

after he passed. I have had many lessons since." I hesitated before adding. "I am to be knighted tomorrow."

She didn't answer at once. Her eyes flickered back toward the fire, and something unreadable passed across her face. When she finally spoke, her voice was quiet. "Congratulations."

A smile tugged at my mouth before I could stop it. "Thank you."

She smiled faintly in return, then brushed a strand of wet hair behind her ear.

"What about you?" I asked. "What is it you do?"

She hesitated, just for a moment, then said, "Oh, me," she caught herself, then gave a quick nod. "I am a healer."

"A healer," I repeated, watching her closely. The word did not seem to fit. There was something too measured in her voice, too practiced. Her posture was straight, her hands still and careful in her lap. She looked nothing like the village medics I had known, worn and weary from their work.

But I said nothing.

Instead, I nodded and looked toward the fire. "Then we share a bit of the same trade. We both try to keep people alive."

For a while, neither of us spoke. The fire continued to crackle, filling the quiet. The warmth had begun to chase the chill from the room, and the tension between us felt easier now, though I still could not quite read her.

She looked peaceful in the firelight. Her expression

was calm and her eyes were half-lidded, yet something in her seemed guard. The way she sat: straight-backed, graceful and deliberate. It belonged to someone accustomed to courts and cloisters, not forest paths. It was as if she had spent her whole life learning how to hide in plain sight.

After a time I said, "I did not catch your name."

Her eyes flicked toward me, the faintest pause before she answered. "Elara."

The name lingered in the air. It was the same name as the queen from the theatre. It suited her, though it sounded like one chosen carefully, not given.

"Elara," I repeated, nodding. "That is a good name."

Her expression softened. "And what about you?"

"William," I said. "William Alaricson."

Her brows lifted slightly. "Alaricson," she echoed. "That means son of Alaric, does it not?"

"It does," I said. "My father's name was Alaric. He built this house long ago."

She nodded slowly, her gaze moving around the room again. "It is strong," she said. "You can tell it was built with care."

A small smile touched my lips. "He believed things should last. He taught me the same."

Elara smiled faintly in return, though it didn't quite reach her eyes. I noticed, but said nothing.

Instead, I turned my gaze toward the window. The rain had not stopped. It drummed against the roof, heavy and constant, a rhythm that filled the quiet between us. Now and then, a low rumble of thunder rolled through the fields, soft at first, then growing until the walls seemed to hum with it.

She turned her gaze from the fire, her gaze finding me again. "William suits you," she said softly.

I looked up from the window, surprised. "Does it?"

She nodded, the faintest smile curving her lips. "It does."

For a time, everything stilled again. The fire crackled. The rain kept its steady song, and the wind pressed against the windows like a restless spirit. The quiet felt almost peaceful, suspended between us.

Then a flash of lightning split the sky, flooding the room with white for a heartbeat. The thunder came close behind, deep enough to make the floor tremble.

She flinched slightly, her fingers tightening around the edge of her cloak.

I straightened from the wall as the decision formed before I could think to weigh it. "You should stay here tonight," I said. "It is far too dangerous for a lady to be wandering alone in weather like this."

She turned her gaze back toward me. For a moment she did not speak. The storm groaned around the walls. Then she nodded once, slow and grateful. "If you are sure I will not be a bother."

"You will not," I said. "The storm will pass by morning. You will be safe here until then."

Her shoulders relaxed, and she turned back toward the fire. For a long moment, she didn't move. Her gaze stayed fixed on the flames, lost somewhere far beyond them.

I found myself watching her again. Something about the way she sat still felt too unearthly. It was too composed for someone soaked and cold, too calm for the storm that battered the walls. The world outside raged, yet she seemed untouched by it, as if chaos itself could not reach her. She was too beautiful to belong to anything as small as this place.

The thought unsettled me. I looked away and pushed from the wall. The floor creaked beneath my boots as I walked toward the back of the house. One of the doors stood half open, its hinges old but strong. I stepped inside.

The room was small, with low ceilings and walls of dark wood. It had once belonged to my parents. My father built the bed himself, solid oak with carvings along the frame. My mother had sewn the curtains that hung at the window, though they had faded with time. The air carried a faint scent of sunflower and pine, something that always reminded me of her.

I pulled an old blanket from the chest at the foot of the bed and shook the dust from it. Then I straightened the sheets, smoothing them until they lay neat. I fluffed the pillows, letting the air fill them again. For the first time in years, the room felt lived in.

A small wardrobe stood beside the wall. I hesitated before opening it. Inside hung a few of my mother's things. Among them was a simple kirtle, pale pink, the color softened by age but still gentle to the touch. She had worn it often, back when the fields outside were full of wildflowers and laughter still filled these walls.

I lifted it carefully, folding it over my arm. It was the only thing I had that might suit the girl sitting by my fire.

When I stepped back into the main room, she was still there, her gaze still fixed on the flames. Her cloak had stopped dripping, but her hair was still damp, clinging to her shoulders in damp blonde curls.

"I found something that might be more comfortable," I said, holding out the kirtle. "It belonged to my mother."

She turned, her eyes softening as she looked at the fabric. For a moment, she didn't move. Then she reached out and brushed her fingers across it, careful, almost reverent. "Thank you. It is beautiful," she murmured.

"It is dry," I said with a faint smile. "That is what matters."

A small yawn escaped her lips before she could stop it. She covered her mouth quickly, embarrassed, and I could not help the quiet laugh that slipped from me.

"You must be exhausted," I said. "Take the room at the end of the hall. It is warm now. You will rest better there than by the fire."

She hesitated, her fingers tightening slightly around the kirtle. "I would not want to take your bed."

"It is fine," I said. "There is more space there, and I am used to sleeping by the hearth when the storms come. Go on."

For a moment, she seemed ready to argue, but then

her shoulders eased, and she nodded. "Thank you," she said softly.

She rose, the firelight catching in her hair as she turned toward the hall. I watched her take a few slow steps, the fabric of her cloak whispering against the floorboards.

Before she disappeared from view, I asked. "Do you need anything to eat or drink?"

She looked back over her shoulder, offering a small, tired smile.

"No, thank you. You have already done more than enough."

I nodded, though part of me wished she had said yes. "Rest well then, Elara."

Her smile lingered for a heartbeat before she vanished into the bedroom, closing the door softly behind her.

For a time I stood there, listening to the rain tapping against the roof. The sound mixed with the steady crackle of the fire until it seemed to fill every corner of the house. The air smelled of wet wood and warmth.

The house felt strangely full now, as though her presence had woken something long asleep. I let out a slow breath and turned toward the hearth.

The fire had burned lower, its glow softer, shadows stretching across the floor. I reached for another log, meaning to add it to the flames.

Before I could, the door behind me creaked open.

I turned, and there she was.

She had changed into the pale kirtle, the fabric

falling neatly to her ankles. It was a little loose on her shoulders, yet somehow it suited her. The color caught the firelight and turned warm against her skin. Her hair was less damp now, though parts of it clung to the kirtle.

For a moment I could only look at her, struck by the quiet simplicity of the scene. She seemed almost unreal in the dim light, like a figure drawn from a fairytale or a dream.

She noticed me watching and looked down quickly. "I am sorry," she said quietly. "I did not mean to disturb you."

"What is it?" I asked.

She stepped closer, holding something against her chest. It took me a moment to recognize the worn leather cover of the book in her hands.

"I found this in your room," she said. "It caught my eye." She hesitated, then looked up. "*The Song of the Willow Bride.* It is my favorite tale."

I blinked, taken off guard. "Mine too," I said softly.

Her fingers brushed the book's spine. "I was wondering," she said, "if I might read it before bed. It has been years since I last held a copy."

"Of course," I said. "You can read anything you find here."

Her eyes brightened, the faintest smile curving her lips. "There is a line from it I always loved," she said, her voice dropping to a whisper. "When the farmer's son says to the queen, *'If exile is the price of loving you, then I will pay it gladly.'*"

Without thinking, I finished the line for her. "And the queen answers, *'Then I will spend every breath mourning the debt I cannot repay.'"*

Her gaze lifted to mine, startled at first, then soft. For a heartbeat, we just stared at each other. It felt as if the whole house had gone still.

She held the book closer, her voice barely more than a breath. "It is always the same," she said. "No matter how many times I read it, that part never loses its ache."

"No," I said quietly. "It does not."

For a moment, she simply looked at me, as though the silence itself carried the rest of what she wanted to say. Then she smiled

again, gentle and fleeting. "Goodnight, William."

"Goodnight, Elara," I said back.

She turned back toward the bedroom, the book cradled carefully in her hands. The door closed softly behind her once more.

I stood there for a long while, listening to the quiet. The storm was still moving across the fields, its voice low and distant now. The fire had burned down to embers, glowing like small, steady hearts in the dark.

It had been years since anyone else had slept under this roof. Yet the house no longer felt empty.

CHAPTER FOUR

IRIS

I closed the door behind me, shutting out the sound of the rain. The room smelled faintly of woodsmoke and lavender. The bed looked warm and neatly made, and for the first time in hours, I let myself breathe.

I set the book on the small table beside the candle. My fingers lingered on its worn leather cover. *The Song of the Willow Bride.* It felt strange to find it here, in his home of all places. Stranger still that he had known the words, finishing the line as if he had read it beside me a hundred times before.

I moved my fingers around the kirtle he had given me. The fabric was soft, worn thin with age, but clean and warm. It smelled faintly of pine and dust. I thought of his mother, whoever she had been, and wondered if she could have imagined her son offering her dress to a stranger on a night like this.

I sat down on the edge of the bed and opened the book. The pages were yellowed, the ink faded at the corners, but the words were still clear. I ran my fingers along the lines I knew by heart and felt a quiet ache rise in my chest.

The story had always been my escape. When I was little, I used to read it by the candlelight until my eyes grew heavy. The queen who walked among her people in disguise, the farmer's son who loved her without knowing her name, the devotion that cost them everything. I had wanted something like that once, something honest and brave.

Now I was not sure I believed in such things.

I leaned back against the pillows, the candlelight flickering against the walls. My eyes were heavy, my body sore from the ride. Outside, the storm still whispered over the roof.

I only hoped I had not sounded too nervous when I told him my name. *Elara.*

It was the first that came to mind, the name of the queen from this very tale, a woman who hid her crown beneath a cloak and wandered the world alone. Fitting, perhaps. Yet the word had caught in my throat the moment I spoke it. I had felt the pause hang there, fragile and sharp, like glass waiting to break.

Even now, I could hear my voice echoing back in the silence, and my stomach tightened. If he noticed the hesitation, he had been kind enough not to ask. Still, I could not stop thinking of it, the way the lie had slipped so easily from my tongue.

I closed the book gently and rested my hand on the cover. The warmth from the fire reached faintly through the wall.

"Thank you," I whispered into the quiet, though I did not know if I meant it for the storm, or for the man who had opened his door to me when he did not have to.

My eyes grew heavier with every blink. The sound of rain softened, fading into the distance. I pulled the blanket close, feeling its weight settle around me.

Within moments, the night pressed down like a gentle tide, and I drifted into sleep.

—

Morning light pulled me from sleep. For a moment I did not remember where I was. A single candle had burned low beside the bed, its wax pooled at the base.

Then I turned toward the window, and my breath caught.

Mist hung over the fields, silver in the light. Through it, dark shapes moved slowly, their outlines shifting with the fog. At first I thought they were farmers or hunters heading for the woods. Then the sun broke through the clouds, and the light caught on metal.

Armor.

A wave of tightness washed over me. The gleam of polished steel, the steady formation, the banners moving with the wind.

Guards. My father's men.

Panic rose sharp and cold, chasing the last traces of sleep from my body. He must have found out. He must have sent them. If they saw me here, if they saw me with William—

I pressed a hand against the wall to steady myself. My pulse beat too fast, every breath shallow.

He could not know they were here, nor could he know who I was.

I pushed the blanket aside and stood quickly, my bare feet cold against the floorboards. My hands trembled as I looked back toward the door. I did not even know why I was still lying. It had begun as fear, but now it felt like something I could not stop.

I hurried out of the room.

William was already seated on a chair by the hearth, his dark brown hair still damp, a cup of tea in his hand. He looked up as I entered, his expression softening.

"You are awake." he said.

"I have to go." The words left me faster than I meant them to. My voice sounded tight in my own ears.

He blinked, surprised. "So soon? Do you not want something to eat first?"

I shook my head, already glancing toward the door. "No. I will eat when I return home."

He frowned slightly. "The village is far. Let me take you back. The roads are still wet, and—"

"No," I said quickly, cutting him off. "My horse is tied near one of the trees. I will be fine."

The silence that followed felt heavier than before. I could feel his eyes on me as I crossed the room, searching for my cloak. My hands moved too quickly, tugging at folds of fabric, trying to keep them from trembling.

When I found the cloak, I gathered it up and clutched it to my chest. "I will just change out of this kirtle," I said, already stepping back toward the hallway.

He rose to his feet, setting the cup aside. "It is fine," he said quietly. "Keep it."

I paused, meeting his eyes for a moment. There was warmth there, steady and kind, the sort that made my heart ache. I wanted to thank him, to say something that would explain the lie I was still living, but the words never came.

So I just nodded, and pulled the cloak tight around my shoulders. "I will go now," I said instead.

Before he could answer, I turned toward the door, praying the guards would not see me before I reached the woods. My hand was already on the handle when his voice stopped me.

"When will I see you again?"

I froze. My fingers tightened around the cloak, and for a long moment I could not bring myself to turn around.

When I did, he was standing near the hearth. The morning light caught his dark hair and his expression was uncertain, hopeful in a way that made my chest tighten painfully.

"I do not know," I said quietly.

His brow furrowed slightly. "Maybe soon?"

I hesitated, then shook my head. "Maybe never."

The words felt colder once they were spoken, but they were the truth. Once I returned, my father would make sure I never left the castle again. He would lock me in my chambers or set guards at every door. This had been foolish, all of it, and I would pay for it soon enough.

William's gaze lingered on me. "I see," he said quietly.

I met his eyes, trying to offer something that might pass for a smile. It felt weak, more like an apology than a farewell. "Thank you," I said. "For everything."

He nodded once. "Safe travels, Elara."

His voice was calm, but there was something in it that caught in my chest. I turned toward the door before it could settle too deeply. I pulled the cloak tighter and stepped outside.

The grass was wet beneath my boots, the wind sharp against my face. I kept my head low, walking quickly toward the tree line.

The guards were still there, their silver armor catching the pale light. They were close enough that I could hear the creak of leather, the soft thud of their horses shifting in the mud.

I swallowed hard and kept walking. Every step felt heavier than the last.

Then a sharp voice broke through the morning air. "Your Highness!"

I froze.

The sound of hooves followed, quick and purposeful. The guards turned their mounts toward me at once, the polished silver of their armor flashing as they closed the distance. I let out a quiet sigh. So they had found me.

A few moments later, the captain reined in his horse beside me. His armor bore the royal crest, its edges damp with rain. He dismounted swiftly and bowed his head.

"Princess Iris," he said, his tone measured but firm. "The King has been worried sick. We have searched all night."

"I imagine he has," I murmured, though I couldn't keep the weariness from my voice.

The captain's eyes flicked to the road behind me, to the faint outline of the house across the field. I straightened my posture, hoping he wouldn't ask questions.

"His Majesty will want to see you at once," the captain said. He extended a gloved hand toward me. "Please, allow me to assist you."

I hesitated only a moment before placing my hand in his. His grip was steady, firm but respectful. He guided me toward his horse and helped me up onto the back of the saddle.

As I settled behind him, I cast one last glance over my shoulder. The small house stood quiet in the distance, the smoke from its chimney rising faintly into the morning air.

For a brief moment, I thought I saw movement at the window, a shadow perhaps, though it was likely only wishful thinking.

Then the captain urged the horse forward, and the fields began to blur around us.

I sighed again, quieter this time. I knew what waited for me at the castle. My father's fury would be worse than any storm.

CHAPTER FIVE

IRIS

The ride back to the castle felt endless. The sun was up, and the air was damp from last night's rain. My cloak clung to my shoulders as we passed through the fields and up the long winding road that led to the gates of Elarion.

The castle rose before us, gray and vast against the dull sky. Its towers pierced the clouds, their tips crowned with banners bearing my family's crest--a white rose over crossed blades. The stone walls were slick with rain, darkened by age and strength. It looked unshakable, eternal, yet to me it had always felt more like a prison than home.

The drawbridge lowered with a groan of iron chains. The sound echoed through the courtyard as we entered. Guards lined the steps, their armor gleaming, their faces unreadable. I felt their eyes follow me as the captain helped me down from the horse.

No one spoke as they led me through the corridors. The floors were cold beneath my boots, and the air smelled faintly of smoke and damp stone. Every step echoed off the walls, joining the faint ring of metal and the faraway clang of a closing gate.

At last, we reached the throne room.

Two guards pushed open the tall wooden doors. The sound rolled through the chamber like thunder. I stepped inside with my head bowed, my heart thudding painfully.

My father sat upon the high throne, his crown of iron glinting under the torchlight. King Henrik of Elarion. His presence filled the room before his voice did. The guards who had brought me in fell to one knee, bowing deeply.

From the corner of my eye, I saw Raven standing near the far wall. Her dark hair was tied back, her healer's robe marked with the silver hawk of Valebran. Her eyes met mine for only a second before she looked away.

"Your Majesty," the captain said, his voice steady but careful. "We found her near the eastern woods. She appears unharmed."

My father rose from the throne. His movements were sharp and heavy with fury.

"Unharmed," he repeated, his voice echoing through the hall. "You brought me great scare, Iris."

I lowered my head. "I am sorry, Father. I—"

"Sorry?" His voice rose, filling the hall. "Do you think sorry erases the danger you caused? Do you think sorry restores what could have been lost if something had happened to you?"

He descended the dais, each step striking the stone. The firelight caught in his eyes, and they burned with anger.

"We are already on the wrong side of two neighboring kingdoms," he said. "A war could start at any moment. I need you whole, safe, and obedient. As I have told you before, once you turn eighteen—a year from now—you will be married to secure an alliance that will protect this throne."

My eyes fell to the floor. The words struck harder than his tone. Of course. It had never been about me, never about love or family. Only power. Only duty.

I said nothing. There was nothing left to say.

He stopped a few paces in front of me. "On your knees," he ordered.

The room fell silent. Even the torches seemed to stop flickering.

My stomach turned cold. I knew what was coming. I had known since I first stepped through the doors.

I closed my eyes and drew in a slow breath. My hands trembled as I lowered myself. The chill of the stone bit through the thin fabric at my knees. I pressed my palms flat against the stone, trying to steady them.

The sound of his footsteps came closer. Then silence.

And then pain.

The strike landed hard across my face. My head snapped to the side, and white heat burst behind my eyes. I did not cry out. I would not give him that.

The sting spread, sharp and deep, from my cheek down to my jaw. My breath came unsteady, the taste of iron at the edge of my tongue.

For a moment, I stayed there, motionless, my eyes closed. The humiliation burned hotter than the pain. I could feel every gaze in the room pressing down on me: the guards, courtiers, Raven—all of them witnesses to my disgrace.

"Open your eyes," my father said.

I obeyed. My cheek throbbed as I lifted my head. The room wavered slightly, the torchlight blurring around the edges of my vision.

He stared down at me, his expression carved from stone. "As your punishment, you will assist the healer for the next several weeks. You will tend wounds, clean the infirmary, and remember what it means to serve this kingdom rather than defy it."

My throat tightened, but I forced the words out. "Yes, Father."

He turned slightly. "Now get out of my sight."

I rose slowly, careful not to meet his eyes again. My legs felt weak and the skin of my face still burned where his hand had struck.

"Raven," he said, without looking her way. "Take her with you."

Raven stepped forward at once. She bowed her

head to the King, then gently reached for my arm. "Yes, Your Majesty."

I let her guide me toward the doors. The guards opened them without a word, and we stepped out into the corridor. The heavy wood closed behind us with a dull thud that echoed through the stone hall.

The moment we were out of sight, Raven exhaled sharply. "Saints above, Iris. Are you alright?"

The question barely reached me at first. The air felt different out there. Cooler, thinner, almost clean after the suffocating weight of the throne room. I swallowed, my throat raw.

A short, bitter laugh escaped before I could stop it. "Do I look alright?"

Raven frowned, her eyes softening. "No. You have a nosebleed."

"Of course I do," I muttered, swiping my sleeve across my face. The fabric came away streaked with red. The sting in my cheek pulsed with every heartbeat.

Raven sighed and reached into the pouch at her side. She pulled out a folded cloth and pressed it gently into my hand. "Here. hold that."

I took it, pressing it against my nose. The cool fabric helped a little.

"Well," she said after a moment, her tone lighter but not unkind, "It seems you are stuck with me for the next few days."

I glanced at her, the corner of my mouth lifting slightly. "Seems I am."

Raven tilted her head toward the hallway. "Come

on. Let us get you cleaned up before we go to the healer's wing."

I followed her down the corridor, holding the cloth to my nose.

My cheek still burned, but the bleeding had slowed. The halls were quiet save for the faint echo of our footsteps and the distant hum of voices from the lower levels.

"At least six knights and three dukes need tending today," Raven said as we turned a corner. "You chose a busy time to get yourself punished."

I gave a weak laugh. "You make it sound like I planned this."

She smiled faintly. "You? Sneaking out when your father forbids it? You plan everything, Iris."

I sighed. "Not this. I just needed to feel something other than these walls."

Raven didn't answer right away. She only glanced at me, her eyes softer now, then faced forward again.

We reached the stairway that led down to the healer's rooms.

The scent of herbs and candle wax drifted up the stone steps. I could already hear the faint sounds of movement below, voices murmuring, metal trays clinking, and water being poured.

Raven paused at the top of the stairs and looked back at me. "Ready?"

I nodded.

She started down first. I followed behind her, keeping one hand on the wall as the light from the upper hall faded. The air grew warmer with every step, carrying the smell of dried herbs and burning oils. My face still ached, but the quiet steadiness of the place eased me a little.

At the bottom, the corridor opened into a wide chamber. Wooden tables lined the walls, and shelves were filled with jars of roots and powders. A few healers were already at work, their voices calm and low. Bowls of water gleamed under the lamplight, and rows of bandages soaked beside them.

Raven led me to an empty table near the back. "You can start here," she said. "Clean the instruments first. It will keep you busy."

I gave a small smile. "You always know what to tell me."

She smiled back, though her eyes stayed serious. "Someone has to."

I sat down and dipped my hands into a basin of clean water. The surface trembled slightly as I moved my fingers through it. My reflection wavered, pale and tired, like someone I barely recognized.

For a while, I just listened to the quiet. It was calm here, a different kind of silence than the one in the throne room.

It would have to do for now.

CHAPTER SIX

WILLIAM

Today was the day.

By nightfall, I would be a knight of Elarion. It meant I would be moving into the castle, living among the king's men, training and resting in the barracks. The thought filled me with a strange mix of pride and unease.

I was twenty years old, and I had lived alone in this house since I was nine. The silence had long become its own kind of comfort.

I packed my things carefully, folding my cloak and setting my sword beside the saddlebag. The morning light slanted through the small window, turning the dust in the air to gold. Every sound seemed sharper: the creak of the floorboards, the soft rustle of cloth, the faint whisper of wind through the shutters.

It felt strange to think I might not see this place again for a long time.

Before I left, my eyes landed on the book lying on the table. *The Song of the Willow Bride.* The cover was still slightly damp from the night before. I picked it up and turned it over in my hands. Her fingers had touched it, too.

For a moment, I hesitated, then slipped it into my pocket.

Being knighted was everything my father had ever wanted for me. He had taught me to fight before I could read, taught me to hunt in the forests until I could move through them without a sound. By the time I turned eleven, I could wrestle men twice my age and win.

He used to tell me that strength was not in muscle, but in restraint. That a man's worth was measured by what he chose not to do. I had carried those words with me ever since.

Outside, the air was crisp and bright. Corven waited by the fence, his breath clouding in the morning light. His black coat shone like polished stone, and the white streak down his nose caught the sun.

I ran a hand along his neck and felt the steady warmth beneath his skin.

"Time to go, big guy," I said quietly.

He snorted, as if he understood.

I saddled him, tightening the straps, and looked back at the house one last time. The roof needed fixing, and the door leaned slightly off its hinges, but it was home. My father's mark was in every beam and every nail. Leaving it behind felt heavier than I expected.

Still, it was the path I had been raised for.

I mounted Corven, adjusted the reins, and turned toward the road that led to the castle. The sun had just begun to rise, washing the fields in pale gold. These were the same fields I had learned to fight, to ride, to live.

The road curved toward the village. Smoke drifted from chimneys, and the faint hum of morning life filled the air. It was the same place where I had first seen her, standing in the crowd with her cloak drawn close.

As Corven's hooves struck the cobblestones, I found myself searching for her without meaning to. My eyes moved from face to face, across market stalls and narrow lanes, looking for a glint of pale blande hair, the fall of a dark cloak—any trace that she had been real at all.

But she was not there.

The streets were busy, filled with merchants opening stalls, children carrying buckets from the well, and townsfolk calling greetings across the square. The theatre stood quiet now, its doors closed, its banners heavy with rain.

I slowed Corven near the corner, watching the spot where she had stood. The stones there looked the same as they had before, yet the air felt different, emptier somehow. For a moment, I stayed like that, listening to the steady rhythm of Corven's breathing, to the sound of me realising that maybe I in fact would not see her again.

Then I drew the reins and rode on.

The castle rose ahead, its towers cutting through the fog. The walls caught the light, turning from gray to gold as the sun climbed higher. The closer I came, the louder the world grew. I could hear the clang of metal, the call of guards, and the steady rhythm of hooves against stone.

When I reached the gates, two sentries stepped aside to let me pass. The courtyard spread wide before me, filled with motion and noise. I straightened in the saddle, feeling the weight of the day settle in my chest. Today, I would swear my vows. Today, I would become what my father had wanted me to be.

A young page hurried toward me the moment I entered. His tunic was too large, his hair damp from the morning mist. He bowed quickly before speaking. "Sir, the captain awaits you in the main yard."

I nodded and dismounted, handing him Corven's reins. "Take care of him."

"Yes, sir," he said, his eyes wide with something close to awe.

The courtyard buzzed with activity. Knights stood in small groups, their armor polished to a mirror's shine. Squires moved between them, carrying shields, spears, and banners that rippled in the soft wind. The smell of oiled metal and fresh hay filled the air.

The captain stood near the steps that led into the great hall. His armor was darker than the others, burnished with age, and his presence carried the weight of command. He turned as I approached, his expression unreadable.

"William Alaricson," he said. "You are to be knighted today."

"Yes, Captain," I replied. My voice sounded steadier than I felt.

He studied me for a moment before nodding. "You have trained under the best swordsmen we have. You have proven your strength in every test. Now, you prove your loyalty. Remember, a knight serves more than himself. He serves the crown, the people, and the code."

"I understand," I said, nodding.

"Good." He glanced toward the hall. "The King will arrive shortly. When the bell rings, you will enter with the others. Kneel before him, speak your vows clearly, and do not look away."

I nodded once more. The captain gave me a final approving look before turning to address another knight.

For a moment, I stood alone in the center of the yard. The rising sun gleamed on every blade and shield, throwing streaks of gold across the stone. My heart pounded steadily, the rhythm of it echoing through my chest.

This was the moment my father had trained me for. Every bruise, every scar, every dawn spent in the fields with a wooden sword led here.

The bell tolled across the courtyard.

Knights began to line up in pairs, the sound of their armor ringing with each step. I joined them, feeling the weight of the sword at my side and the faint pulse of pride in my chest.

The great doors of the hall opened, and light poured through.

We stepped inside.

The air smelled of incense and stone. The walls were draped with banners bearing the white rose of Elarion. At the far end of the hall, the king waited on his throne, the morning light burning against his crown.

My legs felt heavy, but I walked forward with the others. When my name was called, I stepped out of line and knelt before him. The stone was cool beneath my knees. I spoke the vows I had learned by heart, each word steady and clear.

The king drew his sword. The blade shone bright as he placed it against my shoulder.

"With this blade," he said, his voice echoing through the hall, "I name you Sir William Alaricson, knight of Elarion. Serve with honor, with courage, and with faith."

The sword lifted away. The hall went silent for a heartbeat before applause filled the air.

I rose slowly, my pulse still quick, the king's voice still ringing in my ears.

It was done.

I was a knight.

CHAPTER SEVEN

WILLIAM

The afternoon sun hung high above the courtyard when I took my post at the main gate. The stone beneath my boots was warm, and the air carried the scent of the stables and the faint salt of the western wind.

A line of merchants waited to enter, their carts filled with grain and cloth. A few guards stood along the wall, their spears glinting in the light. I kept my eyes on the road ahead, watching for movement beyond the fields.

Footsteps approached behind me. I turned and saw the captain striding toward the gate, his armor catching the sun.

"Sir William," he said, stopping beside me. "Where is the other guard?"

I frowned. "What other guard?"

He sighed, rubbing his temple. "There was supposed to be another man stationed here with you. Seems he has decided to be anywhere but where he belongs." He paused, then shook his head. "You know what, forget it."

He looked out toward the road, his expression unreadable. "You did well this morning. The king was pleased. But being knighted is only the beginning. The real work starts now."

I nodded. "What will my duties be?"

"For now, standard rotations. Guard shifts at the gates and along the walls. Tomorrow, I will have you report to the western post for inspection. After that, you will ride with another to the northern farms. There have been reports of unrest there, and I want a pair of steady eyes on it."

"Yes, Captain."

He studied me for a moment longer. "Good. You will learn quickly. You have got the look of a man who listens more than he talks. Keep it that way."

"I will, sir."

The captain gave a curt nod and turned to leave. His boots struck the stone in even rhythm, fading as he crossed the yard.

I stayed where I was, staring out through the open gates. The road stretched far into the fields, pale under the late sunlight. For a while, I simply watched the wind ripple through the grass and thought about nothing at all.

Suddenly, a voice broke the quiet behind me. "I hope I am not late."

I turned, already expecting trouble.

A knight approached from across the yard. His hair was blond and his armor was a little too polished for someone on duty. He moved with the easy confidence of someone who had never once worried about being in the right place at the right time.

"You must be the one I was supposed to be guarding with," I said solemnly.

He grinned, stopping a few paces away. "That depends. Are you Sir William Alaricson?"

I nodded once.

"Then yes," he said, resting his hand on the hilt of his sword. "Sir Eric of Talwood. Apologies for my late arrival. The kitchen had honeyed bread this morning, and I have a weakness for it."

I looked at him flatly. I had not expected the knights of Elarion to sound so little like the legends. I had grown up to believe they were forged of discipline and silence, not honeyed-bread excuses.

I took a deep breath. "You were expected an hour ago."

He laughed, unbothered. "You sound like the captain already. Careful, or they will start calling you old before your time."

I said nothing and turned my gaze back to the road.

Eric stepped closer, folding his arms as he leaned against the stone wall. "You do not talk much, do you?"

"Not when there is nothing worth saying."

He let out a low whistle. "Cold. I like that. Keeps people guessing."

I ignored him. The air was quiet again save for the distant sound of hooves somewhere beyond the walls.

Eric stayed silent for a moment, then said softly, "So, the newest knight in Elarion, standing guard at the gate. Feels a little strange, does it not?"

I glanced at him. "What do you mean?"

He shrugged. "You train your whole life for glory, then they hand you a post by the gate. Seems the crown likes to test its knights' patience first."

I allowed a faint smile. "Then it is a good test."

He chuckled. "Maybe so."

For a while we stood watching the others cross the yard. The clang of steel and the smell of oil and horse filled the evening air. Sunlight flashed on armor, catching along the walls like a living fire.

After a moment, he leaned closer. "Since you are new, I should tell you a few things. Rules that are not written anywhere but matter all the same."

I raised an eyebrow. "Such as?"

He nodded toward the courtyard. "Rule one. Whatever you do, do not look at the Princess."

I frowned. "What?"

He grinned as if the idea amused him. "I am serious. The King's temper is as famous as his crown. Look at her too long, and he takes it as a personal insult. See that man over there?"

I followed his gaze to a soldier limping across the

yard. His leg dragged slightly with each step, his armor dull with age and scratches.

Eric lowered his voice. "That is him. He made the mistake of looking at the Princess for more than ten seconds while the King was in the room. He has been limping ever since."

I studied the man for a long moment. His face was turned toward the ground and his shoulders hunched as though still carrying the weight of that mistake.

"Noted." I said quietly.

Eric smirked. "Good. I like you. You actually listen."

I turned my eyes back to the gate, though my thoughts lingered on his words. The thought of the princess did not interest me much. I had never seen her, only heard whispers about her beauty, her defiance, and her father's wrath. Every knight had his own version of her story, passed around like a warning or a prayer.

But I had already seen someone far more beautiful. Someone real.

The memory came unbidden: the soft fall of pale blonde hair, the clear blue of her eyes, the quiet strength in her voice. For a moment, the courtyard around me faded. The noise of clashing steel and shouting men softened, replaced by my own thoughts.

I drew a slow breath and looked away from the castle towers.

Some things were better left in memory.

—

The hours passed slowly. The sun sank behind the

towers, and the courtyard emptied until only a few guards remained at their posts. The torches along the wall flickered to life, their flames bending in the cool wind.

Eric stretched his arms and yawned. "Finally. Shift's over. Time to rest before I start snoring on my feet."

I nodded. "You go ahead. I will be there in a moment.

He gave me a knowing grin. "Suit yourself. The barracks are through the west corridor. I'll save you a bed before the good ones are gone."

"Go," I said quietly.

He laughed as he walked off. "Do not get lost, Sir Stoneface."

When he was gone, I looked up at the castle. Its towers reached high into the night, dark against the faint glow of the moon. It felt strange being inside its walls after years of only seeing it from a distance.

I leaned my spear against the gate and began to unfasten the straps of my chestplate. The armor came loose with a dull scrape, heavy in my hands. I set it down beside me and rolled my shoulders. The air was cool against my tunic, and I breathed in deeply. For the first time that day, the weight on my chest eased a little.

I should have gone to the barracks then. Instead, I found myself walking along the outer path, drawn by curiosity. The night was still, and I wanted to see more of the castle's edges, the parts where the noise did not reach.

The path led toward the trees that bordered the

training fields. The wind rustled through the leaves, soft at first, then sharper—like whispers slipping between the branches.

I slowed.

The quiet here was different. Too still. The kind of stillness that listens back.

A prickle ran down my neck. My hand went instinctively to the hilt at my side.

I turned my head, scanning the dark. The moonlight spilled across the path, pale and clean, but the shadows beneath the trees were thick and shifting.

Nothing. Only the creak of wood and the distant sound of water somewhere beyond the walls.

I exhaled, started forward again.

A single step. Then another.

The strike came fast.

A flash of movement, then a deep, tearing pain across my shoulder blade. The shock stole my breath. I stumbled forward, gripping the wound as a voice hissed behind me.

"Told you this was not over."

I spun around, teeth clenched. The moonlight caught the edge of a blade and the sneer of a familiar face. The men from the theatre. The one in front lunged again, but this time I was ready. I drew my sword in a single motion and met his attack with a clash of steel. The force rattled through my arm, but I pushed forward, slamming my shoulder into his chest. He hit the ground hard.

The second came from my right. I turned and

caught his wrist before he could strike, twisting until he cried out. My sword's hilt met his ribs, and he staggered back, gasping.

For a moment, both of them stared at me, eyes wide, breath ragged. Then they turned and bolted into the trees, crashing through the undergrowth until the sound of them was gone.

Cowards.

I stood still for a long moment, the night spinning softly around me. My shoulder burned with every heartbeat, blood running warm down my back. I pressed my hand to the wound. My palm came away red.

The sight steadied me more than it frightened me. Pain meant I was still here. Still standing.

I turned toward the castle. The lights in the distance flickered through the mist, gold against the dark. They looked farther than they should have.

I could still move.

Slowly, I bent to pick up my chestplate, tucking it under one arm.

I started walking again, one careful step after another. Every movement sent a pulse of fire through my shoulder, but the rhythm of my steps helped keep me upright.

I fixed my eyes on the lights ahead. Each step felt heavier than the last, yet the quiet steadied me.

I just needed to reach the walls. After that, I would rest.

CHAPTER EIGHT

IRIS

My white robe was dusted gray, and the headband that kept my hair back had lost its shape hours ago. My hands ached from work, and my shoulders felt heavy. The healer's wing was quiet now, lit only by the soft glow of a few oil lamps. The smell of herbs lingered in the air, sharp and clean.

I let out a long sigh. "Raven, it is dark already. Can I leave now?"

She looked up from the table she was wiping and shook her head. "Not yet. We still need to clean the instruments. You know how the captain gets if he finds so much as a spot on them."

I groaned under my breath but nodded. "Fine."

Together we moved through the room, setting things in order. The metal trays clinked softly as we stacked them. Dust caught the lamplight while we wiped the shelves. My arms felt like lead, but the work went faster with Raven beside me.

When I reached for the top shelf, my sleeve slipped back, and I caught sight of the hawk of Valebran stitched into her robe. The silver thread had dulled over time, but the shape was still clear.

I glanced at Raven. She was focused on a jar of dried sage, her expression calm and distant. I knew her story. Everyone did. She had come from Valebran when she was sixteen, after the man she loved had broken her heart so completely she had left her home behind.

I hesitated before speaking. "Do you ever miss it?"

She paused mid-motion, her fingers resting lightly on the edge of the shelf. For a moment she said nothing, her gaze fixed on the glass jars lined neatly before her. Then a small, thoughtful smile touched her lips.

"Sometimes," she said quietly. "It was beautiful there. Warm, full of music and light. The kind of place where you never thought anything bad could happen."

Her voice softened. "But memories like that hurt after a while, so I stopped holding onto them."

I watched her closely. The light caught her dark hair, turning it almost bronze. There was peace in her face, but something else, too. Something like loss, worn smooth by time.

"But you are happy here, right?" I asked. The question sounded smaller than I meant it to, as if I were asking for both of us.

Raven turned to me, her smile softening. "Oh, of course I am. Happier than I ever thought I would be."

Her tone was warm, but I could hear the faint edge of the weariness beneath it, the kind that comes from making peace with what cannot be changed.

I smiled despite myself. "Good."

She nudged my arm lightly. "Enough talking. The quicker we finish, the quicker we can leave."

I nodded, not wanting to press further. I reached for the next shelf. The room was quiet again, filled only with the soft clatter of glass and metal. I could already imagine the relief of my bed, the feel of sleep pulling me under after a long day.

Then the door opened.

The sound was sharp against the stillness, and both of us turned at once.

A tall, broad-shouldered man stood in the doorway. His hair was dark, and wet from the night and his jaw was sharp beneath the light. His deep brown eyes swept the room before settling on us.

My pulse skipped.

For a moment, my mind refused to name him. I could feel my pulse rise, the sound of it in my ears.

Raven moved first, her tone brisk. "He is hurt," she said, already crossing the room toward him. "Get a table ready."

But I couldn't move. The world seemed to narrow around the sound of her voice and the sight of him stepping into the light. His tunic was torn at the shoulder, blood darkening the fabric. He looked pale, unsteady, but still somehow composed. Too composed for a man bleeding through his clothes.

It was him.

William.

My stomach twisted. Heat rushed to my face, chased by panic.

His eyes found mine almost at once. For a heartbeat, the world seemed to still.

Recognition sparked. His brow furrowed, surprise giving way to disbelief, then to something softer that made my chest tighten.

"Elara?" he said, frowning.

Raven turned at the name, confusion flickering across her face. "Who is Ela—"

I cut her off with a quick glance. The look must have been enough; her words died in her throat

Raven hesitated, her brown eyes flickering between us. Something unreadable crossed her face. Curiosity, maybe suspicion, but she said nothing. Instead, she stepped forward and caught William gently by the arm. "Sit down before you fall down," she said, her tone brisk again.

He did as she told him, lowering himself onto the nearest stool. His breathing was slow but heavy, his hand pressed tightly against the wound.

I forced myself to move. My mind raced, but my body knew what to do. I reached for a clean cloth and a bowl of water as my fingers trembled.

Raven looked over her shoulder. "You take the cloth." she said.

I nodded quickly. My throat felt dry.

Kneeling beside him, I pressed the cloth against his shoulder.

The torchlight glinted along his jaw, tracing the faint sheen of sweat on his skin. Up close, he smelled of iron and rain. He was watching me, really watching me with that same steady intensity I remembered from the night he opened his door.

My heart thudded painfully. I focused on the wound, not his eyes. "Hold still," I said softly.

For a moment, neither of us spoke. The space between us felt taut, as if the air itself were waiting.

Then he said, low enough that Raven couldn't quite hear, "So we do meet again after all."

My heart lurched. I kept my gaze fixed on the wound, afraid of what he might see if I looked up. "It seems we do."

He gave a small, almost disbelieving laugh. "You said maybe never."

The sound of it caught in my chest. I didn't answer. My fingers worked at the cloth, steady but tense, wringing more water from it than needed. Anything to keep my hands busy—anything to avoid his eyes.

He filled the silence with a softer voice. "I thought I would never see you again. You did not mention you were a healer at the castle."

"I did not think it was important," I said, forcing the words out evenly.

"Not important?" His tone sharpened, not cruelly, but with an edge of disbelief. He leaned forward slightly, the movement small but enough to make my pulse quicken. "Even after I told you I would be knighted?"

I drew a slow breath. "I am sorry. I was not thinking. I was just worried because of the storm."

"I see," he said simply.

The words were soft, but something in them made my stomach twist. It wasn't anger, not yet. More like disappointment that cut quieter and deeper. He didn't believe me. He was right not to.

The truth was, I had lied out of panic. I always did when I slipped beyond the castle walls. It had become instinct to hide who I was, to protect myself from the risk of being reported to my father's guards. If someone ever recognized me and sent word back to the castle, the punishment would be severe.

But now, standing before him, that lie felt utterly ridiculous. I hadn't been thinking at all that night. Not when I gave him a false name, not when I told him half-truths about who I was. He had told me he was to be knighted, and I still hadn't realized what that meant.

A knight of Elarion would live within the castle walls. He would guard its gates, dine in its halls, walk the same corridors I did.

And now here he was, sitting right in front of me.

The weight of it sank in, heavy and cold. There would be no easy way to keep this secret now. All it would take was one careless word, one servant calling me by name, and the truth would surface.

I pressed the cloth to his shoulder again, trying to hide the tremor in my hands. The wound was deep but clean, a sharp gash along the muscle. I could feel the heat of his skin through the fabric, steady and strong beneath my fingers.

"Hold still," I said quietly.

He didn't move. The torchlight threw a soft glow over his face, catching on the dark strands of his hair and the faint curve of a smile that wasn't quite there. His eyes were calm, unreadable, but they held mine longer than they should have.

I wondered if he could tell how fast my heart was beating. If he could see how close I was to breaking the silence, to confessing everything before it slipped from my control.

The silence felt fragile, stretched thin between us. I needed to say something, anything, before it broke. "You should be careful next time," I said softly. "It could have been worse."

He gave a faint huff of breath that sounded almost like a laugh. "Oh, yeah? Well, guess who stabbed me."

I frowned and looked up at him. "Stabbed you?"

He nodded once. "Two men. The same ones from the theatre."

My stomach dropped. "You are certain?"

"Hard to forget a face after they try to lay hands on a woman in front of you," he said. His tone was even, but there was a weight behind it. "They found me by the trees. Said I would pay for what I did."

I stared at the wound again, at the red mark cutting across his shoulder. "You could have been killed."

He gave a faint shrug, wincing as he did. "Would not be the first to try. I just did not think they would follow me this far."

"I am so sorry," I said quietly. "They are angry because you defended me."

He looked at me then, his expression softening. "You do not need to apologize for that."

"I do," I said. "You were just trying to help, and now you are hurt because of it."

He held my gaze for a long moment, then his mouth curved slightly. "Well then," he said, a teasing note in his voice, "you better heal it."

The words caught me off guard, and before I could stop it, a small smile tugged at my lips. "Of course," I said softly. "Then do as you are told and take off your tunic."

He raised a brow, but the corner of his mouth lifted higher. "Yes, healer."

Carefully, he slowly pulled the dark tunic over his head. When the cloth fell aside, I saw a body shaped by years of training. His skin was beige with an olive undertone, his abdomen defined and his arms had muscles that looked strong enough to lift mountains.

I swallowed hard and forced myself to focus on the wound, not the man. My pulse still hadn't slowed. Every time I brushed the cloth against his skin, I could feel the warmth of him beneath my fingertips, steady, alive, and far too close.

I dipped the cloth back into the bowl and wrung it out, pretending my hands were steadier than they were. The water had turned faintly red. I pushed the thought away.

"Do not move," I said quietly.

He obeyed. The wound was deep enough to sting when I pressed the wet cloth to it, but he didn't flinch. His breath stayed slow and measured, though a faint line had formed along his jaw where he held the pain in.

"Does it hurt?" I asked.

"Only a little," he said, his voice lower now. "You have a careful touch."

I tried to keep my focus on the wound, not the heat radiating off his skin. "I have had practice."

He studied me for a moment. I could feel his gaze even when I didn't look at him. "You do not look like someone who belongs in

a place like this."

I glanced at him, startled. "What is that supposed to mean?"

"Just that you seem out of place," he said simply. "Too gentle for these walls."

The words hit harder than they should have. "You do not know me well enough to say that."

He smiled faintly, a quiet curve that softened his face. "Maybe not. But I would like to."

The air between us shifted. For a moment, I couldn't breathe. The bowl of water sat forgotten beside me, the torchlight flickering across its surface. I didn't know where to look or what to say, so I reached for the bandage instead. My hands needed something to do, anything to distract from the heat rising in my face.

"You do not need stitches," I murmured. "You are lucky."

"Or maybe those men just were not trying hard enough," he chuckled.

I glanced up sharply. "You think that is something to jest about?"

He shrugged, still wincing. "Humor helps with the pain."

I shook my head, unable to stop the small smile tugging at my lips. "That is a terrible way to deal with pain."

"It works well enough," he shrugged.

I focused on the bandage, wrapping it carefully around his shoulder. The fabric brushed against his skin, warm beneath my fingers. His breathing stayed even, though I could sense the tension in him, like he was holding something back.

"You will need to keep it clean," I said. "Change the bandage tomorrow, and do not lift anything heavy for a few days."

He gave a quiet laugh. "You do realize that is my job."

"Then you will just have to disobey orders for once," I said, tying off the last knot.

"Would not want to upset the captain," he replied, amusement flickering in his tone.

"Then do not get stabbed again," I said simply.

He smiled at that, a small, genuine curve of his lips. "I will try, healer."

The sound of his voice saying the word *healer* made something twist inside me. I stepped back to put some space between us. "There. You are done."

He stood slowly, testing the movement of his arm. "You have got a steady hand," he said.

"Like I said, I have had practice," I replied.

His warm eyes lingered on me. "Still," he said, "thank you."

"You are welcome," I managed, keeping my tone even.

He nodded once, then reached for his torn tunic, draping it over his arm. "Guess I should let you get back to work."

"That would be wise," I said, though part of me didn't want him

to go.

He paused at the doorway, the faintest trace of a smile still on his lips. "Good night, Elara."

My breath caught, but I only nodded. "Good night, ser knight."

The door closed behind him with a soft click.

For a long moment, I stood there, staring at the place he had been. The air felt warmer somehow, touched by his presence. Then the warmth faded, replaced by a hollow quiet. His footsteps echoed down the hall, until they disappeared completely.

I slowly exhaled. My pulse still hadn't settled.

Across the room, Raven was at the table, sorting through her herbs. The sound of her rustling leaves and clinking glass was almost too loud. She didn't look at me at first, and I almost thought she might not say anything at all.

Then she did.

"So," she glanced my way, "why did you lie about your name?"

CHAPTER NINE

IRIS

"Hello?" Raven's voice cut through the quiet. "Are you going to answer, or should I just start guessing?"

I blinked, realizing I had been staring at the door for far too long. My thoughts still echoed with his voice and the sound of my false name on his tongue.

"There is nothing to tell." I said at last.

Raven gave a soft laugh, not unkind. "You expect me to believe that? You froze when he said your name, and he looked like he had just seen a ghost."

I turned away, pretending to tidy the table, though my hands were shaking. "He helped me once. That is all."

"Helped you?" she repeated, stepping closer. "And for that, you gave him a false name?"

Her words struck sharper than I expected. I sighed, the breath coming out uneven. "I did not mean to lie. It just happened."

"Things like that do not 'just happen,'" Raven said gently.

I pressed my hands flat against the table and stared down at them until my vision blurred. "When I sneak out, I cannot risk anyone knowing who I am," I said quietly. "If someone recognized me and reported it, Father would..." My throat tightened. The memory of his hand striking my face flashed hot and cold at once.

"You know what he would do. You saw how he struck me."

Raven's expression softened. "So you panicked."

The truth hung between us like smoke.

"Yes," I said quietly. "And now he is here. A knight of the castle."

Her brows lifted slightly. "That seems... complicated."

"That is one word for it," I murmured.

Raven tilted her head, her tone careful but edged with curiosity. "Well, he did say he wanted to get to know you. And you did not look like you disagreed."

I looked up at her sharply. "Raven—"

She raised her hands in mock surrender. "I am just saying what I saw. If this keeps going, you will have to tell him the truth eventually."

The words landed heavier than I expected. *Tell him the truth.* They echoed in my chest, cold and impossible.

"I cannot," I said at once.

"Cannot or will not?" she asked softly.

I hesitated, my throat tightening. "Both, maybe."

Raven studied me for a moment, her expression unreadable. "He does not seem like someone who would turn you in, Iris."

I almost laughed. "You do not know that. He is a knight now. His loyalty is to the King. To my father."

Raven let out a dry laugh. "You are actually more stupid than I give you credit for."

"Hey!" I said, frowning at her.

She raised a brow. "What? You think he will not notice you sitting beside the King during dinner, or walking behind him during court? He is a knight now, Iris. He will be at every feast, every ceremony, every gathering. You cannot stay hidden forever."

The words settled in my stomach like stone. She was right, but I couldn't admit it. Not yet.

I crossed my arms. "I will tell him. Just not yet."

Raven tilted her head. "Not yet?"

I nodded slowly. "If we ever become friends... if I can trust him, then I will tell him. But not now. Not when I barely know him."

Raven shook her head, half amused, half exasperated. "You really are hopeless."

"Thank you," I muttered.

She laughed under her breath. "Do not thank me yet. You will see how bad this idea this is soon enough."

I rolled my eyes and turned toward the door. "Speaking of bad ideas, Father is probably waiting by the table."

Raven's smile faded. "Right. Best of fortune to you."

I gave a small nod. "I will need it."

She reached out, brushing a bit of dust from my sleeve. The gesture was small but grounding. "Try not to anger him more than he already is."

"I will try," I said, though we both knew it was easier said than done.

I smoothed my sleeve where Raven had brushed it and stepped into the corridor. The air changed the moment I left the healer's rooms. It smelled of roasted meat and wax and stone that had seen centuries. Torches flickered along the walls, their light soft against the stone floors. My footsteps echoed faintly as I walked toward the great hall.

The closer I came, the louder it grew. Servants moved quickly with trays and pitchers. Guards stood still beside the doors, spears at their sides. The murmur of men's voices carried from inside, steady and low.

The hall opened wide before me. Long banners hung from the rafters. The great table stretched down the center, silver and glass gleaming under candlelight. My father sat at the raised end, his crown catching the light. King Henrik. His eyes were colder than the stone beneath his throne.

I moved to my seat quietly. A servant filled my goblet without a word.

My father looked up. "I hope you have learned from your mistakes, Iris," he said. His voice was calm, but it cut deep. "You will not leave these walls again when I have forbidden it."

"Yes, Father," I said.

He watched me for a long moment, his jaw tight. "You will stay with the healer. You will clean, tend wounds, and serve until I say otherwise."

I nodded. "I understand."

He leaned back, his fingers tapping the arm of his chair. "Good. Because if you ever sneak out again, it will not only be my hand that meets your face."

The words hung heavy in the air. For a moment, no one spoke. The hall itself seemed to hold its breath. A few servants paused mid-step, pretending not to listen, though their eyes flickered toward us all the same.

Shame burned through me, sharp and familiar.

I bowed my head. "Yes, Father."

He looked away, already done with me. The talk in the hall rose again with soldiers speaking of borders, harvests, and threats from the north. I ate little. The food tasted like ash.

When I finished, my father dismissed me with a simple wave of his hand.

I rose from the table, bowed low, and turned toward the doors. The guards stepped aside without a word. The sound of my slippers against the stone floor echoed faintly as I left the hall behind.

I always felt nervous after meals with him. His temper was always palpable, even when he said little. Every movement and every glance felt like a test I could fail.

He was strict and unyielding in every way, the king before he was ever my father. I sometimes wondered if he even knew how to be both. His world revolved around the throne, the crown, the endless need to keep power from slipping away. There was never any room for softness there.

My mother had died the night I was born. The world had taken her before she even had the chance to hold me. The servants raised me instead—women with tired eyes and calloused hands who came and went as the years passed. They were kind enough, but never close. I was never truly theirs, and they were never truly mine.

I reached my chambers, the corridor dim and quiet. The guards outside bowed as I entered. Inside, the fire in the hearth had filled the room in a faint orange glow.

I untied the headband from my hair and set it on the table beside the mirror. My reflection stared back: pale skin, tired eyes, and the faint mark still red on my cheek.

For a moment, I just stood there, listening to the soft crackle of the fire. Then I turned away from the mirror and sat on the edge of the bed. The silence pressed close, heavy but familiar.

I let out a slow breath and closed my eyes.

Tomorrow would come with the weight of duty once more.

For now, there was quiet.

CHAPTER TEN

WILLIAM

The morning came cold and still.

The barracks were already stirring when I opened my eyes. Metal clanked against metal. Boots scuffed the floor. Voices rose and fell. The familiar smell of oil leather hung in the air, though it still hadn't settled into comfort.

My bed was in the far corner, away from the noise. Straw mattress, thin blanket, enough to sleep, nothing more.

I sat up slowly, careful with my shoulder. The bandage itched beneath my tunic.

Elara's work.

She'd wrapped it clean and tight, warning me not to strain it for a few days. I'd agreed, though I already knew I'd break that promise before noon.

The pain was dull, manageable, but the thought of tearing it open again made me curse under my breath.

Across the room, Eric was already up. Blond hair sticking up in every direction, armor half strapped, grinning like he'd won a battle before dawn.

"Morning, sir," he said, fastening his belt. "I was starting to think you died in your sleep."

"Not yet," I muttered, pulling on my boots.

I reached for my sword, slinging it over my shoulder. The weight pulled at the wound, sharp enough to make me wince.

Eric noticed. "You all right?"

"Fine," I said. "Just need to be careful."

He nodded toward my shoulder. "The healer's bandages holding up?"

I hesitated. "They are." My hands moved on the leather strap while my mind kept going to the steady press of the cloth on my skin. Elara's face slipped into my thoughts, along with the way she spoke and the calm in her hands. The memory stayed longer than I had any right to let it.

Eric didn't notice. He was too busy talking, too full of energy for the hour. "Captain said we ride north," he said. "The farms near the ridge. There is talk of unrest. Nothing serious, probably some drunk men shouting about taxes."

"Probably," I replied, but the words were thin. My thoughts were elsewhere. I pictured the men who'd ambushed me with their blades. I promised myself if I ever saw them again I would make them regret it. The oath felt hot in my chest.

Still, a part of me acknowledged another truth I did not want to admit. If they had not followed me that night, I would have never been in a healer's tent. I would never have felt her hand steady on my shoulder. I would not have known she worked behind these quiet stone walls, close enough for me to see her again. The thought came with an odd twist of gratitude I could not swallow whole.

Eric clapped me on the arm, jolting me back to the barracks. "You ready?"

I nodded.

We went to the armory. The air smelled of oil and iron. Men were already strapping on armor, buckles snapping, blades sliding into scabbards.

I took my breastplate from the rack and set it against my chest. The weight settled familiar, a kind of reassurance I could understand. Eric fastened his straps beside me, humming something off-key.

When I finished buckling the belts, we crossed the courtyard toward the stables. The mist was lifting, thin threads of it curling above the walls. The sky was pale and washed in light.

Corven waited by the fence. His black coat shone faintly with dew, his breath coming out in small clouds. I reached for his bridle, running a hand down his neck. He was warm and solid beneath my palm.

"Morning, boy," I said quietly.

He tossed his head once, impatient as always. I slid the saddle into place and tightened the girth.

Eric mounted first, his blond hair catching the light. "Let us see if these farms are really as restless as the captain says."

I climbed into my saddle and settled the reins. "If not, at least it is a ride."

He laughed as he turned his horse toward the gate.

The drawbridge creaked as it lowered, the sound of chains cutting through the morning mist. Guards moved aside, their armor glinting faintly in the pale light.

Eric rode first, his horse tossing its head as it stepped onto the road. I followed, guiding Corven forward. His hooves struck against the stone, then fell into a steady rhythm as we reached the dirt path beyond the walls.

Behind us, the towers faded into fog until only their shapes were left in the distance. The fields ahead stretched wide and quiet beneath a pale sky. The road curved north through the open land like a faint scar.

Neither of us spoke for a long while. The sound of hooves and wind filled the space between us. The rhythm of it steadied me more than I expected.

The northern farms waited ahead, and I tried to keep my thoughts on the task. Still, my mind wandered. I remembered the healer's wing and the firelight moving across the stone walls. I could almost hear her voice again, calm and careful as she worked.

When I returned, I told myself I might walk that

corridor again. Only to see if she was there. Only to be sure I hadn't imagined her.

I told myself it would only be curiosity. Nothing more.

Still, as the wind shifted, I knew I was already lying to myself.

CHAPTER ELEVEN

IRIS

The tailors came before sunrise. Their voices filled the room before I had even spoken a word.

They carried rolls of fabric, silk and lace in shades of white and pink. The scent of lavender clung to their hands. One of them circled me with a measuring tape while the others whispered and wrote.

"Height, five foot four," one said.

"Waist, small. Legs slender. The gown must be grand, something to remember."

They spoke of beauty as if it were a duty. I stood still, listening, unsure what any of it meant.

My father had mentioned no celebration—no feast, no guests. Yet the tailors spoke as though everything had already been decided. I wanted to ask, but the words never came. Questions never pleased him.

When they finished, they bowed and promised to return soon. I nodded and smiled politely until they were gone.

Silence filled the room once more.

I turned toward the wardrobe. My healer's robe lay folded neatly on the chair where I had left it. I let my hand rest on the fabric for a moment before turning away.

Instead, I chose a white, off–the–shoulder–dress. It was soft and light, the hem brushing just above my knees. I tied a white ribbon in my hair and let it fall straight down my back, pale against the fabric.

Raven had said we would be outside for most of the morning. That was reason enough.

I looked in the mirror one last time. The faint red mark on my cheek was nearly gone, but I could still feel it when I turned my head. I drew a slow breath and reached for the door.

I stepped into the corridor, the air cool and still. The torches along the walls burned low, and the faint echo of footsteps followed me as I made my way toward the healer's wing.

Raven was already there, sorting jars and bundles of herbs into neat rows. The room smelled of mint and sage, sharp and clean. The moment she saw me, she grabbed a basket from the table and placed it in my hands.

"Perfect timing," she said. "We are going out today.

The Northern farm needs a few supplies, so we will be collecting herbs on the way."

I blinked, surprised. "Outside the castle?"

She nodded, tying her dark hair back. "Yes. We will be quick."

"Will my father not be angry?" I asked, lowering my voice. "You know how he feels about me leaving."

Raven smiled faintly, the kind of smile that said she had already thought it through. "I spoke to him this morning. He said it is fine, as long as it is for duty."

I sighed. "Of course he did."

She arched a brow. "You sound disappointed."

"The Northern farm is a long walk," I said, adjusting the basket in my hands.

"True," she replied. "But at least you get to walk outside the castle walls today."

I looked toward the window. The morning light spilled through the stone frame, soft and cold. It had been two days since I'd last left the castle, but it already felt too long.

A small smile found its way to my lips. "True, I suppose."

"Then come on," Raven said, already moving toward the door. "Before he changes his mind."

We stepped out into the morning light. The courtyard was alive with sound. Servants hurried between the stables and the kitchens, guards called out orders, and the steady clang of metal rang through the air. The scent of baked bread drifted faintly on the breeze, warm and sweet.

Raven walked ahead, her basket swinging lightly at her side. I followed close behind, the sunlight catching on the pale stone walls around us. When we reached the gates, the guards bowed and stepped aside without question.

The moment we passed through, something inside me loosened.

The air beyond the walls felt different. Softer. It carried the scent of pine and wet grass—the promise of distance and quiet. The noise of the courtyard faded behind us until there was only the rustle of trees and the faint hum of the forest.

Birds called from the branches. The ground was still damp from the night's rain, and my shoes sank slightly into the earth with each step. For the first time in weeks, I could breathe without feeling watched.

We walked for a long while in silence. The trees grew thicker as we went, their branches weaving together above us. Sunlight filtered through in small, scattered patches, lighting the moss that clung to the stones like velvet.

After a while, a different, familiar sound reached me.

Water.

I slowed, listening. The murmur grew clearer the farther we went, until through the brush I caught a glimpse of silver light ahead.

The river.

It ran wide and calm, the surface bright with sunlight. The sound of water moving over stone was faint but clear, a sound I knew by heart. The air grew heavy in my lungs. I hadn't seen this place in years, not since

Father forbade me to leave the castle.

I stopped walking. Raven turned to look at me, puzzled.

The riverbank spread out before us, wildflowers scattered along the edge. And there, hanging from the old oak, were the two swings. The ropes looked worn, the wood dark from rain, but they were still there.

"I used to come here all the time," I said softly. "Before..."

Raven frowned slightly. "Before what?"

"Before he said I could not."

I set the basket down, my fingers brushing the handle. The air felt lighter here, familiar in a way nothing in the castle ever was.

Raven's brow furrowed. "What are you doing?"

"Can we stay," I asked, turning to her, "just for a few minutes?"

She looked at me for a moment, then sighed, though there was a hint of a smile at the corner of her mouth.

"Fine," she said quietly. "A few minutes."

I smiled and stepped toward the swings. The ropes were rough beneath my hands, the wood worn smooth from years of use. I brushed a few leaves from the seat before sitting down. The moment I pushed off the ground, the swing moved, slow at first, then higher, the wind lifting strands of my hair.

Raven laughed softly and took the one beside me. "You used to come here a lot, did you not?"

"All the time," I said, my feet brushing through the grass. "If you swing far enough and jump at the wrong moment, you will fall right into the river."

Raven's eyes widened. "You tried that?"

"Once," I smiled faintly at the memory. "It hurt."

She burst out laughing, the sound soft and genuine. "Saints, you must have been fearless."

"Or foolish," I said, though my smile lingered. For a moment, I could almost see the child I used to be. Carefree. Unwatched. Alive.

The water shimmered below us, sunlight breaking over the surface in ripples of gold. The breeze carried the faint scent of wildflowers, the sound of leaves moving like whispers above our heads. For a moment, it almost felt like the world outside the castle didn't exist.

Then the quiet shifted.

At first, it was only a faint rhythm beneath the wind. Then it grew stronger. The sound of hooves on packed earth, slow and steady.

Raven stopped swinging. "Do you hear that?"

I did. The sound pressed through the calm, coming closer. My hands tightened around the rope, my body going still.

The forest seemed to hold its breath. Even the river sounded distant now, buried beneath the rhythm of approaching horses. I felt my pulse rise, each beat sharp against my ribs.

Raven stood beside me, her voice low. "Travelers, maybe?"

"Maybe," I said, though the word came out thin.

The sound grew louder, breaking through the trees. Sunlight flashed against metal. I caught the shape of armor first, then the glint of reins, and finally the outlines of two riders moving through the shadows.

One of them rode a dark, tall and powerful horse. The rider sat straight with with a steady hand on the reins. Even from a distance, something about him made my breath catch. The sharp jaw. The dark hair. The quiet focus in his eyes.

William.

The second man beside him was blond, his armor bright in the light. He looked young, with an easy careless grin as he scanned the riverbank.

But William saw me first.

His horse slowed, then stopped completely. The movement was sudden enough that the other rider glanced over, confused.

The forest seemed to hush. Even the wind quieted. Only the river kept moving, a low and steady murmur beneath the stillness.

Raven straightened beside me, still holding the basket. I didn't move. My fingers gripped the rope of the swing until it bit into my skin. The world around me felt too still, too fragile.

William's gaze didn't waver. His dark eyes moved across my

face, searching and uncertain. I saw the moment recognition struck him.

His expression shifted and his lips parted slightly.

"Elara?" he said at last, the name quiet, almost hesitant.

The sound of my false name sat there heavy, and the air stalled. I opened my mouth to speak, but nothing came out. The name hung in the air between us, soft and heavy, and all I could do was stare at him.

Raven's eyes flicked toward me, then to him, her expression shifting with dawning realization. I felt the heat rise to my face, the same guilt that had haunted me since the lie first left my lips.

William shifted slightly in his saddle, his gaze steady. "What are you doing here?"

My mind raced for an answer. Of all the questions he could have asked, that one felt the hardest to meet. My throat felt tight, my thoughts stumbling over one another.

Instead, I heard myself say, "How is your shoulder?"

He blinked, caught off guard, then gave a small nod. "It is healing," he said. "You did good work." His voice softened, but the question returned, quieter this time. "What are you doing here?"

I forced myself to meet his eyes. "We are headed to the Northern Farm," I said. "To collect herbs."

His brow lifted slightly. "Really?"

"Yes," I said, holding the basket a little tighter. "It is part of my duties."

For a moment, he said nothing. Then a faint smile touched his lips. "Then we are headed the same way. The captain sent us there this morning."

"Oh," I said, unsure of what else to say. My pulse felt loud in my ears.

He studied me quietly, his expression unreadable. The tension in the air felt fragile, like the space between one heartbeat and the next. Then, in that calm, he tilted his head slightly.

"Would you like a ride?"

The question caught me off guard. My fingers tightened around the handle of the basket. "That is kind, but we will walk," I said quickly. "It is not too far."

"It is a long road," he replied. "You will tire before you reach the fields."

"We will manage," I said, though my voice sounded less certain than I wanted it to.

He smiled, the kind that left me unsure whether he was teasing or serious. "At least let me help."

Raven glanced at me, clearly amused. "I think it is best we accept, Iri–" She caught herself. "Elara."

I felt nauseous "Fine," I said quietly, trying not to sound as flustered as I felt.

William reached out a hand. His horse towered over me, muscles shifting beneath his dark coat. I hesitated, tilting my head back just to meet his eyes.

"Come on," he said, voice calm but firm. "He does not bite."

Behind me, Raven stepped toward the blond

knight's horse. She swung herself up with surprising ease, landing gracefully in the saddle behind him.

The knight turned his head, smiling wide. "Well, I do enjoy some company."

Raven smirked. "Do not get used to it."

Their banter faded around me. I could feel William's gaze still waiting. Slowly, I placed my hand in his. His grip was strong and warm, steady as he pulled me upward.

The ground slipped away beneath my feet. His arm came around my waist, guiding me to the saddle. The motion was smooth, but the warmth of him left my heart unsteady. His hand brushed briefly beneath my shoulder before he let go.

The horse shifted beneath us, muscles rippling under the dark coat. I gripped the edge of the saddle, trying to steady my breath.

"Hold tight," he said, glancing over his shoulder.

I nodded, unsure where to put my hands until instinct took over. My palms found his shoulders, solid and warm through the steel of his armor.

"Ready?" he asked.

I nodded again. "Yes."

William gave the reins a light pull and the horse started forward. The motion was smooth at first, then steady as it found its rhythm along the dirt path. The forest stretched out ahead, filled with soft light and the hum of insects waking in the trees.

Behind us, Raven's laughter broke the quiet. "This

is honestly very kind of you gentlemen," she said, her tone half teasing.

The blond knight turned his head slightly, flashing a grin. "Kindness is a knight's duty."

"Oh?" Raven replied. "And what is your name, kind knight?"

"Eric," he said, glancing back at her.

"Well, Eric," she continued, the corners of her mouth lifting, "what are you two doing all the way out at the Northern farm?"

"Reports of unrest," he said simply. "The captain sent us to look into it. Probably nothing, but we will see."

I listened in silence, my hands still resting lightly on William's shoulders. His armor started cooling beneath my palms. The forest air brushed against my skin, and the smell of pine and river water mixed together.

Eric turned his head again, this time looking straight at me. "You know, Elara," he said with a curious smile, "you look a lot like the

Princess."

My stomach dropped. For a heartbeat, I forgot to breathe. The sound of the river faded, and the world narrowed to the rhythm of the horse beneath me. Raven's head snapped toward me, her expression tight and alert.

William's horse slowed a little, the reins tightening in his hand. The sound of hooves on the path dulled.

Eric was still watching me, amused, as if he'd said

nothing out of turn. "Same blonde hair. Same blue eyes. It is uncanny, really."

Raven's voice came sharp, lighter than it should have been. "Careful, Sir Eric. You will make her nervous."

He laughed, easy and unbothered. "Did not mean offense. Just an observation."

I forced a small smile, though my throat felt tight. My fingers curled against William's armor until the edges pressed into my palms. "People say that sometimes," I said softly. "It is nothing."

Eric chuckled under his breath, clearly not finished. "Dare I say," he added, glancing back at me with a grin, "prettier than Her Highness herself?"

Raven's eyes widened and she stared at me, waiting to see what I'd answer.

My heart stumbled against my ribs. The mention of the princess—of me—sent heat rushing up my neck. I could feel my pulse in my hands, in my throat, everywhere. I tried to laugh, but the sound came thin and uneven. "You should not say that," I managed. "It is not proper."

He only shrugged. "I call it as I see it."

Before I could think of what to say, William's voice came, calm but sharp enough to silence him. "That is enough, Eric."

The blond knight blinked and turned forward, muttering under his breath. The air felt heavy again, pressing close.

Then William looked back at me. "He is not making you uncomfortable, is he, Elara?"

The name hit harder than it should have. *Elara.* The lie I had told him so easily now sounded foreign, almost dangerous. My pulse still hadn't slowed. I forced a small nod. "No," I said quickly. "It is fine."

He studied me for a moment, then nodded once. "Good."

The silence that followed felt softer, but it wasn't quite peace. I realized my hands were still tense against his shoulders. Slowly, I let them loosen, and let my fingers slip back to rest against the leather straps of his armor.

I told myself to breathe. To calm down. He still believed the name. He still thought I was only a healer from the castle. It was fine. Everything was fine.

Raven glanced at me over her shoulder. Her look was quiet but knowing. She didn't have to say anything.

I turned my eyes back to the path, letting the quiet fill the space between us. The lie still lingered, but for now, it was enough that he didn't know.

CHAPTER TWELVE

WILLIAM

We reached the Northern Farm just as the clouds began to gather again. The air smelled of soil and grain, and the low stone fences stretched across the fields. A few farmers stood in the distance, watching as we approached.

I pulled gently on the reins, and Corven slowed to a stop. The ride had been long but steady. I swung my leg over the saddle and dropped to the ground, the weight of the armor shifting with a dull clink.

Elara still sat behind me, holding her basket in one hand. I turned and held my arm out to her. "Here," I offered.

She hesitated for a moment before taking my hand. Her fingers were small and cold against my skin. I steadied her as she slid down, her feet landing lightly on the ground.

"Thank you," she said, her voice low.

I nodded once, letting my hand fall to my side. "You are welcome."

Behind us, Eric jumped off his horse, his boots hitting the dirt. He turned to the brunette healer and offered her a grin. She ignored it and hopped down on her own.

Eric laughed softly. "Independent. A fine thing to be."

She rolled her eyes. "Necessity has a way of teaching it."

I turned my attention to the fields ahead. The land stretched wide, lined with rows of wheat and barley swaying in the wind. Beyond them stood a few wooden sheds and a stone farmhouse, its roof patched in places with hay. Chickens pecked near the fence, and a pair of tired-looking oxen grazed by a trough.

Everything looked peaceful enough at first glance, though the air felt tense. The farmers nearby watched us closely, their faces wary, their hands never far from their tools.

Eric came to stand beside me, his hand resting on the hilt of his sword. "It does not look like unrest to me," he said as he scanned the area.

"Maybe not," I replied, scanning the horizon. "But we will check all the same."

I turned to Elara and Raven. "Gather what you

require. Keep to the path and watch your surroundings. When you are done, wait by the horses.

Elara nodded, adjusting the basket in her hands. Raven gave a brief wave of acknowledgement before they started toward the far end of the field, where wild herbs grew along the fence line.

I watched them for a moment. The breeze lifted the edge of Elara's dress as she walked, her pale blonde hair catching the sunlight. Something about it held my attention longer than it should have.

It wasn't just her appearance. It was the careful way she moved, as if every step meant something. There was grace in it, but also distance, like she was somewhere else entirely.

The feeling unsettled me. I drew a slow breath and looked away, pushing the thought aside.

"Come on," I said to Eric. "Let us see what has stirred such unease among the farmers."

He grinned, already walking ahead. "Lead the way, Sir William."

We crossed the field, the soil soft under our boots. The farmers shifted as we passed, their eyes following us but their mouths staying shut. A few nodded in greeting, but most just went back to their work, slower than before.

The wind carried the smell of hay and damp earth. The chickens scattered as we walked past the coops, their wings brushing the dust into the air. A few wagons sat empty by the fence, one with a broken wheel still leaning against it.

Something felt off. Not danger exactly, but unease that hung heavy, the kind that didn't come from simple work.

Eric glanced around, his hand brushing the hilt of his sword. "Strange," he said quietly. "No one is speaking."

"They are hiding something," I replied, keeping my voice low. "Or waiting for it."

We kept walking until we reached the far end of the field. One of

the sheds stood there, its door half open, creaking softly in the wind.

I pushed it aside.

Inside was a mess. Tools thrown in a pile, sacks split open, and the ground was dark with something that looked like tar or oil.

Eric crouched, pressing two fingers into it. "Fresh," he said. "Smells like pitch."

I knelt beside him. The scent was strong, sharp enough to sting. "They were burning something."

He looked at the walls. There were marks there, deep, deliberate.

Not the kind made by accident.

Eric stood, brushing the dirt from his gloves. "I suppose we should report this to the captain."

I nodded, eyes scanning the field again. The farmers had gone back to their work, but every so often one of them looked over their shoulder, watching us.

"Aye," I said quietly. "We will."

I straightened, letting my hand fall from the wall. The smell of tar still clung to the air.

"Our duty is done here," I said. "We will report our findings and move on. The captain expects us in Branhollow before nightfall."

Eric nodded, his expression thoughtful. "Aye. The village near the old mill."

"That is the one."

We stepped out into the sunlight again, the shed door creaking closed behind us. The farmers had spread out across the field, pretending to work, but their eyes followed us all the same.

Eric gave a low whistle. "They are nervous. Either they know know something—or they are the cause for it."

"Does not matter," I said. "The captain will see to it."

We crossed back through the rows of wheat until the horses came into view. Corven snorted softly when he saw me, pawing at the dirt. The two healers were waiting nearby, with baskets filled with green stems and small white flowers.

Raven stood with her arms crossed, her dark hair falling over one shoulder. "Took you long enough," she said.

Eric grinned. "We like to be thorough."

Elara looked up at me. The sunlight caught in her hair, turning it almost gold. Something about her gaze looked nervous, though she tried to hide it. My chest closed around my heart before I could stop it.

"Did you find anything?" she asked.

I nodded. "Enough to keep the captain interested. Nothing for you to worry about."

Her brow furrowed slightly, but she didn't press.

I adjusted the reins and looked toward the sun, already dipping low over the fields. "We will ride you both back to the castle first," I said. "After that, Eric and I will ride for Branhollow."

Elara opened her mouth to protest, but I was already turning toward Corven. "It will be faster that way," I added.

I mounted, the armor settling against my shoulders with familiar weight. When I looked back, she was still standing beside the horse, the basket clutched tight in her hands.

"Come," I said, holding out my hand.

She hesitated only a moment before placing hers in mine. Her fingers trembled faintly against my palm. The sound of the fields dimmed around us, the world narrowing to that single point of touch.

I lifted her easily. This time, instead of settling her behind me, I guided her in front. Her breath caught, soft but clear in the quiet. She straightened quickly, though I could feel the faint tremor in her back as she steadied herself.

My arm brushed her side as I reached for the reins. Her hair slipped against my arm, light against my gauntlet. For a heartbeat, I went briefly breathless.

"Comfortable?" I asked, keeping my voice low.

She nodded. "Yes."

Corven shifted beneath us, his weight rocking gently from side to side. He patiently waited for a signal. My hand stayed on the reins, the other resting lightly at her waist to steady her.

The faint scent of her hair reached me. It wasn't the sharp tang of

herbs most healers carried. It was softer. Clean. Something floral, like lilac or lavender. Too fine for someone who spent her days tending wounds.

I told myself not to notice. Focus on the road. On the fields. On anything but her.

But it was useless. The wind caught her hair and lifted it just enough to brush my chin. My heartbeat stumbled once, hard and quick. Every small movement seemed louder than it should have: the sound of her breath, the rustle of fabric and the warmth of her back against my armored chest.

Corven started forward, and Elara steadied herself quickly. Her hands gripped the edge of the saddle. I could feel her body relax little by little as the tension left her spine.

The forest opened wider as we rode, the trees spreading apart to let the sunlight fall in thin golden bands across the path. The rhythm of Corven's steps steadied beneath us, each stride smooth and strong.

The quiet between us was no longer awkward. It felt weighted—as if both of us were holding our breath for reasons neither could admit.

Her scent lingered. The faintest movement of her hair was enough to pull my thoughts apart. I forced my eyes forward, counting Corven's strides, though it did nothing to steady me.

After a while, her voice broke the silence. "Are we close?"

Her tone was soft, almost hesitant, as if she didn't want to disturb the stillness around us.

"Almost," I replied. "You will see the gates soon."

The path curved, and the sound of running water reached us. The same river that wound beneath the castle's forest edge came into view, its surface bright in the fading light. Two swings hung from an old tree by the water, the same one Elara sat on earlier. They swayed slightly in the breeze, just enough to move the air around them.

Without meaning to, I slowed Corven. His steps grew softer until we came to a stop by the bank.

The others rode on for a few paces before realizing we had halted.

Elara turned around and looked up at me, her voice uncertain. "Why are we stopping?"

For a moment, I didn't answer. I was watching the river, the same one where I'd found her that morning. The light slid over the water like glass, catching on the ripples.

"No reason," I said at last. My voice came out lower than I intended. "It is a good place to rest the horse."

She nodded, though she didn't move. Her fingers brushed the edge of her dress, twisting the fabric lightly. The gesture was small, almost nervous.

The breeze shifted. Her pale blonde hair lifted and

brushed against my arm. I felt it like a spark. Too soft. Too close.

Corven shifted his weight beneath us, impatient to move, but I didn't give the signal. My hand tightened on the reins, not because I meant to stop, but because I couldn't quite bring myself to go on.

I knew I should ride. The road to Branhollow waited. The captain would ask questions if we were late.

But none of that seemed to matter in that moment. Not the orders. Not the distance ahead.

All I could hear was the quiet sound of the river, and her breathing just in front of me.

I told myself it was nothing. Just a simple pause, a moment to rest.

Yet I stayed there, watching the water move in the light.

Maybe I just wasn't ready to take her back to the healer's wing. Not yet.

CHAPTER THIRTEEN

IRIS

I stared at him, uncertain if I'd heard him right. Raven frowned, her arms folding across her chest.

Before either of us could ask again, William stepped down from his horse. The movement was easy, practiced. He looked up at me, sunlight catching the metal on his armor as he straightened.

"Let us stay here for a bit," he said.

I blinked, the words caught me off guard. "But I have duties to attend to. We should head back before—"

"I am sure our friends wouldn't mind covering for us," he said, his voice calm, almost teasing.

Eric's eyebrows shot up. "Now hold on. I never said that."

Raven scoffed, folding her arms tighter. "Neither did I. If the captain finds out, we will all get scolded."

Eric turned to her with a grin. "Then do not tell him."

"Easy for you to say," she replied. "You will not be the one to answer to the king's advisor."

Her words hit me like a cold drop of rain. I looked away quickly, my pulse quickening. *Your father,* her eyes seemed to say.

The air shifted again when I felt William's gaze return to me. It was steady, quiet, almost searching. "You have worked hard enough today," he said softly. "A moment of rest will do no harm."

My heart started pounding faster. I wasn't sure if it was from the way he looked at me or from the thought of what my father would do if he ever found out I'd stayed here with a knight.

"I... I do not think we should," I said, my voice barely steady.

He offered his hand anyway. "You can trust me."

Something in the way he said it made the world go still. The river, the breeze, even the birds seemed quieter. I hesitated, then placed my hand in his. His grip was warm and careful, yet my pulse raced through my fingers all the same.

Raven sighed behind me. "Fine. We may spare a few minutes. But you both owe us for this."

Eric smirked. "Fair enough."

I didn't look back. My eyes followed the river, the

water bright as glass in the light. The swings swayed gently in the wind, the ropes creaking with a sound I remembered from childhood. I used to come here to escape my father's voice, back when this place still felt like freedom.

Raven's sigh came again, sharper this time. "Come on, Eric. Let us give them their moment before the sun sets."

Eric grinned but didn't argue. "Very well, but if the captain ask, I will say it was your doing."

"Sure you will," she said. Her eyes found mine once more before she turned away. It was the kind of look that said: *don't you dare get caught.*

I understood. I could already picture Father's anger and disappointment if he found out I went against him again.

The sound of hooves faded, leaving only the hush of the river and the soft creak of the swings. My hands tightened around my gown. I told myself it was only nerves, only the stillness, but the air felt too close, too heavy.

William turned to me. His dark eyes caught the light turning them amber. "You look nervous," he said.

I tried to steady my voice. "Do I?"

He nodded once. "You do."

"Must be from today's work," I said, forcing a small smile. "It has been a long day."

He studied me for a moment. I couldn't tell what he was thinking, only that his gaze lingered longer than it should have. Then he nodded slowly. "Wait here. I will be right back."

Before I could ask where he was going, he turned toward the narrow path along the forest's edge. His boots pressed softly against the earth. The sound of his steps faded, and I was left alone with the rush of water and the faint rustle of leaves.

I took a breath and tried to calm my nerves. The air felt thick, and every sound seemed louder.

My thoughts kept drifting to the castle. To Father. To what he would do if he learned I'd lingered here with a knight. His punishments were never light. The thought made my stomach knot, but some part of me stayed rooted anyway.

Just a little longer, I told myself. Just a little longer to breathe.

I sat down on one of the swings, the old rope cool beneath my fingers. The wood seat creaked softly as I pushed off, letting the wind brush against my face. The water glittered below, sunlight rippling across its surface. For a few seconds, the world felt gentle again, almost like it used to be.

Then I heard footsteps behind me.

I turned, my pulse quickening.

William was walking toward me. The light slid across his armor, catching at the edges of something small in his hands. When he came closer, I saw the worn leather cover, and my eyes widened.

"The Song of the Willow Bride," I said, unable to hide the warmth in my voice. "My favorite story."

He smiled faintly, the kind of smile that didn't rush. "I know. You told me."

He stopped beside me and brushed the dust from the second swing before sitting down. The ropes creaked softly beneath his weight.

The two swings swayed lightly together, the rhythm, slow and even.

I looked at the book again, at the curled pages and worn edges. "The ending always makes me cry," I said quietly.

He turned toward me, the corner of his mouth lifting. "Then maybe I should skip it."

The sound that left me was half a laugh, half a breath. "Are you going to read it?"

"If you wish," he said, simply.

The space between us felt smaller suddenly, filled only by the sound of the water and the faint rustle of the pages. My hands were clasped in my lap, but my fingers wouldn't stay still. I could feel my pulse in them.

I nodded, lips curving into a tiny smile. "I would like that."

He turned the pages slowly, his thumb tracing the worn edges as if they were something delicate. The breeze tugged gently at the paper, and the sunlight shifted across the book.

Then his voice filled the quiet.

"Once there was a farmer's son named Mike, who loved the queen of his land more than the sun loved the day."

The words were simple, but the way he read them

made them sound like something more. His tone was steady, almost reverent, as if the story meant as much to him as it did to me.

My lungs locked, though I tried not to show it. "Mike was a fool,"

I said softly. "He knew loving her would cost him everything."

William looked up at me then. His brown eyes caught the light, glowing gold. "Maybe. Or maybe he just did not care what it cost."

Something inside me shifted. My face flushed, and I turned my gaze back to the river before he could see the color rising in my cheeks. The water moved slow and silver beneath the sun.

"He should have cared," I said softly. "Love like that never ends well."

He didn't speak at once. The sound of the river filled the pause, quiet but constant. Then gently he said, "Perhaps it is not about how it ends. Maybe it is about having it at all."

The words sank deep, stirring something I didn't want to name. My throat felt tight, my fingers curling against the edge of the swing. For a moment, neither of us looked away.

Then he turned another page.

"The queen, whose name was Elara, wept beneath the willow, for she loved him too, though her crown forbade it."

Hearing my false name spoken like that made something twist inside me. It was only a story, yet it felt too close, too raw.

I looked down at my hands, tracing the lines of my fingers as if that could steady me. "That part always hurts the most," I said quietly.

William's gaze lingered on me for a moment before he closed the book gently. "Then perhaps we shall stop there."

The silence that followed was fragile, like a thread pulled tight between us. The water whispered over the stones, and a bird called from somewhere deep in the trees. I could hear my heartbeat in my ears, quick and uneven.

I didn't know what to do with the quiet, so I filled it. "Why did you not ride to Branhollow with Eric?" My voice came softer than I meant it to. "Will the captain not be angry?"

He leaned back slightly, one hand resting on the book in his lap. "He will only be angry *if* he finds out," he said, calm and certain. "And he will not."

I frowned, though there was a hint of a smile tugging at my lips. "You sound too sure of that."

He looked at me then, eyes warm, almost playful. "Because it is worth the risk."

The words hung there, quiet but heavy.

Suddenly, breathing became difficult. "Worth it?" I asked, my voice barely above a whisper.

He nodded. "I wanted to get to know you better."

For a heartbeat, the air seemed to stop moving. My fingers curled around the edge of the swing, the rope rough against my palms. I didn't know where to look. The ground. The river. Anywhere but at him.

No one had ever said something like that to me before. No one had ever risked anything for me. Not the captain's anger, not even a word of defiance against my father.

But would he risk that too? Would he still look at me this way if he knew who I really was? The king's daughter. The girl locked behind stone walls. The one who lied about her name and title.

The thought filled me with guilt. I looked at the river, its surface bright and shifting, and spoke before I could stop myself. "You should not risk your captain's anger for me. No one has ever done that before."

He turned his head, studying me in silence. Then the corner of his mouth lifted. "Then I will be the first."

Something in my chest sank at his words, heavy and sharp with guilt. He didn't know the truth. He didn't know what he was risking, or who for.

"Perhaps you should not," I said looking down.

He watched me for a moment, the smile fading into something softer. "Perhaps I should."

Before I could respond, he rose from the swing. The wood creaked beneath the sudden stillness. He stepped behind me, his boots brushing through the grass. I turned slightly, unsure what he meant to do, but he only rested one hand against the back of the swing.

"Hold on," he said.

The ropes tightened. Then the swing began to move.

Slow at first. The air brushed against my skin, cool

and light. My hair lifted with the wind and brushed across my face. I gripped the ropes tighter, my pulse quickening as the motion grew. The rhythm carried me forward, weightless for a heartbeat before gravity pulled me back again.

The river shimmered below, sunlight glinting over the surface. I laughed once, softly. The sound barely left my lips.

He pushed again, gentler this time. "You like this place," he said behind me.

I nodded, still catching my breath. "I used to come here all the time. Before..." I stopped.

He didn't ask me to finish the sentence. Thank God he didn't.

Instead, his voice came quiet behind me. "I remember when you were at my house. You said it had been years since you held a copy of this book."

I looked down at the ground moving slowly beneath my feet. "Yes. I first found it in the library. I must have read it a hundred times before I lost it. But I still remember every line."

The swing slowed. He caught the ropes and steadied them until I stopped. Then he stepped around to face me. The book was still in his hands.

"Then keep this one," he said.

I blinked. "What?"

He smiled, soft and certain. "You might as well. My parents read it to me more times than I can count. I know it by heart, too."

The sunlight slipped through the trees, touching his

hair and the edge of his armor. For a moment I could not find words. Tension lingered in me. My heart kept hammering.

"I cannot take that," I said finally. "It belongs to you"

He met my eyes. The smile faded into something gentler. "Please," he said. "I want you to have it."

I hesitated, my fingers brushing the cover. The leather was warm from his hands. "Are you sure?"

"I am," he said, his tone steady, certain in a way that made my chest ache.

I looked at the river to steady myself. "Then how will you read it?" I asked quietly.

He thought for a moment, eyes on the water as if the answer waited there. Then he looked back at me. "Maybe you could bring it here," he said. "Same place. Tomorrow."

I stared at him, unsure whether I'd heard him right. "You are asking me to come here tomorrow?"

He nodded, a faint smile tugging at his lips. "If you would like."

The words turned heavy as I processed them.

Tomorrow. It sounded so simple, yet my father's voice echoed in my head, sharp and cold. He would never allow it. He had barely allowed today.

"I have duties to attend tomorrow," I clutched the book a little tighter. "There is always more to do in the healer's wing."

He tilted his head slightly. "And I am supposed to ride to Nestenwood for inspection."

"Then you will be gone," I said.

"Maybe not," he replied, the corner of his mouth lifting. "I am sure our friends wouldn't mind covering for us again."

I shook my head, though I couldn't keep the small laugh from slipping out. "You will get yourself in trouble."

He smiled wider. "Maybe. But some things are worth the trouble."

Something in his tone made my heart sink. It wasn't what he said, but how easily he said it. As if trouble meant nothing at all. As if he didn't understand how dangerous this was for me.

"You should not speak so," I murmured, lowering my gaze to the book in my hands.

He studied me for a moment, his smile fading into something quieter. "Perhaps I should not" he said softly. "But I meant it."

I didn't know what to do with that. The weight of it sat in the space between us, heavy and unspoken. My throat felt tight, and the air seemed thicker now, as if it had learned how fragile this moment really was.

"We should head back," I said finally. "The hour grows late."

He nodded once. "Very well."

We started walking. The path wound along the river before curving toward the castle, the light fading through the trees. Neither of us spoke. The silence wasn't uncomfortable, just careful, as if a single word might break something we couldn't name.

I told myself I wouldn't come back tomorrow—that I shouldn't.

It would be reckless, foolish. But even as I said it in my head, a part of me already wanted to.

When the castle walls came into view, he didn't ask. And I was grateful for that.

CHAPTER FOURTEEN

IRIS

I tied the white headband my hair and adjusted it until it sat neatly in place. The same white, off-shouldered dress from yesterday brushed lightly against my knees as I moved. It felt strange wearing something so simple again, but I didn't want to draw attention.

The morning light poured through the castle windows, soft and golden, as I made my way to the healer's wing. The air smelled faintly of herbs and warm bread drifting from the kitchens.

I told myself not to think about it, not about the river—but each step I took made the memory louder. The sound of his deep voice. The way the sunlight caught in the water. The way he'd said tomorrow.

It had sounded so simple then. Just a word. But

now that morning had come, the word felt heavier. Reckless. I had barely slept, turning over the same thought again and again. I should not go. Father would notice if I vanished too long. He always did. And yet, every time I tried to convince myself, the same image came back: the book in his hands, his voice reading the story aloud.

By the time I reached the healer's wing, I had already made the choice I knew I should never have made.

Raven was already there, sleeves rolled up, arranging jars on the counter. She turned at the sound of my steps and smiled. "Good, you are early."

"About that," I said, hesitating.

Her brow lifted. "About that?"

I took a slow breath. "I was wondering if you could cover for me today."

Raven set down a jar and turned fully toward me. "Cover for you? Why?"

"Going somewhere?" she crossed her arms.

"Yes," I answered quickly. My cheeks warmed before I could stop it.

Raven's lips curved, amusement flickering in her eyes. "Where exactly?"

I didn't answer. I didn't need to. The way her smile widened told me she'd already guessed.

"Oh," she said, dragging the word out. "I see. You are neglecting your duty to meet that same knight?"

Heat crept up my neck. "It is not like that. I only—

he lent me something, and I wish to return it. That is all."

Raven raised a brow. "Ah, yes—and you chose that pretty dress merely to return a book?"

I sighed. "Raven."

Her teasing expression softened, replaced by something more serious. "No, Iris. I can not cover up for you again."

I blinked. "What?"

"Yesterday, your father kept drilling me about where you were. I told him you slipped in the mud and needed to bathe before coming back." She rubbed the back of her neck. "He barely believed that. If I lie again, he will know something is off."

My stomach twisted at the thought of my father's anger, but I kept pushing. "Please," I said quietly. "Just this once. He will not notice my absence."

She gave me a long look, the kind she used when she was torn between reason and loyalty. "You will truly to get us both killed one day."

"Then at least we will die trying," I said with a weak smile.

Raven groaned, though there was the faintest laugh behind it.

"Very well. But if the king asks, you are helping the midwives. Do not give me the cause to regret this."

"I will not, I swear." I promised.

She pointed a finger at me. "And you owe me a week of work."

"Deal."

Raven shook her head as I turned toward the door. "I hope he is worth all this trouble."

I didn't answer. Maybe because I didn't know yet. I only knew that as I stepped out of the healer's wing, my heart was already racing at the thought of seeing him again.

"Wait a moment," Raven said.

I stopped and turned back toward her. "What?"

She crossed her arms, her tone sharper now. "Does this William know your true identity?"

My throat tightened. "Not yet."

"Not yet?" she repeated, stepping closer. "You did not tell him yesterday? After he abandoned his duty for you?"

I looked down at the cool floor. "I will tell him when I can trust him."

Disbelief flickered across Raven's face. "When you can trust him? Iris, he left his duty for you. He has already proven more trust than most men in this castle."

"It is different," I said quickly. "If he finds out who I am, he will act differently, too. They all do."

Raven's jaw tighten. "So let me understand this," she said slowly. "You are about to sneak off against your father's orders to meet a man who could get you both in serious trouble if you are caught, and you do not even trust him enough to tell him your name?"

The words hit hard. Shame rose up my body. I wanted to argue, but the truth was tangled somewhere between fear and longing, and I couldn't pull it free.

"I do not know," I said finally. "I do not know yet."

Raven studied me for a moment. Her expression softened, though worry still lingered in her eyes. "Then figure it out soon," she said. "Because I will be able to cover up for you forever, not for a third time."

"I will," I promised, though my voice didn't sound as steady as I wanted it to.

She pointed a finger at me. "You owe me for this, Iris. Remember that. I am not dealing with any more of the king's anger."

A small smile tugged at my lips. "I will make it up to you."

"You better," she said, turning back to her work. "Now go before I regret helping you at all."

I nodded and started for the door. My heart thudded faster with each step. Whatever waited for me beyond the castle walls, I knew I was already too far in to turn back.

CHAPTER FIFTEEN

WILLIAM

I leaned against the old tree, the bark rough against my back. It was the same one that held the two swings, swaying gently in the wind.

The river moved slow beneath the morning light, quiet save for the soft pull of the current against the stones. I had been there for a while now, long enough for the sun to climb higher, long enough to start wondering if she would come at all.

Convincing Eric to go to Nestenwood without me had been harder than expected. He questioned me for half an hour before finally agreeing, but only after I promised him my market-day sweets. That was no loss. I had never cared much for sugar.

What I did care about was whether she would show up.

Elara hadn't sounded certain yesterday. Her voice had held that careful distance again, like she wanted to say no but didn't know how. Still, I came. Just in case.

I leaned off the tree, scanning the edge of the woods again. The breeze rustled the leaves, carrying nothing but the sound of water and birds.

Part of me felt foolish for waiting. I was still in my armor, the metal warm under the sun, just in case anyone from the castle happened to see me. It was easier to pretend I was on patrol than to admit I was standing here waiting for a girl.

I told myself I would leave soon. Another minute. Maybe two.

Then movement caught my eye.

A figure stepped through the trees, sunlight spilling around her like it was drawn to her. The same white dress. The same pale blonde hair. The same white headband. She paused for a moment, as if she was still deciding whether to come closer.

Relief hit me harder than I expected. "You came," I said. My voice came out softer than I meant it to.

She smiled faintly and brushed a strand of hair behind her ear. "I almost did not."

"I am glad you did."

Her eyes flicked toward the swings, then back to me. "You waited?"

"Perhaps," I said, trying to sound casual. "I did not want to miss the chance."

Color touched her cheeks as she turned away, pretending to look at the river. The sight made something tighten in my torso. It was a small thing that I didn't quite know what to do with.

My eyes drifted to her hands, to the book she held close against her. My book—no, hers now—the one I had read so many times it felt like a part of me. Somehow, it looked right in her hands, as if it had always been meant to belong to her.

The wind lifted her hair, sending a few blonde strands across her bare shoulder. The sunlight caught them, turning them almost gold. Her pale skin looked soft in the morning light, her eyes bright and alive, the kind of blue that made it hard to look away. She looked nothing like the healers I passed in the castle halls. She looked like she belonged to another world entirely.

She turned back to me, her fingers brushing over the book's worn cover. "Do you want it back?" she asked softly.

I shook my head. "No. I gave it to you."

Her lips curved slightly, but her eyes stayed on the pages. "It does not feel right keeping something that means so much to you."

"Maybe it means more now," I said simply.

The words lingered between us longer than I meant them to.

I sat down beneath the tree. The grass was cool beneath my palms, and the air smelled of river water and sun-warmed leaves. The sound of the current filled the quiet, steady and calm.

"Sit," I said, nodding to the space beside me.

She hesitated. Her hands tightened around the

book, knuckles pale. For a moment, I thought she might refuse. But then she lowered herself beside me. The hem of her dress brushed my arm as she sat, soft against the metal of my armor. The faint scent of roses clung to the air.

I tried not to look at her, but my eyes found her anyway. Light filtered through the branches and caught in her hair, lighting each strand. She seemed close enough to reach out and touch, though I didn't dare.

Instead, my gaze fell to the book resting in her lap. "Well, Elara," I said, keeping my tone light, "would you like to do the honours this time?"

Her lips parted slightly. "You want me to read it?"

I nodded. "I read it yesterday. Now it is your turn."

Her smile came small and uncertain. She opened the book, careful with the worn edges. The parchment crackled softly. "Very well then," she said.

Her voice was gentle when she began, smooth and careful like she'd told the story a hundred times before.

"Once there was a farmer who lived by the willow fields," she read. "His hands were rough from work, but his heart was kind. And every day, he looked toward the palace beyond the hills, wondering what it would be like to see its gardens up close."

Her words filled the clearing, soft and clear. I found myself listening, not to the story, but to the sound of her voice. It was warm, light, carrying something I hadn't known I was missing until that moment. The distance between us felt smaller. I could almost feel the warmth of her bare shoulder against my armored.

She turned another page, her thumb tracing the edge as if she didn't want to lose her place. "Then one morning, the queen came riding through the fields. She spoke to the farmer with kindness, asking about his crops, his home, his dreams. And without asking he fell in love."

Her tone softened. The wind caught a strand of her hair and lifted it across her face. She tucked it back absently, never breaking from the page. I watched the movement, the way her brow creased when she read something that struck her. She seemed lost in the story, caught between what was written and what she felt.

When she reached the part where the king discovered the farmer's secret, she hesitated. "The king sent the farmer away," she said quietly. "Far from the palace, far from the queen. He told him that love was not for men who worked the soil."

Her words faded, and for a long moment, only the river answered.

She closed the book halfway, her fingers still holding the page. "That part always hurts," she said softly.

I nodded slowly. "It is the kind of pain that stays, even when the story ends."

Her eyes lifted to mine, hesitant, searching. "You think it was foolish?" she asked. "The farmer, I mean—to love someone he could never have?"

I hesitated. The truth came quietly. "No. I think he was brave. Maybe the bravest kind of man there is."

She studied me, her expression unreadable. Then, slowly, she closed the book.

The breeze moved through the grass, brushing against her dress. Her hand rested near mine, close enough that I could feel the warmth of it. I didn't move. Neither did she.

For a moment, everything around us stilled: the river, the air, even the light itself.

She spoke again, barely above a whisper. "Do you think the queen ever forgot him?"

I turned my head, meeting her eyes. "No," I said. "You do not forget people who change the way you see the world."

A sound caught low in her throat. It was barely audible, but I heard it. Her eyes flicked away, as if she couldn't bear to hold my gaze too long. A faint color rose to her cheeks, and she looked down at the book in her lap, tracing her thumb along the worn edge.

When she finally spoke again, her voice was softer, almost thoughtful. "It is strange," she said. "A story can hurt, but you still want to read it again."

Her smile was small, delicate, the kind that faded too quickly.

The quiet around us thickened. The river moved slow behind her, its sound a low hum beneath the trees. She sat close enough that I could feel her skin vibrate against mine. The curve of her shoulder brushed the edge of my gauntlet, and something in me clenched.

I wanted to reach for her. To rest a hand on her arm. To pull her closer and tell her that I understood what she meant, that some things were worth hurting for. My fingers twitched at my side, caught between restraint and want.

She turned slightly toward me, her hair brushing against my hand. The sunlight fell through the branches, scattering gold across her dress. For a moment, I almost gave in. I could already feel the shape of her against my chest, and the weight of her leaning into me.

Then the sound of hooves cut through the stillness.

It came faint at first, then closer. The world snapped back into motion. She turned her head toward it, her body tensing. I forced my hand to drop as my jaw tightening when the rhythm grew louder through the trees.

Eric rode into view with his usual grin and reins in hand. "Sir William," he called, his tone brisk. "All knights to the yard. The captain's making an announcement and wants a check."

The words sank into the still air, and for a second, I didn't move. I could have stayed there forever. The river behind her, the book still in her hands, the sunlight turning her hair pale as glass. It was the kind of moment you didn't want to end, the kind that made everything else feel small.

But duty didn't wait for anyone.

"I should go," I said quietly.

Her eyes lifted, hesitant. "You should."

Something in the way she said it made it harder to turn away. I wanted to tell her I'd come back. I wanted to promise it. Instead, I just nodded once and forced myself to move.

By the time I reached Corven, the calm of the river was gone. I swung into the saddle, the weight of my armor settling heavy on my shoulders again. Eric was already mounted, reins in hand.

"Took your time," he said.

"Had a reason," I replied, tightening my grip on the reins.

He smirked but didn't ask. The two of us rode through the forest path. The wind was colder now and the sound of hooves echoed through the trees. The castle walls rose ahead, tall and gray, their flags snapping in the breeze.

The closer we got, the louder the noise became—training calls, the clang of steel, men shouting orders. The world I belonged to. The one that didn't wait for softness.

When we reached the yard, rows of knights were already forming. The captain stood at the center, his voice carrying above the rest.

Eric and I joined the line. I straightened and drew in a slow breath. My shoulder ached beneath the armor, as the wound had not yet healed, but I ignored it.

"Listen closely," the captain began. "The king has received word of unrest beyond the southern borders. So far, the threats are harmless, but they may not stay that way."

The men shifted, some glancing at each other. The tension in the yard grew heavier.

"To strengthen the peace," the captain went on, "His Majesty has arranged a marriage between our princess and the prince of Valebran. It will secure an alliance between our kingdoms and ensure safety for our borders.

"The ceremony will take place within the month," the captain continued. "A royal escort will be needed for the journey. Those who volunteer will receive additional pay, as it will be a long road and a dangerous one. The journey could last a week or a month depending on the weather and the route."

He looked over us, his sharp eyes sweeping through the line.

"Anyone who wishes to volunteer, report your name before the end of the month. That is all. Dismissed."

The yard filled again with noise. Armor rattled. Voices rose.

Eric turned toward me, his grin already forming. "You hear that? Extra coins. I am volunteering."

I barely heard him. Pressure built in my chest. A month away from the castle. A month without her.

Eric nudged me again. "You are not signing up?"

I shook my head slowly. "No."

He gave a low whistle. "You are passing on extra gold? You must be losing your mind."

"Perhaps," I said quietly.

Eric laughed, shaking his head as he walked off toward the captain, already calling out his name to volunteer.

I adjusted my gloves and turned toward the stables. If the others wanted extra gold, they could have it. I had no use for it.

CHAPTER SIXTEEN

IRIS

The morning light spilled through my window as I tied the pink ribbon into place. It sat neatly behind my hair, soft against my scalp. The dress I wore was white, patterned with pale pink flowers and tied with pink lace down the front. The skirt brushed my ankles when I moved, light and easy to walk in. The long sleeves covered my arms, warm in the sunlight.

Raven had not been pleased when I asked her to cover for me again. I had to promise her I would buy her the finest jewels I could find once I was able to. She sighed, muttering that I was a troublemaker, but she agreed all the same.

I went to the healer's wing soon after. At the far end of the corridor was the same door I always used, the one hidden behind the old shelf of herbs. It opened straight into the forest, far from the guards' patrols. The hinges creaked softly as I pushed it open.

Behind me, Raven's voice carried faintly through the hall. "Try not to get caught."

I didn't answer. My pace quickened instead.

The air outside was warm, the sky bright and clear. I followed the narrow path through the trees, the grass brushing my skirts as I walked. The sound of birds rose and fell above me. Each footstep felt louder than it should have.

I knew I shouldn't be doing this. I knew it even as I kept walking.

If Father ever found out I'd left the castle again, his temper would turn sharp enough to draw blood.

But still, I went.

I didn't know what I expected to find, or why I needed to find it. Only that I did.

We hadn't planned to meet today. There had been no promise between us, no word at all. But some part of me hoped he might still be there, waiting by the riverbank like before.

And if he wasn't, I told myself I would turn back. I would return to the healer's wing, pretend none of this had happened, and help Raven with her work.

But I didn't turn back.

The path curved ahead, sunlight spilling through the leaves in quiet, golden lines. The sound of the river reached me before I saw it. My heartbeat quickened.

Through the trees, a figure came into view. He stood

by the water's edge, still and quiet beneath the branches.

William.

He wasn't wearing armor this time. The black tunic he wore fit close around his chest, the fabric tied loosely at the neck. A dark belt crossed his waist, and his sleeves were rolled to his elbows.

The light caught the muscles beneath his skin, strong and well-shaped. When he shifted, I saw the curve of his biceps and the way the fabric strained faintly at his shoulders.

For a moment, I just watched him. He was facing the water, quiet and still, one hand resting at his side. He looked nothing like the knight I'd met in the healer's wing, but more like the man I met at the theatre. So calm and unburdened.

My heart started beating faster.

When his eyes met mine, a grin tugged at his lips. "I did not expect you to come."

The sound of his voice caught me off guard. "I—" I hesitated for a moment, then looked down. "Neither did I expect you."

He smiled, that small, teasing kind of smile. "I am on night watch today, so my morning is free." He paused, his tone softer. "And you?"

"The same as always," I said, brushing a strand of hair behind my ear. "I still have work in the healer's wing. But Raven decided to cover for me again."

His brow lifted slightly, amusement flickering in his eyes. "So you abandoned your duty—to see me? Or should I assume, since we we made no plans, that you came to see the river?"

I shifted my weight, suddenly embarrassed. I looked away quickly, pretending to focus on the ripples in the water. His quiet laugh reached me, low and rough, and it only made my heart beat faster.

"Maybe both," I said softly. My voice didn't sound steady, not even to me.

He chuckled again, the sound deep and easy. "Then I will count that as a victory."

I bit back a smile and looked down at my hands. The air felt warmer now, softer somehow. The river moved quietly beside us, carrying the light across its surface.

Then he said, "You did not bring the book."

I looked down at my hands.. "No. I think I forgot it in my bedchamber."

He nodded once, the faintest smile still playing on his lips. "Good. It suits you better than it ever did me."

The words settled in my chest, warm and confusing. I didn't know how to answer, so I only watched him as he moved toward the nearest tree. He lowered himself to the ground, his movements unhurried, the sunlight catching his dark hair.

I hesitated before sitting, too. The grass was cool beneath my palms, damp from the morning. My dress gathered around my knees as I sank down beside him. The space between us felt small but certain, the kind of space that made it hard to think about anything else.

For a while, we didn't speak. The sound of the river

filled the quiet between us, steady and low. I could feel the warmth of him at my side, close enough that it brushed against my sleeve. Every small shift he made seemed louder than it should have been.

He turned his head slightly, and when our eyes met, he didn't look right away. Something flickered there, hesitation maybe, or the kind of courage that comes before a choice.

Then, slowly, he reached out.

His hand found my waist, light at first, as if waiting to see if I'd pull away. I didn't. His fingers lingered there, unsure, and I saw the faint tremor in his hand, the smallest sign that he was nervous, too.

I froze. My pulse stumbled against my ribs. He looked as though he might pull back, and for a moment, I almost let him. But before I could think better of it, I leaned closer.

My shoulder brushed his arm, and then my head found his shoulder. The movement was instinct, quiet and thoughtless, but the warmth of him under my cheek made something inside me flutter. The butterflies came quickly, wild and restless.

He didn't move. His arm stayed where it was, steady now, no longer trembling. I felt him exhale slowly, the rise and fall of his chest beneath me. When I looked up, there was a faint smile on his lips—almost disbelieving, like he couldn't quite believe I'd stayed this close.

The quiet stretched between us, soft and unhurried.

The air smelled faintly of grass and the river water, the kind of calm that made the rest of the world feel far away. I could hear the steady rhythm of his heart through his tunic, each beat strong and mimicking my own.

I tried to focus on something else, anything else. "What did the captain announce yesterday?" I asked quietly. "You left so early I did not get the chance to ask."

He shifted slightly, his hand brushing my waist as he pulled me a little closer. A small gasp escaped me, but I didn't move away. His arm stayed there, steady, and I let myself lean closer against him. My head stayed resting on his shoulder, and he smiled faintly at the gesture.

"Nothing too serious," he answered. "The captain said they have received small threats along the borders. Nothing dangerous yet, but it could turn. The king is planning to marry off his daughter soon, to one of the neighboring kingdoms. Says it will strengthen ties. Build an alliance if war breaks."

The words struck like ice.

For a moment, I couldn't breathe. The stillness that had settled around us shattered at once. The air that had felt warm now felt sharp, heavy, and wrong.

He kept talking, unaware. "He asked for volunteers to join the trip, but I did not sign up."

I didn't hear the rest. My heartbeat filled my ears, drowning everything else out. Marriage. My father was already arranging it.

He was deciding my life in the same tone he used for border threats and alliances.

My body went still. Then, without thinking, I stood.

"I have to go,"

He rose halfway, confusion flashing across his face. "Elara, what is wrong?"

"Nothing," I said, forcing the word out. "I just need to go."

Before I could move, his hand caught my wrist. The touch wasn't rough, but it stopped me. His voice was quiet, steady. "Something is wrong. You do not look like someone who simply has to go."

My breath hitched. His eyes searched mine, and for a moment I almost told him. Almost. But I couldn't. Not now.

"I just remembered," I said quickly, trying to steady myself. "Raven said she needed extra help. One of the soldiers lost too much blood. I promised her I would come back if she needed me."

He hesitated, still holding my wrist, then finally let go. The warmth of his touch lingered even after his hand dropped away.

"I see," he said, his voice lower now. "Then you should go. Be careful."

I nodded, not trusting myself to speak. "I will."

I turned and ran, the sound of my footsteps swallowed by the forest. The wind caught my hair as branches brushed against my arms, but I didn't slow. My pulse thundered in my ears. Every thought tangled into the words: *marry off his daughter.*

By the time the castle walls came into view, my breath was ragged. I slipped through the back entrance that led into the healer's wing, the same one I always used to sneak out.

Raven looked up from where she was tending to a guard's arm, her sleeves rolled to her elbows. "Saints above, you look—"

I didn't let her finish. I rushed past her, nearly knocking over a stool. "I will be back," I muttered, though I didn't even know if I would.

I pushed through the next door and into the corridor. My steps echoed against the stone as I moved faster with every turn. The hall stretched long and endless, sunlight spilling through the tall windows in bright streaks across the floor.

When I reached the throne room, the guards straightened at the doors. Their eyes flicked to me before they bowed and stepped aside. The heavy doors opened with a low groan.

I stepped inside, the doors closing behind me with a heavy thud. The air felt colder here, sharper somehow.

"Father," I said, my voice steadier than I felt.

He didn't look surprised to see me. His gaze lifted from the parchment in his hands, slow and measured. "You are meant to be aiding Raven in the healer's wing," he said.

I stepped forward as my hands curled into fists at my sides. "You are marrying me away?" The words came out louder than I intended, thick with disbelief. "You said we would wait until I was eighteen!"

His expression hardened, the faintest crease forming between his brows. "Where did you hear this from?"

"That is not important!" I snapped. "Explain it. Now!"

He exhaled through his nose, setting the parchment aside with deliberate calm. "I said," he began, "that you would be married within the next month *if* the threats from our borders grow worse."

My heart pounded in my chest. "What threats?"

"None you should concern yourself with," he replied, his tone clipped.

"That is not fair," I said, my voice rising. "You cannot just decide my life for me. I should have a say in who I marry."

"If it secures the safety of our kingdom," he said, rising slightly from his throne, "then yes. I will gladly do it."

The words hit harder than I expected. My heart sank "So all you care about is the kingdom? Not me?"

He looked down at me, his face carved from stone. "You are a princess before you are my daughter."

Something inside me broke. I stumbled back, trying to breathe, but the air felt too thin. Tears gathered behind my eyes, hot and sharp, but I forced them down. I would not let him see me cry.

He saw anyway. His jaw tightened. "Get out."

I turned and walked away, my steps quick, uneven. The guards lowered their heads as I passed. The servants drew back, startled, their voices falling silent until only my footsteps filled the corridor.

When I reached my chambers, I shut the door behind me and leaned against it. The sound echoed through the room. The fire had burned low, the faint glow flickering over the walls.

He would marry me off within a month. Not when I was eighteen. Not when I was ready. Within a month.

Anger rose sharp in my chest. He didn't see me as his daughter. Only as a piece to trade. A means to strengthen his throne.

The tears came then, no matter how hard I tried to stop them. I pressed my palms to my eyes, breathing hard, until the room blurred.

When I lowered my hands, the firelight caught the tears still clinging to my lashes. The anger in my chest gave way to something heavier, something that ached.

William.

I thought of the way he looked at me, the softness in his voice, the

way his smile always seemed unsure at first, as if he wasn't used to smiling.

Somewhere between those quiet moments, something had changed. I cared for him. And he, in his own quiet way, cared for me. There was no denying it anymore.

But the thought that followed made my chest tighten until it hurt.

Would he still look at me that way if he knew?

If he found out I wasn't Elara the healer, but Princess Iris, the king's daughter, the girl being bargained away like a coin traded for pace?

The question wouldn't leave me. It sank deep, cold and unrelenting. My throat felt tight just imagining his face when he learned the truth. The trust in his eyes. The way it would fade.

I pressed a hand to my chest, trying to steady my breathing, but the ache only grew sharper. Still, beneath the fear, the truth waited quiet and insisted.

He deserved to know.

I turned toward the window. The last light of the day stretched across the sky, turning the glass to gold. The castle was still, the halls hushed in that soft, waiting silence that came before night.

I breathed in, slow and careful.

No matter what it cost me, I had to tell him.

CHAPTER SEVENTEEN

IRIS

The moonlight spilled through the window, pale and cold against the floor. I leaned against the frame, my forehead resting lightly on the glass. The castle was silent at this hour. Even the guards' footsteps had faded from the corridor.

It was well past midnight. I hadn't joined my father for dinner, and he hadn't sent for me. No tray. No servant knocking softly at the door. Nothing. He hadn't cared whether I ate or starved.

My fists curled at my sides. The thought stung more than I wanted to admit.

All night, my mind had been turning over the same thing—the marriage, the threats, and William. How I would tell him the truth. What he would think when he learned who I really was. Would he look at me differently? Would he stop looking at me at all?

The thought made my chest feel tight again, but before I could lose myself in it, a low growl sounded beneath the fabric of my nightgown.

I froze, then let out a quiet sigh. My stomach. Of course.

I tried to ignore it, folding my arms across my chest, but the growl came again, louder this time. I closed my eyes for a moment, feeling defeated.

"Fine," I muttered to myself.

Pushing away from the window, I slipped into my slippers and pulled a light pink shawl around my shoulders. The fire had long died out, leaving the air cool against my skin. I cracked open the door and glanced down the hall.

Empty.

The corridor stretched quiet and still, lit only by a few weak torches. Their flames flickered low, brushing the walls with faint orange light. I walked slowly at first, my footsteps soft against the stone, careful not to wake the guards that sometimes patrolled this side of the castle.

The air smelled faintly of wax and smoke. My shadow moved beside me, long and thin. I turned down the last passage toward the kitchens, where the smell of bread and herbs still lingered from the evening meal.

The door creaked softly as I pushed it open. Inside, the warmth was faint but there. A few coals glowed in the hearth, and the tables were cleared, everything neat and still.

No servants. No guards. Just the hush of the night.

I stepped inside, my fingers brushing the edge of one table as I passed. The wood felt cool beneath my touch. A half loaf of bread sat on a tray, forgotten. I reached for it, more out of habit than hunger.

The air shifted.

It wasn't loud, just the faintest sound at first, leather against stone. Slow, deliberate steps. Heavy enough to belong to armor.

I stopped moving. My hand froze mid-reach. The quiet suddenly felt too deep, like the room itself was holding its breath with me.

"Elara?"

The sound of my false name broke the silence. Only one person called me by that name.

My pulse stumbled. I turned slowly toward the sound.

He stood near the edge of the shadows, his armor catching what little light there was. His helm was still on, the metal dull in the fire's glow, but I didn't need to see his face. I knew that stance. That voice. That stillness.

William.

My chest tightened. The room felt smaller all at once. I tried to steady my breathing, to sound calm even as my pulse thudded hard in my throat. "What are you doing here?"

He stepped closer, the metal of his boots soft against

the stone. His voice came even beneath the helm. "The captain ordered me to patrol the kitchens tonight. Make sure everything is in order." He paused, his head tilting slightly. "And you? What are you doing in the castle this late?"

My throat went dry. "Oh, I—uh—sleep here," I said quickly. "In the barracks. With the other healers."

The words tumbled out far too fast. Saints, it was such a terrible lie, that I could almost hear Raven groaning in my head.

I forced a smile, hoping he wouldn't notice how nervous I sounded. "I came here to find something to eat. The captain said it was alright."

He shifted slightly, the faint sound of armor moving breaking the quiet. "The captain said that?"

"Yes," I said, nodding too quickly. "He... he knows how much I work."

There was a moment of silence. I could feel his eyes on me through the narrow slit of his helm. The longer it went on, the warmer my cheeks felt.

Finally, he spoke. "You are a terrible liar, you know that?"

My brows lifted. "What?"

He took a step closer, his tone softer now. "You start talking too fast when you are hiding something."

I stared at him, unsure whether to laugh or run. "I am not hiding anything," I managed.

"Right," he said, the faintest hint of a smile in his voice. "Then I suppose I should let you eat before you faint from all the honest work."

The corner of my mouth lifted despite myself. "Maybe you should."

He reached past me, grabbed a small loaf from the counter, and held it out. "Here."

I hesitated before taking it, my fingers brushing the cool edge of his gauntlet. "Thank you."

He nodded once. "You are welcome."

I took a small bite, the bread soft and faintly sweet on my tongue. The silence pressed around us, gentle but full.

When I looked up, really looked at him, I forgot how to breathe. The firelight flickered against his armor, catching in the lines of his shoulders and the curve of his jaw beneath the helm. His presence filled the room in a quiet way, steady and certain.

And all I could think about was the lie between us.

He had been nothing but kind. Patient. Trusting. And I had met that with half-truths and fear.

The thought stung.

I set the loaf down on the counter and drew a slow breath. "William," I said, barely above a whisper.

He turned slightly toward me. "Yes?"

My throat tightened. "I—I um..."

The words refused to come. My heart began to pound harder, each beat loud enough that I was sure he could hear it. My palms felt damp. I tried again, but my voice faltered, caught somewhere between my chest and my throat.

He tilted his head. "Elara?"

I couldn't do it. Not here. Not like this. The truth

felt too heavy, too dangerous. I could already see the look that might cross his face once he knew who I really was. A knight's loyalty belonged to the crown, and the crown was my father.

I looked down at my hands, my breath unsteady. "Um... nothing," I said quietly. "It is nothing."

He watched me for a moment, and though I couldn't see his expression beneath the helm, I felt the weight of his gaze. Then he gave a short nod. "Very well."

The tension settled again, softer now but still charged with everything left unsaid. I picked up the loaf, pretending to eat, even though my stomach had knotted tight.

Tomorrow, I told myself. I'll tell him tomorrow. He deserves to know.

But even as I whispered it in my head, I wasn't sure I would.

CHAPTER EIGHTEEN

IRIS

And I was right.

It had been twelve days, and I still hadn't said a word.

We had met in secret whenever we could—at the riverbank, beneath the same tall tree with the two swings that swayed in the wind. We talked. We laughed. We read *The Song of the Willow Bride* until I knew every word by heart. Each time, I told myself I would tell him the truth. Each time, my courage slipped away before I could.

But today would be different. It had to be.

The air was soft and warm. I wore a pale pink dress with short sleeves and white lace tied across the front. The skirt brushed my knees when I moved. A white headband kept my hair back, though a few strands had already escaped.

I sat on one of the branches of the swing's tree, just above where the ropes hung. The bark pressed cool against my legs as I waited, looking out toward the river. The water caught the light, moving slow and silver beneath the morning sun.

We hadn't planned to meet today. Still, some part of me hoped he would still come.

The forest was quiet, save for the usual sound of the river and the faint creak of the old rope below me.

Suddenly, the air changed. Footsteps approached.

I turned.

William stepped through the trees, sunlight falling across his shoulders as if it had been waiting for him. He was wearing a black blouse, the fabric loose at his collar and fitted close across his chest. When he moved, the fabric pulled faintly over his biceps, tracing the shape of muscle beneath.

My eyes lingered longer than they should have.

He always looked different like this. Less like a knight. More like someone real. The kind of real that made my chest feel unsteady.

I leaned forward slightly, smiling to myself. Maybe I could surprise him. Just once.

But the branch shifted beneath me.

It gave a soft creak, and before I could grab the rope, my foot slipped. The world tilted. My heart lurched. A startled breath left my lips—

And then strong arms caught me.

Everything stopped.

I blinked up at him, breathless. His hold was steady, his chest rising against mine. For a heartbeat, I could feel nothing but the warmth of him, the soft thud of his pulse where his arms wrapped around me.

He looked down at me, brown eyes soft with amusement. A small smile tugged at his lips. "Good morning," he said quietly. "Interesting way to greet someone."

Heat climbed to my cheeks before I could think. "I did not mean to fall."

A low chuckle rumbled from his chest. "Then I would say you are lucky I came early."

His arms didn't loosen right away.

For a long moment, neither of us moved. He just held me there, close enough that I could feel his breath against my cheek. The air between us shifted, warm and still, wrapping around us like it didn't want to let go.

My hands rested lightly against his chest. Beneath my palm, his heartbeat was steady and strong, grounding in a way that made it hard to think. I could feel the heat of him through his shirt, the faint shift of muscle when he breathed.

Then his hand moved. Slowly. Carefully. He brushed a stray strand of blonde hair from my face, his fingers grazing my skin. The touch was soft but deliberate, and it sent a shiver through me I couldn't hide.

I almost gasped. I didn't mean to.

His fingers lingered just long enough for my skin to burn where he'd touched. His eyes searched mine before they dropped to my lips.

The space between us tightened.

He leaned in, just a little, and the world narrowed until there was only him. The scent of pine. The warmth of his hand. The sound of his breathing, steady but uneven now. My heart hammered so hard I thought he might hear it.

I couldn't let this happen. Not yet. Not before he knew.

Not when he still thought I was Elara the healer, the girl who didn't belong to a crown or a father's cruel temper. Letting him kiss me now, before he knew the truth, would be wrong. Misleading. Unfair.

I turned my face away, the movement small but enough to break the moment.

The air shifted again. It was cool now where his warmth had been. I drew in a shaky breath, trying to find my voice. "William," I said in an almost whisper.

He stilled, his hand still resting lightly against my back. "What is it?"

I hesitated. The truth sat heavy on my tongue. I couldn't look at him, not when he still thought I was someone else. Someone simpler.

"I need to tell you something," I said finally. My voice trembled, but the words were real this time.

His brow furrowed slightly, but his tone stayed gentle. "Okay," he said. "I am listening."

He set me down carefully, his hands steady until I found my balance. My skirts brushed against his boots as I stepped back, trying to steady the shake in my breath.

I brushed the dust from my dress and lifted my eyes to his. He looked at me with that same quiet patience, waiting for whatever I had to say. I opened my mouth, ready to speak, ready to let the truth out at last.

"William," I began, my voice low. "There is something I—"

"Iris!"

The sound of my real name cut through the air like a blade.

I froze.

Every thought, every breath, stopped at once.

Raven was running toward us, her braid loose, her chest heaving from running. Her eyes darted between us, first to William and then to me.

"You need to come now," she said, breathless. "The kin—" She caught herself, swallowed hard. "The mistress would like to have a word with you. Now."

My blood turned to ice. The way she said it told me everything she wasn't allowed to say.

It wasn't the mistress.

It was my father.

For a moment, I couldn't move. The world around me dimmed, the warmth of William's nearness fading into something sharp and cold. The pulse that had raced for him now thundered for another reason entirely.

Raven's voice came again, softer but urgent. "Iris, please."

I nodded slowly, forcing air back into my lungs. "All right, then."

Behind me, William's brow furrowed. "Iris?"

The sound of my real name from his lips made my chest twist. Hearing it from him was worse than I could have imagined. It sounded wrong in his mouth, because he wasn't supposed to know. Not like this.

I couldn't look at him. I didn't dare.

"Let us go," I whispered to Raven, my throat tight.

Raven grabbed my arm, and we moved fast, the grass whispering under our steps. My pulse pounded in my ears, every beat too loud. I could feel William's confusion behind me, heavy as the silence he didn't break.

When we reached the edge of the forest, I finally hissed under my breath, "Why in God's name did you use my real name? In front of him!"

Raven didn't slow. Her braid bounced behind her as she ran. "I was panicking! The king sent guards looking for you, and I had to tell them something. I said you were helping in the village, but it won't hold for long. Now come on, we have to hurry before he finds out."

The words hit me like cold rain. My father had sent guards. He must already know I'd left again.

I pushed harder, my feet hitting the dirt path as we ran toward the castle gates. The wind tugged at my hair, pulling the white headband loose. My lungs burned, but I didn't stop.

The gates loomed ahead. The guards recognized me at once and moved aside without question. We slipped through, running across the courtyard and into the quiet halls of the castle.

By the time we reached the healer's wing, both of us

were breathless. Raven bent over slightly, one hand pressed to her side.

"He is waiting," she managed, her voice low. "In the throne room."

My pulse beat faster with every step. The corridors felt longer than ever, the air thick and still around me. My palms were slick with sweat, and I had to press them against my dress to steady them.

The guards stood by the tall doors of the throne room, their faces unreadable. When they saw me, they bowed without a word and pulled the heavy doors open. The echo of it filled the hall.

He was there.

My father sat straight on the throne, his expression carved in

stone. His crown caught the faint light from the high windows, but his eyes were colder than the gold that framed them. They locked on me the moment I stepped inside.

My throat tightened. I forced my legs to move forward until I stood before him. The carpet beneath my slippers felt too soft, too quiet. I lowered myself into a curtsy, keeping my gaze on the floor.

"Father," I said softly.

The silence stretched between us. I could hear the faint ticking of the clock above the doors. Then his voice came, calm and sharp at once.

"I have an important matter to discuss."

The words sent a chill through me. They always did.

I lifted my head slowly, afraid of what I would hear next.

His gaze stayed fixed on me, cold and steady. "The decision has been made," he said at last.

Something in his tone made my stomach twist. "What decision?" I asked, my voice barely steady.

He rose slightly, his voice calm but absolute. "Within a few days, you will be married off to Prince Lorenzo of Valebran."

For a moment, I forgot how to breathe. The words hit like a blade pressed against my chest. "What? No. You can not."

"I can," he said firmly, "and I have. The decision is final. The threats against our borders are too great to ignore."

"What threats?" My voice broke as I spoke. "You keep saying that, but I have heard nothing of it."

He looked at me the way he always did when I questioned him, with that same quiet disappointment that felt worse than anger. "None that concern you," he said. "Your only duty is to build an alliance with Valebran."

Tears stung my eyes. I shook my head, stepping back. "I do not even know him. And I'm not eighteen yet!"

He stood then, his shadow falling across the table. His voice rose for the first time, cutting through the quiet like a crack of thunder. "Do you think that matters? Your mother did not know me when we married. She was fifteen. It is your duty to your people."

Tears stung my eyes, hot and useless. "But I do not love him."

"You will learn," he said sharply.

I flinched at the sound of it.

His tone softened only slightly as he looked past me, as though seeing something that wasn't there. "Your mother passed seventeen years ago," he said. "I have not taken another wife since. That is love, Iris. Love built through duty."

I felt the floor tilt beneath me. "That is not fair," I whispered. "I am your daughter. And you are sending me away?"

He looked at me as if my words meant nothing. "I care for my people. We cannot stand against two kingdoms alone. Valebran is our only chance for hope."

My tears blurred my vision, but I still glared at him. He didn't flinch.

"There are tailors waiting in your bedchamber," he said, his tone final. "You will prepare yourself. The announcement will be made tonight."

That startled me. Tonight. He would announce it tonight. In front of everyone. I thought he found out I snuck out, but this was far worse. William would hear. This wasn't how he was supposed to find out.

Before I could speak, he flicked his hand toward the servants. Two of them stepped forward at once, their hands firm on my arms.

"Father, please—"

"Enough," he said.

They dragged me from the throne room. My slippers slid against the polished floor as I tried to steady myself. The great doors shut behind me with a heavy thud that echoed through the hall.

I kept my head low as the servants pulled me through the corridors, my tears falling freely now.

By the time we reached my chamber, my heart felt hollow.

CHAPTER NINETEEN

IRIS

By the time the tailors had finished, I hardly recognized myself.

The gown was pink, soft and heavy at once. It clung tightly around my waist before falling loose past my legs, the silk pooling faintly at my feet. Silver thread traced the hem and neckline, glinting in the light. They fastened silver jewelry around my wrists and throat, cool against my skin. My hair was brushed smooth, but the tears still came, silent and unending.

When the door opened, my father entered. His crown caught the light, his expression as stern as ever. He looked me over once.

"Come," he said. "It is time. And get those tears off your face."

I wiped them quickly, though my hands were shaking. The taste of salt lingered on my lips. He turned without another word, and I followed him into the corridor. Two guards walked beside us, their armor clinking with every step.

The walk felt longer than it should have. My heartbeat filled my ears. I kept my gaze on the floor, afraid that if I looked up, I would start crying again.

When we reached the courtyard, noise met us like a wave.

A tall dais stood in the center, draped in the royal colors of red and gold. The crowd stretched far past the stone walls: lords and ladies dressed in silks, knights lined in their armor, servants standing close together, even farmers and merchants from the outer gates. The murmur of their voices filled the air until it almost drowned out my thoughts.

I followed my father toward the platform, each step heavier than the last. My throat felt tight, my stomach twisted into knots. Every sound in the courtyard felt distant. They were all drowned beneath the pounding of my heart.

I prayed he wasn't here.

That WIlliam had been called elsewhere.

Anywhere but here.

He could not find out like this. Not in front of everyone.

My father climbed the dais, his robes brushing against the stone steps. The guards took their places behind him, their armor catching the morning light. When he spoke, his voice carried through the courtyard, deep and commanding, the voice of a king.

"People of Elarion," he began. "Our kingdom stands at the edge of change. There are threats along our borders, enemies who would see us weakened. But we will not stand alone."

The crowd murmured softly, the sound rising and fading like a breath. Then he turned toward me.

His gaze was heavy, sharp as iron. The people followed it. A hundred eyes fell on me where I stood at the base of the dais.

"To secure peace," he said, "a union has been arranged between our house and that of Valebran.

My chest tightened until I could barely breathe.

"My daughter, Princess Iris of Elarion, will be wed to Prince Lorenzo within the coming days."

The words echoed through the courtyard and then fell into silence. Even the wind seemed to still. Only the banners above us moved, whispering softly in the air.

My hands trembled at my sides. The world around me blurred. Faces became a sea of shapes and color, until one face broke through it.

He was there.

William stood among the knights near the front, his armor gleaming beneath the sun. His eyes were fixed on me. Steady. Unreadable.

The noise of the crowd faded. The speeches, the cheers, the scrape of armor. All of it vanished. There was only the distance between us, and the look in his eyes as the truth reached him.

My heart sank.

This was not how he was supposed to find out.

CHAPTER TWENTY

WILLIAM

The captain had gathered every knight in the yard for the king's announcement. The air was heavy with the sound of armor shifting and the quiet murmur of voices. I stood near the front, my hands resting against the hilt of my sword, the sun pressing against the back of my neck.

I should have been listening. Instead, my thoughts were still on Raven.

The way she had said it. *Iris.*

The name had caught me off guard. It was the name of the princess.

At first, I had dismissed it. Maybe it was a nickname, a private joke between friends. Eric had once said Elara looked like the princess, and I had laughed it off. But the more I thought about it, the harder it was to ignore.

The noise around me began to fade as the king stepped onto the dais. His crown caught the sunlight, his expression calm and unreadable. The crowd quieted instantly.

"People of Elarion," he began. His voice carried easily through the courtyard. "Our kingdom stands at the edge of change."

I barely listened. These speeches all sounded the same: talk of borders, of threats, of loyalty and sacrifice. But then his tone shifted, the kind of shift that makes every soldier lift his head.

"To secure peace," he said, "a union has been arranged between our house and that of Valebran."

I frowned. Another marriage for alliance, another trade of names and crowns. It meant nothing to me. Not until the next words came.

"My daughter, Princess Iris of Elarion, will be wed to Prince Lorenzo within the coming days."

Then I saw her.

She was standing beside the king.

For a moment, the world stopped.

The sunlight hit her hair, that same pale blonde I had seen a hundred times before. The pink of her gown caught the wind. Every line of her face, every flicker of her expression. It was her.

Elara.

No. Not Elara.

Princess Iris.

The name echoed in my head, sharp and hollow. The crowd around me blurred. My fingers went cold around the helm in my hand.

She wasn't looking at me, but she didn't need to. The way her shoulders stiffened told me she knew I was here. That I had seen.

My chest felt tight, every breath rougher than the last.

All this time. Every meeting. Every word. Every look.

A lie.

For a moment, I could not think. The sound of the crowd swelled and faded, as if I stood underwater. The king's voice echoed somewhere far away, meaningless now.

Then her eyes found mine.

Everything I had believed about her shifted in an instant.

Surprise came first, sharp and cold. Then disbelief. It didn't make sense. The healer by the river. The girl who laughed at the smallest things. The one who looked at me like I was something more than a knight.

And then the anger came.

It started low, a flicker in my chest, then rose until I could feel it in every breath. She had lied. Every word. Every quiet moment we shared. All of it built on a lie.

I clenched my jaw, forcing myself to stand still while the others bowed to the king's announcement. The cheers started up again, hollow and distant, filling the courtyard like noise in a dream.

Above them all, she stood in her gown of silk and silver, the princess of Elarion.

The same girl I had held by the river. The same one who caught my eye the first time I saw her.

And I could not decide which hurt more: that she lied to me, or that part of me that still wanted to believe she didn't.

CHAPTER TWENTY-ONE

IRIS

When William's gaze met mine, my heart stopped.

He stood among the crowd, still and silent, his armor catching the sunlight. But it wasn't the light that made my stomach twist, it was his eyes.

They weren't soft like before. They were hard, sharp with disbelief and anger. His jaw was set tight, the muscle shifting beneath his skin. I wanted to look away, but I couldn't.

No. No, this wasn't how he was supposed to find out.

Around us, servants began filling the tables with food, their movements quick and careful. Laughter echoed from the lords gathered near the dais. My father smiled as though he had won some great battle. The scent of roasted meat and honey filled the air, heavy and suffocating.

But for me, this was no celebration.

I could barely breathe. My palms were slick against the silk of my gown. I kept my eyes on my father, silently begging him to finish his speech, to end this before I fell apart.

"Together," he said, raising his goblet high, "our kingdoms will stand stronger than ever."

The crowd cheered, the sound crashing around me. I could feel it in my bones. Still, I looked for William. He hadn't moved. His eyes stayed locked on me, and his jaw clenched harder, his teeth grinding as if he were holding back words meant only for me.

My throat tightened. I wanted to run to him, to explain, to tell him everything. But I couldn't. Not until my father finished his speech.

So I stood there, frozen beneath his stare, praying for the moment to end before the truth between us shattered completely.

I turned my head for only a second, just to catch my breath, but when I looked back, he was gone.

My heart stumbled. The place where he had been standing was empty, swallowed by the crowd.

I looked toward my father, silently begging him to stop speaking. *Please, just finish.* My hands shook at my sides. At last, he lowered his goblet, his tone calm and commanding. "Eat," he said. "Celebrate this future union."

The crowd cheered again, but I barely heard them. I

lifted my skirts and stepped down from the dais, my eyes darting across the sea of faces. I searched for him, through nobles, soldiers, servants—but he was nowhere.

Not near the tables.

Not among the guards.

Not even at the edge of the yard.

My chest felt tight. He couldn't have just disappeared.

I moved faster, weaving through the people until I reached the open gates. Maybe he had gone outside. Maybe he was just trying to breathe like I was.

I broke into a run. The noise of the feast faded behind me, replaced by the sound of my pulse pounding in my ears. The cold air stung my skin as I turned the corner and the hem of my gown caught the stone.

Then a hand caught my bare shoulder.

"Elara."

I stopped. Slowly, I turned.

He stood in the archway, half in shadow, half bright from the torchlight. The wind lifted a strand of his dark hair, but he didn't move. His jaw was tight. His eyes, once warm, were colder than I had ever seen them.

"Or should I say," he said, "Your Highness?"

The words hit hard. For a moment, I couldn't breathe. I looked up at him, my chest tight. He stood close enough that I could see his veins tensing. The space shrinked between us as he stepped closer.

"William," I whispered.

He didn't move. "Your Highness," he repeated, the title sharper this time.

The title made something twist inside me. I swallowed hard. "I know this is startling."

He gave a short, humorless laugh. "Startling?" His laugh deepened. "That is one way to put it. I spent weeks thinking you were someone else entirely. A healer. Someone I could trust. Someone who didn't lie every time she opened her mouth."

My throat burned. "Please," I said desperately. "I did not mean for you to find out this way."

He shook his head, eyes fixed on me. The torchlight caught the line of his jaw, the tension in his neck. "Then how was I supposed to find out?" he asked. "When you disappeared for good? After you married that Valebran prince?"

"I wanted to tell you," I said, my voice trembling. "I tried to tell you today, before Raven interrupted. You would not have understood."

His brow furrowed, disbelief flashing in his eyes. "Would not have understood?" His tone dropped lower, quiet but sharp enough to sting. "Right. So while I was risking my position just to see you, you were hiding a secret that could have me executed."

Tears blurred my vision. "I never meant to lie to you."

He didn't answer. The silence between us felt heavier than his anger.

"I was afraid," I said.. "The first time, when we met

at your house, I lied because I thought you might tell my father. You do not know what he is capable of when he's angry. I would have been locked away for weeks, maybe worse."

He looked at me, his jaw tightening, but I pressed on.

"And later, when we started to talk more, when I started to care about you, I was scared again, because I knew that once you found out who I was, everything would change. You are a knight, William. You serve my father. I thought if you knew the truth, you would look at me the same way he does."

His eyes flickered. The hardness in them shifted for a moment, but not enough to soften it.

"I did not want to be a princess with you," I said quietly. "I just wanted to be me."

The air between us went still. The torches by the wall hissed softly, filling the silence. He looked at me for a long time, and for a moment, I thought I saw something break in his expression. Not anger this time, but hurt.

Then his voice came again, low and sharp. "You should go back inside, Your Highness."

The title cut deeper than any blade.

"William," I whispered, reaching out before I could stop myself.

But he was already turning away. His boots struck the stone with each step, the sound echoing down the corridor until it faded into silence.

I stood there, frozen, staring at the place where he had been. Then the tears came again, falling one by one, each one sharper than the last.

CHAPTER TWENTY-TWO

WILLIAM

The night was quiet save for the hum of the torches above the front towers. My shift had ended, yet my thoughts refused to rest.

Elara—or rather, Princess Iris.

The name felt heavy on my tongue, like a truth I had never asked to taste. I had stood there for hours, staring into the dark, but every time I tried to push her from my mind, she returned. The memory of her voice. Her smile. The way she looked at me when she lied.

My stomach twisted. I clenched my jaw, trying to force the thought away. The sweet, soft-spoken healer I thought I knew had been a lie from the start. I had opened up to her, let her in, and all the while she had been the one person in this kingdom I was sworn to protect above all else.

The sound of footsteps pulled me from my thoughts. Another guard approached, nodding to signal the change of shift. I gave a brief nod in return and stepped aside, barely trusting my voice to speak.

The corridor was still when I walked back toward the barracks. My boots echoed against the stone floor, slow and heavy. The air felt thicker the farther I went, as if the castle itself was watching. My anger burned low and steady, but beneath it, something worse lingered. Hurt.

Every step hurt more than it should have.

I had cared for her. Not the princess. Not the heir to the throne. Just her. The girl who laughed by the river. The one who read from an old book and looked at me like I was something more than a knight.

Now I couldn't tell which parts of her were real.

When I reached the end of the corridor, the barrack doors came into view. I was too lost in thought to notice anything at first, too caught in the ache of what I had just learned. Then I stopped.

She was there.

At first, I thought the light was playing tricks on me. But then she moved slowly, and the torchlight caught her face.

Princess Iris.

The title felt strange even in my head. It didn't fit her the way *Elara* did. But she stood in front of the door, pale in the torchlight, her long white gown brushing the stone floor. Her hair was loose and slightly tangled, and her cheeks were streaked with what looked like dried tears.

For a long moment, neither of us moved. I couldn't. My pulse quickened, and my chest ached with something I couldn't name.

The part of me that still ached for her fought the part that wanted to turn away.

"William," she said quietly. Her voice was soft, broken at the edges.

Hearing it again did something to me. It shouldn't have, but it did. I looked at her, but the words wouldn't come. The anger that had felt clear hours ago was tangled now, dulled by the sight of her.

She took a hesitant step closer, her fingers twisting in the fabric of her gown. "Please," she said. "Just listen to me."

Her eyes were red and tired, but there was something in them. Something that looked too much like hurt. It made it hard to look away.

I drew in a slow breath, steadying myself. "You should not be here, Princess."

She flinched at the word. "Do not call me that. Not when it is just us."

My jaw tightened. "That is who you are, is it not?"

Her lips parted, as if she wanted to argue, but she didn't. The silence stretched between us, filled only by the sound of the torches crackling along the wall.

For a heartbeat, it felt like the river again. Quiet. Heavy. Uncertain.

Then she said, her voice barely above a whisper, "I had to come. I could not let it end like that."

I looked down at her. The torchlight caught the tears on her cheeks, turning them to glass.

Part of me thought I should feel glad to see her like this. She had lied, after all. She had taken the truth and turned it into something I could never trust again. If anyone else had done it, I would have wanted them to feel the same pain they caused.

But that part of me didn't exist. Not when it came to her.

She lifted her eyes to mine, her voice trembling. "I am sorry, William. I care about you. I like you. That is why I lied. I was afraid you would look at me differently. But that is no excuse for what I have done. Please, forgive me."

The sound of her voice, small and desperate, pulled something sharp inside my chest. I wanted to believe her—saints, I wanted to. But I couldn't. Not yet.

I took a slow breath, my hands curling at my sides. "You lied to me," I said quietly. "Every time we met. Every word you said came from a life you hid."

She swallowed hard, her tears falling faster now. "I know. And I hate myself for it."

I looked away, my jaw tight. "You made me think I knew you. You made me believe I met someone I genuinely cared about. You made me believe everything was real."

"It was," she said quickly. "It still is."

I shook my head. "You do not have the right to say that, not after hiding the truth from me."

Her lip trembled, but she said nothing. The silence that followed felt cold, heavy.

I drew a slow breath, steadying the anger that still burned beneath my ribs. I wanted it to stay. It was easier to hold onto anger than everything else—the hurt, the disbelief, the way her voice still clung to my name like it meant something.

I kept my tone level. "You are the princess of Elarion. I am a knight sworn to serve your father. Whatever this was between us, it ends here."

The words came out quieter than I intended, but they cut all the same.

Her eyes widened. She took a step toward me. "William, please!"

"Go," I said, barely above a whisper.

For a heartbeat, she didn't move. Her breathing hitched, and I saw the way her hands tightened at her sides as if she wanted to reach for me but didn't dare.

Then, slowly, she turned.

Her gown swept across the stone, soft and silent, like the ghost of something I had already lost.

When she disappeared down the corridor, the quiet returned,

heavier than before. I stood there, every muscle in my body tense, my hands trembling despite how tightly I clenched them.

It should have been easier to breathe without her. It

should have felt cleaner, simpler—knowing I'd done what was right.

It didn't.

The anger still burned, but beneath it there was something worse:

An ache that refused to leave

CHAPTER TWENTY-THREE

IRIS

Three days had passed.

The mornings felt longer now, colder, too. I had gone to the riverbank each day, hoping he might be there, waiting like before. But he never was. The swings stayed still. The water kept moving.

Now I sat in the healer's wing, the air heavy with the scent of herbs and smoke. My hands were wrapped around the book he had given me. *The Song of the Willow Bride.* I held it so tightly my fingers ached. The pages had started to bend from where my tears kept falling.

The guilt was unbearable. It pressed on my chest until I could hardly breathe. What I had done was cruel. I had lied to him, betrayed the only person who had ever looked at me without expectation or duty. I hated myself for it.

Raven crouched down beside me, her shadow falling over the book. She studied my face for a moment, then sighed. "You cannot spend your days in tears, Iris."

I wiped at my cheeks, though it did nothing to stop the tears. "I cannot help it."

"Yes, you can," she said gently. "You are not the first person to make a mistake."

I looked at her, my voice breaking. "He hates me."

Raven frowned, resting a hand on my shoulder. "Maybe he is angry. But hate? No. I do not think so."

"He told me it was over," I whispered. "He looked at me like I was a stranger."

"Maybe he needs time," she said quietly. "Men like him, they hold things close. But if he cared for you before, that does not just disappear."

I shook my head, staring down at the book. "It should. I lied to him. He deserves better."

Raven sighed and gave a small shrug. "It has been three days, Iris. Maybe he has cooled off by now."

I looked up slowly, still holding the book close to my chest. "You think so?"

"I do not know," she said, her tone soft but steady. "But you will never find out if you sit here in tears."

I bit my lip, uncertain. "He told me to leave, Raven. He meant it."

"Maybe he did," she said, standing now, brushing off her skirt. "But people say a lot of things when they are hurt. Maybe he just needs to hear you out properly."

I hesitated, the ache in my chest tight again.

Raven crossed her arms. "Look, I will cover for you again if you want to go talk to him. But only if you promise not to run away this time."

My head snapped up, eyes wide. "You would really do that?"

A faint smile tugged at her lips. "You think I enjoy watching you cry every day? Go fix this before you make yourself sick."

I let out a shaky breath, my heart already beating faster. "Thank you, Raven."

"Do not thank me yet," she said. "Just go before I change my mind."

I rose slowly, my knees weak beneath me. My fingers brushed the tears from my cheeks as I straightened my headband. The air outside felt sharp, heavy with the weight of everything I had left unsaid.

I clutched the book tighter to my chest as I stepped out of the healer's wing and into the courtyard. The light was bright and open beneath the afternoon. I blinked faster at the sight of it all: the walls, the gates, the place where we had once passed each other in silence.

I told myself I would only walk to the gate—that if he wasn't there, I would turn back. I would let it end quietly.

But I kept walking.

The light was almost blinding, the kind that made everything too clear. The air felt still, expectant, as if the world itself was holding its breath.

And then, through the glare of the sun and the shimmer of steel, I saw him.

He stood near the main gate, tall and steady in his armor. His helm was on, concealing his face, and the wind brushed through his chestplate. The sight of him struck something deep in my chest. Relief, fear, longing. All of it tangled until I could hardly tell one from the other.

He looked the same and yet not at all. There was something colder in the way he carried himself now, something careful and distant.

My heart lurched, but I kept walking.

For a brief moment, his eyes met mine through the slit of his helm. The look was unreadable, sharp as glass. Then he looked away.

I stopped a few feet from him, the book still clutched tight against my chest. "William."

His voice came low and flat, all warmth gone. "Why are you here?"

"Because I want to make things right," I said. My voice was small but steady.

He didn't move. "Well, you can not."

The words stung, sharper than I expected. I could see his eyes through the slit of his helm, the brown I used to find comfort in now cold and distant. His gaze fell to the book in my hands, then back to me.

"You are about to marry a prince soon," he said. "And still you come to me, begging for forgiveness."

My chest tightened until it hurt. The prince. The

marriage. I had almost forgotten in the ache of losing him.

"I do not even want to marry him," I said quietly.

He gave a short, bitter laugh that held no humor. "And you said you did not want to lie to me either. But you did, Your Highness."

The title struck like a blade. My throat burned, but I forced myself to meet his eyes. "I did not lie about what I feel for you."

His expression didn't change. "That is not enough."

The silence between us grew thick, the noise of the courtyard fading around us. I wanted to reach for him, to make him understand, but his armor felt like a wall I could never break through.

I took a step closer, my heart pounding. "Then tell me what I can do to make it enough."

I reached for his arm without thinking. My fingers brushed the cold edge of his gauntlet before I could stop myself. All I wanted was for him to listen. To look at me and see the truth instead of the lie I had built.

But the moment I touched him, he turned.

His eyes met mine, and the air seemed to still. They were sharper than I had ever seen them. Not wild. Not cruel. Just quiet. Controlled. The kind of anger that came from a wound buried too deep to heal.

I froze, not because I was afraid of him, but because I could feel the weight of his pain. It sat heavy between us, a silence thicker than words could fill.

He held my gaze for a long moment before speaking. "There is nothing you can do," he said finally.

Something inside me cracked. "Please—"

The word barely left my lips before an arm snapped around my waist, strong and unrelenting, pulling me backward with such force that the breath caught in my throat.

I gasped, but the sound never reached the air. A gloved hand covered my mouth, pressing hard.

The world lurched sideways. The book slipped from my grasp and struck the ground, pages splaying open with a dull thud.

William's expression shifted from shock to fury, but the world was already blurring at the edges.

And then everything went black.

CHAPTER TWENTY-FOUR

WILLIAM

The moment I saw the masked man grab her, my sword was in my hand.

He was tall and broad, dressed in black, and his face was hidden behind a rough mask. Iris's eyes fluttered shut in his hold, and for a split second I couldn't tell if it was from fear or if he had used something on her.

Rage burned through me.

I charged, closing the distance before he could move another step. The man saw me too late. He dropped her, and I caught her before she could hit the ground. Her body was limp in my arms. I set her down gently and turned back to him.

One strike was all it took. My blade met his chest, and he fell without a sound.

But the moment he hit the ground, more shadows

spilled into the courtyard. Five, then ten—all masked, all armed. The guards shouted, steel clashing against steel, chaos breaking loose across the yard.

I looked down at Iris. Her head rested against my arm, and her breathing was faint but steady. The sight of her like that made something twist hard inside me.

I had to get her out.

I lifted her into my arms. Her white gown streaked with dust now. The noise around us grew louder. Arrows hissed through the air, striking walls and shields.

Then I saw Eric with his sword already drawn, fighting off one of the masked men near the gates.

"Eric!" I shouted. "Take the princess to safety, now!"

He turned, his expression shifting when he saw her. "What happened?"

"Go!" I barked. "Now!"

Eric didn't hesitate. He sheathed his sword, moved to me, and took her from my arms. "I will get her inside."

I nodded, turning to face the attackers again. My grip tightened around my blade.

But before Eric could reach the doors, a figure broke through the chaos. The man was fast as he charged straight for them.

Eric reacted on instinct. He dropped Iris and drew his sword in the same motion, meeting the man's strike head-on. The clash of steel rang sharp in the air.

My heart stopped when I saw her fall.

I took a step toward her, but two men cut across my path, blades raised. I blocked the first strike, the force rattling my arm, then turned my blade and caught the second. They pressed hard, one coming from the side while the other swung for my head.

I ducked low and drove my shoulder into the nearest man's chest, knocking him back. The other swung again, his blade slicing across my arm. Pain burned hot, but I didn't stop.

Across the courtyard, Iris lay still where Eric had dropped her. He was locked in combat, barely holding his ground. I couldn't reach her, not yet.

The man I had shoved lunged again. I turned, parried, then drove my sword through his side. He fell, but before I could move, the second attacker caught my shoulder, dragging me back by the armor. I slammed an elbow into his throat and twisted free.

The courtyard had turned into a war. Smoke stung my eyes and the smell of blood and ash was thick in the air. More guards poured from the castle doors, shields raised, swords in hand. The masked men began to falter, their numbers outnumbered under the king's men.

I didn't wait for it to end. I sprinted across the stones, stepping over fallen bodies until I reached her. She was still lying where Eric had dropped her, pale against the dirt, her hair spread around her like spilled light.

"Your Highness," I breathed, dropping to my knees beside her. I brushed the hair from her face and pressed my fingers to her neck.

Her pulse was there, faint but steady. Relief hit hard enough to steal my breath.

I lifted her into my arms again and turned, running for the castle doors. The sound of battle followed close behind, the clash of weapons echoing against the walls.

Inside, the corridor was chaos. Servants scattered, shouting. The king stood near the throne room entrance, his face pale with fury and fear.

"What happened?" His voice cut through the voice.

"Attackers," I said, breathless. "Masked men. They tried to take the princess."

Before he could respond, the noise outside grew louder, closer. Two guards ran in, blades drawn.

"Protect the king and the princess!" one shouted.

They moved to his side immediately, scanning the hall. One turned to me. "You, sir! Bring her. We'll take her to the safe hold."

I nodded, tightening my grip around her. Her head rested against my shoulder, still unmoving.

Then a voice came from behind. "Iris!"

Raven ran down the hall with wide eyes, clutching her skirts.

"You are with us," I said. "Now."

She didn't argue. She fell in step beside us as we ran, the guards leading the way through the twisting halls. The air grew colder the deeper we went.

We reached the narrow stone passage that led beneath the castle, toward a bunker built long ago for war. The door was thick iron and the walls were rough and damp

"Inside," one guard ordered.

The king stepped in first. Then I stepped in, still holding the princess close. Raven followed, glancing over her shoulder as the door sealed shut behind us with a heavy sound.

The bunker was dusty and smelled of iron. It was colder in here. The walls were built of rough stone, lined with old shelves stacked with weapons and armor dulled by time. In the center stood a long table scattered with maps and broken quills, and beside it—a row of small mattresses, old but stable. The guards lit the torches, casting uneven light across the room.

I carried Iris to one of the mattresses and knelt, lowering her gently onto it. The fabric was torn and dirty, but it would have to do. Her skin looked pale against the dark cloth, her lips faintly parted, her breath slow but steady.

The king came closer, his cloak dragging against the stone. His face was hard to read, caught somewhere between fear and rage. He knelt beside her and shook her shoulder. "Iris," he said, his voice low but firm. "Wake up."

She didn't move.

He looked over his shoulder sharply. "You," he said to Raven.

"Find out what is wrong with her."

Raven was at her side in a heartbeat. She dropped to her knees, her fingers steady as she brushed the princess's hair aside. She opened one of Iris's eyes, checking the pupil before pressing two fingers lightly against her throat. The seconds passed slowly and heavily.

Finally, Raven exhaled. "Her pulse is normal," she said quietly. "Whatever they used, it was not poison. She will wake on her own. They must have given her something to make her weak and easy to carry."

I felt something inside me loosen at those words. The tension in my chest eased, though I didn't let it show. My grip on the sword relaxed only slightly, but I couldn't take my eyes off her.

The king's jaw tightened. His hands curled at his sides, the leather of his gloves creaking. He stared down at his daughter for a long moment, then gave a short nod and stood.

"Good," he said. "She will need her strength when she wakens."

He turned toward the guards standing by the door. "You two, check if the chaos has settled. If the grounds are safe, return and inform me." Then his eyes moved to me. "You stay here."

I bowed my head. "Of course, Your Majesty."

The guards did the same before hurrying out. The sound of the heavy door closing left a silence that seemed to thicken in the air.

No one spoke. The faint drip of water from the ceiling was the only sound for a long while. The king stood near the table, his shoulders straight but his face drawn. Then, without a word, he lowered himself onto one of the mattresses against the wall. The torchlight flickered across his features, carving sharp lines of exhaustion into them.

Raven sat near the princess, her knees drawn close, her fingers twisting together in her lap. She kept glancing at Iris as if expecting her to stir, but she didn't. Her breathing stayed soft and steady.

Meanwhile, I just stood nearby, sword in hand, eyes sharp.

But my gaze never left her.

She was still motionless, lashes dark against her skin, lips parted just enough to draw slow, steady breaths. Every rise of her chest felt like proof she was still here. Alive.

The minutes dragged on. The king's eyes were fixed on the stone floor. Raven shifted now and then, the hem of her dress brushing against the rough ground.

When the sound of footsteps finally came from the tunnel, I turned only slightly. The door opened, and the two guards stepped back inside, their faces flushed but relieved.

"All the attackers have been slain, Your Majesty," one said. "The castle is secure. It is safe to leave."

The King rose slowly, his cloak settling around him. He gave a single nod. "Good."

His gaze dropped to his daughter. For a brief moment, something unreadable crossed his face. Relief, though it was gone as quickly as it came. Then he turned toward the passage. "Then we go."

Raven stood, gathering her skirts, her expression pale but composed. I adjusted my grip on my sword, the metal cool against my palm, and stepped closer to the mattress.

For a moment, I just looked at her.

Iris was still as stone. Her long lashes rested softly against her undereye, and a faint pink returned to her lips. She looked fragile in a way that didn't suit her, a kind of stillness that didn't belong to the girl I remembered by the river.

Without thinking, I sheathed my sword and bent to lift her.

She was light as a feather in my arms, warm against the cold air. A strand of her hair brushed my neck as I straightened, and for a heartbeat, the rest of the world went quiet again.

"I will carry her," I said to no one.

The king gave a short nod, already moving toward the tunnel.

Raven followed close behind, her pace quick and careful.

I fell in step behind them, Iris held close against my chest. Her head rested near my shoulder, her breathing steady now, soft against my collar.

As we walked toward the light of the hall above, the echoes of

battle still hung faintly in the distance. The scent of smoke lingered in the air.

But all I could hear was the rhythm of her breathing and the quiet promise that, for now at least, she was safe.

CHAPTER TWENTY-FIVE

IRIS

At first there was nothing but darkness.

A heavy, quiet kind that felt endless.

Then came the ache, sharp behind my eyes, spreading slowly through my skull. The world began to form in pieces, blurred and uneven. Shapes moved. Voices whispered.

When I blinked again, the ceiling above me came into focus. Grey. Familiar. The smell of lavender and candle wax hung in the air.

My bed.

"She is awake!" someone said. A servant's voice, high with relief.

Before I could speak, Raven was at my side. Her hair was messy, and there were dark circles under her eyes. "Iris," she breathed, gripping my hand. "How do you feel? Saints above, you scared us all."

My throat was dry. My lips cracked as I tried to speak. "I feel… fine," I managed, though my voice came out weak and uneven. "What happened?"

Raven hesitated, her thumb brushing the back of my hand. "You were attacked," she said softly. "A group of masked men tried to take you from the castle. William and the guards stopped them. You have been unconscious since."

William.

The name struck through the haze like a spark, and before I could stop myself, I whispered, "He—he saved me?"

Raven nodded. "Yes. If he hadn't been there, I do not know what would have happened."

Something inside me loosened; a small, trembling breath that felt like relief and guilt all at once.

My heart began to beat faster, the ache in my head fading just enough to let one thought surface. "Where is he?" I asked, my voice quieter this time. "William — is he still here?"

Raven looked away, her expression unreadable. "I do not know," she said finally. "After we brought you back, he stayed downstairs with the guards. I have not seen him since."

The air in my chest went still.

"Oh," I said softly. The single word felt heavier than it should have. I tried to hide the disappointment tightening my throat, but it lingered all the same, sitting there like a stone I couldn't swallow.

Raven didn't say anything. She just looked at me, apologetically.

I closed my eyes as the memory of the shouts hit me. The ache in my head pulsed harder, spreading down the back of my new.

"My head hurts," I murmured.

"I know." Raven reached for a glass of water from the bedside table and held it to my lips. "Here. Drink slowly."

The water was cool and clean, easing the dryness in my throat. I drank until the spinning dulled, then leaned back against the pillows. The fabric felt too soft, too warm, like I didn't deserve the comfort.

Raven set the cup down and gave a small sigh of relief. "Your father told me to send you to him once you are awake," she said gently. "He has been waiting."

Of course he had.

The words twisted in my chest. Waiting, not out of worry, but because there was always something he wanted to control again. There always was.

I turned my head toward the window. The sunlight was faint, weak against the curtains, the kind of light that didn't warm anything. "Of course he has," I whispered.

Raven brushed a strand of hair from my face. "Do not keep him waiting too long. He is in one of his moods."

With effort, I pushed the blanket aside and sat up.

The room tilted immediately, the edges swimming. A sharp pain shot through the back of my skull, and I gripped the sheets until it passed.

Two servants hurried to my side and gently reached for my arms.

"Easy, Your Highness," one of them said softly.

I nodded, though my head still throbbed. With their help, I stood and straightened my gown. My legs felt weak, but I forced them to move. Raven watched from the bedside, her arms folded, worry still lining her face.

"Be careful," she said quietly.

"I will," I said, though I wasn't sure I believed it.

The two servants stayed close as we made our way through the corridor. The castle was quiet, too quiet—the kind of silence that lingered after something terrible. My slippers brushed against the stone, and with each step, the ache in my chest grew.

Still, a small part of me wanted to believe he'd called me for something kind. To see if I was alright. To ask how I felt after nearly being taken from the castle. Maybe, for once, he would sound like a father instead of a king.

When we reached the throne room, the guards straightened at the sight of us. One of them stepped forward and pulled the heavy doors open.

"Her Highness, Princess Iris," he announced.

The servants at my sides bowed deeply. "Your Majesty," they said in unison.

My father was sitting on his throne, the light from the tall windows spilling over the gold embroidery of his cloak. His expression was calm but distant, the way it always was when something troubled him.

"Iris," he said, his tone even. "Come closer. I have an important matter to discuss."

My heart sank. Of course. How foolish of me to think otherwise.

He hadn't summoned me to ask if I was well. Not after what happened. Not even after I'd been unconscious for a whole day.

He didn't want to know if I was alright. He wanted something else. He always did.

"What happened yesterday cannot be ignored," my father began. "The castle was attacked, and who's to say worse will not follow? I believed the threats would remain harmless, but this goes beyond that."

I stood still, my hands tightening around the fabric of my gown. I already knew where this was going, but my chest still tightened when he continued.

"Therefore," he kept going, "we must do what is best for the kingdom. You will be married off. Tomorrow."

The word struck like a blade.

"Tomorrow?" My voice broke. "No, Father, days ago you said within a month!"

He looked at me as though I were a child who hadn't been listening. "I have changed my mind," he said simply. "Tomorrow, we leave for Valebran."

For a moment, I couldn't move. I couldn't even breathe.

Tomorrow. It wasn't just soon. It was final.

I could only stare at him. The sound of my heartbeat drowned out everything else. The room felt smaller. Everything felt like it was pressing on me.

I shook my head, taking a step forward. "That is not fair. You cannot marry me off like this."

"Oh, it is fair," he replied, his tone rising. "And I will. I care for my people, Iris. Valebran's alliance will secure our future. They will fight beside us if more attacks come."

My stomach twisted. "You speak as if I am a bargain," I whispered.

His gaze hardened. "You are my daughter. Your life belongs to this crown, to this kingdom. And if that means sacrifice, then it will be done."

The word *sacrifice* lodged deep, colder than the rest.

I wanted to speak, to tell him what it felt like to have no say, to live as a promise wrapped in silk. But my throat closed around the words.

"You are unbelievable," I said finally, my voice low but shaking. "You would give me in marriage to a stranger!"

His hand slammed down on the armrest of his chair, the sound sharp as thunder. "Quiet!" he roared. "It is final, and it is done."

The silence that followed was heavy enough to crush.

He turned sharply to the servants standing beside me. His hand cut through the air in command. "You two. Go start packing her belongings—and mine. Tell the others to help you."

The servants bowed quickly and hurried out of the hall, their footsteps fading into the corridor.

I stood there frozen in place. My throat burned as I tried to speak. "Please," I whispered. "Do not do this."

His blue eyes stayed fixed on me, cold. The same eyes that belonged to my own father. They looked through me now, like I was nothing more than a piece of his design.

"It is done," he said. "We leave tomorrow."

Something inside me cracked.

The sound of my heartbeat filled the space where his words had been. Tears blurred the world until the throne, the banners, even the light itself dissolved into one unrecognizable haze. All I could see was him. Distant. Unbending.

"Do you even hear yourself?" I whispered. "Do you even care what this does to me?"

He didn't answer. Didn't even blink. The silence between us was the cruelest reply of all.

The tears burned hot now, spilling before I could stop them. "I

hate you!" I said, the words breaking, trembling, but loud enough to echo through the hall.

For a moment, he just stared. Shock flickered behind the anger.

But then his voice thundered across the room. "Iris! Come back here this instant!"

But I was already moving.

The skirts of my gown tangled around my legs as I turned and ran, my slippers slipping on the polished floor. The air tore at my throat, my breath uneven as I pushed through the heavy doors. The guards outside startled, glancing at one another, but none dared to stop me.

The courtyard opened wide before me under a dull, gray sky. The wind hit hard, cold against my face, and I didn't slow. My feet struck the stone, then the dirt, then the grass. The sound of my heartbeat roared in my ears until it drowned out everything else.

I didn't know where I was going, only that I had to keep moving. Away from the throne. Away from the walls that had held me my entire life.

Away from him.

And still, I ran. Faster. Harder, until the air burned in my lungs and the tears blurred the path ahead.

CHAPTER TWENTY-SIX

WILLIAM

The summons came before sunset.

A young guard stood at the barracks door, his voice tight with nerves. "The king requests your presence in the throne room, Sir William."

He left before I could answer.

Eric was sitting on his bunk, sharpening his blade. He looked up when he heard the door shut behind me. "The king, hm?" he said, leaning back slightly. "Good fortune to you. His temper is not something I would wish turned upon me."

I gave a small nod. "I will keep that in mind."

The walk to the throne room felt longer than usual. The corridors were silent save for the faint echo of my boots against the stone. Sunlight crept through the tall windows, streaking the marble floors with pale gold. I tried not to think about why I'd been summoned, but my mind went there anyway.

Two guards flanked the tall doors when I arrived. At the sound of my approach, they stepped forward and pushed them open. The hall inside was vast and cold, every word and footstep swallowed by the emptiness.

I walked until I stood before the dais, then dropped to one knee. "Your Majesty."

The king who was sitting on his throne, regarded me quietly before speaking. "Rise, Sir William."

I obeyed, standing straight but keeping my gaze low.

"I have seen your actions during the attack," he said. "You fought well. You protected my daughter, even when chaos surrounded you. That was an honorable thing to do."

"Thank you, Your Majesty."

His eyes stayed on me. "I have a new position for you."

Something in his tone made my stomach tighten.

"We leave for Valebran tomorrow, for my daughter's marriage," he continued. "You will accompany us as her personal guard. From this day forward, she will not take a single step without you nearby."

For a moment, I forgot how to breathe.

The words sank like stones, one after another. *Her personal guard.*

The air felt too thin, the ground too steady.

To guard her. To stand at her side. To look at her every day and pretend she hadn't lied to me—pretend I didn't still remember the sound of her laughter, the way her eyes caught the light, the softness of her voice when she said my name.

My heart thudded once, hard and sharp. Then again, slower, heavier.

It wasn't fair. None of it was.

She had taken the truth and hidden it from me, and still, some traitorous part of me wanted to see her—to make sure she was safe.

I hated that I cared at all.

The king's tone sharpened. "You will swear by it."

The room felt smaller suddenly. Every thought in my head screamed to say *no,* to walk out before I trapped myself in something I couldn't handle. But that wasn't an option. Refusal would mean dishonor, maybe even execution.

I drew in a slow, steady breath, forcing my voice to hold. "I swear by it, Your Majesty."

"Good," said the king.

I bowed my head, ready to take my leave, but his voice came again before I could move. "Before you are dismissed, there is one more task."

I straightened, hands clasped behind my back. "Of course, Your Majesty."

His tone darkened. "My daughter ran off not long ago. No one knows where she has gone, and I neither the time nor the patience to search for her myself. You will find her and bring her to me—at once."

For a moment, I felt my entire body go still.

I'd seen her a day ago. She was unconscious, pale

against the mattress and my arms. The memory had followed me since.

When Raven said she would recover, I hadn't let myself react then, not in front of the others. But the relief that had hit me was sharp, almost painful. I'd pushed it down. I couldn't let them see it.

And now she was awake. Alive. Running.

A strange, uneven mix of relief and dread settled in my chest. Relief that she could still run at all. Dread that I was the one sent to find her.

Still, there was no refusing the king. Not this order. Not any.

"Do you understand, Sir William?" said the king.

I lowered my eyes, the words heavy in my throat. "Yes, Your Majesty."

He gave a short nod. "Good. Do not return without her."

I bowed once more, the motion stiff and empty. "As you command."

When I turned, the sound of my boots against the stone echoed faintly through the chamber. The great doors closed behind me, their weight ringing through the hall like a final order.

The air outside was cool, and I breathed it in slowly, trying to steady myself. I already knew where she had gone. She always went there—the same place she'd gone when she needed to breathe or feel something.

The forest was quiet as I made my way through it, only the sound of my boots against the dirt path breaking the stillness. The evening light sifted through the trees, painting the ground with patches of gold. My hand rested near the hilt of my sword, though I wasn't sure if I needed it.

I didn't know what I would say when I found her. I didn't know what she would say to me. None of that mattered. The king had given his order, and I had sworn to obey.

When I reached the riverbank, I stopped.

She was there.

Beneath the same tree that held the swings, folded in on herself, small and still. Her gown was wrinkled, her hair tangled, and the light caught on the tear tracks staining her cheeks. Her knees were drawn close to her chest, her face buried in her arms. Her shoulders trembled with every quiet sob.

The sound of it cut through the air.

For a long moment, I couldn't move. The sight of her like that twisted something deep inside me. I had imagined finding her angry, defiant—anything but this. Seeing her broken instead made my chest tighten until breathing felt wrong.

The breeze stirred the leaves overhead, the faint sound of the river threading through her soft, uneven breaths. It was the same place where she had laughed. The same tree where she had looked at me

like I was more than just a knight.

Now, she looked so far from that girl it almost hurt to believe she was the same.

I cleared my throat quietly. "Your Highness."

She lifted her head at once, startled. Her eyes were

red, her lashes wet. For a second, she looked lost. Then she saw me.

"William?"

I nodded once, my jaw set.

She wiped her face quickly with the back of her hand, trying to compose herself. Her fingers shook. The sight was harder to bear than I wanted it to be.

"I should have known," she said quietly, her voice rough from crying. "Of course he sent someone."

"He did," I said, keeping my tone even. "He wants you back at

the castle."

She looked at the river for a long moment, then turned her gaze back to me. "How did you know where I would be?"

I hesitated, glancing toward the water before meeting her eyes again. "Because you always come here."

Her lips trembled. For a moment, I thought she might speak again, but instead she turned away, her gaze dropping back to the water. "Please," she whispered. "Can I stay here a moment longer?"

I nodded once, slow and careful. "Of course."

Silence stretched between us, broken only by the rush of the river. She tried to breathe evenly, but it came out shaky, unsteady. More tears slipped down her cheeks, catching the dying light.

"He is marrying me off tomorrow," she said finally. Her voice cracked on the last word. "To a man I have never met. A man I do not even love."

The words settled heavy in the air.

I took a slow breath, trying to keep it steady. "I am sorry."

It wasn't enough, and I knew it. Still, it was all I could manage without my voice betraying me.

She shook her head weakly. "He does not care about me. Not as his daughter. Only as the princess who can give him what he wants."

Her voice broke, and something in me broke with it.

I wanted to stay angry. Saints I knew I had every right to. She lied to me, looked me in the eye and lied again. But watching her like this—frightened, tears streaking down her face, made it almost impossible to hold onto the anger the way I had before.

It didn't matter that she was the king's daughter. Right now, she looked like the girl who had laughed by the river, the one who had read aloud from an old story and smiled as if nothing could touch her.

I clenched my hands at my sides, forcing myself to stay still. I wasn't supposed to care. Not anymore.

But I did.

And I hated that I did.

The thoughts came slow, one after another, pressing tight in my chest. She had lied. She had hurt me. I should have walked away the moment I found her. I should have turned back and done my duty.

But I couldn't.

Each sound she made chipped away what little distance I had left. The anger didn't vanish, but it dulled, giving way to something heavier. Something I couldn't name without feeling like a fool.

I took a small step closer. Then another.

Still, I hesitated.

The memory of her voice, her laughter, the way she had looked at me beneath the sunlight –all of it rose at once, clearer than I wanted it to be. Before I could stop myself, I knelt beside her.

Her shoulders shook with every breath. She didn't even look up when I reached out. My hand hovered for a moment, trembling with the weight of everything I shouldn't do . Then I let it fall.

She didn't resist when I pulled her in.

Her body trembled against me, small and unsteady. Her face pressed against my chestplate, and I felt her hands clutch at it like she needed something solid to keep from breaking.

"It is alright," I said quietly, my hand resting against her back. "Let it out."

And she did.

Her sobs came hard at first, sharp and uneven, then softened until they became quiet gasps between breaths. Her tears and snot soaked into the leather at my shoulder. I didn't care. No one deserved to fall apart like this alone. Not even her.

After a while, the crying faded. Her breathing evened out, but her hands still trembled. Slowly, she lifted her head. Her face was flushed, streaked red from tears. Her eyes looked glassy, exhausted, but still searching.

"Will you be there?" she asked softly.

I frowned. "Where?"

"At Valebran," she said. "For the wedding."

The word made something twist inside me. I couldn't find my voice right away, but when I did, it came low and steady. "Yes."

Something in her gaze shifted at that. The faintest spark flickered in her eyes, fragile but bright. Hope.

"You will?" she asked, her voice almost a whisper.

"I will," I said quietly. "The king ordered it. I am to be your guard."

Her breath caught, and a small smile found her lips. It wasn't joy, just relief. Maybe comfort. The smallest piece of something that

still felt safe.

She leaned into me again, her head resting lightly against my shoulder. I didn't move. I just let her breathe. Her hair brushed against the side of my neck, warm and soft. For the first time that day, the world felt still.

Moments passed before she stirred. Her voice came quiet but steadier than before. "We should head back."

I nodded. "Very well."

She wiped the last of her tears with the edge of her sleeve and brushed the dirt from her skirts. I rose with her, and together we started down the narrow path through the forest.

For a while, neither of us spoke. The air was cool, carrying the faint scent of pine and damp earth. Leaves crunched beneath our boots and each step felt lighter than the one before.

We were almost past the river when she stopped. Her breath hitched.

"Wait," she whispered. "Do not move."

I froze, my hand instinctively brushing the hilt of my sword. My eyes scanned the trees, searching for movement.

"What is it?" I asked under my breath.

She didn't answer right away. Instead, she pointed ahead. "Look."

I followed her finger.

Two small shapes moved in the grass just beyond the path: a pair of white rabbits. One larger, one small enough to fit in a palm. The smaller pressed close to the other's side, twitching its nose as the mother shifted, alert but calm.

"They are so beautiful," she whispered. "The most beautiful creatures to exist."

I nodded slowly. "Aye."

But I wasn't looking at them.

My gaze stayed on her instead, the way the sunlight touched her face, the soft curve of her features. She looked almost like she belonged here, in the quiet of the forest, untouched by the world that waited beyond its edge. She reminded me so much of 'Elara' at that moment.

The anger in me almost completely dulled. Almost.

If she were a creature of this world, she would have

been like them with her soft jawline, soft features, wide eyes and lips the color of a rabbit's tongue.

The bunnies shifted, then hopped off into the tall grass until they disappeared from sight.

She let out a small breath, almost a sigh, then turned to me. "Let us keep moving."

I nodded and fell into step beside her. The walk was quiet again. The forest thinned little by little until the tall stone walls of the castle came into view.

When we reached the gates, the guards straightened at once and bowed. The sunlight caught on their armor, flashing briefly before fading again.

Iris turned to me, her expression calm but tired. "You have done your duty," she said softly. "You can leave now."

For a moment, I almost spoke. The words sat at the edge of my tongue, *it wasn't all duty.* But I swallowed them back.

I gave a short nod instead. "As you wish, Your Highness."

She hesitated, just for a second, as if waiting for me to say something more. When I didn't, she turned and walked toward the castle doors.

I watched her go until the gates closed behind her. The silence that followed was heavy, settling deep in my chest.

It wasn't all duty. But I kept that truth to myself as I turned away and walked back down the path alone.

CHAPTER TWENTY-SEVEN

IRIS

I kept my eye on my plate. The side of my face was still stinging from where my father had struck me earlier. The red mark burned faintly, but what hurt more was the silence that followed. He hadn't said a single word since then, and I didn't dare speak first.

The meal stretched on. Every bite felt like it lodged in my throat. I tried to focus on the food, but my thoughts kept circling back to tomorrow—to the journey, the marriage, the prince I didn't know. Each thought made my chest tighten harder.

When I finished, I reached for the small plate at the center of the table: honey cakes, my favorite. Their warm, sweet scent was almost enough to soften the ache inside me.

But before I could touch one, his voice broke the quiet.

"Leave that."

I froze. "Why?"

He set down his cup, the movement sharp. "You are to meet Prince Lorenzo soon. You will not go there looking like you cannot control yourself."

I blinked, not sure I had heard him right. "It is one cake."

"You need to be in shape before you meet him," he said flatly. "He cannot see a whale sitting beside him."

The words hit harder than the slap had.

My throat closed up, and for a moment I couldn't move. I lowered my hand slowly, the faint tremble in my fingers giving me away. The honey cakes sat untouched on the plate, glistening under the light.

I looked down again, fighting the sting in my eyes. "Yes, Father."

He said nothing more.

The silence pressed in once again, colder this time. I pushed my plate away, my appetite gone, and waited for him to stand first. When he finally did, I rose, too, keeping my head bowed until he left the room.

When the door closed behind him, I stood there for a long moment, listening to the sound of his footsteps fade down the hall.

I turned away from the table and walked down the corridor. The candles along the walls flickered as I passed, their light brushing against the stone. My reflection followed me in the tall windows, pale and small beneath the glow of the moon.

By the time I reached my bedchamber, the exhaustion had settled deep in my bones. I shut the door softly and leaned against it, my body finally giving in to the weight of the day.

The room was quiet. The fire had burned low, and the soft crackle was the only sound. I moved to the bed and sat down, pulling the covers around me.

For a while, I just stared at the ceiling, trying not to think of tomorrow. But it was hard not to. My eyes burned again, but I was too tired to cry.

Eventually, sleep crept in, slow and heavy. I turned onto my side, curling into the blanket. The last thing I felt before drifting off was the ache in my chest and the taste of the cake that never touched my tongue.

CHAPTER TWENTY-EIGHT

IRIS

Servants moved quickly through my chambers, their hands a blur as they folded gowns and packed trunks. All I could hear was the sound of drawers closing, fabrics rustling, and hurried footsteps against the floor.

Raven entered through the open door, her dark hair tied back, her expression calm but tense. "Are you ready to go?" she asked.

I looked around at the half-empty room, the pieces of my life being taken away one by one. "No," I said quietly. "I do not think I ever will be."

I turned toward the window. Below, the courtyard was alive with movement. Horses pawed at the dirt, their reins held tight by stable boys. Carriages lined the path, their wheels gleaming in the morning light. Too many carriages. Too many people preparing for something I never wanted.

When I looked back, Raven was standing by the table, her fingers fidgeting with the strap of her satchel. Her face was pale, her jaw tight.

"Are you alright?" I asked.

She forced a small smile. "I will be fine."

But I knew better. She wasn't fine. She never was when Valebran was mentioned. It had been three years since she'd left that place, three years since the man she loved had left her in pieces. I could still remember the way she looked that night; like someone who had forgotten what it meant to breathe.

"Do not worry," I said softly. "Everything will be alright."

Raven looked up at me then, her eyes tired and sad. "I am not so sure," she murmured. "Come on. Your father is waiting."

"Hold on."

I crossed the room and reached for the book on my bedside table. *The Song of the Willow Bride.* The cover was still worn, the corners soft from my hands. I brushed the dust from it and held it close to my chest. "I am ready now."

Raven gave a small nod, gripping her satchel tighter. The servants followed behind us, carrying my trunks down the stairs.

When we stepped outside, the morning light was bright, almost cruel. My father was already seated inside his carriage with two of his guards standing close by. The rest of the servants and soldiers were loading supplies into the others.

Raven walked toward the servants' carriage, her shoulders stiff as she climbed in. I turn to mine—a black one trimmed with silver.

I hesitated at the door of the carriage, my hand resting against the polished frame. The steps creaked softly beneath me as I climbed inside.

When I looked up, he was already there.

William sat across from where I was meant to sit, his posture straight, his armor gleaming faintly beneath his black cloak. For a heartbeat, I forgot how to breathe. His presence filled the space like it always did—impossible to ignore.

Our eyes met. Something akin to relief flickered through me, before he looked away.

"Your father," he said, his tone flat, "told me to ride with you. I am to stay in your carriage."

The words sank like stones in my stomach. Whatever light had risen in me vanished just as quickly. Of course my father would do that. He never did anything without reason.

I managed a small nod, though it felt like my throat had closed. "I see."

The carriage jolted forward, the wheels creaking against the cobblestone. Neither of us spoke. The sound of hooves and wind filled the space between us, sharp and endless.

I kept my hands folded over the book in my lap, staring at the worn cover though my mind was far away. Every few seconds, I could feel his gaze flicker toward me, only to turn away again. The distance between us felt larger than the width of the carriage.

I thought of yesterday—the way his arms had felt around me. The

warmth of his voice when he told me to let it out. For one brief moment, I had believed there was still something left between us. Maybe there still was.

"William," I said quietly.

He didn't answer right away. His jaw tightened, his eyes fixed on the passing trees beyond the window.

"Are you still angry with me?"

He turned his head slowly, his expression unreadable. "I do not know."

The honesty cut deeper than anger would have. I swallowed hard. "I am sorry. I never wanted to hurt you."

He looked out the window again. "We should not be speaking in the first place." His voice came low, even. "Not anymore."

My stomach dropped. "Why not?"

"I swore an oath to the king," he said, still watching the world beyond the glass. "My loyalty is to him."

I searched his face, desperate for something that wasn't duty. "And before that oath?" I asked.

He didn't look at me. His next words came steady but hollow. "You are to be married."

That broke something inside me. "To a man I do not even love!" The words came out sharper than I meant.

He didn't flinch. He didn't even turn. "It does not matter."

"Does not matter?" I echoed in a trembling voice. "You can lie all you want, but I know you still care about me—even if I am not Elara, the sweet healer you met. Everything between us was real. Every moment, every word. Only my name was not."

The silence that followed was unbearable. The only sound was the rhythm of the horses' hooves and the faint creak of the wheels. He sat still, staring straight ahead, but I could see the tension in his hands, the way his fingers curled slightly where they rested on his knee.

When he still didn't speak I felt my throat tighten. I pulled the book from my lap and held it toward him. "I am sure you want this back, then."

He looked at the book, then at me. For a moment, something in his eyes softened, but it vanished as quickly as it came.

"Keep it," he said quietly. "It is yours now."

I blinked, lowering my hand slightly. "I do not want to keep something that reminds you of me," I whispered.

He looked away, his jaw tightening. "It is not the book that reminds me."

The words struck deeper than I expected. I couldn't tell if they were meant to wound or to confess. I stilled, and before I could find an answer, he turned back toward the window. His profile was calm, but I could see the tension in his shoulders, the muscle in his jaw still tight.

I pressed the book to my chest, feeling the worn leather against my fingers. The small weight steadied me, even as the ache inside grew heavier.

Silence stretched between us. It wasn't the quiet of peace—it was the quiet of two people holding everything they wanted to say and not daring to say it. The sound of the carriage filled the space instead, the rhythmic creak of the wheels, the muffled thunder of hooves against the dirt road.

Outside, the forest blurred past, turning from gold to grey. The last traces of sunlight slipped through the trees, painting the glass in faint streaks before fading completely.

I stared down at the book again. My fingers traced the edges of the cover, the familiar cracks along its spine. It felt like holding a memory I was no longer allowed to keep.

Every now and then, I could feel his gaze flicker toward me, almost unintentional, but he never let it linger. Each time, he turned back to the window as if the world outside mattered more than what saw right in front of him. Maybe it did.

The air inside the carriage grew colder. I shifted slightly, tucking my hands beneath the folds of my dress. I wanted to speak, to say something that could soften what had hardened between us, but every word that came to mind felt useless. Nothing could undo

what I had done.

Time slipped by in fragments. The rhythm of the

wheels. The steady rise and fall of his breathing. The faint creak of leather when he moved his arm.

Then, at last, the carriage began to slow. The steady rocking faded to a crawl, and the sharp scent of salt and smoke reached my nose. Outside, voices shouted orders, the low crash of waves rising behind them.

With a soft jolt, the carriage stopped.

The door swung open, letting in a wash of cool night air. A guard stood outside, torchlight flickering against his armor. "Your Highness," he said. "We have reached the port. Get ready. We set sail now."

I nodded, though my chest felt hollow. The world beyond the carriage was all shadow and sea, distant docks against the docks and waves churning beneath them. The reality of it settled like a stone in my stomach.

We were leaving.

I glanced once toward William. He didn't look back. His face was turned toward the window, still and unreadable. For a heartbeat, I thought I saw something in his eyes, but it was gone before I could be sure.

So I said nothing. I held the book tighter to my chest, gathered my skirts, and stepped out into the night.

The wind off the water hit sharp, catching my hair. Behind me, the carriage door closed with a final, quiet thud.

CHAPTER TWENTY-NINE

WILLIAM

The ship loomed ahead, its sails tall and heavy against the night sky. Torches lined the dock, their flames bending with the wind. The air smelled of salt and iron, and the creak of ropes filled the silence.

The king boarded first, flanked by his guards. I followed behind, keeping a careful distance until it was my turn to help her.

I reached out my hand. She hesitated for a moment before placing hers in mine. Her skin was soft, cold from the night air. I helped her up, steadying her as she climbed the narrow plank, and then stepped back as quickly as I could.

I didn't enjoy it, and I made sure she could tell. Whatever we had, whatever it was, it had to end here. The secret meetings. The laughter by the river. The quiet moments that felt like more than they should have been. All of it.

Still, it hurt.

But what choice did I have? She was the princess. The king's daughter. And I was a knight, sworn to serve her, not care for her. She belonged to a world far above mine, a world of crowns and alliances, not promises whispered beneath trees.

The ship rocked as it began to move, cutting through the dark water. The stars reflected faintly on the waves. By sunrise, we would reach Valebran.

I led her below deck to her chambers. The room was small but warm, lit by a single lantern that swayed with the movement of the ship. A narrow bed was fixed to the wall, draped with plain sheets. A wooden barrel stood beside it, serving as a table, and the floorboards groaned beneath our steps.

She placed the book on the barrel and lay down without a word. The faint light touched her face, soft and tired.

I stayed by the doorway, sword at my side, the sound of the waves steady in my ears.

I told myself I was watching the room. But the truth was, my eyes never left hers.

—

Light began to spill through the small cracks in the wood, thin and pale at first, then warmer as the sun climbed higher. The steady sound of waves against the hull softened into a calm rhythm.

She stirred. Her lashes fluttered, slow and soft, like

she was caught between dreams and waking. I straightened at once, though I hadn't closed my eyes all night.

For hours, I'd been sitting there, watching, waiting, telling myself to look away. To rest. To forget. But I couldn't.

She looked peaceful like that, almost too peaceful. Her pale blonde hair lay loose across the pillow, and her chest rose and fell in a steady rhythm. It was the kind of calm that never lasts.

It hurt to watch her.

It shouldn't have. I told myself that more than once. She had lied. She had broken trust that shouldn't have been given in the first place. And yet, none of that mattered when I looked at her now. The sight of her breathing softly in that narrow bed hurt more than any wound I'd ever taken.

Because I knew the moment she woke, that peace would vanish. She would remember where we were going. What waited for her on the other side of the sea. She would remember that she wasn't the girl I met by the river anymore, but a princess promised to another man.

Her eyes opened slowly, catching the first thin touch of light. She blinked once, twice, the confusion fading as she turned her head toward me.

For a heartbeat, our gazes met. Then I looked away, too quickly. I fixed my eyes on the window, on the pale horizon stretching over the waves. The sea was calm now, smooth and endless, but inside me the storm hadn't quieted. It hadn't even begun to fade.

The door opened suddenly, letting in a rush of light and movement. Servants stepped inside, holding fabrics and silver. One of them bowed quickly.

"His Majesty sent us," she said. "He wishes for her to look her best when meeting the prince."

I stepped back to give them room. They moved efficiently, speaking in soft tones as they held up a gown of pale pink and white. The silk shimmered faintly in the lantern light, delicate and fine.

The princess—no, Iris rose without a word. She slipped out of her nightgown and into the new dress, letting the servants fasten the lace at her back. They brushed her hair until it fell smooth over her shoulders and clasped silver around her wrists and throat.

I tried not to look. I failed.

When she turned, the breath caught in my chest. She looked unreal, like something carved from light itself. Every movement seemed careful, graceful, though her eyes carried the same quiet sadness I'd seen before.

She had always been beautiful. Since the first time I saw her in that dim theatre, since the healer's wing, since the river. But now she looked like the girl she was born to be; royalty. Untouchable.

She didn't meet my eyes as she walked past me and out of the chamber. I followed at a distance, my boots echoing softly against the boards.

When we stepped onto the deck, the air hit us fresh and cold. The sea stretched wide, the morning light bright across the waves.

Ahead, the shore was close enough to see.

Valebran rose from the cliffs, its castle towering high against the sky. Trees surrounded its walls, thick and green, and behind it, the mountains stood tall, their peaks brushed with white. Parts of the castle reached into the slope itself, the stone blending with the rock.

It was vast. Beautiful in a way that felt distant.

Iris stood at the railing, her gaze fixed on it. I stayed a few steps behind, watching the wind move through her hair and wondering how much of her would be lost to that place once we arrived.

CHAPTER THIRTY

IRIS

"Your Majesty, we have arrived!"

The call rang out from the deck, clear above the waves. My heart lurched.

I leaned forward on the railing, my hands tightening around the wood as the ship began to slow. The water near the shore was calmer, shallower, gleaming beneath the morning sun. Ahead, the docks were lined with banners of blue and silver, fluttering in the wind. A crowd had gathered; nobles, guards, servants. They were all waiting.

My breath came uneven. My fingers fidgeted with the lace at my wrist, the silk of my gown smooth beneath my shaking hands. I could feel the weight of the silver at my neck, too heavy now.

The ship bumped softly against the dock. The sound made my stomach twist.

"Your Highness," one of the servants said again, bowing slightly, "it is time."

I nodded, though the movement felt stiff. My legs were weak as I turned toward the plank being lowered. My father was already waiting, his posture straight, his expression calm. I envied it.

Behind me, I could sense William's presence, silent but steady.

Somehow that steadiness made it harder to breathe.

The plank touched the dock with a dull thud. The wind carried the faint scent of pine and salt.

I drew a breath, one that didn't quite reach my chest, and stepped forward. My gown brushed the wood, soft against the sound of waves beneath. The crowd's murmur grew louder.

"Smile," my father said behind me.

I did as he asked, though it felt wrong. The smile didn't reach my eyes. It was empty, like the painted faces of the women at court.

A man in a deep blue coat approached, bowing low until his forehead nearly touched his hand. "Your Graces," he said, voice smooth and careful. "Welcome to Valebran. The royal family awaits you inside the castle."

I nodded because it was expected. Words didn't come.

We began to move, the wood of the dock giving way to pale stone. The path was lined with trees, tall and green, their leaves moving softly in the wind. The sea stretched close behind us, the sound of it steady and calm. That was the only part I liked, that the sea was close to the castle. It was the only thing that reminded me of home. Of the riverbank.

The guards followed at a steady pace, armor gleaming beneath the sun. Behind them came the servants, their arms full of trunks and satchels. I turned my head, searching the crowd until I saw Raven.

She walked beside the others, her expression tight but her eyes found mine. For a moment, I felt less alone.

The castle gates loomed ahead, tall and carved from silver-gray stone. The walls were high and wide, climbing into the sky like a mountain itself. Banners of blue and silver hung from the towers, their edges fluttering in the breeze.

The guards stationed at the gate wore silver armor inlaid with the crest of Valebran. As we approached, they bowed deeply and pushed the gates open, the sound of metal grinding softly against stone.

"Chin up," my father murmured. "And stomach in."

My stomach was already flat, but I did it anyway. My heart was pounding so hard I could feel it in my throat. My hands trembled against the folds of my gown. I wanted to cry. I wanted to turn around, to run back to the ship—to anywhere that wasn't here. But my feet kept moving.

The castle courtyard was wide and filled with sunlight. Fountains lined the center, their water clear and cold, surrounded by beds of white roses. Beyond it, the main doors stood open, revealing a long hall inside. The floor was marble, polished to a shine, and the walls were covered in paintings of Valebran's kings and queens. The air smelled faintly of salt and flowers.

It was nothing like Elarion. Elarion was old stone and candlelight.

This was darker, grander, colder. Every sound seemed to echo and every step felt too loud.

At the end of the hall stood a pair of enormous doors, silver and tall enough to reach the carved ceiling. Two guards waited before them. They bowed, their hands pressing to their chests, then turned to open the doors.

The sound of them opening filled the air, slow and heavy, revealing the room beyond.

The throne room of Valebran.

And the people who would decide the rest of my life.

CHAPTER THIRTY-ONE

IRIS

We stepped through the doors.

The light inside the hall was bright and cold, spilling across polished marble floors. Four figures stood waiting at the end of the long aisle. My father's hand pressed against the small of my back, firm enough to make me move.

"Chin higher," he murmured. "Smile wider."

I obeyed, though it felt like the muscles in my face might break. My heart began to beat faster, the sound of it loud in my ears.

The King and Queen of Valebran stood at the front, their crowns glinting in the light. Beside them was a small girl, no older than ten, dressed in midnight blue silk. And next to her stood a man—taller than the rest, straight-backed and confident. I didn't need to be told who he was.

Prince Lorenzo.

The King of Valebran stepped forward first, his expression warm. "Henrik," he said, clasping my father's hands in greeting.

"Phelipe," my father replied, his tone even, the faintest trace of a smile on his face.

The Queen approached next, graceful and composed. My father took her hand and kissed her knuckles. "Sonja," he said.

The young princess curtsied politely, her golden curls shining beneath the hall's light.

And then he came forward.

Prince Lorenzo.

I couldn't look at him at first. I kept my gaze on the floor, on the shifting light that danced along the marble. I already knew who he was—the man my life was tied to now, the man my father had chosen for me. The man I belonged to.

When he stepped before me, I felt his presence before I saw him. The air changed, heavier, closer. He bowed gracefully.

I forced myself to lift my eyes.

For a moment, I forgot how to breathe.

His curly, dark blonde hair framed sharp green eyes, the kind of green sunlight gives to a pond. He wore a coat of silver and dark blue, tailored perfectly with gold embroidery tracing every seam. Every line of him spoke of confidence and control.

He reached for my hand, his fingers cool against mine. When he bowed again and pressed a kiss to my knuckles, the motion was gentle but precise, like part of a ritual he'd done a hundred times before.

"My lady," he said. His voice was smooth, careful, rehearsed. "It is an honour to meet you."

I swallowed, my throat dry. "The honor is all mine."

He studied me for a moment, his eyes bright with amusement or maybe curiosity. I couldn't tell. Then a faint smile curved his lips, revealing his dimples. "You are more beautiful than I thought to expect."

Heat rose to my cheeks. I forced a small, polite smile. "You are kind to say so, my lord."

He gave a low laugh, soft and easy, the kind that was meant to charm. "I only speak the truth."

Behind him, both kings watched closely. I could feel my father's gaze like a weight on my shoulder, waiting for me to say the right words, to look the right way.

The silence that followed was mercifully broken by King Phelipe's voice. "You all must be hungry from your journey," he said, spreading his arms with a warm smile. "Come, we had the chefs prepare something special for the occasion."

My father nodded, his hand guiding me once more as the royal family turned toward the grand dining hall. I followed, each step heavier than the last, the smile on my face still painted and hollow.

The dining hall was vast and gleaming, its arched ceiling painted with silver and blue, the colors of Valebran. Crystal chandeliers hung from above, catching the light that poured through the tall windows overlooking the sea. A long table stretched across the room, draped in white linen and covered with plates of food that looked too hot to touch. Roasted chicken glistened beside trays of figs and sugared pastries. Platters of beef and fresh fruit were arranged with perfect precision, as though the meal itself had been rehearsed.

Prince Lorenzo stepped ahead and pulled out a chair for me. "Have a seat, my lady," he said with an easy smile.

I managed one in return, polite but thin. "Thank you."

He waited until I sat before taking his own seat beside me. The others followed—our fathers at the head of the table, Queen Sonja beside King Phelipe, and the little princess near the end. William stood behind me with the guards. His was presence a small comfort.

King Phelipe lifted his goblet. "Please, dine within," he said warmly. "Your travels must have left you weary. Do not be shy."

It wasn't shyness that kept me from reaching for the food. It was the weight in my chest, heavy and dull, that left no space for hunger.

Prince Lorenzo reached for a platter, placing a roasted chicken leg and a small pastry onto my plate. "Eat with a smile," he said lightly, though there was something firm beneath his tone.

My father gave me a look across the table, a silent command. I forced my hands to move, to pick up the fork, to chew and swallow. The food tasted of nothing.

Behind me, I could feel William's gaze, steady and watchful. It shouldn't have brought me comfort, but it did.

King Phelipe rose partway through the meal, goblet raised again. "It brings me great joy to know our kingdoms will be united," he said. "Together, we will build something stronger than before."

My father answered with a smile that looked almost genuine. "May this alliance bring peace to both our lands."

The table filled with talk, and then laughter, clinking glasses, the rustle of silk. Everyone seemed to be speaking at once, yet I heard none of it.

Lorenzo turned to me, his voice smooth. "So, my lady, after we eat, would you like to walk with me? The gardens here are beautiful this time of year."

My stomach tightened. Every instinct told me to refuse, but I swallowed hard and said, "I would love to."

His smile deepened, dimples showing again. "Splendid."

We finished our meal in silence. When the last of the plates were cleared, he rose and offered me his arm.

I hesitated only for a moment before placing my hand on it.

"Shall we?" he asked.

I offered a nod.

He led me toward the open doors of the hall, out into the bright light of the gardens, and I followed quietly, wishing I were anyone else.

CHAPTER THIRTY-TWO

WILLIAM

I followed them from a short distance, close enough to guard, far enough not to intrude. It was my duty, after all. Nothing more.

At least, that was what I kept telling myself.

The gardens were enormous, lined with fountains and marble statues, the air heavy with the scent of roses. Rows of them stretched as far as I could see; pink, red, white and yellow. The sea shimmered faintly beyond the trees, and sunlight fell over the petals like glass.

The prince's hand rested at her waist as they walked.

My jaw tightened before I even realized it. The motion was instinct, not choice. I looked away quickly, fixing my gaze on the path ahead. On the gravel underfoot. On the sound of the sea beyond the trees. Anything but them.

I told myself it didn't matter. That she didn't matter. That this was duty, nothing more. But the words rang hollow in my head, fragile and false.

She looked nervous. Her shoulders were too straight, her steps too careful. Her fingers brushed the folds of her dress every few moments, like she was trying to steady herself. The prince, by contrast, looked perfectly at ease with a stride confidence and a smooth voice. He carried himself like a man used to being obeyed.

They stopped near a tall hedge of roses.

"So, my lady," he said lightly, "which of these do you fancy most?"

Her eyes drifted over the colors, quiet and thoughtful. "The white ones," she answered softly.

The prince smiled, pleased. He plucked a single rose from the bush, brushing the thorns away with careful fingers before tucking it gently into her hair.

"Beautiful," he murmured.

She smiled faintly. It was polite, careful.

My fists clenched before I could stop them. The reaction came sudden, sharp, almost unreasonable. The kind of anger that didn't have a name. It wasn't jealousy. It couldn't be. I had no right to that.

And yet… it burned.

It burned to see her like that, standing in the

sunlight with his hand so close to her face, her eyes lowered in a way I'd never seen before. It burned to realize how easily he could touch her when I could not.

I forced my hands to my sides, drawing a slow breath until the tension dulled, but it didn't fade completely. The ache stayed, low and constant.

They began walking again. The prince's laughter rose softly over the wind as he spoke, his words easy and practiced, meant to charm. She answered quietly, her voice smaller than usual, the warmth I knew replaced with something more careful.

"How old are you, my lord?" she asked after a pause.

"Nineteen," he said with a grin. "And you?"

"Seventeen."

He nodded, pleased by her answer, as though it confirmed something he'd already decided. He kept talking, his voice smooth and steady. He was a year younger than me.

I walked behind them in silence, my hand resting on the hilt of my sword. Each step felt heavier than the last. I watched her from where I stood, how she nodded when he spoke, how she smiled just enough to seem polite, how her eyes fell to the ground whenever his gaze lingered too long.

To anyone else, they might have looked perfect. The prince and his soon-to-be bride, walking through a garden of roses.

But I knew the truth behind her smile.

And it hurt more than I cared to admit.

The distance between us felt both too far and too close. Every time she moved, every sound of her voice, I felt the ache of what I'd lost, and the weight of what I still couldn't seem to let go.

A long while passed before the prince finally turned to her. His tone was gentle, courteous, every word measured like a man who'd practiced charm until it felt like a habit.

"You should rest, my lady," he said. "You have had a long journey. You must be tired."

She nodded. "A little."

He smiled, the picture of grace. "Then come. Let me show you to your bedchamber."

They turned back toward the castle. I followed, as I always did: silent, a shadow where I was meant to be.

The air changed as we stepped into the marble corridors. The scent of the garden faded, replaced by the cold hush of polished stone. Silver and blue stretched in every direction, the light from the tall windows falling across the floor like glass. The candles flickered in crystal sconces, the reflections trembling against the walls.

She walked ahead of me, the train of her gown brushing the floor, her movements light but unsteady. For a moment, I didn't see a princess walking toward her gilded cage.

I saw her.

Elara, the girl by the river, the one who smiled too

shyly when I teased her, the one who held my book like it was a secret worth keeping.

And I realized how much I hated that I still saw her that way.

Because I wasn't supposed to.

Not anymore.

Once we reached her bedchamber, the prince opened them with a quiet smile. "I had the servants decorate it extra special for you," he said.

The room inside shimmered in pink and silver. A large bed stood in the center, draped with silk sheets and gauze curtains that caught the light. A tall closet stood to the side, and beyond it, a smaller door led to a walk-in chamber joined with a private bathing room. A vanity sat near the wall, covered with glass perfume bottles and a silver mirror. There was even a small bookshelf beside the window, its shelves already filled

The balcony doors were open, and the air that came through carried the scent of roses from the garden below. Beyond that, mountains rose in the distance, dark and sharp against the pale sky.

I took my place near the balcony, watching the light move across the floor.

Prince Lorenzo turned back to her. "Rest here, my lady. The servants will come for you when it is time for dinner. You are free to explore the castle before then. Tomorrow, I will take you to the village and give you a proper tour of Valebran."

Iris managed a small smile and nodded. "Thank you, my lord."

His smile lingered a little too long before he inclined his head. "Until dinner, then."

He stepped out and pulled the doors closed behind him. The sound echoed softly through the chamber, leaving only the quiet of the wind and the distant waves.

Iris moved toward the bed and sat down. I stayed near the balcony, pretending to study the view, though my eyes weren't on the sea. I could hear her, the quiet rustle of silk, the unsteady sigh that followed.

Something slipped from her hand and hit the floor. A silver pendant rolled toward me, catching the light. I bent down to pick it up at the same time she did. Our hands brushed.

Her skin was warm, softer than I remembered.

She drew back quickly, a quiet breath catching in her throat. I straightened and held out the pendant. "Here."

She took it without meeting my eyes. "Thank you."

"You are welcome."

Her head tilted slightly. "That is the most you have said to me today."

I let out a slow breath. "There has not been much to say."

She looked at me then, the faintest crease forming between her brows. "You can at least try not to sound like you do not know me."

"I am doing my duty."

Her brows lifted. "Is that all I am to you now? Duty?"

I met her gaze for the first time in what felt like hours. "What else should you be?"

The words landed sharper than I meant. Something flickered across her face. Hurt. I felt it like a blade twisting in my chest.

I shouldn't have said it. I knew that. But it was the only truth I had left. Whatever I felt for her didn't matter. She was the king's daughter. And I was the knight meant to guard her, nothing more.

Still, when I looked at her standing there—the light catching in her hair, her eyes searching mine as if for something that had been lost—I didn't see a princess at all.

I saw her again.

Elara.

The healer.

And it made everything harder.

She straightened, her eyes glinting with something between anger and sorrow. "I need a moment," she said quietly. "Do not follow me."

Before I could speak, she turned and walked toward the door. The silk of her gown brushed softly against the floor, the sound fading as she slipped into the corridor.

When the door closed, the room fell silent again.

I stood where I was, staring at the empty space she'd left behind.

I told myself to move. To breathe. To remember what I was here for.

But all I could see was her face, all I could hear was

her voice, all I could feel was that brief touch of her hand against mine.

And for a moment, I forgot everything else.

Because no matter what name she bore, or what crown waited on her head, she would always be Elara to me.

CHAPTER THIRTY-THREE

IRIS

I walked faster down the hall, my skirts brushing against the marble. My pulse was still quick, anger threading through every step. *A duty.* That was what he'd called me. Nothing more, nothing less.

I bit down hard on the inside of my cheek, holding back the sting in my eyes. This was exactly why I hadn't wanted to tell him the truth—why I'd hesitated again and again. Because now that he knew who I was, that was all I could ever be to him. His duty. The princess. The king's order.

I turned a corner, desperate to clear my head, when a faint sound caught my ear. It came from one of the open barracks down the hall. I stopped, glancing in, and froze.

Raven was there, curled up on one of the benches, her shoulders trembling. The sight made my heart drop.

"Raven," I said quickly, hurrying to her side.

She looked up. Her dark eyes were red and swollen, her hands gripping the fabric of her skirt. I sat beside her without a second thought and pulled her close. "Oh God, Raven, what is wrong?" She shook her head, wiping at her cheeks. "It is nothing."

"Clearly it is not nothing," I said softly. "Please, tell me."

Her breath hitched. "I cannot."

"Raven—"

"I saw him," she whispered.

I stilled. "Who?"

She hesitated, her eyes darting to the floor. "My past lover. The one who broke my heart." Her voice cracked on the last word. "He is here, Iris. He is living in the castle."

My eyes widened. "What? Who is he?"

Raven shook her head again, pressing her palms to her eyes. "I do not want to tell you."

I wanted to push, to ask more, but the look on her face stopped me. Whatever she'd seen had shaken her deeply. I just placed a hand on her arm. "You do not have to," I said quietly.

She nodded, though she didn't look up.

I stayed beside her, my thoughts spinning. He must have been a servant, a knight, a lord. But it didn't matter. All I knew was that Raven had just seen a ghost from a past that still haunted her. And for now, that was enough.

I stayed beside her and didn't say a word. Sometimes silence was the only comfort that worked. Raven's breathing came in short, uneven sounds, and every so often she pressed her sleeve to her face. I didn't know how long we sat like that, but time seemed to stretch and fold in on itself.

At some point, servants passed by the open doorway. Their eyes lingered on us for a moment, but one look from me was enough to make them look away. None of them said a word.

The light outside began to fade. The shadows lengthened across the floor until the room dimmed into a soft blue. Raven had been crying for hours. I had not moved. I just sat beside her, stroking her hair now and then, letting her lean against me when she needed to.

It was nearly dark when a servant finally appeared at the door. "There you are, Your Highness," she said. "Dinner is ready in the hall."

I nodded. "I will be there in a minute."

When she left, I turned to Raven and gently lifted her chin. "Accompany us for dinner?"

Raven shook her head immediately. "No. I cannot.."

"Oh, come on," I said softly. "Some food might do you good."

She gave a weak laugh that didn't reach her eyes. "I am not noble enough to sit with royals."

My chest tightened. "Raven, do not say that. I do not care about your title. You are my friend."

She looked down, her voice small. "Still no. I would rather eat by myself tonight."

I hesitated but nodded. "Very well. But tell me if you need me, okay? You can come to me whenever."

She nodded once. I leaned forward and hugged her tightly. She didn't say anything, but I felt her grip my hand before letting go.

I stood, smoothing my skirt and glancing toward the fading light outside. Then I gave her one last look before turning toward the hall. The castle was quiet, and my footsteps echoed softly as I made my way to dinner.

CHAPTER THIRTY-FOUR

IRIS

I sat at the long table, my hands folded neatly in my lap. The hall shimmered beneath the glow of silver chandeliers, the air filled with laughter and clinking glasses. Across the table, King Phelipe rose from his seat, his goblet raised high.

"My friends," he said, his voice carrying easily through the room, "it brings me great joy to announce that the wedding between our beloved Prince Lorenzo and Princess Iris of Elarion will take place in less than seven days."

A wave of cheers followed, loud and bright against the marble walls. Laughter filled the air. Goblets clinked. Music stirred in the corners.

I tried to smile. I tried to look every bit the happy bride they all expected. But my throat locked instead.

Seven days. Only seven days until everything changed.

Lorenzo turned toward me, his smile wide and polished. He slipped an arm lightly around my shoulders, the movement practiced, effortless. The guests cheered louder at the sight. The sound pressed against me until I could hardly breathe.

I kept my head lifted, my face calm, my hands steady in my lap.

But inside, everything trembled. His touch felt foreign, too gentle, too sure. My stomach knotted.

Across the room, beyond the flicker of candlelight, my eyes found him.

William.

He stood among the guards, helm tucked beneath his arm, posture straight, gaze fixed ahead. His expression didn't waver, didn't shift. He could have been carved from stone.

Still, the sight of him made my breath catch. For one fleeting moment, I wanted him to look at me. To see me. To see *her,* the girl from the river, the one who had once made him smile.

But he didn't.

He never looked my way.

A duty. The words echoed in my mind, sharp and cold.

Fine then. I would play my part.

I turned toward Lorenzo and leaned closer until my head rested lightly against his shoulder. The movement was small but deliberate. He smiled, clearly pleased, his hand tightening gently at my waist. The crowd clapped again, delighted.

The noise blurred around me. The music, the voices, the laughter. It all melted into a dull hum.

When the servants brought out another round of food, I focused on the simplest thing I could. The tray nearest to me gleamed with sugared figs, their syrup catching the light.

"They look good," I said softly, because I needed to say something. Anything.

Lorenzo followed my gaze, amusement tugging at his lips. "Do they now?"

"Yes," I said. My voice came out steadier than I felt. "They do."

He picked one up delicately and held it toward me. "Then try one, my lady."

For a moment, I hesitated. Then, because there was no choice, I leaned forward.

The fig was sweet. Too sweet. The kind of sweetness that made it hard to swallow.

I smiled through it anyway. "It is lovely," I murmured.

He laughed softly, satisfied. "Good."

I glanced over my shoulder, trying to catch his eyes. William, still standing among the guards, didn't move his gaze. Not once did he look at me. That brought a flicker of irritation through me.

The feast carried on long after the announcement. The clinking of goblets, the rustle of silk, and the constant hum of conversation filled the air. Every sound pressed against my skull until it all began to blur.

Lorenzo spoke easily beside me; confident, composed, perfectly trained in charm. He asked if the journey had been long, if I liked the palace, if I preferred the gardens of Elarion to those of Valebran. I answered each question softly, careful not to reveal how hollow the words felt leaving my lips.

He laughed often. I did not.

When the final plates were cleared and the guests began to rise, King Phelipe called the attendants forward to escort us to our chambers. Lorenzo offered his arm again, his smile unfaltering.

"Come, my lady," he said. "You must be tired. The night has grown long."

I placed a hand lightly on his sleeve. "A little."

As we walked through the corridor, the sound of our footsteps echoed faintly against the stone. The hall was lit by tall, silver sconces that threw long shadows across the floor. William followed several paces behind, quiet as ever, the faint jingle of his scabbard the only sign of his presence.

Lorenzo glanced sideways at me, his voice smooth and low. "My chamber is only a door away from yours," he said. "Perhaps we should go there first. There is something I would like to show you."

The words caught in my throat. I managed a small, careful smile. "Of course."

Lorenzo's chamber was grand yet quiet. The walls were paneled in deep blue silk, trimmed with silver embroidery that shimmered faintly in the candlelight. A tall window overlooked the sea, its glass reflecting the pale moonlight that bled through the curtains.

The scent of salt and burning wax filled the air.

A wide bed stood near the center of the room, its frame carved from dark wood. The sheets were soft and dark, the kind that seemed almost too fine to touch.

He closed the door behind us. The faint click of the latch made my chest tighten.

"Please," he said gently, motioning to the bed. "Sit."

I hesitated for a moment before obeying. The mattress sank slightly beneath my weight, cool and smooth beneath my palms.

He sat beside me—not close, but near enough that I could feel the warmth of him. For a long moment, he said nothing. The silence between us was calm but uncertain, and I could hear the distant hum of the sea outside.

When I finally looked at him, he was already watching me. His green eyes caught the candlelight, soft and curious rather than commanding.

Days ago, I wanted nothing to do with him. I still didn't. Not truly.

But he was kind. Gentle, even. There was no cruelty in his gaze, no arrogance in his smile. Only patience.

I could not change what was coming. The marriage would happen whether I wanted it or not. The least I could do was try to find something to hold on to.

He was handsome. That much was easy to see. His features were sharp, but not harsh. His voice was smooth, his posture relaxed, as though nothing in the world could unsettle him.

Perhaps I could learn to like him.

I drew in a quiet breath and forced myself to speak. "Your chambers are beautiful," I said softly. "The colors suit you."

His lips curved into a small smile. "You think so?"

I nodded. "Blue and silver. Calm, but strong. Like the night sky."

He studied me for a moment before speaking again. "I am glad you like it. I had them prepared for when you arrived. I wanted you to feel at home."

The words surprised me. "You did that for me?"

"Of course," he said. "You will be my wife soon. It is only right that this place feels like yours, too."

I looked down at my hands, unsure what to say. It felt strange to hear the word *wife* spoken aloud. Strange, but real.

When I looked up again, he was still watching me with a gentle expression. "You do not need to be afraid," he said quietly. "I know this is new. You do not have to like me yet."

My blinking slowed at that. "Yet?"

He smiled faintly. "I only ask for time."

Something in his words made my shoulders ease, just a little. Not much, but enough to breathe without feeling like my chest might crack.

Maybe he was right. Maybe time would help.

Not yet. But soon. I had to like him. I had to know

him. In less than a week, he would be my husband. That was reason enough to try.

I lifted my gaze to his again, trying to steady my voice. "You said there was something you wanted to show me?"

He nodded, rising from the bed. "Yes. This."

He crossed the room to a polished wardrobe near the window and opened it. Candlelight glinted off silk as he drew something out and folded it carefully, the fabric smooth and dark. He turned and held it toward me.

It was a gown.

The color was the same as his chamber: midnight blue with silver thread winding through the bodice and sleeves like fine vines. Tiny pearls caught the light, faint as stars.

I stood slowly, reaching out to touch it. The fabric was cool beneath my fingers. "It is beautiful," I murmured.

He smiled, clearly pleased. "I want you to wear it tomorrow."

"Tomorrow?"

"Yes," he said. "I am taking you to one of our finest villages. It sits along the coast, not far from here. I want you to see Valebran for what it truly is—its people, its streets, its food." His eyes warmed slightly. "You will try our best breads, our pastries. I think you will like them."

I glanced at the gown again. "And this is for that?"

"It is," he said. "The colors are the royal shades of Valebran. I thought they would suit you."

The candlelight caught the silver thread as I turned the fabric in my hands. It shimmered softly, almost alive in the light.

"I will wear it," I said at last.

His smile deepened, dimples visible now. "Good."

He placed the gown carefully on the chair beside the bed, smoothing the fabric as if it were something precious. Then he turned back to me and extended his arm.

"Come," he said softly. "Let me take you to your bedchamber."

I hesitated, just for a breath, before resting my hand lightly on his sleeve. His arm was firm beneath the fabric, his movements unhurried as he led me toward the door.

The corridor outside was dim and quiet. Only the faint sound of the sea drifted through the open arches, carrying the cool scent of salt and stone. We walked in silence, our footsteps echoing against the marble floor.

When we reached the next door, Lorenzo pushed it open for me, his hand resting briefly on the frame as he stepped aside.

The moment I crossed the threshold, my mood shifted. The room was softly lit by the glow of lanterns near the balcony, and standing just beyond them was William. His armor gleamed faintly in the light, his helm hiding his face, his posture straight and still.

My heart hammered without reason. I forced my gaze away.

Lorenzo paused at the doorway, his eyes tracing the direction of mine. For a moment, he said nothing. The quiet stretched thin between us. Then his voice came lower, softer than before.

"You are so beautiful," he said. "I could look at you all day."

The words settled over me like warmth I didn't ask for. My throat went dry. "Thank you, my lord."

"Ah, just Lorenzo." He corrected with a smile. "There is no need for formality between us. Not when we will be wed soon."

I hesitated before nodding, trying to calm the quick flutter in my chest. "Of course, Lorenzo."

Something in his expression eased at that. The distance between us seemed smaller now, the candle-light touching the sharp lines of his face, softening them.

"May I stay with you for a while?" he asked quietly.

I wasn't sure how to answer, so I simply nodded.

His smile deepened. He reached into the pocket of his coat and drew out a small white rose. Its petals looked fresh, perfect, as though it had just been plucked from the garden.

"I remember how you said these were your favorite," he said.

He stepped closer. My eyes widened as he lifted his hand and tucked the flower just behind my ear, his fingers brushing against my skin.

I stood still, not knowing what to say.

Lorenzo smiled again, satisfied. "It suits you," he said softly.

I managed another small smile, though my heart was pounding too hard for it to feel real.

"Oh I cannot wait for our wedding," said Lorenzo. "I already know we will make the perfect royal couple."

I forced another small smile, though my chest felt tight. "Yes, of course we will."

His dimples deepened, pleased with the answer. "That is what I like to hear."

He sat down on the edge of the bed, then reached for my hand.

Before I could think, he gave a gentle tug, pulling me toward him until I was sitting on his lap. His arm slid around my waist, his breath brushing close to my ear. My stomach did something at that. I wasn't sure if it knotted or if it were butterflies, but either way, it was enough for me to feel the steady rise of his chest. His arms tightened faintly around my waist, making it a little difficult to breathe.

"You will make a fine queen," he murmured.

I smiled, uncertain how to respond. My fingers tightened in my lap, and I tried to ignore the strange rush of warmth climbing up my throat.

Then—

"Her Highness is to be in slumber before midnight."

The voice cut through the quiet like a blade. I stopped breathing before I even turned.

Lorenzo's hand went still against my waist, the

warmth of it replaced by sudden stiffness. We both turned toward the sound.

William stood near the balcony, with his helm now tucked under one arm. His expression was calm, but there was something dangerous beneath it, something that made the air heavier.

"The King's orders," he said

Lorenzo's brows lifted slightly. "Oh?" His voice carried a note of amusement. "And why was I not informed of this?"

William didn't blink. "Because I was informed only moments ago," he replied. "His Majesty wished it to be enforced at once."

My pulse quickened, though I didn't know why. A part of me knew William was lying. There was no such order, there couldn't be. But he stood there with a quiet conviction that almost made me believe him.

Almost.

I clenched my jaw, heat crawling up my neck. What was he doing? Trying to humiliate me? Or worse, trying to remind me of the control he still held, even after everything? The thought made my chest burn.

Lorenzo's smile returned, smaller now, sharper. "Surely," his fingers tightened faintly at my side, "the King would not mind his daughter's future husband spending a few moments after midnight with her."

"He will," William said simply.

The words landed heavy, final.

The room seemed to shrink around us. I could feel the tension rolling off them both: Lorenzo's pride,

William's restraint, the sharp friction of two men circling a line neither dared cross.

And I was caught between them with a heart beating so fast I was sure they could hear it. I could feel William's gaze on me, and that only made it worse.

Something twisted in me. Anger. Embarrassment. Confusion. I didn't know which one was stronger.

I lifted my chin, the words slipping out before I could stop them. "Actually," I said, forcing my voice steady, "he will not."

That silenced William. For a heartbeat, no one moved.

Then his jaw flexed, his voice low but firm. "King Henrik expects all attending to be well rested for tomorrow."

I turned to him slowly, irritation flaring sharp and fast. I'd had enough of his coldness. "Oh?" My tone sharpened. "And what exactly happens tomorrow?"

William's eyes flicked toward me. "Something important," he said. "So the Prince must leave."

Lorenzo gave a short laugh under his breath, his fingers still resting lightly at my side. "Is that so?"

But before either of them could say another word, I stood. My voice was calm, though the air felt like it might break. "No," I said. "You must leave."

For a long moment, no one moved.

The silence pressed heavy between us, thick enough to feel. The wind outside brushed faintly against the balcony curtains, but even that seemed distant.

William didn't speak. He only stood there, his jaw

tight, his fists curling once at his sides. The faint blaze in his eyes said everything his voice didn't.

For some reason, that look brought a flicker of satisfaction to my chest. He'd lied. There was nothing important beyond a simple visit to a village. He made it up, and we both knew it.

I turned toward him fully, my voice steady now, deliberate. "Well?" I said. "Get out, *knight*. My fiancé and I are trying to have a moment."

Lorenzo's smirk returned, slow and sure. "You heard her," he laughed. "Out."

William's gaze lingered on me for a long, burning moment. The air between us felt heavy, too still, like the world itself was holding its breath.

His fists stayed tight at his sides, knuckles pale against the light. For a second, he looked seconds away from punching the wall behind him, from saying something he'd regret. But he didn't.

Instead, he drew in a slow, loud, breath. His eyes met mine one more time, sharp and unreadable.

"As you wish, Your Highnesses," he said quietly.

The words came out tight, controlled, but there was something in them that felt like the crack of a blade.

Then he turned. The door closed behind him with a dull, final sound, leaving the air thick with everything he hadn't said.

CHAPTER THIRTY-FIVE

WILLIAM

The sun slipped through the tall windows, painting the chamber in soft streaks of gold. I stood near the balcony door, my hands clasped behind my back, pretending to be focused on the view outside.

Servants moved quietly around the room, fastening the ties of the princess's gown and adjusting folds of silk until it draped perfectly. I told myself to keep my eyes forward to stay still, to be what I was; her guard. Nothing more. But every time one of them brushed her hair over her shoulder or pinned the silver at her throat, my gaze betrayed me.

She looked radiant. And untouchable.

The gown was the color of Valebran's sea, its silver thread catching the morning light. When she turned slightly, I caught the faint shimmer of pears along her sleeves. She didn't even have to try. She was born to look like this. A princess. A prize. Someone who didn't belong to men like me.

And yet the memory of her voice from last night echoed sharp in my head. *You must leave.*

The words burned deep. Now I watched another man's arm settle around her waist, and the heat of it came roaring back.

Lorenzo leaned close, smiling at her reflection in the mirror.

"You look beautiful," he said softly.

Something inside me twisted. My jaw locked until I could feel the ache in my teeth. The same girl who had once cried against my chest, who had looked at me with something real in her eyes, now stood perfectly still under his hand.

I turned my gaze away before it showed, before she could see what it did to me. But in the mirror, her eyes flicked toward mine for the briefest second. A heartbeat of silence. Then she looked away.

"Very well," Lorenzo said, his tone bright. "Ready to see Valebran's finest village?"

She nodded, a faint smile softening her face. "Yes, I think so."

He offered her his arm, and she took it.

I quietly followed as they left the room. Every movement was a quiet war between duty and everything else I wasn't supposed to feel.

The walk through the corridors was quiet save for the faint sound of their footsteps and the echo of laughter from servants preparing for the day. When we reached the courtyard, sunlight spilled across the stone, catching the silver of the carriages lined before the gates.

A few other guards joined us. Lorenzo took Iris's hand, helping her up the step with a smile that made my jaw tighten once more.

She placed her fingers in his, her voice soft as she thanked him.

The sound of it stirred something sharp in my chest.

I climbed in after the others, taking my place across from then. The door shut. The horses started forward, and the wheels creaked against the cobblestones as the castle fell away behind us.

The carriage swayed with the rhythm of the road. Lorenzo's arm slipped easily around her waist again, like it belonged there. His voice came low, smooth. "You are absolutely stunning," he said. "And I will say it every time I see you."

She giggled, light and quiet. The sound hit harder than it should have. "Thank you, Lorenzo."

"Ah," he said, smiling wider. "I love hearing you say my real name."

She said it again, softer this time, and I felt it like a blow. *Lorenzo.* The word hung in the air—too intimate, too easy.

My hands curled into fists against my knees, the leather of my gloves creaking with the strain. My jaw clenched until it hurt. I stared at the floorboards, focusing on the faint scuffs in the wood, anything to keep from looking up. Every word they exchanged felt like salt rubbed into an open wound.

I reminded myself what I was. A knight. Her guard. Nothing more. But the reminder did little to dull the ache.

Silence stretched after that. The only sounds were the steady rhythm of the horses and the faint rustle of fabric as she leaned against him. I kept my eyes fixed on the floor, each second feeling longer than the last.

Then the carriage slowed. The noise of voices grew louder outside. The wheels rolled to a stop.

We had arrived.

The door opened with a faint creak, letting in the bright warmth of the sun and the smell of the sea mixed with earth. Lorenzo stepped out first, his boots hitting the ground with a soft thud before he turned and held out his hand.

"Careful, my lady," he said with a smile. "You will love the village."

She placed her hand in his and stepped down, her gown brushing lightly against the stone. The guards followed, one after another, their armor catching the light. I was the last to leave the carriage, my sword at my side, the weight of duty heavy on my shoulders.

The village stretched wide before us, more alive than I expected. Narrow streets wound between small houses of pale stone and red-tiled roofs. The air smelled faintly of baked bread and hay. Children ran along the road, laughing, and merchants stood at wooden stalls draped with fruit, flowers, and handwoven cloth.

When the people saw us, they stilled. Then, one by one, they bowed. The sound of it was soft, a rustle of movement and reverence.

Lorenzo held Iris's hand, his smile easy and sure. "Come,"

She nodded and let him guide her through the street. The other guards followed close behind, forming a loose circle around them. I walked a few steps back, eyes shifting between the rooftops, the crowd, and the pair ahead.

Everywhere they passed, villagers knelt or offered flowers. The Prince greeted them warmly, his hand never leaving hers. She smiled back at them, polite and kind, though even from a distance I could see the stiffness in her shoulders.

Lorenzo led her toward a stall where the scent of warm bread filled the air. The baker bowed low, his face lighting up as the Prince approached. I stayed back, a few paces away, near another stall lined with woven baskets. Leaning against it, I crossed my arms over my chest and tried to look anywhere but at them.

Lorenzo said something to the baker, and a moment later, the man handed him a small loaf still warm from the oven. Lorenzo tore off a piece, smiling as he turned to Iris. "Try this," he said.

She hesitated, then leaned closer. He held the bread to her lips, and she took a small bite. Her smile was soft, her eyes lowering as she swallowed.

Something in me twisted at the sight. It was sharp

and unexpected, like being struck from inside. For a second I didn't even understand

it. Then I did.

It ached.

I had known this would happen. I had known from the moment the king announced her betrothal that I would have to stand by and watch her become his. But knowing it and seeing it were not the same. Watching her laugh with him and seeing the way he looked at her like she was already his, made it real. Too real.

I thought I could finally bury what I felt for her. I thought I had cut it clean. I told myself she was the king's daughter, a duty, nothing more. *Not Elara.* Not the girl who used to sit by the river and smile like she had no idea how dangerous it was to look at someone that way.

I told myself I was loyal to the king and would obey him, and wouldn't think of her again.

But in that moment, standing there while he fed her bread and she smiled like she meant it, I realised how wrong I was. I realised how much it hurt to see her with another man. To know she would be married soon. To know I would still be here, guarding her, watching, pretending none of it mattered.

Lorenzo tore off another piece, brushed a crumb from her chin, and she laughed again. My stomach sank. I clenched my fists at my sides and forced my gaze toward the street. I tried to focus on anything else; the chatter of the villagers, the sound of hooves, the cries of vendors selling fruit. But all I could hear was her voice. Her laugh. Her softness.

I swallowed hard, trying to steady the feeling that had built in my chest. I had sworn to serve the king, to protect his daughter. But right then, I realised how little I cared for any of that. None of it mattered. Not when the only thing I wanted—the only thing I could not have—was standing a few feet away, smiling at someone else.

CHAPTER THIRTY-SIX

IRIS

Lorenzo was still smiling as he fed me another piece of bread. I smiled, too, though it felt faint and practiced. The villagers watched us closely, whispering to one another as they passed.

Then I looked up.

And saw him.

William stood a few feet away, half hidden, leaning against a wooden stall. His arms were crossed, his shoulders tense beneath the armor, his expression carved in stone. The only thing that gave him away was the faint spark in his eyes. Anger. Quiet but sharp.

It wasn't new. He had looked the same all morning. Angry in the carriage. Angry when Lorenzo approached me after the servants had finished dressing me. Angry now.

My smile faltered before I could stop it.

For a moment, neither of us looked away. His gaze held mine, steady and unflinching, and something inside me twisted. I turned back to Lorenzo before he noticed, forcing another polite smile when he said something about checking another stall.

"I will be right back," he said warmly, brushing his fingers against mine before walking off.

As soon as he turned away, I looked back. William was still staring.

And just like that, every memory from the night before came rushing back. His voice, cold and distant. The way he said I was nothing more than duty. The way I'd told him to leave.

The look in his eyes before he did.

A dull ache pressed at my chest. I told myself I shouldn't care. That I had every reason to be angry with him after the way he'd spoken to me. But guilt crept in anyway, suffocating me.

He had only been trying to follow orders. And I had thrown him out like he meant nothing.

The market noise dimmed around me, fading into a distant hum. My steps slowed as I moved toward him, unsure what I was even going to say.

He didn't move. Didn't speak. He only watched as I came closer, the muscles in his jaw tight, his eyes darker than I remembered.

When I finally stopped in front of him, the space between us felt heavy. Too heavy.

"William," I began quietly, taking a small step closer. "About last night—"

His gaze cut to mine, sharp and sudden, silencing me before I could finish. The look in his eyes was enough to make my breath catch. It wasn't just anger. It was something deeper, something raw and unguarded that flickered only for a second before hardening again.

I flinched, my words faltering.

He spoke finally, his voice low and tight. "There is nothing to speak of, Your Highness."

The title—as usual—hit like a slap.

My eyes glistened, lighting something sharp inside me. "What?" I said, my tone rising before I could stop it.

He didn't answer. His eyes were still fixed on me, his silence louder than any insult. The muscles in his jaw worked as if he were holding something back.

I took a breath, anger creeping in to hide the hurt. "Well, then why have you been looking so angry all day?" I asked.

Still nothing. Not a word.

I took a slow breath, anger creeping in to hide the ache beneath it. "You have been looking angry all day," I said quietly. "In the carriage, at the castle, even now. I've seen it. So what is it, William? Why have you been looking like that if there's nothing to speak of?"

Still nothing. Not a word. His silence cut deeper than if he'd shouted.

The space between us felt like it was closing in, filled with things neither of us dared to say. My pulse thudded in my ears, my voice lowering to something softer, steadier. "If you hate me, then say it," I said. "But stop looking at me like that."

He didn't move. His arms stayed cross and his gaze stayed locked on mine, unflinching. It burned through me, cold at first, then something else entirely.

I swallowed hard, refusing to look away. "If I am just your duty, then do your duty. Stop acting like I am worth looking at."

Still, no answer. His eyes lingered on me for a heart-beat, then he turned and started walking away.

"Come back here!" I called after him. My voice was loud enough for people to turn back and stare.

He didn't stop. He didn't even look back. He just kept walking, his steps steady and unhurried, until he disappeared into the crowd.

My chest ached with the words I wanted to say caught in my throat. Before I could move, Lorenzo's voice came from behind me. "There you are," he said with a bright smile, his arm slipping easily around my waist.

I forced a nod, trying to steady myself.

"Where to next, my lady?" he asked.

"To the castle," I said quickly.

He tilted his head. "So soon?"

"Yes. I am not feeling too well."

Concern flickered across his face, though it looked practiced.

"Very well then." He offered his arm again. "Let us get you back."

He guided me through the crowd. The air smelled of salt and spice, but I could hardly focus. My thoughts were still on William, on the look in his eyes before he walked away.

When we reached the carriages, the guards were already waiting. Sunlight glinted off their armor as they moved aside to let us pass. William was seated inside ours. His posture was rigid, his hands resting on his knees. When our eyes met, I felt my breath catch. His expression was cold, distant, but his gaze didn't waver.

A day ago, he could barely look at me. Now, he didn't seem able to look anywhere else.

Lorenzo helped me up the step and took his seat beside me. The guards followed, closing the door behind them.

"Let us ride," Lorenzo said.

The driver gave a sharp nod, and the carriage began to move, wheels rumbling softly over the stone road.

Lorenzo's arm slid around my waist, pulling me closer to him as the carriage swayed. His tone was light when he spoke to one of the guards, but I could feel how close he was, how every inch between us disappeared.

Across from me, William's gaze hardened. He said nothing, yet I could feel it. Sharp, heavy, and fixed on me. His eyes held the same coldness he'd worn all day, but beneath it, something else lingered—something that made it difficult to breathe.

I kept my eyes on my hands, fingers twisting together in my lap. I looked down at my hands, my fingers twisting together in my lap. I wanted to tell him to stop staring. I wanted him to say something. Anything. But not here. Not in front of Lorenzo.

So I sat still, silent, as the wheels rolled on, the air inside the carriage thick with words neither of us could say.

CHAPTER THIRTY-SEVEN

IRIS

The dining hall was bright and full of sound. The long table gleamed beneath the chandelier, silver platters spread with roasted meats, fruits, and bread still warm from the oven. The scent of herbs and honey filled the air.

My father sat beside King Phelipe at the head of the table, the two of them deep in conversation about alliances and borders. Their voices carried easily, low but confident, the way men spoke when they believed the world was firmly in their grasp.

I sat to their right, across from the Queen. Lorenzo was beside me, cutting into his steak with practiced ease. He looked relaxed, comfortable in his place, occasionally leaning toward me to say something polite.

I nodded when expected, smiled when I had to, and tried to focus on the plate in front of me. The chicken was tender, the sauce rich, but I could hardly taste it. The weight in my stomach had nothing to do with the food.

Laughter rose from further down the table. Servants moved quietly between us, refilling goblets and clearing plates. The light flickered against the walls, soft and golden, and for a moment, I wished I could melt into it, become part of something so simple.

Lorenzo turned to me again, his voice gentle. "You should try the wine. It is from our vineyards."

I gave a small smile, lifting the cup to my lips. "It is lovely."

He looked pleased, and I looked back to my food, pretending to eat, pretending everything was fine. But the hollow ache in my chest stayed. It always did.

When the meal ended, the Kings were still talking, their voices rumbling over the clatter of plates. Lorenzo wiped his mouth with a hankerchief, then stood and turned to me with a smile.

"Allow me to walk you to your bedchamber," he said.

I nodded, setting my napkin down. "Of course."

He placed a hand at the small of my back, guiding me gently out of the hall. The corridors were quiet now, the echo of our steps following us through the long stretch of marble and silver.

We were halfway to my room when a sound stopped me. It was faint but sharp, a muffled cry coming from somewhere down the servant's hall. I turned my head, listening

"Is something wrong?" Lorenzo asked.

"I thought I heard—" I hesitated, glancing toward the narrow corridor ahead. "I will be just a moment. You can go on, I will not be long."

He chuckled softly, shaking his head. "I will wait by your door. Cannot have my future bride wandering alone."

His words made my stomach tighten, but I forced a polite smile. "As you wish."

I turned toward the sound, following it down the narrow corridor. The castle was quiet here, far from the warmth of the halls. Only the faint light of a lantern guided me. When I pushed open the door to the servants' barracks, the smell of soap and damp cloth filled the air.

Raven was sitting on one of the cots, her knees drawn up, her face hidden in her hands. Her shoulders trembled as quiet sobs escaped her.

"Raven," I said softly, moving closer.

She lifted her head, eyes red and wet. "I am fine," she whispered. "Please, just go, Iris."

I shook my head and knelt beside her. "No. This is the second time I have seen you like this."

"It does not matter," she said, turning away. "You should leave."

"Is it because you saw him again?" I asked quietly.

She froze for a moment before nodding. "I cannot,"

she said in a broken voice. "It hurts to see him. I thought I was past it, but I am not."

My heart sank. I sat beside her and pulled her into my arms. "Oh, Raven."

She clung to me, crying harder. I stroked her hair, letting her cry as long as she needed. "Everything will be alright," I said softly, though part of me doubted my own words.

Her pain reminded me too much of my own. The way it hurt every time I saw William, the way my chest ached knowing he wanted nothing to do with me. But I pushed it aside. This wasn't about me.

So I stayed with her, holding her until her sobs turned quiet. "You will be alright," I whispered again.

Raven nodded weakly, her voice hoarse. "I hope so."

I gave her hand a light squeeze. "You will be," I said, even if I wasn't sure either of us believed it.

Moments passed in quiet. The air in the barracks felt heavy, filled with the faint sound of Raven's soft breaths between tears. Outside, the last light of day slipped away, leaving the small room in a haze of shadow and candlelight.

Finally, Raven sat up, wiping at her eyes. "I should head to bed," she yawned,

I stood with her, brushing the wrinkles from my dress. "Are you sure you will be alright?"

She nodded faintly. "I will. I just need some rest."

I stayed beside her until she lay down, curling beneath her blanket. Her breathing steadied slowly, the tension easing from her face. I watched her for a while longer, waiting until her eyes finally closed. Only then did I move.

Quietly, I slipped out of the room and pulled the door closed behind me. The corridor outside was dim, lit only by a few torches along the walls. My footsteps echoed softly as I made my way through the long halls toward my chamber.

When I reached the door, I froze. Lorenzo was there, standing beside it, his arms crossed casually.

"Took you long," he said, a hint of amusement in his voice.

"You waited," I replied.

He smiled, unbothered. "I would wait as long as one could."

I nodded faintly, unsure how to respond. He stepped forward and opened the door for me.

"After you," he said.

I stepped inside, the soft light of the chamber washing over the silver walls and pale curtains. The scent of roses drifted faintly from the balcony. William stood there, his helm tucked beneath his arm, watching us with that same unreadable expression. His gaze was steady, cold, and far too heavy to ignore. I hated how much it still affected me.

Lorenzo followed close behind, his steps quiet. "I will stay for a bit," he said lightly. "It feels wrong to leave so soon."

I hesitated but gave a small nod. "If you wish."

He smiled, moving closer. His hand found mine, his touch warm and certain. "You look tired," he said softly.

"I suppose I am," I murmured.

He lifted my hands between his, brushing his thumb over my knuckles before leaning in and pressing a kiss to them. I froze. His lips were gentle, lingering just long enough to make my heart stutter.

When he looked up again, his green eyes met mine, soft and searching. "You really are beautiful,"

I tried to smile, though it felt strained. "Thank you, my lord."

"Lorenzo," he corrected with a faint grin. "I already said it is Lorenzo. No titles between us, not when we will soon be wed."

I nodded, forcing a faint smile again. "Of course."

He stepped closer, closing the space between us until I could feel the warmth of him against my skin. His voice dropped lower. "Rest well, dear," he said, his breath brushing my cheek. "I will need you looking radiant tomorrow."

Every part of me wanted to pull away, to step back, to breathe again. But I didn't. I only nodded, my voice thin and quiet. "I will."

Lorenzo smiled, pleased, and finally released me. He turned toward the door, the faint sound of his boots echoing on the polished floor. Before leaving, he looked back once more softly. "Goodnight, Iris."

"Goodnight," I whispered.

When the door closed behind him, silence filled the room again.

William was still standing by the balcony. The faint lantern light touched the edge of his armor, glinting off the metal and tracing the lines of his face. His jaw was clenched, his shoulders squared, every inch of him tense. His eyes were hard, steady, and burning with something I didn't want to name.

He looked the same as he had all day. Cold. Controlled. Angry.

And I knew, at least part of that anger was mine to carry.

My throat tightened. The guilt pressed down hard, but so did the irritation. He had no right to look at me like that, unless it's because I lied about who I was, though I doubt that's the reason.

He crossed his arms over his chest. For a moment, I thought he might say something. But he didn't. He only kept staring, silent and unmoving, as if daring me to speak first.

The air between us felt like a live wire. I could hear my heartbeat, quick and uneven. I could see the faint rise and fall of his chest as he breathed, slow but deep, as though fighting for control.

I held his gaze, my pulse hammering in my throat. Every second felt longer than the last. I wanted him to look away. I wanted him to say something. Anything.

But he didn't.

The quiet became unbearable.

Without thinking, I turned sharply and crossed the room. My fingers closed around the door handle, pushing it shut with more force than I meant to. The lock clicked into place, the sound cutting through the stillness like a spark.

The tension seemed to thicken, coil tighter around us both.

I turned back to him, my hands trembling at my sides. He didn't move. He just stood there, eyes following me with that same quiet, smoldering anger.

Enough.

If he wanted to keep staring at me like that—if he wanted to stand there as though I were some stranger, then he was going to face me now.

CHAPTER THIRTY-EIGHT

WILLIAM

She was standing right in front of me now, eyes bright with anger, chin tilted up to meet my gaze. The air between us felt thick, too heavy to breathe. I kept my arms crossed, staring down at her, my pulse steady but hard.

"Why do you keep looking at me like that?" she asked, her voice low but sharp.

I didn't answer. I couldn't. If I opened my mouth, I wasn't sure what would come out. Something cruel, maybe. Something I would regret. I couldn't tell her that every time I saw her with Lorenzo, it made something in me twist—that I hated it more than I had any right to.

Her tone rose. "Say something! You've been angry

for so long, and I know it cannot just be because I lied to you about who I was."

I drew a heavy breath through my nose. She was right, and I knew she was. She seemed to know a truth I didn't want to face. Something burned in my chest, fierce and unwanted. I tried to keep it still, to swallow it down.

"Answer me!" she said again, louder this time. Her hand came up, her small fist ready to hit me in the chest or shove me. Anything to make me react.

But I moved before I could think. My hand caught her first before she could land the strike. Her skin was warm beneath my fingers.

We both froze.

Her breath hitched, and my grip tightened slightly, not out of force but from the effort it took to keep control. Her eyes met mine, wide and defiant, and I could feel my heart hammering against my ribs.

"Let go!" she said in a trembling voice, not from fear, but anger. She pulled at her wrist, but I didn't move.

"I said let go!" she shouted again, louder this time.

The sound of her voice cracked something inside me. I could see the anger in her eyes, the frustration, but behind it there was something else. Hurt. The same hurt I had been trying to bury under duty and silence. I had been holding it all in for too long, and now I couldn't hold it anymore.

"Do you want to know why?" The words came out harsh and low.

She stilled. "Why what?"

"Why I look at you like that. Why I cannot stand seeing you with him."

Her lips parted slightly, but before she could speak, I went on. "Because I hate every part of it," I began. "I hate the way he looks at you like you belong to him. I hate the way he smiles at you, the way he touches you, and how you let him. I hate that you laugh with him the same way you used to laugh with me. Every time I see you beside him, it feels like something inside me is tearing apart."

Her eyes widened. She didn't speak, just stood there frozen, her breath uneven.

"It feels like hell," I said quietly. "Like living through punishment every time I see his hand on you, every time he calls you his."

For a long moment, she said nothing. Then, her voice came out barely above a whisper. "But you hated me for lying to you. You said I was nothing but a duty."

The words hit hard. I looked away, jaw tight, every muscle in me strained to keep steady.

When I didn't answer, she said, "If you are so angry at me, and if I am nothing but a duty to you, then why do you care?"

That question struck deeper than anything else.

Because I did care. More than I had any right to. More than I could ever admit.

I could feel something burning deep in my chest, something that had been building for too long, pressing against the walls I had tried to keep up. I wanted to stop it. I wanted to swallow it down like I always did, but it was too much. I couldn't.

"Because–" The words tore out of me before I could think. I stopped, breathing hard. My pulse was loud in my ears.

She took a small step closer, eyes fierce, demanding an answer. "Because what, William?"

It snapped. The last of the restraint I had been holding broke apart.

"Because I am in love with you," I said.

The words came out low, ragged, and absolute. I had never spoken anything truer in my life.

She froze. Her lips parted slightly, her blueeyes wide, breath caught somewhere in her throat.

I took a step back, running a hand through my hair as if that could undo what I'd said. "I tried not to," I said quietly, my voice strained. "God knows I tried. Especially after I found out who you were. You are the king's daughter, a princess, and I am just a knight. It should have ended right there. But it did not."

Her eyes glistened, her voice barely a whisper. "You… you love me?"

I didn't answer. I just looked at her, unable to lie anymore. The truth was too heavy to swallow back down.

She took a small step forward, her voice shaking. "Since when?"

The question cut through the air, pulling something deeper out of me. I looked at her, really looked, and the memories came like a tide I couldn't stop.

"Since the first day," I said finally. "Since you came into my home pretending to be a healer. You smiled at me like you were not afraid, like I was more than a soon-to-be-knight. And at the riverbank, you read by the river, you asked about my past, you laughed when I said something foolish. I did not know your true name, but I knew I was done for."

She swallowed hard, her hands trembling as she clutched her skirts.

I stepped closer, my voice lower now. "And when I found out the truth, when I realised who you really were, I told myself to stop. To hate you. But I could not. I still saw Elara. The girl who sat by the river, the one who looked at me like I mattered."

Tears gathered in her eyes. She didn't try to hide them.

For a moment, I just watched her—the way her breath caught, the way her shoulders trembled. Something inside me cracked open.

"I do not know if you love me back," I said, "but I cannot do this anymore. I cannot pretend I have forgotten you. I cannot act like you do not matter to me, because you do. More than I ever thought anyone could."

Her breath caught, and she shook her head as her hands tightened at her side. "But you look at me like I am the one to blame," she said, trembling. "Like I wanted this marriage. I never did. And you know it. You held me when I cried about it back in Elarion. You know I am being forced into it."

I stared at her, my chest tightening. The room felt smaller. "It was the way you started getting closer to him," I said quietly. "Smiling at him. Letting him touch you. Every time I saw it, it felt like a knife."

Her lips trembled. "At the start I did it because I had no other choice. We are getting married either way. But then I did it–" she paused softly, "to make you jealous."

A quiet laugh escaped me. It was so sudden despite everything that had happened. "Well, it worked."

That pulled a small laugh from her too, unsteady but real. It broke something heavy between us. I found myself smiling, just a little.

"Come here," I said.

She hesitated for only a heartbeat before stepping closer. I wrapped my arms around her, drawing her against me. She felt small and trembling in my hold, her cheek warm against my chest. For a long time, neither of us said anything. The only sound was her uneven breathing and the steady beat of my heart.

"I am sorry," I said finally. "For everything I said. When I called you a duty, I did not mean it. I was angry and feared the King a little. I wanted to push you away, but now I do not. I do not care about any of that."

Her hands gripped my arms tighter. "I am sorry, too," she whispered. "For lying about who I was. If I had not, maybe none of this would have happened."

I shook my head. "Do not say that. I would have fallen for you no matter what name you gave me."

She looked up then, her blue eyes soft and wet. "You forgive me?"

"I already have," I said quietly. "I forgive you, Iris."

Her lips parted slightly at the sound of her real name. "It feels good to hear you say it," she whispered. "Not 'your highness.' Just Iris."

I brushed a thumb across her cheek, wiping a tear that had escaped. "Then Iris it is," I said.

That drew another smile from her. She leaned into me, her forehead resting lightly against my chest. I held her tighter, my arms settling around her as if they belonged there. Which they did.

"It feels so good to finally be able to hold you again," I said softly.

She tilted her head slightly, her voice muffled against me. "It feels so good that you sre not avoiding me anymore."

I smiled faintly. "Then let us see to it that way."

Her quiet laugh filled the room, soft and tired. "Agreed," she said.

A yawn escaped her, quiet and unguarded. I loosened my hold and stepped back slightly. "You should probably get some rest," I said. The words felt heavy. I didn't want the moment to end. I wanted to stay here, to hold her, to tell her everything she meant to me, to ask if she felt the same. To ask if she loved me, too. But that could wait. Tomorrow would come soon enough.

She nodded, her eyelids already drooping. "I should," she murmured, moving to sit on the edge of her bed.

I straightened, my hand resting on the hilt of my sword.

"You should rest, too," she said, glancing up at me.

"There is no resting when it comes to your safety," I replied.

She gave a tired smile. "But you have been awake for so long."

She was right. I could feel the weight of exhaustion pressing at the edges of my thoughts, though years of training had taught me to stay awake through worse. Still, I only said, "I will rest when you have fallen asleep."

Her eyes softened. "You promise?"

"I do."

She smiled again, faintly this time, and lay back against the pillows. The covers rose to her chin as her breathing slowed.

"Goodnight," she whispered.

I watched her for a moment longer before answering quietly, "Goodnight."

Then I took my place by the balcony, sword still at my side, and listened to the sound of her breathing until the room fell silent.

CHAPTER THIRTY-NINE

IRIS

I wasn't asleep. I couldn't be.

The room was quiet save for the sound of the curtains rustling and the comforting rhythm of the waves outside. William had kept his promise. He was sitting on the wooden chair near the window, his head leaned back, his hand resting loosely on the hilt of his sword. The lantern's light touched his face in a soft glow. He looked so peaceful for once, his guard down.

He loved me. That was what he had said. Since the first moment he saw me. The words kept circling in my mind, over and over, until I didn't know what to do with them anymore.

I cared for him. I knew that much. I trusted him more than anyone. The thought of him angry or hurt tore at me in ways I didn't understand. But love? I wasn't sure yet. It was something deeper, something I hadn't had time to name.

Maybe I just needed time. Maybe I needed a moment with him without the walls, the guards, the duty. Just us.

I shifted slightly under the blanket, my heart beating faster at the thought. He was right there, only a few steps away, close enough to reach if I wanted to. But I stayed still.

For now, it was enough just to watch him.

Moments passed. I had been staring at him for so long that I lost count of time. The room was quieter, and the sound of his steady breathing only made my thoughts louder. I couldn't lie there any longer. I needed to move, to think, to breathe.

I slipped from the bed and put on my slippers. The floor was cold, and the air carried a faint chill that made me shiver. Carefully, I opened the door. The faint creak of its hinges seemed loud in the stillness, but William didn't stir. He was still there, sleeping upright, one hand loosely on his sword.

The hall was dim, lit only by a few torches along the stone walls. My footsteps echoed softly as I walked, arms wrapped around myself for warmth. I took a few deep breaths, trying to clear the noise in my mind.

Then I saw her.

Raven stood at the far end of the corridor. My brow furrowed. She was supposed to be asleep. No one should have been awake at this hour.

"Raven?" I called quietly.

She jumped and turned, her face pale in the low light. "Oh—oh, Iris! You startled me."

"What are you doing here?" I asked, walking closer.

Her hands fidgeted with the fabric of her skirt. "I am just... looking for something. I lost my satchel."

"Do you need help finding it?"

"No—no, I am fine. Go back to bed, really." Her voice was quick, uneven.

I stopped a few feet from her, narrowing my eyes. "Raven..."

She blinked rapidly. "Y–yes?"

"I can tell you are hiding something," I said. "You are far too nervous for someone who just lost a satchel."

She let out a slow sigh, her shoulders sinking. "Fine. You caught me."

"Caught you doing what?"

Her voice dropped to almost a whisper "Meeting someone."

My stomach turned. "Meeting who?"

Her gaze lowered to the floor. "My past love," she said quietly. "The same one who broke my heart. He found out I was here... and wanted to talk."

"What?" I said quietly, my eyes narrowing. "Who is he?"

Raven shook her head quickly, her fingers twisting together. "I cannot tell you. Not yet."

I wanted to press her, but something in her tone stopped me. That was her secret, not mine to pry open.

"Can you please leave before he comes?" she asked. "He should be here any moment."

I sighed, glancing toward the shadows at the end of the corridor.

"Fine," I said. "I will go."

Her eyes softened. "Thank you."

I gave her one last look before turning away. My slippers made almost no sound against the stone floor as I walked farther down the hall. The castle felt colder here, the torches fewer, the air still.

Behind me, I heard something. The sound of footsteps. Heavy and deliberate. A man's. My heart picked up for a moment, but I didn't turn around. It had to be him, the man Raven once loved. I wanted to turn my head to see who he was. But I couldn't. Not after I had promised to give her space. So I kept moving.

The hall stretched long and empty until it opened into the dining room. The faint scent of wine and roasted fruit still lingered in the air. I walked to one of the long tables and sat down, my hands resting on the smooth wood. A bowl of grapes sat near the center, left from dinner, and I took one without thinking.

The sweetness filled my mouth, but it didn't ease the unease in my chest. I waited, hoping that by the time I returned, Raven would be done and back in bed.

Minutes passed. Then more. The hall stayed silent. My eyelids grew heavier with each breath. The chill of the room and the stillness made it harder to stay awake.

Finally, after what felt like a long while, I pushed the bowl away and rose from the chair. It had to be enough time. They must be finished by now.

I took a steady breath and started back toward the corridor.

The walk back felt longer this time. The halls were colder and the shadows were deeper. I moved carefully, not wanting to wake anyone, my fingers brushing the cold stone walls for balance.

When I turned the corner toward the direction of my bedchamber, I slowed. The sound of voices reached me. I took another step, peering through the dim light.

And then I froze.

A gasp caught up in my throat, a sharp sound escaping before I could stop it.

Raven stood near the wall, her hands trembling slightly as someone held her close. His figure was familiar, tall and dressed in fine clothes that caught the light from the torch above. His hand cupped her face, and his lips were on hers.

Lorenzo.

My mouth fell open, a soft gasp breaking the stillness around me. I didn't move. I couldn't.

The prince.

The man who was meant to be my husband.

The same man, now kissing my dearest friend.

CHAPTER FORTY

IRIS

They broke apart the instant they saw me. Both of them froze like they'd been struck.

Raven's eyes went wide. "Iris! What are you doing here?"

I took a step forward, my heart pounding. "No, the question is what are *you two* doing?"

Neither of them spoke at first. The air felt too heavy, too sharp. Lorenzo straightened, his face pale but composed. "My lady," he began carefully, "it is not what it looks like."

I let out a short, disbelieving laugh. "Then what does it look like, Your Highness?"

Raven drew in a shaky breath. "Please do not be angry," she said quickly. "You remember the man I told you about—the one who broke my heart?"

I frowned, my voice barely steady. "Yes?"

Her next words made my stomach drop. "It is him. The Prince. Prince Lorenzo."

For a moment, I could only stare. The world seemed to tilt beneath my feet. "What?" I whispered. "You are saying *he* was the one?"

Raven nodded weakly, eyes full of guilt.

My chest tightened. My betrothed. My supposed future husband.

The same man who had hurt my best friend so deeply she still cried at night. And Raven hadn't told me.

"Why did not you say anything?" I asked, my voice trembling. "You should have told me, Raven!"

"I could not," she said, her words barely more than a whisper. "I did not know how."

Before I could speak again, Lorenzo wiped the corner of his mouth with his thumb. His voice came calm, too calm. "Because there is nothing between us anymore," he said flatly. "It was a mistake. A long time ago."

The words sunk deep into me. I could hardly breathe. twitched, searching both their faces. I was desperate to understand what I was seeing, what I was hearing.

Raven stepped forward, shaking her head. "Lorenzo, please do not say that," she whispered, her voice breaking.

He turned to her, his jaw set. "No, I have said it

once and I will say it again. There is nothing between us anymore."

"Then why were the two of you kissing?" I asked, my voice sharper than I meant it to be.

He looked at me then, guilt flickering across his face before he spoke. "Because I loved her once," he said quietly, "and I still do. But the two of us do not work."

Raven's face crumpled. Tears filled her eyes, spilling down her cheeks as she shook her head. "Please," she said, her voice trembling. "Do not say that."

"I already have."

Then his eyes turned to me. "You are the one I want now."

The words struck me like a blade. My heart began to pound so hard I thought he might hear it. I didn't move or speak. All I could do was stare at him and listen to the sound of Raven's quiet sob.

Lorenzo drew in a breath and looked between us. "But that does not mean I will stop loving you, Raven. It just means I have my priorities."

Raven let out a broken laugh through her tears. "And that is exactly why you broke my heart," she said, her words shaking. "That is why I left Valebran. Because of you."

Lorenzo's jaw tightened. "What do you want me to do?" he said sharply. "You are a servant, Raven. My father wants me to marry someone of noble birth. Someone who can help secure the future of this kingdom, not a peasant."

Raven shook her head slowly, tears still falling.

"And that is the only reason you want her," she said bitterly. "For your kingdom. For your crown."

The truth cut through the air. And for the first time, it made sense to me. The way Lorenzo looked at me. The way he spoke about marriage. It wasn't just admiration or affection. It was duty. The

same duty that had once torn him from her.

I looked at raven, at the pain in her face, and something inside me ached for her. They must have loved each other once, truly and deeply, until he chose his title over her.

Lorenzo exhaled, his tone softening. "I love you, Raven," he said quietly. "But I will always put my kingdom and my people first."

Raven's head snapped up, her eyes blazing through the tears. "To hell with you," she said, her voice breaking but fierce. "I wish I never met you."

She wiped her cheeks with the back of her hand and turned sharply, walking down the hall. Her footsteps quickened with each sound.

"Raven!" I called, already stepping forward, but Lorenzo's hand caught my arm.

"Do not," he said firmly.

I tried to pull free. "No, let me go after her. She is my friend—she needs someone right now."

His grip didn't loosen. "And you are going to be *my* wife soon," he said, his voice sharp. "We will be married in a few days."

I twisted in his hold, anger rising in my chest. "That does not mean she does not need me."

He held my gaze, his own expression unreadable. "I may look like a monster," he said slowly, "but I am doing the right thing."

"The right thing?" I said, my voice trembling. "If you love her, why do not you want to be with her?"

His eyes hardened. "Because I love my people, too," he said quietly. "I cannot choose one person over many. I have a duty to my kingdom, and that must come first."

He finally let go of my arm, his fingers sliding away. I looked at him, my chest heavy, unable to form a response.

"Go back to bed, Iris," he said, his tone final.

For a long moment, I stood there, my breath shallow, my thoughts scattered. Then I turned and began walking back down the corridor.

I could hardly believe what I had just seen and heard. Lorenzo, the man I was meant to marry, was the same one who had broken Raven's heart. The same man who made her cry in the dark and tremble at the sound of his name.

And worse, he had admitted it himself. He was marrying me for the crown. For the title. For the power that came with my name.

Something inside me clenched painfully. I knew our marriage was meant to form an alliance, to strengthen two kingdoms. I had known it since the moment my father first spoke of Valebran. But hearing it, truly hearing it from Lorenzo's mouth, made my heart beat faster and heavier.

I had never wanted to marry him, not from the

beginning, and now the thought of it filled me with dread. I had always dreamed of something more. I grew up reading stories about love that was real and alive, the kind that burned bright even when the world stood against it. *The Song of the Willow Bride* had always been my favorite. Elara and Mike had chosen each other against everything, bound by love, not duty.

That was what I wanted. True love. Deep love. The kind that made your heart ache in the best way. But that was not something my father would ever allow. To him, love meant nothing if it did not serve the throne.

The halls were silent as I walked back to my chambers, my thoughts heavy and tangled. When I reached the door, I opened it quietly and stepped inside. William was still there, asleep on the chair, one hand resting on the hilt of his sword.

I stood for a moment, watching the slow rise and fall of his chest. Then I crossed the room softly, careful not to wake him, and slipped beneath the covers.

Sleep did not come easily. My mind refused to rest. All I could think about was the love I wanted and the life I was being forced to live instead.

CHAPTER FORTY-ONE

IRIS

Two days had passed since that night, yet the memory of it still lingered in my mind. The tension, the truth, the way Raven's voice broke when she cried. It haunted me quietly, sitting just behind every thought.

Now I sat at the long dining table, the silver plates reflecting the soft glow of the candles. The room was quieter than usual. Lorenzo sat across from me, focused on his meal, his expression calm but distant.

I cut a small piece of meat, trying to keep my tone light. "Will we be doing anything tomorrow?"

He looked up briefly, then back at his plate. "No. I will be helping my father with the wedding preparations."

The word hit me harder than I expected. *Wedding.* It

was only a few days away now. Every corner of the castle buzzed with excitement and movement. Servants hurried through the halls, florists carried armfuls of white lilies, and tailors rushed to finish my gown. Everyone seemed thrilled. Everyone except me.

My chest sank as I nodded slowly. "Of course."

He gave no reply, only took another bite of his food. His voice, his eyes, even his posture had grown colder in the past two days.

Perhaps guilt, or duty, or something else entirely. I wasn't sure.

But I didn't mind it. His distance felt like a strange kind of comfort.

The meal passed quietly. My thoughts were louder than the silence between us. When I finally finished, I placed my fork down and stood. Lorenzo remained seated, his gaze fixed somewhere past me.

He didn't offer to walk me to my chamber. Didn't even look up.

I waited for a moment, expecting he might look up or at least say goodnight. But he didn't. So I finally turned and walked out of the hall.

The corridors were quiet as I made my way back to my chambers. When I opened the door, the room felt colder than usual. Empty. William wasn't there. The chair he slept on stood by the balcony, but there was no sign of him. I assumed he had been called to stand guard elsewhere.

I let out a slow breath and began to move toward

my vanity. I was reaching for my brush when something on the floor caught my eye.

A single white rose.

It just lay inside the balcony door, the petals pale as snow beneath the dim light. My brows drew together as I stepped closer. Then I saw another one. A pink one, lying a little farther ahead. And another white one beyond that. A trail.

My pulse quicked. I opened the balcony doors. The night air was sharp and cool, brushing against my skin as I stepped outside. The roses continued, one white, one pink, one white again, forming a path across the stone floor over the balcony's edge.

I leaned forward and looked down. The drop was steep, but below I could see the same pattern of roses leading toward the garden, winding down a narrow ledge that looked just stable enough to climb.

A chill ran down my spine.

Lorenzo. It had to be him. He was the only one who ever gave me white roses.

I hesitated, staring at the roses. Should I follow them? Every rule I had ever been taught said no. I wasn't allowed to leave my chambers alone, especially not at night. The castle walls were supposed to be my safety.

But the trail looked so deliberate, so tempting, almost calling to me.

I glanced toward the door, half-expecting William to appear and stop me. He didn't. The room was still. The only sound was the wind brushing through the balcony curtains.

I took a deep breath. Then another.

Before I could change my mind, I fastened two white clips on either side of my hair to keep it from blowing into my face. I draped a soft pink shawl over my white gown and stepped out onto the balcony again. The air was cool against my skin, and the moonlight made the roses gleam like drops of pearl and blush scattered across stone.

Carefully, I climbed over the railing. My fingers gripped the carved edge as I lowered myself down to the ledge below. It was narrow, but solid enough beneath my slippers. I kept one hand on the stone as I followed the trail, each step slow, careful.

When I finally reached the ground, my breath came in short bursts. I glanced around. No guards in sight. The torches on the walls burned faintly in the distance, leaving most of the garden in shadow.

I gathered my shawl closer and followed the roses across the grass. The petals glowed faintly in the moonlight, leading me through rows of trimmed hedges and flowering trees. The farther I went, the quieter it became. The wind had died down, the air heavy and still.

At last, the roses led me to the farthest corner of the castle grounds, a place I had never been before. There were no guards here, no lights, only the high stone walls and the soft rustle of leaves.

And then I saw something.

A tall, muscular figure stood leaning against the wall as if he had been waiting for me. His posture was calm, almost casual, but something about it made my pulse quicken. The moonlight caught his outline, and for a moment, I couldn't move.

The figure straightened, stepping out from the shadows. The moonlight caught his face, and my heart nearly dropped.

William.

He was leaning against the stone wall, his arms crossed, a faint smirk tugging at the corner of his mouth. The look in his eyes was calm but unreadable, the kind that made my pulse trip over itself.

"William?" I managed, my voice barely above a whisper.

"I did not think you would actually come," he said with something that sounded like amusement.

I blinked, glancing down at the trail of roses at my feet before looking back up at him. "You put those there?"

"I did." His smirk deepened slightly. "I remember you said you liked the white ones. But I also saw the way you looked at the pink ones that day in the gardens."

For a moment, all I could do was stare at him. The night air pressed cool against my skin, and my heart was still racing, caught between confusion and something else entirely.

"You remembered that?" I said softly.

He nodded once, his gaze steady on mine. "I remember a lot of things about you."

My eyes drifted to his hands, and that was when I saw it. The book. The same one we had read to each other by the riverbank.

My fingers clenched. Memories flooded in all at once. The sound of his voice. The warmth of sunlight through the trees. The feeling of peace I hadn't known in so long. My heart began to beat faster.

He lifted the book slightly, noticing my stare. "If you would like to stay," he said quietly, "we could read this together. Just like we did back in Elarion."

My heart skipped. I looked up at him, and for a moment, everything else fell away. The castle, the crown, the worry. All that mattered was this. Him, me, and the book.

"I would love to," I said softly.

A faint smile curved his lips. He held out his hand. I hesitated, then took it. His hand was warm and steady.

"I know the perfect place for this," he said.

I followed him to the far end of the courtyard, where the walls met the shadows. He stopped in front of a small wooden door built into the stone. When he pushed it open, a rush of cool night air brushed against my skin.

"Secret door," he said with a small grin.

We stepped through, and I could barely breathe for a moment. Trees surrounded us, tall and silent, their leaves whispering in the breeze. We walked further until the sound of water reached my ears.

The trees thinned as we walked, and soon the sound of water grew louder. The air carried the smell of sea salt and wet stone.

When we stepped past the last line of trees, the sea stretched before us, calm and dark beneath the moonlight.

William walked ahead and sat down near one of the trees, the same way he used to by the riverbank. I stood there for a moment, just staring. The soft rush of waves, the shimmer of the moon on the water was all too familiar. For a heartbeat, I almost believed I was back home.

I took a slow breath and moved closer. Before I could sit, I felt his strong arms slip gently around my waist. The warmth of his touch was steadying and grounding.

"I thought you would like this," he said quietly, his voice near my ear. "It reminds you of home, does not it? You loved the river."

My chest ached at his words. It was true. I always had. But what I loved most was that he remembered.

I turned to face him fully, my voice soft. "Yes. It does remind me so much of home."

He smiled, and something in that smile eased the tightness in my chest. He sank down near the tree and gently pulled me with him until I was seated on his lap. The warmth of him against the cool night air made me shiver, though not from the cold.

He reached into his dark cloak and pulled out the book. The worn leather cover caught the silver light of the moon. "Then let us read," he said quietly.

I nodded, unable to stop the smile that rose to my lips. I leaned closer, until my head rested against his chest. His tunic was soft beneath my fingers, and I could hear his heartbeat, steady at first, then quicker, stronger, as if it were trying to speak for him.

He rested his chin lightly on the top of my head and began to read. His voice was low, careful, the same voice that had once carried across the riverbank when everything between us was simple.

The words from the book were familiar, yet they felt different now. Maybe it was the way he said them, slower, gentler, like each one carried something unspoken.

Butterflies stirred in my stomach. I tried to ignore them, but the warmth of him behind me made it impossible. The rhythm of his voice, the sound of the sea, the faint brush of his breath near my ear—it all blurred together until I could not tell what was the story and what was real.

I tilted my head slightly and glanced up at him. The moonlight touched his face, softening it, and I felt my chest tighten in a way I had not before.

I could not explain what I was feeling. It was quiet but strong,

settling deep in my chest and refusing to leave. Everything else faded until there was only his voice and the sound of the sea.

He kept reading, his tone calm and even. I watched him for a moment, the way his lips moved, the way the light caught his face. Something inside me ached, and I looked away before he could notice.

The air was cool, but I felt warm. Too warm. His arm brushed against mine as he turned a page, and I forgot to breathe.

For a while, neither of us spoke. Only the waves filled the silence.

I closed my eyes when he began to continue reading. And though I did not understand what it was, I knew I did not want it to end.

CHAPTER FORTY-TWO

WILLIAM

This moment felt precious in a way I could not describe. Her resting against my chest, her head just beneath my chin, and the faint scent of the roses lingering in her hair. The night was quiet save for the sea and her soft breathing.

I kept reading, though the words began to blur. My focus was on her—the way her fingers rested lightly on my arm, the way she leaned closer whenever the wind grew colder. I could feel her heartbeat through the fabric of her gown, soft and steady against me.

It struck me then how rare this was. Peace. After everything that had happened, this silence between us felt fragile, like something I didn't deserve but would never forget.

I looked down at her. Her eyes were half closed, her

lips curved in the faintest smile. I wanted to reach out and touch her face, to trace the softness of her skin, but I didn't. Some moments were meant to stay as they were.

I kept reading until the story came to an end. My voice grew quieter with each line until I finally closed the book and set it beside me on the grass. The night was still, the sea calm beneath the moonlight.

When I looked down at her, her eyes were half lidded, her lashes heavy with sleep. She looked tired, but peaceful. I didn't want the moment to end, though I knew I should tell her to go back before anyone noticed she was gone.

"It would be best if you returned," I said quietly.

She shook her head against my chest. "Not yet," she murmured. "Just a little longer."

A warmth spread through me at her words. I smiled, unable to help it. "Then stay."

She leaned closer, her head tilting up toward the open sky. For a while, we said nothing. Then she lifted a hand, pointing toward the distant peaks outlined in silver. "What do you think is up there?" she asked softly.

I followed her gaze. The mountains stood tall and dark, their tips lost in the mist. "Maybe nothing," I said. "Or maybe something worth finding."

She hummed quietly, thoughtful. "Do you ever think about leaving? Going somewhere far?"

"Sometimes," I said. "But not tonight."

She smiled as her eyes drifted toward the stars.

Their reflection shimmered across the water, soft and distant.

"What about them?" she asked, her voice barely above a whisper. She pointed up at the sky. "What do you think they really are?"

I followed her gaze again. The stars scattered across the dark like spilled silver dust, endless and unreachable. "I am not certain," I said after a moment. "Maybe candles. Ones God lights so people do not get lost in the dark."

Her lips curved. "That is a comforting thought," she said. "Lights to guide us when the world feels too dim."

Then her gaze deepened, her voice softer now. "But maybe they are something else. Maybe they are a piece of us. A mark of every soul that has found peace in heaven. Each one a reminder that no one is ever truly gone."

I looked at her, unable to speak for a moment. The wind carried the scent of salt and earth, her words lingering like a faint hum of the sea.

"That is beautiful," I said finally. "I like your way better."

She smiled again and leaned closer, her shoulder brushing mine. "Then we will keep both," she whispered.

The stars shimmered above us, like shards of light across the sky. She kept her gaze on them, blue eyes wide and full of wonder. But mine stayed on her.

Her hair glowed faintly beneath the moonlight, a soft halo against the silver sky. I drew her closer without thinking, my arms tightening around her. The quiet between us felt warm, steady.

"They are beautiful," she said softly.

"I know," I murmured. But I wasn't looking at the stars.

She tilted her head slightly, still watching the sky. "The stars are the most beautiful things ever," she said.

A faint smile tugged at my lips. "And yet, you outshine them."

She turned her face toward me, her eyes catching the light, and for a moment I forgot to breathe. A soft color rose to her cheeks, warm and delicate against the cool air. She looked away quickly, but I saw the small smile forming on her lips.

We sat in silence after that. She was still watching the stars, her head resting lightly against my chest, and my heart beat faster than I wanted it to.

So this was love. Not the kind sung in taverns or written in stories, but something quiet. Real. It rooted itself deep, the way the tide clings to the shore.

I reached beside me and picked a small dandelion growing near the tree. Its petals trembled in the breeze as I twirled it between my fingers.

She tilted her head, watching it spin. "Do you have a favorite flower?" she asked softly.

I froze. The question was simple, yet caught me off guard. I had never thought about it before. Flowers had just been things that grew and wilted without meaning.

But then I looked at her, really looked, and I realised I've never had a thing for flowers until the most beautiful one was sitting in my arms. She blossomed like a flower, just like how my love blossomed for her.

She hadn't told me she loved me. Not yet. Maybe she never would. The thought made my chest sink, but it shouldn't have mattered. What I felt for her was already too deep to fade, too rooted to be undone by silence.

She looked up at me again, her eyes curious. "So," she said softly, "what is your favorite flower, then?"

I looked at her for a long moment, the repeated question hanging between us. Her eyes caught the moonlight, soft and clear, and something inside me gave way.

"You," I said quietly

She blinked, surprise flickering across her face. "Me?"

I nodded, my voice steady now. "You asked what my favorite flower is. It is you."

Her lips parted, but no words came out. I could see the faint color rise deeper into her cheeks as she looked away, her fingers tracing the fabric of her gown.

"I am not a flower," she whispered.

A faint smile curved my lips. "You are to me."

Neither of us spoke after that. She simply leaned against me again, her head resting on my chest. The quiet surrounded us, soft and calm, and I could feel her breathing match mine. I didn't move. I didn't want to. I knew I had spoken the truth, and for the first time, it didn't scare me.

Time passed, though I couldn't tell how long. The

stars above us shimmered faintly, the waves whispered against the shore, and the night felt endless. Then her voice broke the stillness.

"We should return," she said softly.

I nodded, though every part of me wished we could stay. "Of course."

Before she could stand, I looked at her. "May I have the honour of seeing you here again tomorrow?"

She hesitated, her eyes searching mine. Then she smiled, gentle and small. "Yes."

My heart quickened, and I couldn't stop the smile that formed on my face. "Thank you."

We stood and began walking back toward the castle. The moonlight followed us through the trees. After a few steps, I slipped a hand behind her back and another beneath her knees.

She startled, her voice rising in protest. "William—what are you doing?"

"Carrying you," I said simply.

"I can walk," she murmured.

"You can," I said, meeting her gaze as I held her closer. "But maybe I just like carrying you."

She looked at me, caught between a frown and a smile. I felt her relax in my arms as the wind moved through the trees and the castle lights came into view.

CHAPTER FORTY-THREE

IRIS

My stomach was tight with nerves. Lorenzo sat at the edge of my bed with his green eyes fixed on me as the tailors moved around, adjusting fabric and pins. I stood before the mirror in yet another gown. This one was white silk with heavy lace and soft pearls stitched along the hem.

Three days. Only three days left until the wedding. The thought alone made it hard to breathe.

"It is alright," Lorenzo said, his voice even. "Next."

The tailors exchanged glances and hurried to change the gown. One after another, they brought out more. Five dresses later, I felt the weight of each one pressing down on me. On the eighth, Lorenzo finally stood.

"That one," he said, a faint smile touching his lips. "It is perfect."

I turned to the mirror. The gown shimmered under the light, its bodice trimmed with silver thread that caught every movement. Layers of white and pale pink tulle flowed to the floor, soft and light, like drifting clouds. Tiny jewels glimmered across the neckline, catching the light each time I moved.

Lorenzo stepped closer, nodding in approval. "It suits you," he said, then turned to the tailors. "Now, go prepare her ball gown."

They bowed quickly and left the room, the door closing behind them.

I stood still, my reflection staring back at me. I didn't feel beautiful. I felt trapped.

Lorenzo came up behind me and placed his hands on my shoulders. "You look beautiful," he said quietly, his breath brushing the side of my neck.

I didn't flinch, but I didn't hide my discomfort either. "Please," I said softly, keeping my eyes on the mirror. "Can you leave?"

His hands lingered for a moment longer before he stepped back. "As you wish," he said. Then he turned and walked out, leaving me alone with the suffocating silence that followed.

—

By the time dinner ended, the hall was alive with talk of the wedding. Laughter and conversation filled every corner, words of alliance and prosperity passing from one noble to another. Servants hurried about, clearing plates, pouring wine, and polishing silver that already gleamed.

But I wasn't listening. Not really.

All I could think about was him. William.

The sound of his voice, the steadiness of his arms around me, the warmth of his presence. It had been a day since that night by the sea, and the memory of it had not faded. If anything, it had only grown sharper. I ached to see him, to hear him speak my name again. My heart fluttered at the thought, quick and restless, and I didn't know why it felt stronger now than it ever had before.

I left the dining hall quietly and made my way through the corridors, the soft echo of my footsteps keeping me company. When I entered my bedchamber, I half expected him to be there, standing by the balcony as he always did.

But he wasn't.

The room was still, dimly lit by the candles near the vanity. I exhaled softly until my eyes caught something near the balcony doors.

Roses.

A trail of them, just like before. White and pink, scattered across the floor, glinting faintly in the candlelight.

Excitement filled me so quickly it almost felt like a rush of wind through my chest. I reached for my shawl and wrapped it around my shoulders, then fastened my headband, my fingers trembling slightly. My heart was beating fast, almost too fast, as I pushed the balcony doors open.

The night air was cool and smelled faintly of roses. I followed the trail down, carefully climbing over the stone rail and finding the same narrow ledge as before. My slippers touched the grass softly when I reached the ground. The roses continued, white and pink, winding through the garden toward the hidden door.

When I stepped through it, the world opened again to the sea.

The waves whispered faintly against the shore, and the moon painted everything silver.

Halfway down the path, I stopped. The air was cool and quiet save for the sound of the sea below and the faint rustle of the trees. I pressed a hand to my chest, trying to calm the quick, uneven beat of my heart.

A thought came so suddenly it almost took my breath away. William. The memory of his voice when he said he loved me returned so clearly that it felt like he was standing beside me. He had said it with such honesty, as if he had been holding it in for far too long. My heart began to race, not from the climb, but from what I was feeling.

He was the only one who had ever truly seen me. Not a crown, not a title, not a duty. Just me. He had cared for me long before he knew who I really was. And even after finding out, even after everything that should have pushed him away, he still looked at me like I was someone worth loving.

He had told me he loved me, yes, but it was not just

in words. It was in the way he guarded me without being asked, the way his eyes softened when they met mine, the way he treated me like I mattered more than the world he served. He had shown me what love was long before I understood it.

And somewhere along the way, the care I had for him had changed. It had grown into something deeper, something I could feel in every part of me. I did not know what to call it yet, but I knew it was strong, and it was real.

I kept walking, my slippers brushing softly against the grass as the roses led me farther into the night. The air grew cooler, carrying the scent of salt and sea. The sound of the waves grew louder until it filled the silence around me. The trail ended where the trees met the shore, just as before.

And there he was.

William sat beneath the same tree, his cloak draped over his shoulders. One leg was bent, the other stretched out before him. His head rested slightly to the side, as if he had been listening to the water. The moonlight touched his face, soft and calm, and for a moment I could not move.

When he looked up, his eyes met mine. A faint smile appeared, quiet and knowing. I failed to inhale, and something deep inside me stirred. My heart began to race, faster and faster, until I could hear it in my ears.

I really looked at him then. The man who had stood beside me through everything, who had loved me when he had every reason not to. The man who saw me for who I was, not what I was born to

be.

And it hit me all at once, quiet but sure. I loved him, too.

The truth settled in my chest, warm and steady, and I knew nothing could ever change it.

CHAPTER FORTY-FOUR

IRIS/WILLIAM

IRIS

Joy spread through me so quickly it almost hurt. For days, I had told myself I didn't want to marry Lorenzo because I barely knew him, because it wasn't right to marry someone I didn't love. But now, I understood it was more than that. I didn't want to marry him because my heart already belonged to someone else. Because I loved William.

The thought filled me with warmth, with something that felt both terrifying and beautiful. I was in love with him. Truly, deeply—in a way that made everything else fade.

Before I could think, before I could stop myself, I

ran to him. My slippers barely touched the grass. All I could see was him. His face lifted in surprise as I reached him, but I didn't slow down. I crashed into him, my arms wrapping around his shoulders, and he caught me, steadying me before we both tumbled backward into the grass.

He was still sitting, his cloak pooling around us. For a moment neither of us spoke. His hands stayed at my waist, holding me still, as if afraid to let go. I could hear the sound of his heartbeat under my ear, strong and real, and it made mine beat even faster.

He raised a brow, his voice quiet but curious. "Iris?"

I looked up at him, breathless. "Sorry," I whispered. "I had to."

A soft chuckle left him, low and warm. "Had to?"

"Yes," I said, nodding slightly. "I just... had to."

His smile deepened, and without another word, he pulled me closer. I let him. My head found its place against his chest, the steady rhythm of his heart echoing in my ears. His hand moved slowly up my back, gentle and certain, and I felt something inside me loosen, something that had been wound tight for far too long.

The world around us seemed to fade. The sound of the sea, the whisper of the wind through the trees, it all became distant. There was only this: his warmth, his heartbeat, the safety of his arms.

I closed my eyes and let myself sink into him. For the first time in what felt like forever, everything was quiet. I was where I was meant to be.

I had never felt so safe. So sure of something in my life.

I loved him. Completely.

WILLIAM

We sat together in silence, the sound of the sea filling the spaces between us. Her breathing was soft against my chest, her scent a mix of roses and lavender that wrapped around me like something I never wanted to let go of. I could stay like this forever, holding her while the world faded away.

Her warmth pressed against me, and for the first time in years, I felt at peace. My hand rested lightly on her back, rising and falling with every breath she took.

Then she spoke, quiet but clear. "William?"

"Mm?"

There was a pause, long enough for me to feel her heartbeat quicken against my chest. Then she said it, barely louder than the wind. "I love you."

For a heartbeat, I forgot to breathe. Her words sank into me like sunlight through cold water, filling every space I hadn't known was empty. I pulled back just enough to see her face. She was looking down, shy almost, her fingers curled in the fabric of my tunic.

"Iris," I said quietly, her name more of a breath than a word.

She finally looked up, her eyes meeting mine, uncertain but full of warmth. "I mean it," she said. "I love you."

Something in my chest tightened, then eased all at once. I had imagined this moment a thousand times, hearing those words in my head, wondering what they would sound like from her. But nothing came close to the way they felt now.

"Say that again," I whispered.

"I love you."

My breath came out rough. My heart was pounding so hard it almost hurt. "You do not know what that means to me."

"Then tell me," she said softly.

"Everything," I murmured. "It means everything. It means this."

Before I could think, I pulled her to me and kissed her.

For a heartbeat, she went still. I felt her breath catch against my lips, her hands tightening against my chest as if she wasn't sure what to do. Then she kissed me back. Slowly at first, almost hesitant, but then with more certainty, as if the hesitation had broken.

The sea faded. The wind stilled. All I could feel was her. The softness of her lips, the faint tremor in her fingers, the warmth of her pressed against me. My hand found her waist, pulling her closer. She leaned into me, her body fitting perfectly against mine as if it had always been meant to.

I deepened the kiss, slower this time, my thumb brushing along her jaw. She tilted her head slightly, her lips parting to meet mine again. I could taste the salt from the air, the faint sweetness of her breath.

Without meaning to, I rose, bringing her with me. Her hands gripped my shoulders, steadying herself. When her back brushed the tree, I paused, but she didn't move away. The look in her eyes told me everything I needed to know.

I kissed her again, harder now. My hands slipped around her waist, lifting her without thought. Her legs wrapped around me for balance, and I held her there, steady and secure.

She laughed softly against my lips, a sound that made something in me ache with joy. I kissed her again, gentler this time, slower, like I wanted to memorize the shape of this moment.

When we finally broke apart, she was still in my arms. Her forehead rested against mine, her breath quick and warm.

The night was quiet around us. Only the sea moved, calm and endless in the distance. My thumb brushed her cheek, tracing the warmth of her skin, and she leaned into my touch.

We stayed like that, saying nothing. There was no need for words. The silence said enough.

And as I held her there, I knew one thing with absolute certainty. Whatever came next, whatever the world demanded of us—I would love her for the rest of my life.

I would never love anyone else the way I loved her.

CHAPTER FORTY-FIVE

IRIS

I lay still with my head resting on William's bare chest, listening to the rhythm of his breathing. His arms were around me, heavy and warm, holding me close as if the world outside did not exist.

Neither of us had moved for hours. The quiet felt endless, peaceful in a way I never thought peace could be. His heartbeat was steady under my ear, a sound I could have listened to forever.

Then came the knock.

I flinched, my heart lurching. Another knock followed, firmer this time. "Your Highness?" a voice called through the door.

I sat up quickly, panic sparking through me. William was already awake, his eyes sharp though his body stayed still.

"They are going to open the door," I whispered. My voice trembled.

He glanced at the handle, then at me. The knock came again.

"Just a moment!" I called louder this time.

I turned to him, my pulse racing. "You need to put on your armor. Quickly."

He nodded once, silent but focused. He reached for his tunic, slipping it over his head in one swift motion. The faint light caught the silver of his armor as he fastened each piece, his movements quick but precise.

The knock came again, impatient now.

"Hurry," I whispered.

He secured the last clasp, then took his helm from the table and pulled it on. Within seconds, he looked every bit the knight he was supposed to be.

When he finished, he crossed the room and took his post near the balcony door, standing tall and composed as if nothing had happened at all.

I took a deep breath, trying to calm the storm in my chest. My lips still tingled from his kiss, and my heart was beating far too fast.

"Come in," I finally said, forcing my voice steady.

The door creaked open, and two servants stepped inside, bowing their heads politely. One of them—a young man in a green livery—glanced briefly at William before speaking.

"Sir William, His Majesty requests your presence," he said. "You are to join the other guards in preparation for tomorrow's station at the wedding."

The word *wedding* struck like a stone to my chest. For a moment, the world seemed to quiet. I had almost forgotten about it, forgotten that in less than a day I was to stand beside Lorenzo, wear white, and vow myself to him before the entire court.

My heart sank, and I looked toward William. His expression didn't change, though something flickered behind his eyes. He gave a short nod, his voice calm. "Understood."

He turned to me for only a second. It was brief, but I saw it, the faint ache in his eyes, the same one that was now in my own heart. Then he slipped past the servants and out the door. The sound of his boots faded down the corridor until there was nothing left but silence.

The servant turned to me. "Your Highness, His Majesty also asks that you begin practicing your vows. The royal scribe is preparing the final script, and the King wishes for you to be ready by this evening."

I nodded faintly, though my chest felt hollow. "Of course."

They bowed again and left me alone in the room.

I stood there for a moment longer after the servants left. The room was quiet, yet my heart was not. It pounded so hard it hurt. The thought of tomorrow—of vows and ceremony—pressed down on me until I could barely breathe.

Then the door opened again.

I turned, startled, and saw Lorenzo step inside. He held a small mug in his hand, steam rising faintly from it. His smile was calm—too calm, as he crossed the room and sat on the edge of my bed.

"Tomorrow," he said, his tone light, "our kingdoms will finally be united."

He slipped an arm around my shoulders. I stiffened at his touch.

He held out the mug toward me. "Drink this."

I looked down at it, uncertain. "What is it?"

He smiled, as though the answer were obvious. "A tea with a special herb. Every queen and princess in Valebran drinks this before her wedding night. It ensures she bears a son."

My lips barely moved. "A son?" I repeated quietly.

"Yes," he said. "When you drink this, you secure our future. Our heir. My mother drank this before she married my father, and not long after, she bore me."

I could barely find my voice. The steam from the mug curled between us, sweet but bitter in scent. My stomach turned.

He looked at me expectantly, smiling, but all I could feel was the fear growing in my chest.

When he noticed I wasn't moving, his smile thinned. Slowly, he lifted the mug closer until the rim brushed my lips.

"Drink," he said.

I froze. The scent of the liquid turned in my stomach. My body refused to move. My hands trembled slightly at my sides.

"Lorenzo," I said, my voice unsteady. "I just need to step out for a moment."

His expression changed in an instant. "I am sure nothing is more important than securing an heir," he said sharply.

Before I could take a step back, he moved closer. His hand came up behind my neck, the other still holding the mug. "Drink," he repeated, firmer this time.

I shook my head, panic rising. "Please—"

He didn't listen. The mug pressed against my mouth, the bitter liquid spilling past my lips. I tried to turn away, to spit it out, but his grip tightened. He clamped his hand over my mouth, forcing me to swallow. The taste was sharp and metallic, burning as it went down.

When I finally gasped for breath, he lowered the cup, his eyes calm again as if nothing had happened. "Good," he said quietly.

"I will see you at dinner," Lorenzo said calmly, as if nothing had just happened.

He set the empty mug on the table and walked to the door. His steps were steady, quiet, and deliberate. The door closed behind him with a soft click that felt far too gentle for what he had done.

I stood there frozen. My throat burned from the taste of the drink, and my heart beat so hard it made my chest ache. The room felt smaller, colder. I wanted to move, to scream, but I couldn't.

I didn't want this. Not the gown. Not the vows. Not the man. None of it.

Tomorrow. The word echoed in my mind. Only one

day left. One day until I was no longer free. One day until I married someone I didn't love.

I pressed a hand to my chest, trying to steady my breathing. My heart belonged to someone else. It always would. The thought made my throat tighten.

And then, the realization came, sudden and sharp. After the wedding, my father would return to Elarion. He would take his guards and his servants with him. That meant William would leave, too.

My pulse quickened. That might be the last time I ever saw him. The last time I would hear his voice or feel his arms around me. The thought was unbearable.

Anger replaced fear. It burned through the haze of panic until I could almost feel it in my fingertips. I needed to speak to my father. He had to listen this time. He had to understand.

He had ignored me before, brushed off my pleas as childish worry, but this was different. I couldn't let him decide my life for me. Not now. Not when my heart already belonged to someone else.

I took a deep breath, my hands trembling into fists at my sides. Tomorrow might change everything, but tonight, I might have a chance to fix this.

I needed to find him.

I found him in one of the council rooms, speaking with King Felipe. The air was heavy with talk of alliances and trade routes, their voices low but firm. I hesitated in the doorway, then stepped inside and curtsied to both of them.

"Your Majesties," I said softly.

My father turned first, his brows lifting. "What is it, Iris?"

"I need a word," I said, trying to keep my voice steady.

He sighed, glancing at Felipe before answering. "I am busy right now."

"Please," I said. "It will be quick."

"Iris..." His tone held warning, but before he could finish, King Felipe raised a hand.

"That is fine," Felipe said kindly. "I will be waiting outside."

He stood, the gold of his cloak brushing the floor as he walked out. Two guards followed him, the door closing behind them with a dull thud that echoed through the chamber.

My father turned back to me, his expression unreadable. "Make this quick," he said.

I drew a slow breath and stepped closer, my hands tightening around the folds of my gown. My heart was pounding, but I forced the words out anyway. "I do not want to marry him, Father."

"So you have said," my father replied, his tone flat, almost bored. "You said the same thing back in Elarion."

"Yes," I said quickly. "And I meant it then, and I mean it now. After spending these days with him, I have realised that I not only do not want to marry him, but I cannot."

He turned away, adjusting the cuff of his sleeve as

though my words were nothing but noise. "You can leave now."

I didn't move. My throat tightened, but I forced myself to step closer. "Father, please. I cannot marry him."

His eyes flicked to mine, cool and tired. "Enough, Iris."

"No, listen to me!" I said, the words spilling before I could stop them. "He gave me a drink this morning. He said it would help me bear him a son. He expects me to carry his child already. Father, I am too young—"

His head snapped toward me, his gaze suddenly sharp. "You ungrateful one," he hissed. "Your mother was sixteen when she had you. Do not speak to me of 'too young.'"

The words cut deep. I flinched, but I stood my ground. "This is not about age," I whispered. "It is about choice."

"Your only choice," my father said, his voice cold and sharp, "should be worrying about the future of your people. If this marriage does not continue, if you fail to do your part, our people will suffer because of our enemies." His tone hardened, rising with every word. "Because of you."

I stood frozen, my chest tight. His words struck harder than I wanted them to. "Then how am I supposed to live my life?" I asked, my voice shaking. "If I marry someone I do not love, how am I supposed to live a happy life?"

He didn't answer. He just stared, eyes full of disappointment, as if happiness were something I should have never dared to ask for.

For a heartbeat, I thought about telling him. About William. About the way my heart beat faster every time I saw him, the way he looked at me like I was more than a crown. Maybe if Father knew, maybe if he heard me say I loved someone else—he would understand. But the look in his eyes stopped me. I knew he wouldn't. To him, love was a luxury, not something worth risking kingdoms over.

He stood suddenly, the sound of his chair scraping across the stone echoing around us. His palm slammed against the wall, and the sound made me jump. "Your mother was just like you before she married me," he said, his voice rough with anger. "She said she could not marry me because she didn't love me, because she did not know me. But she married me anyway."

"That is because she was forced—"

"No!" His voice cracked through the air like lightning. "Because she cared about her people. Because she knew her duty came before

her heart. And guess what, Iris? After our marriage, she learned to love me. And I loved her deeply back. Just like you will with Lorenzo."

I stared at him, the words sinking like stones in my stomach. *Learned to love*. As if love could be taught, as if it could be forced. He was wrong. I knew it in every part of me. My mother might have learned to love him, but that didn't mean I could do the same.

"And what if I love someone else?" The words

escaped me before I could stop them. They hung in the air, trembling between us. My voice shook, but I didn't take them back. I couldn't.

My father turned sharply. His eyes narrowed, cold and unreadable. "Unless it is a lord, a prince, or a duke —the marriage will continue anyway."

My stomach sank. "And what if he is not?"

He stilled. His tone sharpened. "What are you saying?"

My throat tightened. I hesitated, but the words pushed out anyway. "What if he is not one of them?"

The air grew tense, heavy. I could see something flicker in his eyes. "What are you trying to say, Iris?"

My heart pounded so fast it almost hurt. I could barely breathe. But I refused to stay silent. "I am saying that I love someone."

Silence. A deep, cold silence that made the room feel smaller. My father's gaze hardened, his jaw set. "Are you saying you love someone?"

I nodded. "Yes."

His voice dropped low. "Who?"

My hands trembled, but I straightened my back. "I am not telling you."

His tone rose. "I asked you a question."

"And I am not answering it." My words came out shaky but loud enough to echo.

He took a slow step forward, then another, until he was standing directly in front of me. The space between us disappeared. I could smell the faint scent of wine on his breath, the heat of his anger pressing against my skin.

For a moment, I thought I should move back, bow my head or say sorry. But I didn't. My legs wanted to buckle, yet I forced them still. He looked furious, but I met his eyes anyway. My hands were shaking, my throat tight, but I wouldn't look away.

My mind raced. I thought about William. About the way he looked at me like I wasn't a crown or a duty. About the way his voice softened when he said my name. I thought about how he held me like I was something worth protecting, not something owned.

I couldn't tell my father his name, not yet. Not when I knew what he could do. But I also couldn't let him believe I would marry a man I didn't love. Not when my heart already belonged to someone else.

He took another step closer, his boots scraping against the stone floor. His eyes were hard and sharp as steel. "I will not ask again," he said, his voice low but filled with warning. "Who?"

I swallowed hard. "I am not telling you."

For a moment, there was a heavy, unbearable silence. Then he began to laugh—a sound that sent a chill crawling up my spine. It wasn't kind. It wasn't amused. It was dark and cruel, the laughter of someone who already knew he held all the power.

"You are such a fool," he said, still laughing. "You really think I won't find out? You think you can keep something like that from me?" His eyes flashed. "Iris, I will find out. And when I do, I will have his head. And you will still marry Lorenzo. So do not play smart with me."

My whole body trembled. I wanted to shout, to tell him he was wrong, but no sound came. My throat tightened, and all I could do was stare at him, my vision blurring.

"But," he continued, stepping closer until the heat of his anger pressed against me, "if you tell me now, maybe I will show mercy. Maybe I will spare him a cruel death."

Still, I said nothing. My lips parted, but the words wouldn't come. I could barely breathe. I just stared at him, feeling the pounding of my heart and the weight of the silence that followed.

His expression darkened. I saw it happen, how his control snapped. His hand came up before I could even move. The sound of the slap filled the room, sharp and final.

Pain bloomed across my cheek, bright and searing. My head turned with the force of it. For a moment, the world spun, and I tasted blood on my tongue. My eyes burned, but I refused to let the tears fall. I would not give him that.

He stood above me, chest heaving, his voice harsh and shaking. "You will do as you are told. You will marry the Prince, and you will not speak another word of this foolishness."

I met his gaze through the haze of pain, my chest rising and falling with every ragged breath. There were no words left. No pleas. Just the hollow ache of knowing that whatever love I had found was now in danger because of me.

"Leave," he said at last.

I turned, my steps unsteady. The room spun as I reached for the door, my cheek throbbing with every heartbeat. When the heavy wood shut behind me, the echo followed me down the hall, chasing me like a shadow I couldn't escape.

And for the first time, I truly understood what it meant to be powerless.

CHAPTER FORTY-SIX

IRIS/WILLIAM

IRIS

Dinner passed in a blur. I barely tasted the food on my plate. Around me, the hall was filled with noise. The nobles talked about the wedding, about how grand the ceremony would be and how strong the alliance would make our kingdoms. Their words ran together, meaningless and hollow.

My thoughts were somewhere else.

William.

I hadn't seen him since this morning. Not during the day, not during the evening. I kept searching for him among the guards, hoping I would catch a glimpse of his face or hear his voice. Nothing. He was gone, and the distance was unbearable. The idea that this might be our last day together made my chest ache. Tomorrow, everything would change. I would stand beside a man I didn't love, while the one I did might be forced to leave forever.

I tried to eat, but every bite turned heavy. My hands shook slightly as I lifted the fork, and my throat felt tight. I wanted the dinner to end. I wanted to run from the hall, from the voices, from the eyes that saw me only as a bride, not as a person.

When the nobles began speaking again, louder now, I quietly rose from my seat. My father didn't look at me. Lorenzo didn't either. That was fine. I didn't want their attention.

I left the hall quickly. My footsteps echoed through the corridor. The air was cold and smelled faintly of smoke and candle wax. I walked faster, clutching the sides of my gown, my heart beating faster with every step. I needed to see him. I needed to find him.

The thought repeated in my head, over and over. If I didn't see him tonight, I might never get the chance again. The fear of that thought made my eyes sting.

By the time I reached my bedchamber, my breath came quick and shallow. I closed the door behind me and leaned against it for a moment, trying to calm my racing heart. The room was quiet. Too quiet. Only the soft rustle of the curtains moved in the still air.

I turned toward the balcony. My hands were trembling when I reached for the curtain.

And then I saw them.

Roses. White and pink. A trail of them scattered across the floor, shining faintly under the light of the moon.

A small gasp left my lips.

Without thinking, I grabbed my shawl and hurried toward the balcony. My heart felt alive again, wild and trembling with hope. I didn't care what waited beyond those doors. I just needed to see him.

The moment my feet touched the ground, I didn't walk. I ran.

The night air was cool and sharp against my face, but I didn't care. My heart pounded so hard it filled my ears, drowning out the sound of the waves and the wind. I ran faster, following the faint light of the moon across the grass until I saw him.

William.

He was standing by the same tree near the sea, the one that had become ours. When he saw me running toward him, he straightened and took a few steps forward, surprise flashing in his eyes.

For a moment, everything else disappeared. There was only him.

I ran faster until I was in his arms. He caught me easily, his hands firm around my waist. A soft laugh escaped him as he lifted me from the ground and twirled me once before setting me back down.

"Someone is excited to be out here," he said, his voice warm and teasing.

I didn't answer. I couldn't. My chest felt too tight,

my heart beating too fast. I reached up, touched his face, and kissed him.

It was soft at first, uncertain, but then his hands moved to my back, pulling me closer. The warmth of him spread through me, steady and sure. The scent of salt and sea filled the air, and everything else fell away.

When we finally pulled apart, the world felt still. The waves moved gently against the shore, and the night air was cool against my flushed skin. His hands lingered at my waist, as if he wasn't ready to let go—and truthfully, neither was I.

I looked up at him, the moonlight catching the quiet smile on his lips. For a moment, nothing else existed. Not the castle, not the wedding, not the crown waiting to bind me to a life I didn't want. There was only this. Him and me.

I rested my forehead against his chest, feeling the steady rhythm of his heartbeat beneath my palms. It was calm, sure, and it made me feel safe in a way I hadn't known I needed.

He said nothing, and neither did I. Words would have only broken what we had in that moment.

When the wind shifted and the sea whispered against the rocks, I felt something ache inside me. I wished time could stop here, beneath the stars, where nothing else mattered.

But it couldn't.

So I held him tighter, just for a little longer, knowing that when I let go, it would hurt. Knowing that no matter what tomorrow brought, this night would be ours.

WILLIAM

We had been in each other's embrace for what felt like hours.

Now we sat beneath the same tree we always did. My arms were still wrapped around her waist, and her head rested on my shoulder. Neither of us had spoken. We didn't need to. The quiet between us was enough.

But then her voice broke through the stillness.

"I will be married tomorrow."

The words sank deep, cutting through the air like a blade. I didn't move. I couldn't. For a moment, it felt as though the ground had vanished beneath me. My chest tightened until it hurt to breathe. I wasn't ready for this. I would never be ready. Nothing could prepare me for losing her.

My grip around her tightened. I could feel her breath catch slightly, but she didn't move away. I didn't let her. I couldn't. The thought of her standing beside another man, wearing his ring, his name, hearing the world call her his, tore something raw inside me.

"Saints, I cannot," she said. Her voice trembled, breaking something deep inside me.

I looked down at her. Tears had already filled her eyes, spilling over and streaking down her cheeks.

"Iris..." I breathed her name, but it was all I could manage.

"I am forced to marry someone I do not love," she said, her voice shaking. "And that means we will ever see each other again."

Before she could fall apart, I pulled her closer into my arms. Her body pressed against mine, soft and trembling. "I would take it all away from you if I could," I whispered. And I meant it. But even as the words left my lips, I knew I couldn't. I couldn't take away her crown or her title or her duty. I couldn't give her the life she deserved.

A commoner like me could never stand against a prince or a king. I knew it. She knew it. But knowing didn't make it hurt any less.

Her tears soaked into my tunic, and my own threatened to fall. I had to stay strong for her, to make her believe that everything would be alright, even when I didn't believe it myself.

"But I will not see you again," she whispered.

I tilted her chin up, forcing her to meet my eyes. "Do not speak like that," I said softly. "Of course we will. I will write to you, and I will visit whenever I can."

She shook her head, her lip trembling. "But that is not enough."

Her words sank deep, heavier than anything she'd ever said. I knew she was right. It wasn't enough. It would never be enough.

My heart sank, but I tightened my hold around her anyway, as if that could make it true.

I brushed my thumb across her cheek, wiping away another tear. "Then I will find another way," I said quietly. "Whatever it takes. I will find a way to see you again."

Her eyes softened, her breath catching as she looked at me.

"I promise, Iris," I said, my voice barely above a whisper. "This is not the end."

She closed her eyes and pressed herself against my chest, her fingers curling tightly around my arms as if afraid I might vanish. I held her there, feeling the steady beat of her heart against mine, each thud echoing through me. For a moment, there was nothing else. Just us, breathing the same air, holding on like the world could not touch us.

Then she lifted her head again. Her eyes met mine, wide and searching. "If there was a way for us to be together," she said softly, her voice barely more than a whisper, "if a new law suddenly came that I could marry whoever I wanted, would you wait for me? Even if it took ten years?"

Her words lingered in the air. She swallowed, her gaze flickering down for a second before meeting mine again. "Or would you already have found someone else?"

I stared at her, struck silent. The thought of waiting for her, even a lifetime, did not frighten me. What frightened me was how easily I knew the answer. Her face was so close now, her breath warm against my skin, and I could see the fear behind the question. The fear of being forgotten, of losing this.

I let out a quiet breath, my hand moving up to the

side of her face, fingers tracing her jaw. "Iris," I said, "I could wait ten years. I could wait longer. There is not anyone else for me."

Her eyes shimmered, her lips parting as if to speak, but no words came. So I pulled her closer again, holding her as the waves whispered against the shore.

"If the world ever gives us a chance," I murmured, "I will be there. I will always be there."

She looked up at me, her voice barely a breath. "You promise?"

I nodded, my hand still on her cheek. "I promise," I answered. "I will never leave you."

Her eyes glistened in the faint light, and for a moment, everything around us disappeared. I could see nothing but her, hear nothing but her breath.

"Even in death, I will be with you," I whispered. "You are my first love and my last. My only love. So I will wait an eternity if I must, because a life without you is no life at all."

Her lips trembled, and tears filled her eyes again, but this time they weren't from sorrow. She leaned forward until her forehead rested against mine, her breath mingling with mine.

"William..." she whispered, her voice breaking.

I closed my eyes, my hands gently tightening around her waist.

"I mean it," I said. "Even if the world changes, even if everything else fades, you will still be the one I love."

She let out a soft sob and buried her face in my neck. I held her close, feeling the warmth of her tears against my skin. The night around us was still and endless, but it didn't matter. For that moment, time had stopped.

And in that silence, I knew nothing could ever make me let her go.

When she finally spoke again, her voice trembled. "So we are just like Elara and Mike," she said. "Two who love, but can never have each other."

Her words hit something deep inside me. The story we loved, the one that ended in a heartbreak. Two souls meant for each other, torn apart by the world that refused to let them be.

I pulled back just enough to see her face. "No," I said, shaking my head slowly. "Not like them."

She looked up at me, confusion glimmering in her eyes.

"They gave up," I said softly. "But we will not."

Her eyes softened, though her tears still clung to her lashes. "But what if we are not given a choice?"

"Then we will make one," I whispered. "No matter what happens, I will keep finding my way back to you. Even if the world keeps us apart."

She looked at me for a long time, her eyes searching mine as if trying to hold on to every word. Then, slowly, she nodded. The faintest smile touched her lips, small but real.

The sea whispered behind us, the sound mingling with the wind. She leaned forward until her head rested against my chest again, her hands clutching her skirt as though she could anchor herself there.

I ran a hand through my hair and closed my eyes. For that moment, nothing else mattered. Not the crown, not the vows, not the morning that waited us. Only her heartbeat against mine, and the quiet promise that lived between us.

If the world tried to tear us apart, I would still find her. Somehow.

CHAPTER FORTY-SEVEN

WILLIAM

I had been right about one thing. I would come back for her. If it took a lifetime, I would find her again. I would wait a hundred years if I had to.

But staying? That wasn't something I could do. Not to her. Not to myself.

After she left for her chambers, I stayed by the water for a while. The night was quieter, the sea stretching endlessly under the moon. Every sound, every breath felt heavier than the last. I tried not to think, but everything reminded me of her—the way she smiled, the way she said my name, the way her hand had fit in mine like it had always belonged there.

Eventually, I moved toward the small dock behind the castle. There were a few boats there, tied loosely against the posts. I found a small one, worn from years of use but still sturdy. It would be enough. I checked the ropes, the oars, the boards. I worked in silence, letting my hands move while my mind stayed far away.

I would stay for the wedding. I owed her that much. I would stand among the guards, silent and still, and watch her walk down the aisle in white. I would watch her say vows she didn't mean to a man who didn't deserve her. And when it was over, when the ball had ended and the castle had gone quiet again, I would leave before the morning light touched the sea.

I would give up my title, my knighthood, my life here. None of it mattered anymore. Not if she wasn't in it. But staying would only break us both. I couldn't look at her and pretend that I was fine. I couldn't stand there and watch her become someone else's forever.

I straightened and looked toward the castle. The lights glowed softly in the distance, gold against the night. Somewhere inside those walls, she was preparing for her wedding. For a life she didn't choose.

My chest ached. When God allows it, I'll find my way back.

I stood, listening to the sound of the sea for a moment longer. Then I turned away.

Tomorrow, I would watch her marry another man.

And then I would leave.

Possibly forever.

CHAPTER FORTY-EIGHT

IRIS

The servants were hurrying around me. One fastened a necklace around my neck while another adjusted the silver pins in my hair. The gown was white and heavy, embroidered with silver thread that shimmered with every move. It was beautiful, but it didn't feel like mine.

"Hold still, Your Highness," one of them said as she tied the corset tighter. I could barely breathe.

Meanwhile, the others continued to fuss around me, their chatter blending into a dull hum. Somewhere below, I could hear the faint rhythm of footsteps and laughter as others prepared the grand hall for the wedding ball. The air carried the scent of roses and fresh polish. Every corner of the castle was coming alive for the day that would change everything.

My chest felt tight, and I couldn't tell if it was from the corset or from everything pressing down at once. My hands were trembling slightly in my lap when the door opened.

Raven stepped inside.

It had been days since I had last spoken to her, since I found out the truth about her and Lorenzo. She looked unsure, standing near the door like she wasn't sure she was welcome. Her eyes darted the room before landing on me.

"You look beautiful," she said hesitantly.

I met her eyes. For a moment, I saw something fragile there, something almost like pain. It struck me that this must be just as hard for her as it was for me. She was about to watch her friend marry the man she loved.

"Thank you," I said quietly.

The servants clipped more jewelry around my wrists and neck. Raven stayed still, her hands clasped tightly together. She said nothing, but the sadness in her face spoke louder than words.

"Will you be alright?" I asked.

Her eyes widened before she gave a small, nervous laugh. "Alright? Oh, of course I will." The sound of it wavered.

I didn't believe it.

Raven's gaze flickered away for a moment before she spoke again, her voice smaller this time. "You are not angry at me? That I did not tell you that your prince is—"

"It is fine," I said quickly, cutting her off.

"No, Iris, I should have—"

"I did wish you had told me sooner," I said, keeping my tone steady, "but it is fine."

I wasn't sure if I meant it, but what right did I have to judge her?

I had lied, too. I had lied to William about who I was. I had hidden my name, my title, my life. So I, out of everyone, couldn't hold it against her.

Suddenly, a servant stepped into the room. Her voice was hurried. "Is she ready?"

"Almost," one of the others replied, fastening the last clasp on the back of my gown.

"Well, hurry then," the first servant said. "The King is coming."

The King. My father.

My stomach twisted, and for a moment, I couldn't breathe. My heart began to pound so hard I could feel it in my throat. The room suddenly felt smaller, heavier, like the air itself was pressing down on me.

Raven's head turned toward me, her face pale. The servants kept moving around, smoothing the folds of my gown, fixing the silver pins in my hair, whispering about perfection and duty. None of them knew that every touch, every word, made me feel more trapped.

He was coming to walk me down the aisle.

To give me away.

Once he stepped into this room, everything would change. There would be no more time, no chance to run, no moment left for second thoughts.

That would be the end of Iris, the girl who once laughed by the river, who dreamed of love and freedom.

And the beginning of someone else entirely.

The servants moved quickly around me now, their hands tugging, straightening, perfecting every last detail. One of them leaned in to fasten the final clasp at my neck, her fingers trembling with haste.

"Hold still, Your Highness," she murmured.

I tried, though my hands wouldn't stop shaking. The air felt thick, the sounds distant, as if the world outside the room had already moved on without me.

And then the door opened.

The servants froze.

My father stepped inside.

He filled the doorway, dressed in his formal attire, the crest of Elarion glinting on his chest. His face was calm, unreadable, though his eyes were sharp as they swept across the room before landing on me.

For a heartbeat, no one spoke. The only sound was the faint rustle of silk and the pounding of my heart.

He gave a single nod, the kind that left no room for choice. "It is time."

And just like that, the last piece of air left my lungs.

This was it.

The moment he took my arm, my life would no longer be mine.

I looked down at the gown, at the diamonds, at the glimmering white fabric that felt more like a chain than a dress.

And I knew that once I stepped through that door, there would be no turning back.

CHAPTER FORTY-NINE

WILLIAM

The courtyard was alive with noise. Bells rang from the towers, their sound carrying across the city. Silk banners hung from the walls, bright in the morning light. The air smelled of roses, sea salt, and burning candles. People gathered shoulder to shoulder, whispering, smiling, waiting for the ceremony to begin.

And I stood among the guards.

My armor felt heavier than ever. The helm hid my face, which was good because I could not trust myself to look calm. The others stood tall beside me, proud to serve, proud to witness history. But all I felt was a hollow ache in my chest.

The Prince was already on the dais beside the priest. King Phelipe stood next to him with a proud expression and hands folded behind his back. The blue and silver decorations glittered in the sun. It should have been beautiful, but to me it looked like a cage.

This was not the life I imagined. I never thought I would fall in love with someone far above my station. I never thought I would have to stand and watch her marry a man chosen by her father.

Iris had not arrived yet. The long path of petals leading to the dais was empty. I stared at it until my chest ached. My heart beat faster with every passing second.

This was the worst day of my life.

When it was over, I would stay until the ball if I could. Then I would leave. I would take the small boat waiting at the edge of the bay and sail away. Somewhere quiet. Somewhere far.

I would go back to my parents' home—the small cottage in the deserted area, the one Iris first ran into when she came to me as Elara the healer. It was quiet there, untouched by crowns or courts. I thought maybe I could find peace there, but even that house would remind me of her.

Everything would carry her memory. I could almost see her there again, draped in a wet cloak as she sat by the fire to dry herself. The thought hurt more than any wound I had ever taken.

Even if I waited my whole life for her, I knew the truth. That chance might never come. A princess belonged to a prince. And any man who dared love her was a fool who challenged the throne itself.

Just then, the heavy bells began to ring. Their deep

sound echoed through the courtyard, rolling across the stone walls and the gathered crowd. The signal that the bride was coming.

My hand tightened on the hilt of my sword until my knuckles turned white. I told myself to stay calm, to breathe, to stand tall and still like every other guard. My heart was a storm beneath the armor, but I could not let it show.

Then she appeared.

Iris stepped into the courtyard beside her father. The light caught her as if the heavens themselves had turned to look. For a moment, the crowd, the bells, even the priest faded into silence. She looked ethereal, almost unreal—like something from a dream. Her gown shimmered with silver thread that glowed beneath the morning sun. Her straight, pale blonde hair fell long down her back, brushed smooth and held by pins of silver and crystal that caught the light with every step.

She walked slowly, her chin lifted, her hand resting lightly on her father's arm. Each step looked graceful and measured, but I saw the faint tremor in her hands, the way her breath shook as she neared the dais.

When they reached it, King Henrik said something I could not hear. Then he took her hand and placed it in Lorenzo's.

And that was it.

She stood beside him now, facing the priest. Her white gown brushed against his dark coat, the two of them framed by flowers and banners. It was perfect, just as everyone wanted.

But for me, it was ruin. Something inside me cracked open, silent but deep. It was the sound of everything I had ever wanted slipping away from me forever.

The priest's voice smoothly carried over the courtyard, calm and measured. "Do you, Prince Lorenzo of Valebran, take Princess Iris of Elarion to be your lawfully wedded wife, to honour and protect her for all the days of your life?"

Lorenzo proudly lifted his chin. "I do."

My stomach twisted. I told myself to stand still, to keep my eyes forward, to remember that I was only a guard among dozens. But it felt like the world had gone silent, as if every sound had been swallowed by those two words.

Then the priest turned, his gaze falling on her. "And do you, Princess Iris of Elarion, take Prince Lorenzo of Valebran to be your lawfully wedded husband, to honour and serve him for all the days of your life?"

The courtyard waited.

For a moment, she did not speak. I could see her lips trembling, her hands clenched at her sides. My heart pounded so hard I could hear it in my ears. Then, so softly I almost wished I hadn't heard it, she said, "I do."

That was when it broke.

A tear slid down my cheek, hot and heavy, hidden behind the steel of my helm. I blinked hard, but another came, and another after that. The inside of the helmet grew damp, and the sound of my breathing filled the space around me.

I was grateful for the armor—grateful that no one could see me like this. But even as I stood there, I knew the truth. There wasn't a single piece of armor in the world strong enough to protect me from this.

This was a wound no blade could give, no healer could close. It wasn't just heartbreak. It was the feeling of watching your whole soul belong to someone you could never touch again.

Every vow they spoke cut deeper, every cheer from the crowd pressed heavier against my chest. It was unbearable, this kind of pain. I wanted to scream, to run, to tear the armor from my body just to breathe again, but I couldn't. I had sworn to serve, to stand, to protect her—even now.

So I did what I had always done. I stayed still. I stayed silent. I let the tears fall where no one could see them, each one a reminder of the life I would never have.

And in that silence, I understood. This was the price of loving her. This was the cost of a heart that belonged to a princess.

CHAPTER FIFTY

WILLIAM

The priest stepped back as the two kings moved forward. The crowd fell silent again, the air heavy with ceremony and expectation.

A servant stepped from the side, carrying a silver blade on a small velvet cloth. He bowed low, then held it out to King Henrik. My king took it without hesitation. The blade gleamed in the sun, sharp and spotless.

He turned to King Phelipe, his expression solemn. "In blood we seal this bond."

Without flinching, Kink Henrik cut his palm first. A thin line of red followed. He then offered the blade to King Phelipe who did the same, the blood beading along his skin.

They clasped their hands tightly together.

"In blood we bind ourselves," Henrik said, his voice strong and sure.

Phelipe nodded, his tone matching his own. "And may this alliance last forever."

The crowd erupted into cheers, the kind that rolled through the courtyard like thunder. Trumpets sounded from the balcony, and rose petals fell from the upper windows.

Everyone looked joyous. Everyone but me.

Their cheers felt distant, muffled—like the world had moved on without me. I kept my stance, sword at my side, eyes on the ground. The blood binding their hands was meant to mark peace between two kingdoms, but all I could see was what it cost.

It had cost her.

And as their voices rang out in celebration, I stood there in silence with a heart breaking for a peace that had taken everything from me.

CHAPTER FIFTY-ONE

IRIS

The wedding was over.

I stood before the mirror again, unable to recognize the girl staring back at me. My cheeks were wet, and no matter how many times I wiped my face, the tears kept coming. They slid down one after another, falling onto the silk of my gown and staining it with dark marks.

The servants moved around me once again, helping me into my ball gown. One fixed the ribbon at my back, another adjusted the corset until I could hardly breathe. The gown was soft pink, soft as morning light, and the off-shouldered fabric shimmered under the candles. Silver sparkles caught the glow and scattered across the floor like dust from the stars. It should have made me feel like the princess I am, but I only felt lost inside.

My heart beat too fast, and I could not tell if it was from the corset or everything itself. Each breath felt heavier than the last.

Behind me, Raven sat in silence. Her hands were folded tightly in her lap, her eyes glassy. She had been there for a while, watching as the servants worked. When she spoke, her voice was quiet and uneven. "You look beautiful," she said.

I did not feel beautiful. I felt broken. But I forced a small smile anyway. "Thank you."

She nodded, though her lips trembled. Her gaze dropped to the floor, and I saw how close she was to crying too. It hurt to look at her. I knew this must be just as hard for her as it was for me. She watched the man she loved marry her closest friend.

One of the servants straightened and said, "She is ready."

Just then, the servants around me froze and bowed low. Their sudden movement made my heart jump. I turned, my pulse quickening, and saw him standing in the doorway.

My father.

His eyes swept over me, sharp and cold, and the look on his face made my stomach twist. There was no pride in his gaze. Only something close to disgust.

"Those better be tears of joy," he said, each word striking like a stone.

I tried to speak, but nothing came out. The silence stretched between us, heavy and unbearable.

He took a slow step forward, the sound of his boots

echoing against the floor. "You just did Elarion a great honour," he said. "You secured your people's safety and formed an alliance that will protect us from our enemies. That is not something to cry over. That is something to be proud of."

I swallowed hard, my hands trembling in front of me. "Proud?" I said quietly. "I have lost everything I wanted. How am I supposed to feel proud of that?"

His expression hardened instantly. The air in the room seemed to grow colder. He took another step closer until the shadows from his figure covered me.

"You better be grateful," he said, his voice rising slightly. "If this were any other day, I would remind you how a princess should behave. But I will not have your face bruised for your ball tonight. Not when your new husband will be watching you."

My throat burned, but I couldn't hold back the tears that kept falling. He looked at me once more, shaking his head as if even my sadness was an inconvenience.

"Now hurry up," he said. "Wipe those tears, Iris. You are a princess. Act like one."

He turned toward the door, his cloak shifting behind him. "I will be waiting outside," he said without looking back. His footsteps echoed down the hall until the sound faded completely.

The room felt colder the moment he left. For a second, no one moved. Then the servants hurried to my side, their hands gentle but frantic as they dabbed at my face with handkerchiefs and cloths. Their voices were quiet, trembling, as if even the sound of their sympathy might anger him if he returned.

Raven stood where she was, her eyes full of sorrow. "You are allowed to cry," she whispered.

I let out a shaky breath, trying to steady my voice. "I know," I said softly. "But I cannot. Not now. Maybe once the ball is over."

The words came with a nervous laugh, one that sounded wrong even to my own ears. None of this felt real, and yet I was trapped inside it.

Raven's face didn't change. She stepped closer, the faint rustle of her dress the only sound in the room, and before I could say anything else, she wrapped her arms around me.

For a heartbeat, I stood still, and then I melted into her embrace. My arms went around her, holding her as tightly as she held me. The tears came again, hot and heavy, soaking into her shoulder.

Raven's breath hitched, and soon her own tears began to fall. "Oh God," she said with a broken laugh, "I need to stop crying. I am making this about myself."

I shook my head quickly. "No, please do not say that," I whispered. "We have both lost pieces of ourselves today."

Her arms tightened around me again, and I held her close, my heart aching in ways I didn't know it could.

We stayed like that for another long moment, neither of us speaking. The air in the room felt heavy with unspoken words and grief neither of us knew how to name.

Then slowly, Raven loosened her hold. I did too. We stepped back, and I turned toward the mirror again.

The servants were waiting, hands trembling as they lifted fresh handkerchiefs to my face again. They dabbed carefully at the corners of my eyes, brushing away the last traces of my tears until my skin was smooth again. I watched them in the reflection, watched as they erased the only proof that I was breaking inside.

Raven stood behind me, her expression soft but full of worry. I gave her a small nod, though my chest felt like it was caving in.

When the servants finally stepped back, I drew in a deep breath and straightened my shoulders. My reflection stared back at me—a princess dressed in silver and pink, eyes dry, lips calm. Someone who looked ready. Someone who wasn't me.

"I am ready," I said quietly.

The servants bowed their heads and moved toward the door. Raven's eyes glistened, but she didn't say a word.

I turned away from the mirror, forcing one last breath into my lungs, and walked out to face the life I never wanted.

CHAPTER FIFTY-TWO

IRIS

The sound of my father's boots echoed beside mine as we walked down the long, candlelit corridor. The hall was silent save for the faint murmur of music drifting from beyond the great doors at the end. My gown brushed the marble floor, heavy and soft, and my pulse thudded in my ears with every step.

When we reached the doors, my father stopped. His hand gripped my bare arm, tightly. I turned my head to meet his sharp gaze.

"You will smile," he said in a low voice. "You will tell everyone how honoured you are to be a part of this union. Do you understand?"

It took all my strength to nod. "Yes, Father."

His expression softened only slightly. "Good."

The grand doors opened with a deep, echoing creak, and light flooded the corridor. My heart skipped a beat.

"Go," he said simply.

I stepped forward.

A herald standing at the threshold raised his voice, clear and strong, announcing, "Her Royal Highness, Princess Iris of Elarion."

The ballroom fell quiet for a breath. Then the soft hum of strings continued, and I walked in.

The sight before me almost stole my breath. Chandeliers hung high above, their crystals catching the silver moonlight and scattering it across the marble floors. The walls were lined with silk drapes in pale gold and rose, and garlands of white roses wound around tall pillars. Guests in fine attire filled the space, their jewels glittering like stars. The air smelled of honeyed wine and burning candles.

Every eye turned toward me. Conversations stopped. Laughter faded.

And then I saw him.

Lorenzo stood near the center of the room, dressed in deep blue and silver, a goblet in his hand. His head turned at the sound of my name, and when his eyes found me, they widened slightly. For a brief moment, admiration flickered across his face.

I forced a smile and took another step forward. My heart pounded faster with every movement and I wished I were anywhere but here.

As I stepped down from the dais, Lorenzo met me halfway. His eyes swept over me in quiet appraisal before he gave a small smile, the kind meant for the crowd as much as for me.

"You look beautiful," he said softly, taking my hand and lifting it toward his lips. His mouth brushed against my palm, a gesture that drew approving murmurs from the crowd nearby.

The touch made my skin crawl. I forced my lips to curve into a faint smile. "Thank you," I whispered, though the words caught somewhere in my throat.

He raised his hand then, signaling the musicians. The sound of violins swelled through the hall, filling the air with a melody so elegant it almost hurt to listen. The harp joined next, its strings trembling like sunlight over water, and all around the room the guests turned toward us, their eyes full of expectation.

Lorenzo's hand found my waist. "We will lead the first dance," he said quietly.

There was no choice but to nod.

He stepped closer, drawing me into the center of the ballroom. The nobles parted in graceful formation, leaving a wide circle of polished marble for us to dance upon. I could feel their gazes following every step, weighing every movement, judging every inch of my posture.

The music deepened, rich and full, and we began to move. His hand guided mine, his other pressing firmly against the small of my back as he led me into the rhythm. Our steps were slow and measured at first, sweeping across the floor in elegant arcs. My gown shimmered in the candlelight, the pink silk catching silver sparkles each time I turned. The fabric brushed the floor like waves, and my breath came shallow beneath the tight corset.

Around us, the rest of the court began to follow suit. Couples in velvet and silk glided across the floor.

Lorenzo leaned closer, his voice low near my ear. "They are watching," he murmured. "Smile, Iris. You are their princess. They need to see their future queen happy."

I lifted my chin, forcing the corners of my lips upward. My smile felt painted on, fragile as glass. We turned again until everything spun into a blur of color and light. My chest ached, and I could barely keep my breath steady.

The melody rose to its peak, faster now. He turned me sharply, his hand never loosening its hold. I could see our reflection on the polished floor, the perfect picture of grace, the perfect illusion.

Then, at last, the music slowed. He pulled me closer for the final step, bowing slightly as he brought my hand to his lips again. The musicians struck the last note, and the ballroom erupted into polite applause.

Lorenzo smiled for the crowd, and I mirrored it. But as I looked around the glittering room, the silver and crystal and smiling faces, all I could feel was the hollow ache in my chest.

"Perhaps I should get us something to drink?" Lorenzo said in a light and pleasant tone.

Before I could answer, my eyes caught on a familiar figure standing among the servants near the wall.

Raven. Her hands were folded neatly in front of her apron, her face still and polite, but her eyes met mine for the briefest moment. There was sadness there, but something softer, too. Understanding.

It felt good to see a familiar face after the suffocating dance, after the applause that rang hollow in my ears. I gave her a small, almost invisible nod.

Lorenzo followed my gaze. When his eyes found her, I saw the faintest flicker in his expression. Something unreadable but heavy. His eyes dropped for a heartbeat, then lifted again. His face returned to its composed charm.

I wanted to look away, to focus on anything else, and then I saw him.

Standing near one of the marble pillars, dressed in full armor, helm on and posture straight as a blade. Even through the crowd, I knew him. I would know him anywhere. William.

My breath caught in my throat. The light from the chandeliers gleamed faintly off the steel of his armor, but it wasn't that I saw. It was the way he stood, steady and proud, as if the chaos of the world couldn't touch him. Even from across the room, my heart knew his presence.

For a moment, I forgot where I was. Forgotten titles, vows, and everything I was supposed to be. I wanted to go to him. To reach for him, just once more.

I turned back to Lorenzo quickly before my thoughts could betray me. "A drink would be nice," I said, my voice softer than I intended.

He smiled, pleased by the answer. "Excellent," he said.

Without hesitation, he turned and began to weave through the crowd toward the long table of silver cups and crystal decanters.

As soon as Lorenzo's back was turned, I exhaled a shaky breath, my pulse hammering so loudly I was certain someone would hear it. I didn't think. I couldn't. My feet moved before reason could stop them, slipping through the shifting crowd, past nobles in gold and silk, past the gleaming chandeliers and the sound of laughter that suddenly felt far away.

When I reached him, the words left me in a rush. "William."

He turned at once, and before I could stop myself, my arms were around him. The cold metal of his armor pressed against my chest, and his arms came around me all the same, strong and sure. For a heartbeat, I let myself breathe. For a heartbeat, I was safe.

I felt the weight of eyes turning toward us, whispers already rippling through the air, but I didn't care. Not tonight. Not when this could be the last time.

"Come," I whispered urgently, pulling back just enough to look up at him. "Please."

He didn't hesitate. He only nodded once, a silent understanding passing between us.

We moved quickly past the crowd until we reached the open balcony. The night air outside was cool, but it felt like the first real breath I had taken all night. The wind brushed against my bare shoulders, making me shiver, though I hardly cared. All that mattered was him.

The music from the ballroom faded behind us, replaced by the soft rush of the sea below and the faint hum of the night. I turned to face him. My heart was beating so fast and my chest rose too fast. His armor and helm caught the line of the moon, hiding a face I longed to see.

Without speaking, I reached up. My fingers brushed over the cold metal before finding the clasps at the sides. He didn't move or speak. The soft click as I unfastened it, sounded far louder than it should have. I lifted the helm away and set it carefully on the edge of the balcony.

There he was. His face. His beautiful, beautiful face.

For a heartbeat, we just looked at each other. Neither of us dared to breathe.

Then I stepped closer. My hand touched his jaw, and he leaned into it, eyes softening as he exhaled. My breath trembled, my heart racing faster than ever. I rose on my toes and kissed him.

It was gentle at first before his hand slid to the back of my neck as he drew me closer. The other settled at my waist, firm and steady. The taste of salt lingered on our lips, carried by the sea breeze and maybe the tears I hadn't realized were falling.

The world around us disappeared. There was no sound but our breathing, no light but the moon, no one but us. His lips moved against mine, slow and full of feeling, and I felt something deep in my chest unravel.

When we broke apart, our foreheads stayed pressed together. His hand was still at my waist, holding me there as if letting go would undo everything. I closed my eyes, trying to memorize the warmth of his skin, the scent of him, the feel of his arm around me.

"I love you so much," he whispered, pulling me closer. "More than anything in this world."

My heart twisted painfully. "I love you, too," I said, my words barely reaching him. It was all I could manage, and yet it felt like everything.

He exhaled slowly, his thumb brushing over my jaw. "No matter what happens," he said softly, "remember that."

For a moment, I thought he meant to hold me again. But then he stepped back. My eyes opened, confused. He moved toward the balcony railing, standing far too close.

"William," I said quietly with a shaky voice. "What are you doing?"

He turned, and there was such calm in his face it made my heart break. "May the world give us another chance," he said. "I will be waiting."

Then he turned away. I froze, watching as he planted a hand on the railing. My chest tightened so painfully I could barely breathe.

"William, please," I whispered. But he didn't stop. He swung his leg over the edge, steady and sure.

And then he was gone.

"William!" I screamed loudly, running forward until my hands hit the cold stone of the balcony edge. I panicked when I looked down. He was there below, moving quickly through the courtyard. The night swallowed him bit by bit as he passed through the gates.

"William, come back!" I screamed on the top of my lungs. The tears came fast, spilling down my face, blurring everything in front of me. I couldn't think. I couldn't breathe.

All I knew was that my heart was breaking. The pain was so sharp it stole the air from my lungs and forced me onto my knees. The tears wouldn't stop. My fingers gripped the cold stone until they ached.

He was leaving.

Leaving me.

The thought ripped through me like a wound that would never heal. I pressed a trembling hand to my chest as if that could hold it together—as if I could stop the ache from spreading.

"No," I whispered. The word came out cracked and small. "No, please."

I stumbled to my feet, wiping at my face even though it did nothing. The gates were still open in the distance, his shadow fading further with every heartbeat. My mind screamed at me to move. To run. To stop him before it was too late.

I climbed onto the railing, my hands shaking as I pulled myself up. The wind hit my face, cold and sharp, but I didn't care. All I could think about was reaching him, finding him, begging him to stay.

But before I could climb over, a pair of hands grabbed me.

CHAPTER FIFTY-THREE

IRIS

The tears were still stinging in my eyes when I turned to see who it was.

"Raven?" My voice cracked on her name.

She stood behind me with her hands locked around my arms. The sight of her made my chest tighten even more.

"Raven, let me go!" I shouted, trying to wrench free, but her grip only tightened.

"I cannot," she said, her voice trembling. "Iris, please do not—"

"Let me go!" I screamed again, twisting, clawing at her wrists. "He is leaving! I have to go to him!"

She shook her head, her voice breaking. "I am sorry. He told me to stop you."

I froze for a heartbeat, the words barely sinking in.

"I do not care what he told you," I cried, my voice hoarse. "Raven, please, let me go!"

I tried again to pull free, but she only held tighter. Her arms wrapped around me like iron bands, dragging me away from the railing. My tears came harder, falling so fast I could barely see. My breaths were sharp and uneven, and my whole body shook.

"Raven, please," I whispered again, my voice raw. "He is all I have."

But she didn't move. Her grip only tightened more, making my arms hurt. "I know," she said. "I know, Iris. But I cannot let you go. You will get hurt. Please."

Her words were a blur in my ears. My mind could only focus on the silhouette moving in the distance. I could see him through the open gates, walking toward the ocean.

"William!" I screamed, thrashing in her hold. "William, come back!"

"Iris, please stop," Raven said between trembles. "Let us go back inside."

But I couldn't. I didn't even hear her properly. My breath came in sharp, broken gasps, the air catching painfully in my throat. I could not breathe. My lungs burned as if the world itself had turned against me. All I could see was him, far ahead, his figure growing smaller and smaller until the night began to swallow him whole.

The man I loved. The man who had held me like I was the only thing that mattered. He was walking away, and I was frozen, watching the life I wanted slip farther and farther from reach.

My body gave in before my mind did. My knees buckled, the strength leaving me completely. The world blurred through my tears. Raven caught me before I could fall by steading her arms around me.

"Iris," she whispered. "Come on, please. Let us go back inside."

I couldn't respond. My heart was pounding so violently it hurt. The ache in my chest grew heavier, spreading until I thought it would crush me entirely.

"Come," she said again, more firmly this time. Her hand brushed through my hair in a trembling attempt to comfort me. "Please, Iris. It is over. He is gone. Let us go back inside."

Her words stabbed deeper than she could know. *Over. Gone.* The very sound of them made something inside me twist painfully.

She pulled me closer, wrapping her arms tighter around me, and for a moment I let her. I let my forehead rest against her shoulder, my tears soaking into her dress. My arms rose weakly and circled her as I sobbed against her.

But then something inside me snapped.

The thought of never seeing him again, of letting him disappear forever, struck like fire through my veins. The pain turned into panic—the panic into something fierce and uncontrollable.

"No," I whispered against her shoulder. Then louder. "No!"

Before she could react, I pushed against her. My

hands gripped her arms and, with all the strength I had left, I shoved her away.

Raven stumbled back with a gasp, her eyes wide with shock. "Iris—"

I didn't hear the rest. My feet were already moving. I ran for the railing, my skirts tangling around my legs, my tears blinding me. The world narrowed until all I could see was the open night beyond the balcony and the faint silver glow of the ocean where he had gone.

I threw myself at the railing and climbed before I even realized what I was doing. My hands gripped the cold stone, my skirts dragging and tearing against it. The night air bit at my skin, sharp and cold, but I didn't care.

"Iris, stop!" Raven's voice rose behind me, breaking with fear. "Come back, please!"

But I didn't stop. I couldn't. My fingers found another hold, and I climbed lower, the stone rough beneath my palms. Her voice grew fainter behind me, but I refused to look back. I dropped the last few feet and landed hard on the ground, my knees jarring from the impact.

Pain shot through my legs, but it didn't matter. I pushed myself up and ran.

The wind rushed against my face, pulling at my hair and skirts as I sprinted across the courtyard. I could hear Raven behind me, calling my name again and again. But that only made me run faster.

"William!" I cried, my voice tearing through the night. "William, stop!"

My heart pounded so hard it hurt, the sound thundering in my ears.

I could see the gates ahead, wide open, the world beyond them silver and dark. My slippers slipped against the dirt, but I didn't slow. My tears blurred everything, yet I could still see him.

He was there.

Down by the water, the faint moonlight glinting off his armor. He was standing in a small sailboat, his hands working to untie the rope from the dock post. The boat rocked gently in the waves, ready to leave.

"William!" I screamed again. "Stop!"

He froze.

For a moment, the world seemed to go still. The wind quieted, the sound of the sea softened, and everything between us felt suspended in time.

My breath came in sharp gasps as I stumbled onto the shore, my skirts heavy with sand and water. My tears mixed with the salt in the air.

He turned slowly toward me. His expression shifted from confusion to disbelief, and then to something softer, something aching.

I took another step forward. "Do not go," I said, my voice breaking. "Please."

"Iris—"

Her voice came faintly from behind me, broken and shaking. I turned sharply to see Raven running toward us, her hair loose from its braid, her face pale in the moonlight.

"No!" I cried, my voice hoarse. "Leave!"

She froze where she stood, her eyes wide with shock. For a moment, she looked like she might come closer, but the look on my face stopped her. Her lips parted as if to speak again, then closed. She took a slow step back.

The waves crashed softly against the shore, the sound filling the silence between us.

"Iris," William said finally, his voice quiet and heavy. The way he said my name made my heart twist, but it only fueled the storm building inside me.

"No," I said again, louder this time, my voice trembling. "You do not get to do this."

He took a hesitant step toward me, his eyes searching mine, but I didn't let him speak. The words came rushing out of me, raw and angry and full of hurt.

"You lied," I said, my chest tightening with every breath. "You lied about saying you wouldn't give up. You said you would never leave me, and look what you are doing." My voice broke, and I pressed a trembling hand to my chest. "You are leaving, William. You are leaving and hiding behind the excuse that you will wait for me."

He flinched as if I had struck him, but I didn't stop. The tears came faster now, hot against my cheeks, and I could hardly breathe through them.

"You said you love me," I whispered. "You said nothing would keep you away. But you are walking away. You are choosing to leave me."

His jaw trembled, and for a moment he couldn't speak. Then, through the sound of the waves and my own ragged breathing, I saw his tears fall. Slow, silent, and full of everything he was trying to hold back.

"Iris," he said at last, his voice breaking. "I never wanted to hurt you. But if I stay, it will destroy us both."

"Please," I whispered, shaking my head as more tears slipped down. "Do not say that. I need you, William. I need you, and you need me. You are all I have."

He closed his eyes as if the words hurt to hear. When he opened them again, the moonlight caught on the tears still clinging to his lashes. For a long moment, neither of us spoke. Only the sea filled the silence, its soft roar wrapping around us like a heartbeat.

Then he reached out a hand toward me. His voice was quiet, trembling but sure. "Then come with me."

There was a beat of nothing. Everything stilled.

"Come with me, my love." He reached his hand out farther, the plea trembling with every word.

Something inside me broke.

When I turned, Raven was still standing a few steps behind. She looked terrified, torn between stopping me and letting me go. For a moment, I saw my own pain reflected in her face: the same kind of helpless ache that came from loving someone you could never truly have.

I turned back to William.

There he was. My William. Standing at the edge of the sea, the wind tugging at his cloak, his tears catching the moonlight as they fell. His hand was still outstretched, waiting. He looked at me like I was his whole world, like nothing else existed beyond this moment.

"Come with me," he said again, his voice shaking. "Please."

My heart slammed against my chest so hard it hurt. The sound of the waves faded until all I could hear was that pounding inside me, quick and uneven, urging me to move.

I didn't know what to do.

If I went to him, I would lose everything—my title, my crown, my wealth, my father's favor. Everything I had been raised to protect would vanish the moment I took his hand. But what did any of it matter if I was never happy again? What was a kingdom worth if it meant a life without love?

I looked at him. His face was wet with tears, his hand still outstretched, trembling.

Love was more than wealth. More than duty. William was worth more than all of it.

But my thoughts still tangled. If I stayed, I would live a life of silence and sorrow. I would smile for the court, bear the prince's heir, and die a little more each day. My heart would belong to someone I could never touch again. Staying would mean surviving, not living.

If I went with him, I would lose the world. But I would have him—my world. The one person who had ever seen me for who I truly was. The one who loved me before he knew my name.

My breath came out shaky. My decision came before my mind could catch up.

I stepped forward.

His eyes widened, glistening in the moonlight.

And then I placed my hand in his.

The world seemed to exhale around us, the sea roaring louder as if it knew what I had just done. His fingers tightened around mine, warm and certain, and I knew there was no turning back.

I had chosen him.

I had chosen love.

And everything else would come after.

CHAPTER FIFTY-FOUR

WILLIAM/IRIS

IRIS

Raven had helped us. Not easily. She had argued, begged even, her voice trembling as she tried to make me stay. But when I reminded her of the love she once lost, of how she knew what it felt like to ache for someone she could never have, something in her softened. She had promised not to tell my father, though tears filled her eyes as she watched us leave. I still saw that image whenever I blinked.

Now I sat wrapped in William's cloak, staring at the horizon. The air was cold and sharp, biting at my cheeks. The water shimmered like liquid glass beneath the moon, and I tried to steady my breathing against the rhythm of the oars.

William's movements were calm and even. His arms flexed with every stroke, the quiet splash of water breaking the stillness. After a while, he turned to me, his face half hidden by the shadows.

"Are you sure?" he asked, his voice low. "We can still go back."

I met his eyes. "No," I whispered. "I do not want to go back."

A tear slipped down my cheek. I didn't bother wiping it away. My chest hurt, tight with all the things I couldn't say. I had made the right choice, but it was still hard. Harder than I imagined.

William slowed the boat until it drifted gently with the tide. His gaze stayed on me, full of worry and tenderness all at once.

I looked down at the sea, then back at him. "Where will we go?" I asked quietly.

He looked toward the horizon, his jaw tightening as if he were choosing his words carefully. The boat rocked softly beneath us, the moonlight stretching over the water like a path only we could see.

"A place no one can find us," he said finally. "My parents' home. It is far from the cities, far from civilization."

My eyes lit up. I remembered. The same little house I had run into on that stormy night, drenched and trembling, when I first met him. The smell of the fire, the sound of the rain on the roof, the warmth in his voice when he offered me shelter. It all came rushing back like a dream I never wanted to end.

I looked at him and the ache in my chest softened just a little. The sea stretched endlessly ahead, but for the first time, it didn't feel so terrifying.

His eyes met mine again, gentle and sure. The wind caught his hair, and the faintest smile tugged at the corner of his lips.

"We are going home," he said quietly.

And I believed him.

Because with him, everywhere was home.

The boat drifted forward, carried by the tide, until the castle lights disappeared behind us completely.

WILLIAM

She had chosen me.

The thought alone nearly brought me to my knees.

I watched her for a long while, barely trusting my own eyes. The Princess of Elarion had chosen me; a knight, a commoner with nothing but a sword and a fading name to share her life with. She had given up her crown, a palace, and the safety of everything she'd ever known—all for me.

A single tear slipped down my cheek before I could stop it. I let it fall, tasting the salt as it mixed with the sea air. The sound of the waves against the boat filled the silence, soft and steady, like the world itself was holding its breath.

She was asleep now, her head resting on the side of the boat, wrapped in my cloak. The moonlight touched her face, turning her hair pale as silver. I couldn't look away. Every so often, her lips parted slightly, and she would breathe out a soft sigh.

We had been rowing for decades. My arms ached, but I didn't care. I would have rowed across the ends of the world if it meant keeping her safe.

—

More time passed. The horizon turned gold, the soft glow of dawn spreading over the open sea. My arms burned even more with every pull of the oars. I could feel the muscles in my shoulders tearing, but I didn't stop. I had rowed through the night and I would keep rowing as far as it took. Every stroke took us farther from the life we had left behind. Farther from duty and pain.

The water was calm, glinting like molten glass under the rising sun. She was still asleep beside me, her head still resting against the side of the boat. The sight of her made me forget the ache in my arms. For a few minutes, there was nothing but peace.

A light breeze brushed against my face. Seabirds cried in the distance. She stirred slightly in her sleep, her hand shifting until it rested near mine. I watched her for a long time, memorizing the softness of her expression, the faint color of her cheeks. I had never known something could feel this still, this right.

The sun climbed higher, painting the water in streaks of orange and gold. I slowed the oars, letting the boat drift. I wanted her to rest a little longer. I wanted this moment to last.

Then it happened.

A sharp hiss broke through the air.

Something hit the water beside the boat, sending up a spray of foam. My head snapped toward the sound, my chest tightening. Another hiss followed, then another, each one closer. The sound was all too familiar.

Arrows.

I turned toward the horizon. Far off in the distance, a dark shape was cutting through the sea. The sun glared against its sails, but even from here I could see the symbol painted across them. The crest of Elarion.

Cold dread flooded through me.

Another arrow struck the side of the boat, the wood splintering inches from my hand. I dropped the oars and reached for the sword lying near my feet. My heart was pounding so hard I could barely hear anything else.

She stirred in her sleep, her brow furrowing. I wanted to tell her to stay down, to stay still, but my voice wouldn't come. The calm that had surrounded us only moments ago was gone, shattered by the sound of arrows and the splash of water.

The once gentle sea now felt cruel and endless.

Another arrow hissed through the air.

And then the world around us erupted.

CHAPTER FIFTY-FIVE

WILLIAM

More arrows flew through the air, slicing past my head and thudding into the wood beside me. I ducked low, the boat rocking hard under the force. One arrow splashed into the water near my arm, spraying salt water against my face.

Iris stirred awake, her voice weak at first. "William, what is happening?"

Before she could sit up, I reached for her shoulder and pushed her gently back down. "Stay down," I said sharply. "Do not move."

Her eyes darted around in panic. "What is going on?"

"Just stay down," I repeated, grabbing the oars again. My arms burned with every pull, but I forced the boat forward through the waves. The sea felt heavier now, dragging us backward like it wanted to keep us trapped.

Arrows kept flying. One hit the edge of the boat and split the wood. Another found its mark. It struck my shoulder and drove through the fabric. Pain shot through me and I hissed, my grip faltering.

"William!" she cried, trying to rise, but I caught her wrist and pushed her down again.

"It is fine," I said between shallow breaths. "Stay down. It is just a scratch."

Blood ran down my arm, but I ignored it. The air burned into the wound, and every movement sent pain through my body. I would not stop. Not while she was still in danger.

More arrows came. Some struck the water, others missed by inches. I hunched lower, rowing faster. The sound of my heartbeat drowned everything else.

"Who are they?" she asked, her voice shaking.

I didn't answer. My eyes stayed on the horizon. I had to find land. I had to get her somewhere safe.

She turned slightly, and her voice broke. "William, my father. He is on that ship."

I froze for a moment. The sun hit the crest painted on the sails, the royal emblem of Elarion shining bright. And there he was. The King himself stood at the front, his crimson cloak billowing in the wind. Soldiers surrounded him, and even from here, I could feel his fury.

Her father.

The King.

He was watching us.

The sight cut deep, but I didn't have time for anger. Not now. I gritted my teeth and forced the oars through the water again. My shoulder screamed in pain, but I didn't stop. I couldn't.

The sea crashed around us, pulling at the boat. My blood dripped down the oar handle, mixing with the salt. The pain meant nothing. Only she mattered. Only getting her away from that ship.

Then, through the morning light, I saw it—a thin strip of dark green.

Land.

I pushed the oars through the water with everything I had left. My arms burned, my wounded shoulder felt like it was on fire, but I didn't stop. I couldn't. Each pull brought us closer to that strip of green, closer to safety.

The waves slammed against the sides of the boat. My vision blurred from sweat and blood, but I kept my eyes locked on the shore. Nothing else mattered. Not the pain, not the arrows, not even the roar of the sea behind us.

Another arrow came. I saw it too late. It struck my arm, deep and fast. The force of it nearly tore the oar from my hand. I gritted my teeth, a hiss escaping through them as blood ran warm down my forearm.

"William!" Iris cried. "Oh God, let me see it!"

"No," I barked, keeping my grip tight on the oars. "Stay low."

"You will bleed to death!"

"You can check it once we are on land," I said, the words rough between shallow breaths. "Not now."

She didn't argue, but I can feel her panicking beneath the crash of the sea. The feeling tore through me worse than the pain in my arm.

The shore was closer now, so close I could see the line where the waves met the sand. I dug the oars deep again and again. My muscles screamed. My shoulder throbbed with every movement. The blood made the wood slick under my palms, but I refused to let go.

A voice carried across the wind, sharp and commanding. "Release my daughter!"

King Henrik's voice.

So that was what he thought. That I had stolen her. That she hadn't chosen this. The anger hit me hard, but I didn't let it break my focus.

The arrows came again, slicing through the air, hitting the water just behind us. The boat rocked hard, and I nearly lost balance, but I steadied it and pushed on.

The sand was only a few feet away now. My arms felt like lead, my breath short and uneven, but I didn't stop. One more pull, then another.

The bottom of the boat scraped against the sand, jerking us forward. We were there.

I let go of the oars and slumped forward, my chest heaving. My arms trembled from the effort. The arrows still came, but they fell short now, splashing harmlessly into the shallow water.

We had reached land.

I turned to her, breathing hard. "Come on," I said, reaching out my hand.

She took it without hesitation, her fingers trembling against mine. Together we stepped off the boat, our feet sinking into the wet sand. The sea pulled at our ankles, the salt biting at my wounds, but we didn't stop. The air smelled of iron and smoke and fear.

Then it came.

An arrow struck me in the back. The force drove the breath from my lungs. For a second, I froze. The pain flared sharp and deep, but instinct took over. I moved in front of Iris, forcing her behind me, my body shielding hers.

Another arrow flew, hitting my shoulder. The shock of it almost made me fall, but I gritted my teeth and steadied myself.

"Run," I said, my voice breaking. "Run!"

She hesitated, shaking her head, panic rising up her face. "No, I am not leaving you—"

"Go!" I shouted, pushing her forward. "I am right behind you."

The pain was unbearable now, spreading through my back like fire, but I ran. The sand shifted beneath my feet, slowing me down. Iris stumbled ahead of me, looking back with wide, terrified eyes.

Behind us, I heard shouting. The heavy sound of boots hitting the shore. The king's ship had landed. His soldiers were coming.

Another arrow hit, this one lower, near my ribs. My

legs nearly gave out, but I forced them to move. I couldn't stop. Not while she was still running.

The forest line was close. Just a few more steps.

But another arrow struck, then another. The impacts blurred together until I couldn't tell how many there were. My back burned, the weight of them dragging me down.

Still, I ran.

The only thing that mattered was keeping her safe.

If this was the price of loving her, then I would pay it without regret.

My vision blurred. Every breath came shorter than the last, every heartbeat louder than the one before. The trees ahead swayed and shifted, and for a moment, I thought I might collapse right there on the sand.

Then I saw it. A shadow cut into the cliffside, half hidden by overgrown vines. A cave. Shelter.

"Iris," I rasped, my voice barely audible. "Over there."

She turned, following my gaze. The moment she saw it, she nodded and sprinted ahead, her ballgown brushing the sand as she ran. I stumbled after her, the weight of the arrows in my back dragging me lower with every step.

The shouting behind us grew louder. The soldiers were close. Too close.

I forced one more push, each movement sending pain through my chest. My breath came ragged and uneven. I could see her just ahead, standing at the cave entrance, her hand reaching for me.

"Come on!" she cried, her voice desperate.

I reached her. The cool shade of the cave swallowed us, dimming the blinding sun outside. For a second, I felt relief, brief and fragile.

Then my knees buckled. The strength drained from my legs, and I hit the ground hard. The world tilted, spinning around me. I could hear her gasp, could feel her hands on my shoulders, but I couldn't lift my head.

My chest rose and fell in short, shallow breaths. The sound of the sea faded into something distant, like a dream slipping away.

Everything grew quiet.

And then, nothing.

CHAPTER FIFTY-SIX

IRIS

My hands were shaking so badly I could hardly breathe.

William lay face down in the dirt, his eyes closed, his back a mess of blood and broken arrows. There were so many of them. Too many. The shafts rose from his skin like dark thorns, the blood pooling beneath him already beginning to soak into the cave floor.

For a moment, I froze. Panic clawed at my chest, and my mind went blank. I wanted to scream, to cry, but I couldn't. If I lost control now, he would die.

I forced a breath in, then another.

I remembered the hours in the healers' wing with Raven—how she had made me crush herbs, clean wounds, pack moss into cuts to stop the bleeding. My father had forced me to help back then, to punish me, saying a princess should know the value of healing and pain. I had hated it at the time. Now it was the only thing keeping me from losing him.

I crawled closer, my knees scraping the cold stone, and pressed two fingers to his neck. His pulse beat faintly beneath his skin. Weak but still there.

"Thank God," I whispered.

I looked around the cave frantically. There, near the wall, green moss clung to the damp stone. I ripped it free, squeezing it to drain the water, then turned back to him.

I reached for the first arrow. My fingers brushed the shaft, slick with blood. I hesitated only for a second before gripping it tightly and pulling.

He jolted awake, gasping sharply, his body tensing under my hands.

"Stay still," I hissed. "Please, they will hear you!"

His teeth clenched, his breath coming in harsh bursts. I pressed the moss over the wound and held it there. Blood seeped through my fingers, but I didn't stop.

"This might hurt," I warned, pressing the moss deeper into the open wound.

He let out a low, broken sound, his voice strained in pain. I bit down on a sob. "I am sorry," I whispered. "It will stop the bleeding."

I moved to the next arrow, grabbing it firmly and pulling it free. More blood. More pain. His body trembled under my hands, but he didn't cry out again. I pressed another piece of moss over it and applied pressure.

My heartbeat thundered in my ears. My hands were slick and shaking, but I didn't stop. One by one, I pulled the arrows out, whispering small apologies each time.

When I reached the last one, my arms were trembling from exhaustion. His breath came shallow and weak.

"Just one more," I whispered. "Then we will go. We cannot stay here too long, they will find us."

His head turned slightly, his face pale and slick with sweat. "No," he whispered, his voice hoarse.

I froze. "What?"

"I cannot run anymore," he said quietly. "I can hardly even sit." He struggled to lift his head but couldn't. "You have to go. Go to them and tell them I tried to abduct you."

For a moment, I couldn't breathe. His words didn't make sense. They couldn't.

"What?" I said again, shaking my head. "No. Are you out of your mind? My father will kill you!"

He gave a weak, broken laugh that made my chest tighten. "I am already going to die as it is," he said softly. "So just go. Please, Iris. I cannot stand."

"No!" My voice cracked, and the tears started falling again. "Please, do not say that. I will help you. Just lean your body toward me, I will put my arms under your shoulders, and we will run together. We will make it."

He turned his head slightly, his eyes meeting mine. They were tired, heavy, but still full of that same gentleness that had always undone me. "That will slow us both down," he murmured. "And when they see you, they will think—"

"I do not care what they think!" I snapped, shouting. "I am not leaving you, William!"

He tried to speak again, but the sound died in his throat. His hand twitched, reaching for me.

And then the air shifted.

The faint sound of footsteps grew louder outside the cave. The crunch of boots on sand. Voices calling to one another.

I turned toward the entrance, my heart slamming against my ribs. Shadows filled the mouth of the cave. One by one, soldiers stepped inside with their swords drawn.

There were too many of them

I felt William's fingers brush weakly against mine, and I reached for his hand.

The steel glinted in the dark, the sound of swords unsheathing filling the silence.

We had been found and were now surrounded.

CHAPTER FIFTY-SEVEN

IRIS

One of the guards stepped forward, lowering his sword slightly. "Your Highness! Are you alright?"

Before I could answer, another voice shouted from behind him, sharp and furious. "Get him! He tried to abduct the Princess!"

The sound of boots scraped against the stone as several soldiers moved forward, their weapons raised. Panic shot through me.

"No!" I cried, stepping in front of William before they could reach him. My arms spread wide. "Stand back! He did not do anything!"

"Iris," William rasped weakly behind me, his voice barely a whisper, "do not—"

"No!" I turned, my voice rising with desperation. "All of you, stay back! He has done nothing wrong!"

The guards hesitated, glancing at one another uncertainly. The sound of metal shifting echoed through the cave as some lowered their blades while others kept their grip tight.

Then the air changed. The heavy rhythm of boots approaching filled the cave.

And there he was.

My father.

King Henrik stepped through the circle of guards. His gaze flicked from me to William, who lay bleeding behind me.

"Someone," he said, his tone cutting through the air, "tell me what happened here."

No one spoke. The silence stretched, heavy and unbearable.

His eyes narrowed. Then they landed on William.

"You," he said, taking a step forward, his voice low with fury. "You dared to lay your hands on my daughter? To abduct the Princess of Elarion?"

My heart twisted. "He did not!" I said quickly, the words tumbling out before I could stop them. "He did not try to abduct me."

My father's gaze snapped to mine, sharp and furious. "Then what happened?"

I swallowed hard. My hands were trembling. I could feel every eye on me, waiting for my answer.

"I ran away with him," I said.

The words echoed through the cave.

Gasps broke out all around. The guards exchanged startled glances. Even the air seemed to stop moving.

My father's eyes widened, his face darkening as the weight of my confession settled. His voice came out quiet but dangerous, each word trembling with fury.

"You what?"

"I could not live the life you wanted me to live," I said, my voice trembling. "I cannot live with a man I do not love and have him call me his wife. No, Father. I could not."

For a moment, he only stared at me. His jaw tightened, his breath sharp and controlled. Then, slowly, he turned his gaze toward William.

"And you," he said, his tone low and dangerous, "you helped my daughter escape?"

"No," I said quickly, stepping in front of William again. "He did not help me! I chose this. We did this together. Because I love him!"

The last words seemed to hang in the air, heavy and final.

My father's eyes widened, and for a heartbeat he was silent. Then his face darkened with a rage so fierce it made the soldiers flinch. He looked as if thunder itself had struck him.

"Do you have any idea what you have done?" he roared, his voice echoing through the cave walls.

"I do not care what I have done!" I shouted back, my voice breaking. "I did what was right!"

The crack of his hand against my cheek was so sharp it echoed. My head snapped to the side, but I didn't move otherwise. I didn't even touch the sting. I refused to give him the satisfaction of seeing me fall.

His breathing was harsh, uneven. "Guards," he barked. "Seize this traitor."

"Father, no!" I cried, stepping forward, but his hand shot out and gripped my arm, holding me back.

Two guards moved toward William. He didn't resist. His body was limp, his olive face now pale, his eyes barely open. They grabbed him by the arms, dragging him across the dirt toward the mouth of the cave.

"Please!" I screamed, thrashing against my father's hold. "Stop! Do not touch him!"

He didn't listen.

The guards hauled William outside. I could see his blood leaving a trail behind him, dark against the sand. They reached the carriage waiting near the shore, the same one we had taken when we left for Valebran.

My father turned to me then, his expression full of fury and something worse: disappointment. His grip on my arm tightened until it hurt.

"You will never see him again," he said, his voice shaking with restrained anger. "Not as long as you live."

"What are you going to do?" I said, my voice breaking on the last word.

He looked at me as if I had asked whether the sun would rise.

"There is no light punishment for this," he said. "He will be taken back to the castle. He will be healed enough to stand, and then he will be executed on the breaking wheel."

Air stalled in my chest. *The breaking wheel. Executed.* Not only did he want to kill him, but he wanted to torture him first. My eyes widened in horror. "No," I whispered, shaking my head. "No, you cannot."

"Yes, I can. I am the king." he said, his tone like stone. "He will be healed first so he can feel every bit of it. And then he will die. You will watch it happen and learn to never disobey me again."

The tears blurred my sight. I could hardly breathe. "Please," I begged, my voice cracking. "Please do not do this."

He ignored me completely. "And after that," he said, his voice quieter but cruel, "you will face your punishment, too. Then you will return to Valebran and become Lorenzo's queen. As planned."

Before I could say another word, his hand shot out. His fingers wrapped tightly around my arm. I tried to pull back, but his grip only tightened.

"Father, stop, please!" I cried.

He didn't answer. Without another word, he dragged me toward the carriage. My feet stumbled across the dirt, my body fighting him even as the guards forced William inside. William didn't resist.

His head hung low, blood dripping down his side. His eyes were half-closed, barely conscious.

"William!" I screamed, trying to reach for him.

My father yanked me back before I could touch him. "Enough!" he shouted, his voice echoing across the beach. "You have shamed your family, your crown, and your people."

Tears streamed down my chest. "Please," I said one last time. "Do not do this. Spare him. I will go back to Valebran and be Lorenzo's queen–"

"You made your choice, Iris," he cut me off. "Now you will live with it."

He pushed me toward the carriage, and before I could resist, the door slammed shut behind us.

CHAPTER FIFTY-EIGHT

IRIS/WILLIAM

IRIS

The carriage rattled through the gates of Elarion's Castle, its wheels scraping against the stone path. The sight of the tall towers and gray walls made my stomach twist. The place that once felt like home now looked like a prison.

When the doors opened, my father stepped out first. His voice was sharp and cold when he spoke. "Take this traitor to the healers," he ordered, pointing at William. "Once he is well enough to stand, take him to the dungeons. His execution will be set for tomorrow."

The words echoed through me like a knife. *Tomorrow*. He was going to die tomorrow.

Two guards dragged William out of the carriage.

His head hung low, his legs barely holding him upright. Blood had soaked through his tunic, leaving a dark trail behind him as they pulled him toward the east hall. I tried to move after him, but my father's next words stopped me.

"And take the Princess to her chambers," he said. "She will remain there until I decide she can leave."

Before I could react, two guards stepped forward and seized my arms. Their grips were strong, unrelenting. "Let go!" I shouted, thrashing against them. "Let me go!"

They said nothing. Their hands only tightened as they dragged me up the stairs. My feet scraped against the steps, my voice raw from screaming. "Father, please!" I cried. "Please do not do this!"

He didn't turn around. He didn't even look at me.

When we reached the corridor, I could still hear the sound of boots behind us, the guards pulling William in the opposite direction. I turned my head, desperate to see him one last time, but the hallway was already empty.

The guards shoved open the door to my bedchamber and threw me inside. I hit the floor hard, the breath knocked out of me. The sound of the lock turning was loud, final.

I scrambled up, running to the door and pounding my fists against it. "Let me out!" I screamed. "Let me out this instant!"

Silence answered me.

My hands fell to my sides, shaking uncontrollably.

The silence pressed in on me, thick and suffocating. Then something inside me snapped. I turned around and screamed, the sound tearing out of my throat until it burned. It was anger, pain, and despair all at once, echoing back at me from the cold stone walls.

I slammed my fists against the wall. Once. Twice. Again. The impact sent sharp pain up my arms, but I didn't stop. I hit harder, faster, until I couldn't feel anything but the sting of raw skin. The sound of it filled the room, a rhythm of grief and fury.

William was going to die tomorrow. The thought echoed in my head like a curse. He was going to die, and I would be forced to watch. Tortured. Broken. His pain would be paraded before me while I stood there helpless.

The anger grew until it swallowed everything else. My fists met the wall again, blood streaking across the stone. My knuckles split open, crimson against gray. The pain barely registered. It was nothing compared to the ache in my chest.

He was going to die because of me. Because I ran. Because I chose him. Because I was too selfish to let him go when I should have.

I slid down to the floor, my legs too weak to hold me. My breath came in shallow bursts, my vision blurring. My hands throbbed, and blood dripped onto my gown, staining it. My chest hurt so much it felt like it might tear open.

If I hadn't gone with him, none of this would have happened. He would still be free. He would still be alive. The weight of it crushed me until I could barely think.

The fire flickered across the walls, but I felt no warmth. Only cold. Empty, endless cold.

I pulled my knees close, pressing my head against them. The tears wouldn't stop, no matter how hard I tried. And as they fell, one thought burned through the haze of pain and guilt.

I couldn't let it end like this.

WILLIAM

I could hardly feel my body. It was as if the world around me had dissolved into nothing but pain and fading sound. My eyes fluttered open, though my vision blurred and shifted, colors bleeding together into pale shapes. The smell of herbs and metal filled the air.

The ceiling above me came in and out of focus. I blinked slowly, trying to make sense of the movement around me. Then I heard voices, rushed and urgent.

"The King wants him healed before dawn. Hurry!"

Their words cut through the haze like a dull blade. Healed before dawn. I knew what that meant. Not mercy, not kindness. Just a cruel preparation for what came next.

Hands pressed against me, cold and firm. The faint sting of liquid on my skin made me flinch. Someone tore away the moss Iris had placed, and the brief comfort of her touch vanished with it. My breath hitched, a hoarse sound escaping my throat.

Everything burned. My shoulder, my back, my chest. The pain was so deep it felt carved into my bones. I tried to move, to speak, but my limbs wouldn't listen.

More voices shouted. The words blurred together, growing distant, like they were sinking beneath the sea. My vision swam again. Faces hovered above me, their mouths moving, but I couldn't hear them anymore.

Then, slowly, everything went quiet.

The light dimmed, the pain dulled, and the world slipped away into black.

—

When I opened my eyes again, the world was dim and silent. For a moment, I didn't know if I was still alive. My body felt heavy, my head pounding, and the air around me was thick with dampness and the faint scent of stone and rust.

I forced myself to sit up. My muscles protested, but they worked. The sharp pain that had once burned through my back was gone, replaced by a deep, dull ache. I looked down and saw that I was bare from the waist up, only my trousers left. My skin was clean, though faint red marks dotted my shoulders where the arrows had been.

The healers had done their work. They had saved me.

But not for mercy. Not for life. Only so I could face what waited next.

I looked around. Bars rose high in front of me, cold and black, their edges wet with condensation. The light came from a single torch fixed outside the cell, flickering weakly against the walls. The floor beneath me was rough stone, uneven and cold.

There was a small slab of rock against the wall, some sort of makeshift bed and a rusted chain looped through the iron ring around my wrists. In the corner sat a dented chamber pot. The stench of it mixed with the damp air.

I was in the dungeons.

My pulse quickened as the realization sank in. The silence here was different. Heavy. Final. This was where they kept men who had already been sentenced. Men waiting for death.

I leaned back against the wall, the chill of the stone biting through my skin. The faint sound of footsteps echoed somewhere in the distance, fading as quickly as they came. I closed my eyes for a moment, breathing slow and shallow.

Then I turned my head slightly and saw a crack in the far wall. A thin line of light spilled in. It was faint, weak, but enough to tell me what I didn't want to know. Morning.

The night was gone.

The faint hum of voices carried from somewhere above—guards changing posts, the low clatter of armor echoing through the halls. The world outside was waking, but down here, time felt still. Cold. Unforgiving.

I turned my head toward that small crack again. The light shifted slightly, spreading across the floor in a slow, golden streak. Dawn. The start of a new day for everyone else. The end of mine.

My hands trembled in the chains. I flexed them slowly, testing the strength of the iron. It didn't matter. There was no escaping this.

A quiet breath left me. I closed my eyes, letting the light brush against my skin one last time. The warmth was faint, but I could almost imagine it was her. Iris. The way she felt in my arms, the way her voice sounded when she said my name.

The light grew stronger, spilling further into the cell.

It was the next day.

And today, I would die.

CHAPTER FIFTY-NINE

IRIS

The light poured through my window, soft and golden, but it felt cruel. I had not slept, not even for a heartbeat. My body ached, my eyes burned, and my heart felt like it was being torn apart with every passing second.

I had changed hours ago into a simple white gown covered in small, pink embroidered flowers. My hair was pinned back with two pink clips, though my hands had trembled as I put them on. The mirror reflected nothing but red, swollen eyes and a pale, hollow face.

William would die today.

The thought struck me again and again until I could barely breathe. I moved toward the balcony, my legs weak, my hands gripping the frame for balance. The morning air was cool and heavy.

And then I saw it.

The courtyard below was already filled with people. Guards. Servants. Townsfolk gathered by the gates. In the center stood a tall wooden post, and upon it, a wheel. The sight made my stomach twist. A sound escaped my throat before I could stop it.

They were preparing his execution.

A public one.

"No," I whispered. My hands clutched the railing, my knuckles white. "No, no, no."

I turned toward the door. Still locked. The guards had sealed it last night. I hit it once, twice, but it didn't move. My mind raced. I needed to get out. I needed to reach him before they did. God, I couldn't let him die. I wouldn't.

Then my eyes landed on the balcony.

I remembered the one in Valebran. The roses, the ledge, the path he had once made for me. My heart hammered in my chest. This one was higher, and the fall was much worse. But it didn't matter.

I swung one leg over the railing, gripping the cold stone tightly. The wind tugged at my gown, but I kept climbing, inch by inch, down the far corner where the wall curved and the rocks jutted out thick enough to hold my weight. My hands slipped twice, scraping my palms, but I didn't stop.

When I was finally close enough to the ground, I took a shaky breath. The distance was still high enough to hurt, but I had no choice.

I jumped.

The air rushed past me. My feet hit the grass hard, and pain shot up my legs. I stumbled forward, gasping, before steadying myself.

I was free.

I gathered my skirts and ran. The grass was wet with morning dew, soaking the hem of my gown, but I didn't care. Every breath burned my lungs, every step sent a sharp pain through my legs, yet I kept moving.

Two guards stood near the courtyard gates. I bowed my head, my hair falling forward to hide my face, praying they wouldn't recognize me. My heart pounded so loudly I was sure they could hear it.

They didn't stop me.

I slipped through the archway and into the castle's main hall. The corridors were mostly empty, though the sound of distant footsteps echoed somewhere behind me. I moved quickly, keeping close to the walls until I reached the heavy door at the end of the corridor—the one that led below.

The door creaked softly as I opened it. A rush of cold air met me, smelling of damp stone and decay. My pulse quickened. I closed it behind me and descended the narrow staircase, the sound of my steps swallowed by the darkness.

It was colder down there. The air was heavy, thick with the scent of mold and iron. Cobwebs brushed my face as I passed through the narrow corridor lined with barred cells. I whispered his name once, but the sound barely left my lips.

I ran faster. My slippers slid against the rough floor

as I searched each cell, peering into the shadows. Some were empty. Others held only broken chains or old straw.

Then, near the end of the corridor, I saw him.

William.

He was slumped against the far wall, shirtless, the faint light from the torch outside his cell brushing across his skin. His head rested to the side, eyes closed, his body still.

A choked sound escaped me. I pressed a hand to my mouth, my knees weakening with relief.

He was alive.

I had made it before they came.

I rushed to the cell, my footsteps echoing off the stone walls. My fingers wrapped around the cold iron bars as I pressed myself close to them.

"William!" I cried, my voice breaking.

His eyes snapped open. For a second, he looked dazed, his breathing uneven, and then he pushed himself up with trembling arms. When he saw me, his whole face changed. He crawled forward, the chains on his wrists clinking as he reached the bars.

"Iris," he breathed, his hand finding mine through the narrow gap. His touch was cold but steady. "You should not be here."

"I need to get you out of here," I said, my words tumbling out too fast, too desperate. "I can find something sharp, maybe a key—there has to be something!"

He ran a shaking hand through his hair, his eyes tired and full of sorrow. "Iris, it is over," he said quietly.

"You have to leave. There's nothing you can do. They will be here soon."

"No," I said, shaking my head so hard it hurt. "I will not let them! I cannot!" My voice broke again. I looked around frantically, searching the floor for anything I could use to pry the lock open. My hands shook. "There has to be something!"

He leaned his head back against the wall and closed his eyes for a moment, his breath coming shallow and uneven. When he spoke again, his voice was softer, almost peaceful. "Look at me, my love. There is nothing we can do now. It is over."

Tears ran freely down my cheeks. I shook the bars, my voice trembling. "What do you mean it is over? No, it is not! Please, do not say that!"

He looked at me again, and even through the dim light, I saw the faintest smile on his lips. "You know what I feared the most while I was locked up?" he asked. "Not death. Not the pain. But the thought of not seeing you again. Not even once." His thumb brushed my hand through the bars, his touch so gentle it made my heart ache. "And now you are here, right in front of me."

"Do not talk like that," I whispered, sobbing now. "You are not going to die, I promise. I will get you out. I swear I will."

He shook his head slowly. "Iris, if I die, at least I die knowing you loved me. That is more than I ever thought I would have."

"Stop it," I said, my voice breaking apart. "Please stop saying things like that."

His hand tightened on mine. "Then promise me something," he whispered. "Promise me you will live. That you will keep going, even when I cannot."

I pressed my forehead against the bars, closing my eyes. "I cannot promise that," I said. "Not if you are gone."

He gave a faint, broken smile. "Then let me go knowing I meant something to you."

"You do," I whispered through my tears. "You mean everything."

And I held his hand tighter, as if my grip alone could keep him alive.

The sound came suddenly. The deep creak of the dungeon doors opening above, followed by the echo of heavy boots on the stone steps. My heart stopped.

They were here.

The torchlight flickered along the walls as shadows moved closer, growing larger with every step. I turned toward the sound, my breath catching in my throat.

"No," I whispered. Then louder. "No!"

William's hand tightened around mine one last time. His voice was soft, almost calm. "It is okay, my love."

I shook my head violently. "No, it is not okay!" My voice broke into a sob. "They cannot take you! Please, they can't—"

I stared at him, unable to breathe, my whole body trembling.

Tears blurred my vision until I could barely see his face.

The boots drew closer. The keys rattled.

He gave my hand a weak squeeze, the faintest smile on his lips. "Everything is going to be alright."

But it wasn't. Not for me. It never would be.

The cell door burst open. The clang of metal struck through the air, sharp and final. Guards filled the narrow space, their armor glinting under the torchlight. Then he appeared. My father.

His expression was hard as stone. His eyes met mine, cold and furious. "How did you get here?" he demanded.

My throat closed. "Father, please," I said, falling to my knees. "Please, spare him. I beg you. I will not ever disobey you again, I swear it. I will go back to Valebran, I will be Lorenzo's wife. I will do everything you ask, just please do not kill him."

His jaw tightened, his glare cutting through me. "What is done is done," he said, his voice low but full of anger. "And nothing can change it. He did the unforgivable. He loved you when you already belonged to another. And then he had the audacity to try and take you away from him."

"He did not take me away—"

"Silence!" The word cracked like thunder. I flinched, my heart pounding so hard I thought it might stop.

He turned from me to the guards, his tone sharp and commanding. "You two," he said, pointing toward me, "take the Princess to the yard at the front. She will witness his execution fair and square."

Then he looked toward William, his voice colder still. "And you two, take this traitor to his post."

"No!" The word ripped out of me, raw and trembling. Panic rushed through my veins like fire. My breath came fast and shallow as they stepped forward, seizing William by the arms. His head tilted weakly toward me, his lips parting as if to speak, but no words came.

I struggled, thrashing in the guards' hold as they grabbed my arms and pulled me away. "Please! Do not take him! Please!" My voice broke with every cry, but it didn't matter.

The sound of chains, the scrape of boots on stone, and the cold certainty in my father's eyes filled the air.

I had to do something. Anything.

Because if I didn't, this would be the last time I ever saw him alive.

CHAPTER SIXTY

IRIS

The sunlight hit my eyes the moment they dragged me outside. The air was heavy, filled with the murmur of a restless crowd. Hundreds of faces stretched across the courtyard. Some looked eager, others afraid, but all were watching.

The breaking wheel stood in the center like a monument to cruelty. The sight of it made my knees weak.

The guards at my side didn't let go. Their hands were rough on my arms, keeping me in place. I lifted my head and searched the yard until my eyes found him. William.

They were dragging him forward. His shirt was still off, his steps slow and uneven. He looked so pale. So tired. Every movement seemed to take all the strength he had left.

When they reached the wheel, the guards threw him down and began tying his arms and legs with thick rope. I bit my lip so hard I tasted blood. I wanted to scream for them to stop, but no sound came out.

When they lifted his head, his eyes met mine across the yard. For a heartbeat, everything went still. His gaze held mine, calm and steady, though I could see the pain in it. It was that look that shattered me.

My heart pounded in my chest until it hurt. I couldn't breathe. If I didn't do something, I knew I would break apart right there.

Then my father stepped forward. The guards straightened as he passed, and the crowd quieted.

"Father, please!" I cried. "It is not too late to stop this. Do not do it, I beg you!"

He didn't look at me. His eyes stayed on the people before him.

"My people," he began, his voice carrying clearly through the courtyard. "This man—a knight who once swore loyalty to our crown—has betrayed that vow. He has betrayed us all."

A ripple moved through the crowd, soft murmurs spreading like wind.

"He loved my daughter," my father said, his voice colder now. "And in his selfishness, he sought to take her away from her husband, to break the alliance that keeps our lands safe. He put every one of you in danger. And now he will die for his crime. Let this be an example."

My throat burned. My pulse thudded in my ears.

I turned to William again. His head was bowed, his chest rising slowly. My father's words faded into a blur as panic began to fill me. I needed to stop this. I needed to think.

But I couldn't. My thoughts scattered like leaves in the wind. All I could see was the man I loved, bound to the wheel. All I could hear was my father's voice, calling for his death.

Then my father turned to William.

He says, "And as for you, know that this punishment is exactly what you deserve. You dared to defy those above you and now you will suffer the worst death because of it. I hope you regret your decisions."

William slowly lifted his head. When he spoke, his voice was sudden and unexpected. "No, I do not."

A loud gasp erupted from the crowd. My father's head sharply turned towards William. "What did you just say?"

William met his eyes. "You asked me if I regret loving your daughter and my answer is no."

My father's face twisted with rage. "You dare call it love when you have dishonored my name?"

William drew in a deep breath. "Yes, because I do not care about you or your dishonor. I will never regret loving your daughter or dishonoring your rules to be by her side. If I were given a thousand lives, I would spend each and every one of them finding her again."

My father's jaw tightened, but William pressed on, louder now, so the whole courtyard could hear.

"In every place, in every age, no matter the chains

you bind me with, my heart will always find hers. And if you strike me down now, know this. My love does not die. It will echo through the years, through the very stones of this kingdom, until time itself forgets your name."

He raised his head higher. "You say you will execute me with the worst punishment? Well, I do not fear your blade nor your wrath. I fear a life without her." He moved his gaze toward me. "I may have served you, but know this. Princess Iris holds my heart. No command, no threat, no force of arms shall tear it from her. Try to stop me if you dare. I will cut down any man or threat who dares stand in my way, even if that man is *you*."

My father's face darkened. "You dare speak such indolence at the hour of your death? You dare defy me even now?"

William gave a faint smile, one meant only for me. "I would defy kingdoms, thrones, and kings like you if it meant one more moment with her."

My heart beat faster. I couldn't believe what he had just said. In front of everyone. Even though he was going to die.

My father's expression hardened. "Start. The. Wheel," he ordered.

"No!" I screamed, but it was too late. The wheels began to turn.

My stomach tightened so badly I could hardly breathe. I needed to do something, anything! But there was nothing I could do.

The wheel moved again. William didn't even flinch.

He didn't cry out or beg. He just looked at me, calm and steady, like he was already at peace.

Something inside me broke. It wasn't a thought or a plan. It was a raw, unstoppable pull that took hold of me before I could think twice. My body moved on its own, powered by terror and love. I yanked my arms free from the guards, their startled shouts echoing behind me, and before they could grab me again, I lunged for the sword at one of their sides.

The weight of it nearly made me drop it. My hands shook, slick with sweat, but I held on. The crowd gasped, their voices rising like a wave. The sharp scrape of the wheel slowed for a second, but my father's furious shout brought it spinning again.

"Stop the wheel this instant!" I screamed, my throat tearing with the force of it. "Stop it!"

My father turned sharply toward me, his face hard with disbelief. "What are you doing?"

I raised the sword and pressed the point to my stomach. It burned cold against my skin. "If he dies, I die, too," I said. My voice was shaking, but my words were clear.

William's voice carried through the noise, rough and broken. "Iris, no! Do not! Please!"

I didn't look at him. I couldn't. My eyes stayed on my father.

His jaw clenched. He took a slow step toward me, his tone sharp and low. "You would not kill yourself."

Tears stung my eyes, but I didn't look away. "If you kill him, then I will."

A cruel laugh broke from his lips, short and bitter. He thought I was bluffing.

To prove him wrong, I pushed the sword forward. The blade bit through skin, sharp and cold, and a burning pain spread through my abdomen. Something painful left my lips. The sound was part gasp, part cry. My knees trembled, and I felt something wet and warm spreading through the white fabric of my gown.

William's voice cracked through the chaos. "Iris! Stop!"

I didn't. I pressed it in deeper. The pain blinded me, white-hot, but it didn't matter. Watching him die would hurt far worse.

My father's face turned as pale as bone. His voice rose, no longer calm or commanding but desperate. "Iris, put that sword down. Give it to me now."

"Not until you let him go," I said. My voice was thin and trembling, but the steel in it didn't waver.

"Iris, I said give me that sword!"

I could hardly breathe. My arms were shaking violently now. Every muscle in my body begged me to stop. But I didn't. I pushed the blade in another inch. More blood spilled out, running down my gown, staining it deep red. The pain was unbearable. I bit my lip hard to keep from screaming.

My father's eyes widened in panic. "Stop the wheel!" he shouted, his voice echoing across the courtyard. "Stop the wheel this instant and release William!"

The guards rushed to obey. The wheel stopped turning. The sword slipped from my hands, and my knees gave out beneath me.

I fell forward, my vision blurring.

The only thing I could see was William. He was free. He ran toward me, shouting my name. I tried to reach for him, but my arms wouldn't move. He dropped to his knees beside me, his hands pressing hard against my stomach to stop the bleeding.

"Iris," he said, his voice breaking. "Why did you do that–Iris! Stay with me!"

I gritted my teeth, the pain making my whole body tremble. "I had to," I whispered.

He held me tighter, blood covering his hands. He looked terrified, but his eyes stayed on mine, full of love and fear all at once.

Then a shadow loomed over us. My father. His face was pale, his expression cold and furious.

"You, Sir William," he began, anger visible in his voice. "You are hereby stripped of your title and your honours. You hold no rank in my court from this moment forward. If I see you again, I will not hesitate to kill you."

William didn't look up. He didn't even flinch. All his focus was on me. He pressed harder on the wound, whispering my name over and over as if saying it could keep me alive.

Then my father turned to me. "And you," he said, his voice colder than I'd ever heard it. "You are banished from this kingdom. If you ever return, I will have you killed. If I hear your name again, I will hunt you both down myself."

I forgot about the pain for a moment. His words cut deeper than the sword ever could. Banishment. From my own home. From my father.

He stepped closer. "Leave now," he said "before I change my mind and put you both on the wheel."

I felt the world crumble inside me. The pain in my stomach was nothing compared to the ache in my chest. My Father. My own father was threatening to kill me.

William's arms wrapped around me, steadying me as I swayed. I could see the fear in his face, but he said nothing.

We both knew what we had to do.

He lifted me gently, his arms trembling slightly. The crowd parted, silent now. My gown was soaked in blood, and each step left a dark mark on the stones. I looked once at my father. He didn't look back.

William held me close as we walked away from the courtyard. Away from the crowd. Away from everything I had ever known.

And though my body was weak, I clung to him. Because even in the ruin of everything, he was all I had left.

CHAPTER SIXTY-ONE

IRIS

He carried me through the courtyard, his steps uneven but steady. The guards didn't stop us. No one dared. The only sound was the soft trail of blood dripping from my gown onto the stone.

We reached the stables. The scent of hay and earth filled the air. His horse—Corven—neighed softly as if sensing the storm around us. William moved quickly, his breath heavy, his face pale.

He lifted me onto the saddle, settling me in front of him. I felt his arm wrap around me, his hand pressing firmly against my wound. His other hand gripped the reins. He didn't speak. He didn't need to. His silence said everything.

The gates loomed ahead—the same gates that had

once welcomed me home now stood like a wall between who I was and who I had become.

The wind brushed against my face. My vision blurred, not from pain but from the weight of everything I was leaving behind. My father. My kingdom. The life I once knew.

William clicked his tongue softly, and Corven moved forward. The hooves struck the cobblestone, echoing through the courtyard like a heartbeat fading away.

He held me close, his hand still pressed against my stomach, warm and trembling. I could feel the rise and fall of his chest against my back, the steady rhythm of his breath keeping me awake.

Neither of us spoke. There was nothing left to say.

As the castle disappeared behind us, I rested my head against him. The night swallowed us whole. The pain dulled for a moment, replaced by something deeper.

Grief. Love. Freedom.

And as the wind carried us into the dark, I knew this was the beginning of something neither of us could ever escape.

—

We had been riding for hours. The wind had grown colder, the sky painted with streaks of orange and red as the sun dipped behind the trees. My head rested against his chest the entire way, my body weak, my vision hazy. I was surprised I hadn't bled out, but William's hand never once left my wound. He held it tight the whole ride, whispering my name whenever my eyes began to close.

When he finally pulled on the reins, I lifted my head weakly. My eyes widened.

We were there. His cottage. The same small house in the middle of the wilds, surrounded by forest and quiet. The place where everything had begun.

Nostalgia filled me. I remembered the first night I had come here, the rain, the fear, the warmth of his fire. It felt like another lifetime.

He climbed down first and then lifted me carefully from the horse. I could feel the strain in his arms, the trembling, but he didn't say a word. He set Corven loose to rest near the fence and carried me inside.

The moment we entered, the familiar scent of smoke and pine hit me. It almost broke me.

William moved to the bed, the same one where I had once slept the night we met, and laid me down as if I were made of glass. His hands trembled as he reached for the torn fabric of my gown.

"I am sorry," he whispered, and tore the blood-soaked cloth away from my stomach. The air hit my skin, cold and sharp. He froze when he saw the wound. For a moment, the world seemed to stop with him.

"You should not have done this for me," he said "You were never meant to. I would have faced every blade before letting this happen."

I looked at him, my chest rising and falling with effort. "I did, William."

He pressed a hand against the wound, desperate to

stop the bleeding. "No," he whispered fiercely. "Now look at you. You are bleeding out, you are banished. There as a kill order on your name. You have lost everything."

A faint smile touched my lips, even as my body trembled from the pain. "But I didn't lose you," I said softly. "They would have killed you if I had not."

He shook his head, his jaw tightening as tears welled in his eyes. "You should have let me die. At least then you would still be safe."

"Safe?" I whispered, a weak laugh slipping through the pain. "There's no safety without you."

He swallowed hard, his voice barely holding together. "I do not deserve you."

My eyes met his, glassy, fading, but still filled with him. "Neither do I," I whispered. "That is why we fit perfectly together."

For a moment, he said nothing. Then he leaned forward, resting his forehead against mine, his breath trembling against my lips.

"If you die here, Iris…" His voice cracked as if that was something he refused to imagine. "Then God will have to take me with you."

My fingers trembled as I wiped his tears away. "I am still here," I whispered. "And I am not leaving this world while you are in it."

He let out a shaky breath, his forehead still pressed against mine, as if afraid that letting go would make me vanish.

For a moment, everything was silent. No guards. No

courtiers. No crown. Just him and me, breathing in the wreckage of what we'd become.

Outside, the wind whispered through the pines, carrying with it the scent of the kingdom I could never return to. It didn't sting the way I thought it would. Not when his arms were around me.

"You are safe now," he murmured, though his voice trembled. "Even if you don't have your old life anymore, we will build something of our own."

And as the night closed around us, I believed him. I always would. For the first time, exile didn't feel like an ending. It felt like the beginning of *us*.

CHAPTER SIXTY-TWO

WILLIAM

I worked quietly, my hands moving the way she told me to. The cut was deep, and every time I pressed the cloth to her skin, I saw her flinch, even though she tried to hide it. I hated it. I hated that she had done this for me.

She guided me through each step with a weak voice, telling me how tight to wrap the bandages, how to fold the cloth so it wouldn't reopen the wound. I listened, but my mind wasn't really here. All I could think about was how I wished she hadn't done it.

She was a princess. She belonged in a palace, surrounded by gold and silk, not in a forgotten cottage with blood on her hands. Not like this.

It would have been better if she had let me die. At least then, she would still have her title, her crown, her safety. But now she had nothing. Because of me. Because she chose me.

I tightened the last bandage, my chest aching with guilt. I would protect her. No matter what came next, I'd make sure no one ever touched her again. If I had to fight every soldier in the kingdom, I would. I would kill for her. I would die for her.

"That is enough," she whispered, breaking through my thoughts. "I think that is good."

I nodded, my hands still on her. For a moment, I couldn't move.

Then I leaned forward and pulled her into my arms.

She gasped softly, but her arms came up around me. I held her close, afraid that if I let go, she would vanish.

"I love you," I whispered against her hair. My voice trembled. "I love you so, so much."

She didn't answer right away, just rested her head against my chest, her heartbeat weak but steady. Then she whispered back, barely audible.

"I love you, too."

Something inside me broke then. Not from pain, but from the unbearable truth that love like this could survive even ruin. I buried my face in her hair and held her tighter, as if I could shield her from the world that had already cast her out.

Outside, the wind howled through the pines, carrying the echoes of a kingdom that no longer wanted us.

Let them have their thrones.

I had her.

That was enough.

—

It had been seven days since our exile. Seven days since the castle walls disappeared behind us and the world grew quiet again.

I was outside, working the soil by hand, the sun already low in the sky. The air smelled like pine and damp earth. My hands were rough and raw, but I didn't mind. It felt good to build something again, even if it was small. The garden would give us food in time, and the work kept my thoughts still.

Behind me, the door creaked open. I looked up and saw her standing there. Iris. She was wearing one of my old tunics, her hair loose, her face pale but glowing in the light.

"Do you need help?" she asked softly.

I straightened, frowning. "No. Get back inside. You need rest."

She smiled faintly but didn't move. "I have been lying down all day."

Then I saw her hand clutch her abdomen. The smile faded, replaced by a wince. The spade fell from my hand before I even realized it. In an instant, I was at her side.

"Easy," I said, slipping an arm around her. My hand pressed gently to the small of her back as I guided her inside. She didn't argue, just leaned against me, her steps slow but steady.

When we reached the bed, she sank onto it with a tired breath. I knelt beside her, brushing a strand of hair from her face. Her eyes met mine, soft and tired, but filled with something that made my chest ache.

We didn't need to say anything.

This was our life now. No crowns, no swords, no titles, no gold,no silver armor. Just the two of us in a small cottage in the middle of nowhere.

And maybe that was enough.

Because we had each other.

And we always would.

EPILOGUE

IRIS

Three months had passed.

Three quiet, beautiful months.

I had never known happiness like this before. Not the kind that comes from grand halls or silk gowns, but the kind that fills the air with peace. The kind that made me feel safe, and whole, and loved.

Every morning I woke up to the sound of birds and William's arms around me. Every night, I fell asleep to his heartbeat. The memories of the palace, of my father, of all that had been taken from me. They felt distant now, like a dream fading in the morning light.

William had become a farmer. He worked the fields every day, hands calloused, face sun-touched, yet he never once complained. I went to the village from time to time, helping the sick as a healer. It wasn't much, but together we made enough to survive. Enough to live.

And that was all we needed.

Now, we were lying together in bed, the soft light of the fire flickering across the walls. William's arm was draped around me, a book open in his other hand. His voice was steady, low, and warm as he read.

It was *The Willow Bride*. Our story.

As he neared the end, I nestled closer to him, resting my head on his shoulder. I knew how the story ended. Mike and Elara didn't get to be together, but that no longer hurt me. Because William and I were. We were together, and that was enough.

When he finished the last page, he closed the book and smiled down at me. "The end," he said softly.

I smiled back, my fingers tracing lazy circles over his chest. "It is still my favorite story," I whispered.

He tilted his head slightly, a faint grin tugging at his lips. "Because it is ours now?"

I nodded. "Because we changed the ending."

He laughed quietly, that deep, gentle sound I'd grown to love more than anything. Then he leaned in.

Our lips met, soft and slow. The kind of kiss that didn't need words, that said everything instead.

When he pulled back, his forehead rested against mine. The fire crackled beside us, and the world outside went still.

For the first time in my life, I didn't think about tomorrow. Only this moment. Only him.

He then pulled back, smiling and brushed a thumb along my cheek. "I will go make supper," he said.

I stretched, the sheets rustling as I sat up. "I will help," I said, reaching for his hand.

He laughed under his breath and helped me out of bed. The floorboards creaked faintly beneath our feet as we walked toward the door. Everything felt calm: the golden light from the window, the smell of the fire, the peace we had built here.

But then William stopped.

He froze mid-step, his shoulders going rigid. His eyes widened, fixed on something beyond the doorway.

My heart quickened. "William?" I whispered. "What is it?"

He didn't answer.

I followed his gaze, my breath catching in my throat.

Outside, through the open window, stood a line of castle guards. Their armor gleamed in the dying light. Each one held a sword, drawn and ready.

For a heartbeat, the world seemed to hold its breath.

Then one of them stepped forward and burst through the door.

The warmth of the fire lingered for only a moment before fading, leaving nothing but the sound of steel and the echo of everything we were about to lose.

End of Book One.

Love survives exile.
Hope survives ruin.
And somewhere beyond the ashes of Elarion… their story continues.

A WORD FROM THE WRITER

Thank you so much for reading and reaching the end of this story. I started writing it during my summer break, never expecting it to grow into something this meaningful. Every chapter, every scene, every sleepless night was worth it because of readers like you.

Thank you for giving Iris and William a place in your heart. Their story isn't over — and neither is mine.

TikTok: @Calisaazmelle
Snapchat: @Calisaazmelle
Instagram: @Calisaazmelle
Email: calisaazmelle@hotmail.com

Follow my socials for book 2.

KEEP READING FOR
A SNEAK PEAK AT

THE KNIGHT
AND
THE CROWN

The first book in the new princess x knight, prince x servant doulogy!

ARABELLA

I looked at myself once before turning away from the mirror.

The mask sat perfectly against my face–pale pink enamel brushed with gold along its edges. It covered my forehead and nose while leaving my mouth and blue eyes bare. My blonde hair fell loose down my back in soft, shining waves. Gold pins shaped like small flowers held the front strands away from my face.

My gown pooled around my feet, silk layered over silk, light enough to stir when I breathed. The bodice was fitted and embroidered with fine gold thread that shimmered in the candlelight. The skirt faded from blush to ivory, like a rose opening petal by petal. It was my favorite color. Before my mother passed, she said pink made me look kind, and I had worn it ever since.

I smoothed my hands down the fabric and lifted my chin.

Tonight was not about duty. At least, that was what I told myself.

When the doors to the ballroom opened, sound spilled out to meet me.

Music rose first, strings and flutes woven together, followed by laughter and the low hum of conversation. The ballroom glowed beneath hundreds of candles set into golden sconces and hanging chandeliers. Their light reflected off the marble floor and the painted ceiling above, where saints and kings looked down in silent judgment. Silk banners hung along the walls, each bearing the crest of Sanctia–a silver sword holding a golden crown.

Masks filled the room.

Feathers and jewels, lacquered wood and polished metal, painted smiles that hid familiar faces. Some were simple cloth, others elaborate works of art. I could not tell who was who, only who they were. Nobles wore velvet and gemstones, their posture straight and practiced.. Lesser lords favored fine wool and careful embroidery. Servants passed quietly through it all, dressed in darker cloth, their backs a little hunched.

Some couples were already dancing, moving in careful circles across the floor. Others lingered at long tables laden with sugared fruit and pastries, cups of wine pressed into waiting hands. The air smelled of honey, wax, and perfume.

I stepped forward and rested my hand on the banister.

The grand staircase curved down into the heart of the room. As I began my descent, heads turned. Even masked, I was recognized. Pink and gold gave me away. They always did.

Halfway down, an arm slipped easily through mine.

"Running off without me?" a familiar voice asked.

I smiled before I looked.

"Nathaniel," I said.

My brother walked beside me, tall and straight, his steps confident and unhurried. His mask was deep, rich blue edged with silver, and his doublet matched perfectly, the fabric fitted neatly at his shoulders. He looked every inch the crown prince. He always had.

"You look pleased with yourself," I told him.

He laughed softly. "I am pleased with you. Father insisted you attend, and I insisted you enjoy it."

"That was not insisting," I said. "That was commanding."

"Same thing," he replied, unfazed.

We reached the bottom of the stairs together, and the crowd parted without being asked.

"You will dance tonight," Nathaniel said, though his attention was already drifting across the room.

"I do not feel like it," I replied. I hated dancing with strangers.

"You never do."

"I never have to."

He leaned in closer. "Well, lucky you, for I have been instructed to dance with Lady Elowen."

My brows lifted. "By whom?"

"The archbishop's secretary," he said. "Apparently her lineage is impeccable."

I rolled my eyes. "The Church would have you married before Father finished his supper." Even though there was amusement in my voice, I wished part of what I said wasn't true. The Church always pressured Nathaniel into getting married, saying if he doesn't, Sanctia won't have a king after Father passes. Being the crown prince came with responsibilities, and one of them was securing a queen. The only way to become king or queen was to marry someone of noble birth. Thankfully that wasn't something I had to worry for, though my heart still ached for my brother.

"They forget you are human," I said quietly.

"They never cared," he answered.

The music swelled again, and a hand was placed on his shoulder. He turned, already smiling.

"Enjoy yourself, Ara," he said. "Try not to steal any pastries."

"I made no promises," I replied.

He left me with a final glance and disappeared into the crowd.

I stood alone for a moment, surrounded by motion and sound, and felt suddenly tired even though I had just arrived. I did not want conversation, nor did I want expectations wrapped in silk.

My gaze drifted instead to a silver tray weaving through the room.

Sweets.

I followed it without shame

The butler paused when he saw me and lowered the tray. Small pastries were arranged with care–candied almonds, honey cakes, and marzipan–pale and shaped into delicate fruits.

I took one.

The almond sweetness mixed on my tongue and for a world, the world softened.

I closed my eyes and breathed.

Perhaps the night would not be so terrible at all.

After eating the entire tray, I decided I needed a drink. Preferably something sweet. Wine was tolerable, but only when it sparkled. I scanned the room until I spotted another butler standing near one of the pillars, a tray balanced easily in his hands. Crystal glasses caught the candlelight, filled with liquids in shades of gold and rose.

Exactly what I needed.

I moved toward him, careful not to step on trailing hems or brush too close to strangers. The music had shifted to something slower, the dancer turning in measured steps. I reached a tray and lifted my hand.

Then I walked straight into something solid.

My head struck a hard chest, and the impact sent a jolt through me. I stumbled back half a step, my hand closing on nothing.

"I am so sorry," I said at once.

I looked up.

He was tall, taller than most men in this room. His shoulders were broad and his arms well-shaped. Black hair framed his mask, which was dark and plain, cut cleanly to follow the lines of his face. Pale green eyes watched me through it, steady and sharp. He wore a black doublet fitted to his chest and arms, the fabric stretched lightly over muscle. A sword hung at his side, real steel, not decoration.

For a moment, I forgot about the drink.

"I was not watching where I was going," I said, heat rising to my face.

My gaze dropped, and that was when I saw the faint splash of wine against the dark fabric of his chest.

"Oh," I breathed. "I am truly sorry."

Before I could think better of it, I reached for the butler beside us. He had already lifted a handkerchief from his sleeve. I took it and turned back to the man.

"Please," I said, holding it out. "I ruined your doublet."

He hesitated only a moment before taking it from me.

His fingers brushed my own. They were warm.

His eyes remained on mine as he began to wipe, which made me nervous. I hoped he wasn't angry, as anger often meant complaint, and complaint landed me in trouble.

"I did not mean to," I said again, hoping it would soften him.

He nodded then, slowly.

"It seems," he said calmly, "that neither of us was looking where we were going."

Relief rushed through me so quickly it left me lightheaded.

I let out a breath I had not realized I was holding, my shoulders loosening as if his words had untied something tight in my chest. He was not angry. He was not calling for a guard, *though I doubt he would if he knew I was the princess.* And he was not turning toward the crowd with complaints on his tongue.

For a moment, I thought that was the end of it.

Then his mouth curved, just slightly.

"But....I will not allow this to pass," he said.

The world seemed to tilt.

My heart dropped. I thought of the Master of Ceremonies, of his sharp eyes and quicker punishments. I thought of the whispers who watched from corners and remembered everything. A single complaint could travel far in a room like this.

"I am so sorry," I said again, quickly. "I did not mean any disrespect. I will pay for it. The doublet, I mean. I will make it right."

He studied me for a moment, his expression unreadable behind the mask, his eyes still fixed on mine as his hand slowed against the dark fabric.

"As pleasant as that sounds," he said, "there is something else you can do."

My stomach tightened.

But I nodded anyway because there was nothing else to do. "Name it."

He folded the handkerchief neatly and returned it to

the butler, who had lingered nearby. Then he straightened and held out his hand to me.

"A dance," he said.

I did not say anything for a long moment.

I stared at his hand instead. It was waiting. Strong fingers, scarred at the knuckles, the olive skin rougher than silk or parchment. I never planned to dance today, as that demanded too much attention and too many eyes. I usually endured it out of courtesy and escaped as soon as I could.

Yet something pressed against my chest, telling me to say yes.

I knew it was not only because I had ruined his doublet.

Slowly, I placed my hand in his.

His fingers closed around mine, careful, as if he were aware of how easily I could pull away. The corner of his mouth curved beneath the mask, just enough that I noticed.

Nerves fluttered through me, sharp and unexpected.

He guided me toward the floor without a word. The music wrapped around us, and when he placed his other hand at my waist, it was done with practiced ease. Not presumptuous. Not hesitant. Certain.

I had been taught to dance since I could walk. Years of lessons rose up without effort, and I followed his rhythm as though I had been waiting for it. Our steps aligned, smooth and unbroken, my pale skirts brushing his boots as we moved.

He led, and I let him

The crowd blurred around us.

Everything faded and his eyes never left mine, and I found that I did not want them to.

The space between us felt smaller than it should have.

For a time, neither of us spoke. The music carried us, and I followed each shift of his body without thinking. There was comfort in it, an ease that unsettled me more than nerves ever could.

I wondered if he felt it, too.

His thumb shifted slightly against my hand, a subtle movement that sent a strange warmth through me. Then, at last, he spoke.

"You dance as if you listen."

The words were unexpected, making me blink faster. "Listen to what?"

He tilted his head, considering me as we turned. "To the music," he said. "And to the person leading you."

Something about the way he said it made my breath catch.

"I was taught well," I replied, though the words felt thin.

His hands loosed slightly at my waist, just enough that I noticed the change.

"Perhaps," he said, his voice softer now, "we began on the wrong foot."

My brows furrowed. "How so?"

He glanced down briefly, then back at me. "An introduction would have been kinder than spilling a drink."

That drew a small laugh from me. It slipped so freely before I could stop it, surprising us both.

The corner of his mouth curved again. "Callias," he said. "Of Dominia."

The name settled in my mind at once. Dominia lay a sea away from Sanctia, its borders etched in thick ink on the maps I had studied as a little girl. I had traced its coastline more than once with idle curiosity, though I had never imagined meeting someone front here in this way.

"I am a knight," he continued, as we moved slowly with the music. "High ranked. I was sent to guard my king while he is here."

"That sounds important," I said. Him being a knight explained the well-shaped muscle beneath his doublet.

"It is," he replied, without pride or apology.

He studied me then, his expression thoughtful. "And you?"

I hesitated for only a moment. "Oh–me–I am Arabella, the prin–"

A hand landed on his shoulder.

The interruption was so sudden. I looked up and found myself facing a man in a crown, his mask worked with gold and dark jewels. Even without the regalia, the way the crowd shifted around him would have given him away.

Callias released me at once and bowed deeply.

The king leaned in and said something low, meant only for him.

I did not need to be told who he was. It was clear he was the king Callias came here to guard.

Callias straightened and turned back to me. "My apologies, my lady," he said. "I would very much like to continue, but it seems duty calls."

Then he stepped back, and before I could answer, he was gone.

The space he left behind suddenly felt too large.

Printed in Dunstable, United Kingdom

80039517R00258